SEVEN ARCHANGELS: ANNIHILATION

SEVEN ARCHANGELS: ANNIHILATION

Jane Lebak

Philangelus Press
Boston, MA USA

ISBN: 978-1-942133-00-1
Kindle ASIN: B00NCKEMFY
Library of Congress Control Number: 2014950436

Cover: C.K. Volnek

To Pauline Griffin,
who always encouraged my writing

November 8, 2007

Gentle Readers,

I trust this finds you growing in God's love. Angels and our stories are a lot of fun, and I hope you will enjoy the time you spend with us.

That said, human beings fail to correctly interpret a significant portion of our interactions with you, and rather than allow confusion, I've asked to compose the forward to this volume. Feel free to proceed directly to the story. If you find yourself confused by our terminology or social structure, return at that time to my introduction. I will lay it out below.

One can divide creation in a number of ways. For purposes of this forward, we'll consider angel versus human. You, presumably, are human. I am an angel. That's a division in rough strokes.

One can divide angels into two groups as well, the first being *angels* with a lowercase A, meaning any angel, and the second being *archangels*, also in lowercase, meaning angels in a position of authority. The Seven all qualify as archangels, as do the heads of the choirs .

The most frequent and useful classification system divides the angelic world into nine orders or choirs. (We do sing, but don't read too much into that unless you also believe fish go to school and lions are proud.) The nine choirs are, in order from most powerful to least: Seraphim, Cherubim, Thrones, Dominions, Powers, Virtues, Principalities, Archangels, Angels. Relax. You won't be tested on that.

Each choir has its own characteristics and responsibilities. Seraphim are the "fiery ones." The word *Cherubim* means "fullness of knowledge." I'd give an exhaustive list, but Jane is only allowing me 800 words, and you'll figure it out for yourself if you pay attention.

Here's where I start getting a headache. I didn't invent English, so don't complain to me. (The one who invented English doesn't have a comment box out, so don't complain to him either.) The last two orders, you'll notice, are Archangels and Angels. With capital letters. Why this happened is beyond me, but I think the purpose was to test our patience. The upshot is, if you're referring to Raphael, you can call him a Seraph, an archangel, or an angel, and you'd be right; not every angel is an Angel (although every Angel is an angel); Michael is the only archangel who's also an Archangel. Where's my Excedrin?

Another point of order: you know those baby faces with miniature wings at the neck? Those are not Cherubim. I'm sure Satan wanted to stick it to me when he came up with those cutesy figures. A real Cherub could blow the roof off your house with one beat of his wings. Looking at him, you'd be transported with awe, not ga-ga and wanting to give him a smooch.

And while we're on the topic of Cherubim, the *-im* suffix is how you form a plural in Hebrew (מי). It makes me nuts when someone says "Cherubs" or "Seraphs." It's not that hard. Seriously. Raphael asks me to be patient because how are you supposed to know if no one tells you. Well, I'm telling you now.

Next: for the love of little green apples, please quit calling me Gabbie, Gabe, Gabey, or Gabri. We won't even discuss what happened to the woman who tried calling me "Brie." Just, don't. God gave me a perfectly good name. Two, in fact, so if you're feeling really formal you can call me Gebher'el rather than Gabriel, but the rest of the time, my given name is just fine. It means *Strength of God*, and it's perfect the way it is. The only one allowed to use a nickname for me is my Creator, who substitutes 'el with 'li to make it *Strength of Mine*. (May all of you be so blessed as to one day hear Him say something similar.)

Similarly, Remiel is sick of hearing *Rem-ee-yell*. She's *Ree-mee-el*. I never trifle with her, so be sure to pronounce her name correctly. For that matter, archangel is *ark-angel* and not *arch-angel*. I didn't invent spelling either.

About angelic bodies: we have some control over our forms, so we can turn insubstantial, semi-solid, or solid. Usually we stay in a semi-solid angelic body, no need to sleep or eat, and unable to be killed. We cannot become human without God's help. Nor can humans become angels. Perhaps in my next 800 words I can ruminate about the theoretical three "choirs" of humans (Saints, Martyrs and Innocents) but I'm out of space.

800 words isn't a lot. If any of this doesn't make sense, email me, but I've covered the basics.

Enjoy the book. Be God's own, and remember I pray for you.
Sincerely,
Gabriel (Cherub)

PS: Raphael wants to say hi with my last ten words.

One

The mirrors around the semi-circular studio reflected endless variations of a dancing angel, the only angel to have cried when she received her name. Unleashing the power of a tornado, Remiel spun to music loud enough to rattle all twenty windows. Arms, legs and six gold wings pumping to the rhythm, she whirled about the room.

During a pause in the cacophony, Remiel turned to find Saraquael, of the choir of Dominions, standing against the corner. The volume lowered instantly, and then the music stopped as the frown of her previous concentration transformed into a grin.

He inclined his head, as if to say, *You can continue.*

She opened her hands, communicating reassurance in the nonverbal manner of angels. Then, a smile still adorning her angular features, she shrugged.

"What were you playing?" Saraquael, like Remiel, was one of the Seven archangels that stand directly before God.

"I'm not sure. Israfel said it's a trend poised to dominate American radio, so she asked me to figure out if it fell under her dominion as the angel of music." She rubbed a hand through her cropped hair, then along the gentle slope of her neck. "I can dance to it, so I'd say yes." As she lowered her arm, a half dozen bracelets jangled. "What brings you?"

"I just wanted to stop by." He gestured at the dance floor. "Keep going."

"I'm done." Her clothing changed from a black leotard into jeans and a red t-shirt, but her hair remained the same, standing away from her neck to reveal a row of piercings in each ear. "Are you sure everything is all right?"

Saraquael squinted, his six teal-speckled wings opening. "Is something the matter?"

"I just... I get a sense, a danger." She shook her head. "It's probably nothing. But the universe keeps vibrating with tension like an overwound violin string."

Saraquael moved closer to her, concern clouding his green eyes. "Do you have any idea why?"

She shook her head. "No, and I'm tired of banging my head against the problem. The music didn't make it go away." Her eyes glinted like garnets as she slapped his arm. "Tag. Find me."

She vanished. Saraquael grinned before flashing away too.

He appeared in a dark exhibit hall of the New York Aquarium at Coney Island. Remiel's presence, although dampened, sparkled like a repressed giggle. He let his attention expand to cover the whole hall, all the tourists. Focusing on one end of the hall, he concentrated in turn on each of the people and things. He turned his attention to one golden fish in a lighted tank. *Gotcha!*

Remiel's laugh sparked in his mind, and again she vanished. The whole search had taken five seconds.

He followed. This time, the place where Remiel felt strongest was a barred-spiral galaxy about 700 million light years from the Earth. He "felt" around for her signature, the wild smile and the trail her thoughts left in reality like the wake cut by a lake-faring sailboat. He could sense how compressed she wasn't, how she shed power like a star, how she almost wanted him to find her. Her heart felt like a beacon, but for the moment he couldn't settle on a method of pinpointing her.

All right, he prayed. *How am I going to do this?*

It's your game, God replied. *We already know I know how to find her, Saraqua'li.*

Saraquael laughed.

"Need some help?"

Saraquael turned his attention to a square-jawed angel with only two green wings. "Hey, Michael. Remiel's trail leads to here, but I'm stumped."

It had taken ten seconds so far. Michael added his strength to Saraquael's, who used the Archangel's power to enhance his senses. As he opened his heart, Michael served as a lens to focus his thoughts, and in that moment Saraquael felt one star out of place. He targeted it with his will. *Tag!*

"You stinker." Remiel appeared before them as the manufactured star system vanished. "You'd never have found me without help."

Michael ran a hand through saffron-toned hair. "It would only have taken him a minute or so."

"Yeah, I'm sure." Remiel smacked him on the shoulder. "You're it!"

Both Remiel and Saraquael vanished, and Michael flashed after in pursuit.

The Heavenly sunlight streamed through a window in the library of the Cherub Gabriel, lighting the pages of the book holding all his attention. He remained in a hush interrupted only by turning pages.

Some people don't understand why angels might read books. For himself, Gabriel didn't understand how Heaven could be Heaven without them.

Gabriel didn't look up when Raphael entered the room, just continued reading while extending a welcome to the Seraph. His soul flooded into Raphael's, and the two of them mingled for a moment with Gabriel's sedate and logical Cherub nature curling around Raphael's zealous Seraph-soul in a perfect fit, before it withdrew all the stronger.

The nine choirs each embodied a different aspect of God, typifying that characteristic and returning love to God in a way uniquely its own, a diamond with nine facets. As God's light filtered over them all, they lifted and amplified God's infinity in their own ways, Thrones for example by fully engaging in worship, or Dominions by their understanding of systems and strategy. No one angel could perceive all of God simultaneously, of course—but working together, all of them could hope to learn one thing or another about God and over the course of eternity perhaps—perhaps—know him in entirety. At least, so Gabriel hoped.

Raphael's brown eyes gleamed. Gabriel finally looked away from the book.

Concentrating, he reached through their bond to feel Raphael's request: a group of the angels were playing a creation-wide game of hide-and-seek, and Raphael was going too. Would Gabriel like to come?

Gabriel glanced back at his book, at his notes. Michael was concerned about some unusual activity in Hell, and being the investigators of the nine choirs of angels, the Cherubim wanted to figure out what Satan was keeping so shrouded. Generally the demons would brag, but right now the highest-order demons were strutting around creation with only a glint in their eyes, as if they could already taste a victory, and it didn't make sense. No clues. Whatever they'd planned, they'd planned it big.

Then he looked at Raphael, one of the most powerful Seraphim and his fellow angel among the Seven who stood directly before God. The Seraph sparkled at him. He was tall and broad-shouldered even as Gabriel was slight; soft-eyed where Gabriel was angular; chocolate-haired where Gabriel was blond—and yet despite all that, they resembled one another. Gabriel's grey eyes glinted.

Would it be all right if I went? he prayed.

God told him it would make no difference.

Gabriel closed his book, and then both were gone.

By now the game had picked up a large number of players: six of the Seven, plus the leaders of three of the nine choirs. A "who's who" of the angelic world would have been filled with their identities. They hid as flowers in a field, raindrops in a thunderstorm, a painting in a museum, a new Jovian moon, an electron, and a word in a book.

Gabriel had just been located as the PM dot on a digital clock accidentally set for AM, so he joined Remiel and Raphael in a New England barn. He sprawled on the ground floor looking up at Remiel perched on a bale of hay in the loft. The hay's spicy scent mixed with the horsey odor, and the air carried a harbinger chill. Outside, the leaves had just begun to paint themselves orange and red.

"The game was a good idea." Raphael sat on one of the beams above the loft.

Remiel smiled her thanks.

Raphael nodded. "God told me to come—that we should enjoy this world to the fullest for as long as we have it." He paused. "Although now that I think about it, that was an odd thing to say. We don't have to live like humans do, as if every day might be the last."

Shadows haunted Remiel's sharp eyes. "Maybe an indicator of the end times? I've been uneasy."

Raphael glanced between his knees at Gabriel. "What do you think?"

Gabriel was staring out one smudged window at the cloudless sky. "It can't be a terrorist attack they're plotting, because they'd brag about that, and the guardians in the affected areas would know."

Remiel giggled behind her hand.

"You know how Cherubim get when they're engaged with a problem?" Raphael winked at her. "I figured I'd at least try to draw out our absent-minded professor with a theory question."

Gabriel focused suddenly. "A theory question?"

"Forget it."

Gabriel leaned against a hay bale and stared at the rafters holding up the roof, tracing the lines of force in his mind.

Remiel asked what Raphael had been up to lately, and Raphael said he'd prevented a convenience store robbery by three armed bandits.

"Three armed bandits," Remiel drawled, going semi-solid and plucking a small handful from a hay bale. "How many of them were there?"

Raphael tilted his head. "Three."

"Three three-armed bandits." Remiel's voice distorted as she tried not to giggle. "That's nine arms total."

Raphael's shoulders were shaking, and he looked down with his eyes closed and his lips pursed. "I wonder how they all met up. Maybe some kind of three-armed support group?'

"They have twelve-step programs for that sort of thing?"

"To have that," Raphael said, struggling to keep the laughter from his voice, "they'd need four three-legged bandits, and there weren't any of those."

Gabriel looked away from the wooden beams and directly at them both. "What exactly are you two talking about?"

Remiel sprinkled a few pieces of hay in the air and flashed them over Gabriel so they dropped onto his hair, then passed through his insubstantial form.

Raphael laughed out loud. He swung from the rafter so he hung from his knees, then grasped the wood and flipped to dismount.

"I'm so mean," Remiel said. "It's not fair to do that to the sense-of-humor-impaired."

"He does so have a sense of humor!" Raphael exclaimed.

Remiel hurled a double handful of hay at Raphael.

Even Cherubim can't foretell the future, but sometimes you don't have to be psychic to know what's about to happen. Gabriel sent his awareness out through the entire hay loft and noted the exact position of every bale of hay, every piece of straw, every bit of rope.

The Blizzard of 1888 might have resembled what happened next if only snow were green and gold.

Raphael flashed up into the hay loft, semi-solid and armed with hay. Remiel shrieked as he tackled her. The ensuing furor saw hay tumbling over the side of the loft while twelve flailing wings thumped against the roof, the bales, and the floor boards.

One of the horses looked at Gabriel. "Don't ask me," said the Cherub. "I just followed them here."

Gabriel flashed up onto one of the beams so he didn't become a friendly fire statistic courtesy of the hay shrapnel.

From behind him he heard, "Oh no, you don't," and abruptly he was nabbed between Remiel and Raphael, who catching him off-guard were able to force him solid. They shoved him into the loose piles.

Brilliant with joy, Raphael laughed. Gabriel discharged enough energy to blow them off, then fixed his eyes on the Seraph. He drank in Raphael's soul-fire, empowering himself and at the same time getting giddy. He could feel God smiling on them, laughing along with the game. Grinning, Gabriel tore hay from the closest bale and jumped Raphael, shoving him into the sliding straw and dodging the return volleys.

Raphael struggled away from him. "You lunatic! On the best day of your life I could pummel you into the ground!" And Gabriel, knowing in his heart how much power he really had, replied by tackling and pinning him.

Remiel sang aloud, "She'll be buried deep in hay-seeds when she comes—when she comes!" More angels arrived, more bedlam ensued, and Gabriel ached from the laughing. It was good. He suspected it would take several hours to comb the last straw bits out of his wings and hair, but so far he'd avoided having it stuffed down the back of his shirt, although not for want of Raphael trying.

Raphael whistled, bringing everyone up short. "Someone's coming."

"Tag!" Remiel slapped Gabriel on the shoulder. "You're it! Everybody run!"

All the other angels flashed out of the hay-piled barn except for Remiel. "Say," she said, "would you mind...you know, taking care of this?" Then she vanished too.

Gabriel shook his head, considered the piles of loose hay all over the loft and the barn floor (knee-deep in some places) and recalled where all of the baled hay had been at the start. A moment's concentration returned every blade of grass, every piece of hay, every sliver of straw, back into the place it had been when they'd begun.

"Sure," Gabriel said to God, shifting his sight to the Vision of God, breathtaking and even more joyous than Raphael up to his waist in flying hay. "She starts the fight, but whose responsibility is it to make sure everything gets cleaned up again?"

God smiled at him.

He glanced around to make sure everything had its right place, then straightened one string where it looked less tight than it had been when they started. As the farmer opened the door, Gabriel vanished, leaving the man to wonder why the hay scent was so strong this afternoon and why the horses looked vaguely amused.

Now it was Gabriel's turn to find everyone.

He opened his senses. Immediately Gabriel felt Raphael's presence like a beacon through their bond, but it wasn't fair to single him out first. Raphael's soul was attached to his so tightly that at times they seemed like one angel. Together both were stronger and more balanced than if they'd remained separate and extreme, but at the same time, it meant Raphael couldn't possibly hide.

It wouldn't be sportsmanlike to nab him first.

Avoiding Raphael's presence for now, Gabriel released his senses and picked up echoes of all the angels, though not all of them were easily identifiable. The strongest was a signature of Michael's power, but when he traveled to the location (a dresser drawer in an apartment in Prague) it was only a ring: a sigil. Michael had divested part of his soul into the object, giving it his power even though it wasn't him.

That was a good ruse. Gabriel pocketed the ring and turned his attention outward again, and again the clearest sense he got was Raphael.

Raphael had taken the form of a chain link on a park swing, and he vibrated with tension as he awaited capture. At least two others were nearby.

Gabriel coalesced at the park, invisible in the October air as he settled to the ground. Children shrieked as they raced through the equipment while in a field alongside, three older boys played Frisbee.

Gabriel's mouth twitched. The others were waiting for him, but really, it was just a game. He would tag Raphael and send him to get the rest of them. No one would object, and there were books in the library, or maybe an afternoon ahead where he could find an unused living room with comfortable chairs.

Raphael zinged him through the bond. *Get your head out of the clouds.*

Gabriel clenched his heart back to himself.

It's just a game. Raphael sounded frustrated. *God can keep the universe running without you for ten minutes.*

Gabriel folded his arms, and his grey eyes darkened even as he pulled his six grey wings tighter to his back.

Why bother playing a game if you're going to be thinking about ten other things when you're with us? You might as well not even be here!

Gabriel cut the contact and released himself to find the others.

Once he focused his perception on Remiel, he immediately—and not unexpectedly—found two signatures. He "felt" through both of them, each terribly close, observing rather than probing: one of the two was evil, and Gabriel didn't want to touch it.

Remiel's twin.

God sent him reassurance, and Gabriel briefly shifted to the Vision, brushing God's own sorrow over the fall of Remiel's twin. Two bright lights, so inscrutable that together they formed one angel constantly bi-locating—so united that when one chose a different master, the other nearly lost its mind. Gabriel felt now and always had that one of the greatest tragedies of the winnowing had been the separation of the twins known only as the Irin.

You're doing it again, God told him.

One moment, two Irin. The next, one demon calling itself Camael and one screaming angel whom God named Remiel and promoted to the Seven.

Gabri'li, God said gently.

Gabriel couldn't help but smile when God used his nickname; while *Gabriel* meant "God's Strength," by adding 'li instead of 'el, God could turn it into "Strength of Mine."

I know: I'm doing it again.

God chuckled.

I ought to apologize to Raphael. He's right.

Although Remiel's signature came from a field beside the play park, Gabriel moved in the opposite direction. A kid jumped off the swing where Raphael hid, and Gabriel drifted over to sit on it, rocking with the leftover momentum.

I knew you'd find me first, Raphael sent.

About to respond with an apology for being distracted before, Gabriel stopped. He looked across the park to a group of kids clustered around a young boy and something he held in his hands. Focusing his hearing on the group, he grinned, then prayed, *God, could you put me in a body for a few minutes?*

A moment after that, a slight boy, grey-eyed and blond, slipped off the swing and inserted himself into the gathering.

"Eew!" one kid was saying.

"It's not eew," said the one in the center. "It's my baby tooth."

Gabriel got up close to the kids, shorter by a head than most of them. He studied the white wonder on the boy's palm, then took the boy's hand and drew it closer.

"Don't touch it!" said one of the boys, louder. "It's disgusting—it used to be part of his body."

"No, it's cool," said another.

Gabriel could hear guitar music, which he filed away as out-of-place at the park, but for now he got up close to the boy with the tooth and said, "Life is like a tooth, you know?" He kept his voice soft so the bigger kids turned to look. "Now is this life, and then we go ahead to a bigger and better one after we die, and that one lasts forever." Gabriel looked at the boy with the tooth. "That's like a baby tooth that falls out, and you get a better tooth that's stronger and lasts the rest of your life."

"That's even cooler!" said the kid, and then the other kids all started chattering at the same time about how they wanted to lose their teeth now, and the one boy still calling it disgusting. Gabriel retreated toward the benches, and as he did, he saw the source of the guitar music. Raphael had taken the form of a teenage boy and was strumming. He looked up from his guitar.

"Oh, right," Gabriel whispered. "Tag."

Raphael flashed him an amused look, and Gabriel quirked a smile.

Raphael sent back, *I should know better than to try distracting a Cherub engaged with a problem.*

Gabriel came closer, about to share all the things he'd already deduced, but then an older boy started talking to Raphael about his guitar technique, asked what brand guitar it was (Raphael had his name in Hebrew, "God Heals," where it ought to say "Martin") and within minutes both excitedly compared techniques, discussed different fingerings, and then talked about alternate ways to handle bar chords.

Gabriel waited for a break in the exchange, but it only got faster and more furious. He gave up when the boy's kid sister showed up requesting songs. When Raphael started playing "Shoo Fly, Don't Bother Me," Gabriel turned the rest of his attention toward the field to find Remiel.

He could feel her in a clover patch, and shortly he stood there, staring around his feet.

Two of the other boys approached, one of them the "disgusting" boy. "What are you doing?"

Gabriel didn't look up. "I'm searching for a four-leaf clover."

"How do you do that?" said the smaller of the two, who appeared to be six.

"It's actually not that hard." Gabriel grinned. "You've got to figure that statistically speaking, there would be about one four-leaf clover in a patch this size."

"I'd have estimated two." The smaller boy's eyes peered out curiously from under his curly hair. "I think it's about one in three hundred, although there's obviously some variance due to genetics."

The bigger boy rolled his eyes.

"This species of clover tends to have fewer four-leaf variants," Gabriel said, waving a hand out over the plants, "maybe one in five hundred, and given the square footage of this patch, I estimate we have about five hundred clovers here. Knowing that, you look at the patch and unfocus your eyes and concentrate on the shapes rather than the individual leaves themselves."

"Oh!" The smaller boy seemed to get a bit taller. "You're pattern-matching rather than actually looking."

Gabriel grinned. "It's as simple as picking out a square in a field of triangles."

The boy looked breathless. "Do you find you can train the human eye to register only the squares?"

"Absolutely!" Gabriel turned his attention back to the plants at his feet. "Human vision is very easy to fool because the brain interprets visual patterns the way it expects to and rejects any data it doesn't expect—"

"You don't have to tell me," said the boy. "I take advantage of that all the time."

The bigger boy said, "You'd better quit it. Now."

Immediately the younger boy fell silent.

Gabriel brightened. "Got it!"

As he picked the four-leaf clover that was Remiel, the bigger boy jumped Gabriel. The smaller one throttled him, jamming a cloth against Gabriel's mouth so a sweet chlorine fog flooded his lungs and left him coughing. A stabbing heat scorched up his thigh. Then came a haze over his eyes and a binding around his lungs.

Demons!

Even as Raphael leaped from the bench and Remiel exploded from the clover, the smaller boy raised both hands and threw up a shimmering Guard around them like a bubble.

Gabriel tried to call for God but couldn't think clearly, couldn't find a way to get out of this solid body and back into his angelic form, and in the next instant his vision blackened.

Gabriel fell limp, insubstantial, and before Raphael could get close, they'd flashed him from the field.

Two

Raphael exploded away from the park in pursuit, Remiel following. Raphael immediately outdistanced her, but she streaked behind, trans-forming her clothing to armor, forming her sword in her hand. The demon pair "bounced" rather than flashing straight to Hell, passing through five locations in an attempt to throw off their hunters. In the time it took to think of their next location, they were already there.

After the third bounce, Raphael tackled the nearer of the demons mid-transfer, and he hurled him to the ground on a snowy field in Antarctica. Remiel rose up behind him, sword aflame, and looked down to find Raphael had captured her twin.

God— Her heart seized. *What are they doing?*

Raphael slammed Camael into the ground by his shoulders. "What did you do with him?"

Camael looked Raphael in the eyes and laughed.

Remiel concentrated so her armor changed into Camael's armor, her sword to his sword, and then her body changed from female to male. Her earrings plinked out of her ears onto the surface of the snow.

Raphael spun to face her. Projecting her determination, Remiel streaked after the other demon.

She followed the traces of his passage, but even that brief hesitation had caused the trail to dissipate. She could feel only hints of Gabriel's power, and she thought his captor was the Cherub Mephistopheles. But it was impossible to verify.

At some point she felt the trail angle into Hell, so she tried to follow, but Hell bounced her back.

Stupid regulations. Remiel flashed into Hell's lobby. Demons flanked the stone columns as she advanced to the sign-in book, complete with pen on a chain, where demons checked in and out on order of the commanders of the army. Closer inspection revealed that pen was missing and the chain dangled limp. Remiel formed a pen out of her soul material and signed. "Camael, Mephistopheles, and Guest."

The demon guarding the entrance huffed. "Guest? You have to specify."

"Bite me." Remiel turned to enter. The stone floor clung to her feet as she moved.

The demon drew his sword. "By Belior's orders, you have to sign in exactly—"

"Are you countermanding Mephistopheles' orders?" Remiel snapped. "You will let me inside now!"

The torches lining the room poured smoke to the ceiling where it gathered, unable to escape. The demon said, "Belior doesn't care about Mephistopheles and his little projects."

"He'll care about this one soon enough," said a silky voice from an alcove. Remiel turned to find Mephistopheles, his wings tucked exquisitely at his back, his armor gleaming, the only part of him not in total control his blond curls. "Kindly admit my officer, and we won't have to escalate the matter."

The demon slid his sword into its scabbard.

Mephistopheles turned to Remiel. "Don't stand on ceremony with these peons. I remember when you stabbed someone through the heart rather than deal with Belior's idiocy." And Mephistopheles flashed them both into central Hell.

They arrived in a chamber utterly lightless. Remiel resisted her urge to glow: they were in the Lab Area where the chief torment was the living darkness. Demons couldn't disperse it with their glow, and although she suspected she could, to do so would immediately give away her deception.

"Is he secured?" Mephistopheles asked.

"I just finished," came a deeper voice which Remiel guessed belonged to Beelzebub, Mephistopheles' bonded Seraph and Satan's other advisor.

She could hear the hiss of feathers against one another, the sliding of fabric against fabric as someone walked, and then the clank of metal against metal. "Insufficient. This much play in the chains allows for too much movement. We need a five-point restraint. Once we begin, you'll have to run a Guard over him in a V from each of his shoulders to between his legs and across his chest."

"Easy enough," Beelzebub said.

Remiel-as-Camael said, "When will we do it?"

"We can't proceed until he regains consciousness," Mephistopheles said. "That could be fifteen minutes. Maybe longer. It's tricky to predict how medications carry over from human bodies to angelic bodies, but Gabriel's notorious for having no tolerance to drugs."

Beelzebub said, "I'll stay here. You can tell Lucifer we've got him."

"I'll stay," Remiel said. "It doesn't make sense for you to stand watch over a sleeping prisoner."

Beelzebub's sense of annoyance crawled over Remiel, who cringed.

"Accompany me," Mephistopheles said, sounding as if he were standing close to Beelzebub. "He's bound to be pleased that we captured Gabriel so easily."

"You got him at all because of Camael," Beelzebub said. "Camael could use the political capital."

Mephistopheles sounded irritated. "Since when have you concerned yourself about anyone else's political capital?"

Remiel opened her hands and created a paper cup of coffee and a donut, which she handed to Beelzebub. "I didn't realize we paid you to be a rent-a-cop."

Even in the darkness, he was able to recognize what she'd done. "Good one! And it's chocolate frosted, too."

Remiel bit her lip. "Really, I can stay. Sa—Lucifer won't speak to me anyhow."

How am I going to get Gabriel out of here if he doesn't leave? she prayed, but God didn't answer. They were in Hell. The room was Guarded, preventing unwanted people from entering or communicating. Because God adhered to His own rules, she wouldn't get a clear response.

Well, the insane could get through Guards. But God would remain stubbornly sane, and so would Gabriel.

Mephistopheles and Beelzebub weren't projecting at each other, so Remiel knew they must be trading thoughts and energy through their Seraph-Cherub bond. Finally Mephistopheles said, "Stay if you wish. Let me know the instant he awakens."

In the next moment, Remiel found herself out of the lightless cell and in an equally lightless corridor with Mephistopheles.

"He's more useful elsewhere," Remiel said.

"Don't try to talk sense to a Seraph," Mephistopheles said. "But you're right that Lucifer won't bother speaking to you."

"Wait!" Remiel's heart raced. "I'm important to this. You'd better bring me inside when you do it."

"Oh." The blandest sense of laughter laced his voice. "Is that the case?"

Remiel's heart faltered. "I deserve to be there!"

Mephistopheles still sounded as if he were smirking. "I'll recommend you to him, but don't count on it. I don't care if you serve as the focus. Anyone would do." And away he flashed.

Alone in the corridor, Remiel slammed her fist into the wall, then kicked it, then stood with her hands clenched, struggling to get a grip on herself.

She was just on the outside of that little room where they had Gabriel. This much was something, at least. She formed a sigil of her power and placed it against the wall, then flashed to the top of the room (having to desolidify herself through meters of stone) and placed another one there. Then a third on the opposite side of the first. That would at least enable Michael to find the room.

Remiel sat in the corridor and folded her arms. She couldn't slip here. One mistake and she'd be chained alongside Gabriel and probably get the same treatment—whatever it was that required they keep him still and use someone as a power-focus.

If they used her as the focus, she'd get back inside. But then she'd find herself face to face with Satan, and while it had been easy to fool Mephistopheles (let's face it—most Cherubim had the social skills of a smart brick) she'd never be able to fool Satan.

I'm not leaving Gabriel. Not when I'm this close. Ten more minutes.

She sat in the corridor, concentrating on her own heart. Camael. Twins. Irin. She and her brother had been indistinguishable before the winnowing, and so far she'd been able to pretend to be him, but if she wanted to fool Satan, she couldn't pretend. She had to become Camael. More than just his gender, more than just his clothing. She had to put on his thoughts, put on his perceptions, and try to layer all that over a soul that still refused to reject God.

Help me.

She hoped that was God's assent in her heart.

The first way to be Camael was to hate Remiel—it was something easy enough to do, to loathe that ineffective slave of their Creator, the one God had bought off with status in exchange for rejecting the other half of herself. And once Camael hated Remiel, the rest flowed easily: to hate the things Remiel loved, to hate the things that reminded him of her, and then the logical next step, which was to despise himself because it was one of the things she had loved and because Camael himself reminded himself of Remiel.

Stupid Cherub, Camael thought to Gabriel. *Why did you have to get yourself captured and put me in this position to begin with?*

And now, Camael thought, it was his job to get Gabriel out of there.

Raphael's enraged soul emitted a shock wave like a depth charge the instant Gabriel was taken, and within seconds Heaven responded.

Michael arrived in the park, armored, and he looked around at all the guardian angels. "Where did they go?"

Raphael returned in that instant with Camael, bound with his will, even as more angels arrived: Israfel, Raguel, Saraquael, Uriel, and Zadkiel. They picked up the information wordlessly as Raphael's heart swirled out the details in no coherent order, and Michael laid his hand on his sword.

Saraquael said, "Raguel, come with me," and they flashed away.

Michael turned to Raphael. "Can you get any sense from Gabriel?"

Raphael's eyes were wide as tea saucers. He shook his head.

"If Raphael and I can't pick up anything from him," Israfel said, running a hand through her waist-length black curls, "then he's still unconscious."

Michael huffed. "Did you get an idea of where they were headed?"

Raphael opened his hands. "They were bouncing, and I caught Camael on the third bounce. Remiel followed the other one. I'm not sure where in Hell they went."

Raguel and Saraquael returned. "Wherever they've got him, he's Guarded. I can't get a good feel of where he might be."

Raphael flashed to the clover field, and Michael followed. "This is where it happened."

"The second signature feels like Mephistopheles'." Michael looked back at Saraquael. "Hunt out a Guard set up by Beelzebub. They're bound to be working together."

Saraquael vanished again.

Raguel squared his shoulders, flared his broad wings, and looked down at Michael. "Do we want to invade? I'll summon the army."

The Throne Uriel, who up to now hadn't spoken, said, "Why did they want Gabriel?"

Michael inadvertently projected that he didn't frankly care why they'd abducted Gabriel, but immediately he paused.

With a typical precision and concern on Uriel's heart-shaped face, the Throne added, "Their motive should have a direct impact on how much force we bring to bear."

Michael pointed from Raguel to Camael, who still struggled against Raphael's binding. "Secure and question him."

Raguel took hold of Remiel's twin and flashed him to Heaven. Israfel followed.

Michael returned his attention to Raphael, the color of whose eyes and wings had intensified as his emotions started frothing. His whole form vibrated with tension.

"Any luck reading him?"

Raphael shook his head.

"Try to keep calm." Michael laid a hand on Raphael's arm. The Seraphic heat had begun to escape control, and the resonance of his soul emitted a high-pitched whine. Without a bonded Cherub to absorb his fear, he was discharging power unchanneled.

"You need another Cherub."

Uriel had reached the same conclusion as Michael at the same moment and called into the air, "Ophaniel?"

"No!" Raphael took a step backward. "I'll need all my energy when Gabriel wakes up—"

"And until then," Michael said, "we can't have you rattling a hole in the Earth's mantle."

Ophaniel, head of the order of Cherubim, had already appeared.

Michael turned to him, saying, "Raphael needs—"

Ophaniel locked his steely eyes with Raphael's, and Raphael's brightness subsided even as Ophaniel began to glow.

"You must realize Israfel's suffering too," Ophaniel said. "She's Gabriel's other primary bond."

"Stick close to Raphael for now," Michael said. "Has Raguel figured out what they want with Gabriel?"

Ophaniel folded his arms and focused on the ground. "Camael said it's annihilation."

For a minute, Michael heard nothing.

When he managed to break free of the shock, he realized he was standing alongside an emotional volcanic eruption: Raphael's terror and urgency to act. Uriel and Zadkiel were right up next to Ophaniel questioning and questioning.

Israfel and Raguel had returned. Israfel was white as ash, her black hair limp. Saraquael appeared, and additionally two human souls arrived in the park, standing invisible in the clover while children played and parents chatted and insects darted and early rainbow-painted leaves let go their branches.

The two human souls were Peter, Jesus's first apostle, and Mary, Jesus's mother. Uriel caught them up on the facts while Ophaniel led Israfel and Raphael away from the rest of the group.

"Listen," Michael said, and because he was the head of Heaven's army, everyone turned to him. In ordinary times Gabriel out-ranked him, and Raphael too—Uriel would if Uriel ever cared to exert any authority. But for now, they'd yield to him. Michael lowered his eyes, clenched his fists, and tightened his wings to his back.

"Raphael and Israfel can't contact Gabriel, so we have to assume he's out cold, and therefore unreachable to the enemy as well." Michael looked at the other archangels and the two humans. "That at least gives us some time." He turned to Saraquael. "What else do you have to report?"

"There are three of Remiel's sigils surrounding what seems to be a Guarded storage closet. I couldn't slip through."

Israfel drew close. "Is annihilation even possible? What makes them think they can do it?"

Raguel said, "Camael was convinced."

"But didn't God tell us we were eternal, that he would never end our existence?"

Uriel took a step forward and tried to touch her, but Israfel stepped backward, intoning, "Just clarify it for me. I don't remember if he told us we were eternal, or if eternity in his glory was a grand assumption on our part."

Michael waved her down. "If they think they can do it, we have to assume they can. I'd rather react as if it were possible only to find out it's not than assume Gabriel can't be destroyed and find out later he was." He looked at Raguel and Saraquael. "Suggestions?"

Raguel said, "While we're breaking down one door, they might be smuggling him out the back into another place. We need to pull him out of there, and I hate to say it, but a large-scale attack won't facilitate that."

Israfel shook her head as if to knock the panic to the sides and let her think clearly in the center. She glanced at Ophaniel, and he must have drawn off some of the fire because suddenly she regained her focus. "They must have chosen Gabriel because if they get one shot, they want to make it worthwhile. Can we turn the tables and abduct one of theirs?"

"Unless we grabbed Satan, I can't imagine it would help," Michael said. "And even if we did, it might not."

"I still don't think it's possible," Zadkiel said.

For the first time, Mary spoke. "Are you guys aware of what it sounds like you're saying?"

"Annihilation." Michael faced her squarely. "Destroying his soul as if it were never created by God so that the only thing to remain would be our memories. If that. No chances at an afterlife."

"Ezekiel 28," Uriel murmured.

As she wrapped her hands in the hem of her sweater, Mary's olive-toned skin lost color. "Oh."

"Camael meant it," Michael said. "So we mean it too."

Raphael and Ophaniel rejoined them. "I still can't reach him." Raphael's voice quavered. "Working together, we can't reach him."

"That's a good thing." Michael laid a hand on Raphael's arm. "Keep that in mind—if you can't reach him, they can't either."

With a matter-of-fact lack of inflection unique to Cherubim, Ophaniel added, "Either that or he's already destroyed."

Raphael and Israfel both ignited.

"Thank you," Raguel muttered. "It always helps to have a Cherub cover all the bases."

Ophaniel shifted his feet and looked down.

Mary stepped nearer. "Michael, are you all right?"

"I don't have the time not to be all right." He huffed. "If anyone needs the help, it's Raphael. He and Gabriel are like one person."

Israfel glared at Michael. He noticed her look but only said, "Can you sense him?"

"Still nothing."

Michael turned to Ophaniel. "Ideas?"

"Remiel gave us a location," Ophaniel said. "Israfel and Raphael give us a connection. You and Raguel have the power. Once Gabriel is awake, we have enough going for us to slip him out of there. And Remiel, if possible, can send us a signal."

Michael turned to Saraquael. "Can you make contact with Remiel?"

"Not without potentially exposing her."

"Good point." He frowned. "You and Zadkiel question Camael again and see if you can get any other useful information from him: the procedure, who will be involved, how long it takes, and whether they've tested it on anyone."

The two Dominions vanished.

Michael took a deep breath and realized he didn't have a clear path at the moment. He looked up at Raphael, who had flames around his eyes and his wings. Ophaniel himself was trembling with the energy he'd drawn off Raphael and Israfel, so Michael summoned Raphael's bonded Cherub Sidriel, and also Zophiel, another Cherub bonded to Israfel. Then he looked at Uriel, who stood beside Mary, an arm over her shoulders.

Mary looked careworn, strands of grey in her black hair. "What's next?"

"We pray," said Uriel. "We wait for Raphael to make contact, and we pray."

Three

Gabriel became aware that he was becoming aware. For an angel, that liminality was a new experience, so he made note of the heaviness of his eyes, the weight of his chest, and the dull sound of his body.

The spiritual body he inhabited was held fast, and Gabriel extended his consciousness to probe the world around him. That he'd been taken prisoner he could remember. It was unconscionably stupid not to have realized a six-year-old didn't typically have that kind of vocabulary or scientific perception of the world. They'd clearly singled him out for capture. But where he was and what they intended, that he didn't know, and like an empty basin plunged against the surface of a pool, he trembled for knowledge to fill the emptiness.

Gabriel's form remained limp, but his mind had already shifted into the highest gear with an urgency. Where was he? Chains suspended him upright, arms spread, legs together, wings pressed against a stone wall. One outcropping of rock jutted into the small of his back, but he didn't shift to get it into a more comfortable place. For now he wanted to appear unconscious. He could detect another presence entombed with him.

Next his senses spread to the corners of the room, rolling up against the edge and filling it without overspilling. If he'd spread his six wings to their fullest, Gabriel would have brushed the opposite walls with his primary feathers, and the ceiling he could have touched with his wingtips while standing. He stopped breathing, then stopped his heart in order to hear better. The room sounded empty, but he still could feel someone on guard—distracted, but waiting. Coffee and sugary fake chocolate scented the air. Gabriel opened his eyes the barest amount to see nothing.

The lab area.

Gabriel trembled at the intransigent darkness as thick as tar, then stilled himself, re-closing his eyes because he'd rather not see the hungry dark. His highest output of light would emerge grainy here, like light six fathoms deep. The damned couldn't achieve even that much.

God, how am I doing?

The answer came only faintly. He was, after all, in Hell.

What do they want with me? Why am I here? Where are they? Gabriel took a deep breath as slowly and silently as he could. Stay calm. If Gabriel wanted more of God in here—and he did—he'd have to find a way to let in more of God.

He reached for Raphael through their bond but couldn't get a sense of the Seraph.

First things first. Gabriel sent his mind into the chains on his wrists and ankles, then asked the metal to lengthen. It started to, but pulled tight around the centers. This much he had expected: the chains were laced through the core with the disembodied will of a minor demon, and it had been told to hold tight.

Gabriel focused his attention on the chain, then commanded, *Lengthen!* After a pause, he thought, *Aha!* even though nothing had happened.

Disheartened to think it had failed, the will-lacing let go of the chain.

Yeah, give him a challenge next time. Gabriel then pointed out the lengthened one to the others, and they gave up too, dropping him unceremoniously to the floor.

The chain links clanked against one another, and Gabriel tensed. He tried to pull his hands from the cuffs, but a higher order demon must have made those: they held fast no matter how Gabriel tried to change their shape or his own.

"Oh, you're awake," said a deep voice which Gabriel realized was Beelzebub's.

Being obviously awake made reconnoitering more difficult. In retrospect, he ought to have put up with the chains until he'd studied everything else.

The scrape of a chair as Beelzebub stood. Gabriel rushed his mind through the chamber to figure out where in the lab area he was. He felt along the walls, which naturally were Guarded so no one could enter.

Although angels seldom Guarded anything, demons set Guards as a matter of course to prevent their enemies (or their allies) from searching their private chambers. Guards permitted entry only to those on good terms with those who had set them, being created directly by the will of the owner, and they were capable of containing a conscious, sane angel. This Guard resonated with a prickliness Gabriel found unusual. He pushed on the Guard to learn more.

"You're wondering why you're here." Beelzebub drew closer. "You haven't got much time, so listen to me."

Gabriel tried to recoil into the stone. The demon Seraph stood so close Gabriel could feel his body heat.

Gabriel pushed again on the Guard. —ah. The prickliness was due to the apparently-single Guard's being composed of several different ones—the one at his back having been set first, then the one on his right. Those felt ancient. The one before him and the one to his left were approximately the same age, with the ones on top and bottom set last of all, only this week, finished off by someone weaving them together.

Beelzebub said, "Why don't you shine a bit so we can have this talk face-to-face?"

Turning his head, Gabriel projected that darkness was just fine for now.

Gabriel knew how to set Guards, and this wasn't the way to do it. Having it set piecemeal could leave chinks for an enemy to exploit. It could be squeezed until one buckled because they were all of different strengths. *It makes no sense.* If Mephistopheles had arranged this—a good assumption, considering which demon stood here now—he knew better. Gabriel would have expected such shoddy work only from a minor demon, not from one who pre-winnowing had been among the smartest Cherubim.

Beelzebub shook Gabriel. "Don't take your brain away. Stop thinking. If you have questions, ask me. I'm standing right here."

The way the room was Guarded made sense, Gabriel thought, if this room wasn't really a room, just an unused space carved from the rock by omission rather than intention. Yes, this theory worked, with the wall to one side reeking of Beelzebub and the one on the other tingling of Mephistopheles. At his back it felt like Satan's own offices, his secrets so tantalizingly close but unable to be broken open. Personal notes, plans, perhaps even a private conference taking place, and no other options remained for Gabriel other than reconnaissance.

This theory meant they'd been preparing for his capture as long ago as the age of the youngest Guard: about a week.

"Pay attention!" Beelzebub sounded frustrated. "Mephistopheles is going to annihilate you!"

Gabriel focused abruptly.

"That's what it takes to get you to look?" Beelzebub folded his arms and shifted his stance so he leaned back on one leg. Like most Seraphim, he was tall. "Mephistopheles figured out how to annihilate an angel. We're starting with you. I can let you free. Are you willing to listen?"

The sudden glow from Gabriel's spirit illuminated Beelzebub's dark eyes and square jaw. "I knew there was something to Ezekiel 28:18! How is he going to annihilate an angel?"

An infinite exasperation passed over Beelzebub's face. "Who cares? We have to do this fast if you want to escape."

Gabriel said, "Do what?"

Beelzebub erupted in flames, and his Seraphic power surrounded Gabriel like a cloud of swarming bees. He rested the heels of his hands against the wall on either side of Gabriel's head, and he smirked.

Gabriel's heart recoiled from the energy. "I'm not going to bond with you!"

Beelzebub was looking right into his eyes, and Gabriel extinguished his light, but the demon was so close he could feel eddies from his eyelashes as he blinked. The heat crawled over him.

"Even if I agreed to, I'm not sure we'd be able to cross-bond. All the pre-existing bonds between angels and demons were broken by the winnowing."

"Give it a try," the Seraph murmured.

"I think—" Gabriel swallowed. "I think I'd rather die."

Beelzebub hit him. Gabriel gave a relieved sigh as the Seraphic energy let off.

The demon said into the air, "Mephistopheles, he's awake."

Was it true? Was it even possible? Certainly it fit with his suspicions about the demons, that they'd devised something tremendous. This information helped it make more sense that they'd keep their discovery quiet, just in case the attempt failed. But to make the attempt at all, their theory must be sound. Mephistopheles was generally sober.

At that moment, Mephistopheles appeared, and Gabriel heard him gasp. The energy in the air vanished as the fallen Cherub pulled it all inside. Gabriel geared up his light in time to see Mephistopheles turn toward Beelzebub, vibrating into an angry blur. "What are you doing? He's going to die! Why would you bond with a thing that's doomed?"

"If we could access his power—"

"In fifteen minutes he won't have any power left to access, you idiot! If Lucifer finds out what you—"

Mephistopheles froze, then turned to face Gabriel, who wore a tremendous smile.

The fallen Cherub's almond eyes narrowed.

"I'll tell him whatever I like," Gabriel said. "I don't stand to lose anything more, unless you're all bluster."

Mephistopheles and Beelzebub stood frozen for a moment, and Gabriel envisioned their bond, soiled but a bond nevertheless, and abruptly he realized that if they were telling the truth, how horrible his loss would be for Raphael.

Beelzebub said, "He'll never believe you. You'd say anything to save your life."

"Shut up!" Mephistopheles snapped, startling Gabriel. "You've said enough already." He turned back to Gabriel. "He's right, of course. You're going to die regardless."

"Then why should I care what happens afterward?"

Mephistopheles flinched. "He's my Seraph."

Gabriel wished he could smirk the way Beelzebub could, but instead he stayed deadpan. "He was nearly mine too."

Mephistopheles glared at Beelzebub in time to stop him from charging toward Gabriel. "Get out of here."

The fallen pair locked gazes, and then Beelzebub vanished.

Silence continued for a moment.

Mephistopheles went to Gabriel and searched his pockets. "Lucifer won't spare you no matter what you say, and at this point, I daresay he wouldn't expect anything else from Beelzebub. Nor from you. It would be easy enough to counter that you'd offered to bond him to save your own life. Oh...?" He pulled Michael's sigil ring from Gabriel's jeans, and his eyes glimmered. "I thought I detected something. I would have believed you'd know better than to allow Michael to divide his power." He slipped the ring onto his finger, then returned his full attention to Gabriel. "Lucifer will initiate the proceedings as soon as he's ready, whenever that is. Timing is a game for him."

Gabriel said, "Did you really figure out how to annihilate an angel?"

Mephistopheles assented.

"And you're certain it's possible?"

"We haven't actually performed one yet," Mephistopheles admitted, "but the theory checks out. You're our test case."

"That makes sense," Gabriel said. "If God's going to punish you for annihilating someone, you ought to make sure it's someone important."

"Exactly." Mephistopheles rubbed his chin. "When it came time to select a subject, we settled on a few targets, but I argued for you, and now you're here."

Curiosity sparkled inside. "But how do you intend to destroy soul material? It regenerates."

Mephistopheles' eyes glistened. "It's not destruction so much as it's disconnection. If you disunite a soul's parts, they continue drifting away from one another until they can't regain any sort of cohesion."

Gabriel's head raised. "Oh! So one would still exist, only in an infinite number of pieces!"

"With entropy drawing those further apart."

Gabriel tried to brush that aside with his hand, but he was still chained, so he only shook his head. "Entropy belongs to the fallen world. With a celestial creature, the parts might well reconstitute themselves. That's why dismemberment isn't permanent."

"The soul-fragments would try to reunite," Mephistopheles said, "but lacking cohesion, how would they adhere?"

Gabriel's eyes widened. "You've discovered how a soul is more than the sum of its parts?"

Mephistopheles opened his hands and created a screen of light, on which he illuminated a series of filaments and dots. "Consider this a model of a soul, extremely simplified for purposes of instruction. The various attributes are these dots, and this—" he changed the color of the filaments, "—is the string which binds them all together, fastening them to one another and giving them order."

Gabriel struggled to lean closer. When he tried to point, his hands hit the end of the chain again, so he created a light pointer of his own and selected parts of the diagram. "You unhook it from one end and begin unraveling—"

"It's not raveled," Mephistopheles said. "The knitting reference in psalms is a metaphor, although maybe human souls are knit. I haven't tested theirs. Ours resemble beadwork."

Gabriel frowned. "What anchors the ends?"

"Nothing, ironically. The ends of the 'string' coil around themselves. The soul parts do have a natural attraction to one another, but it's not terribly difficult to pinch them apart."

"I wouldn't have guessed that." Gabriel hummed. "Have you mapped which parts of the soul are which?"

"It wasn't necessary for our purposes."

Gabriel's pupils widened. "If I were you, I'd attempt inactivating them one at a time to determine what attributes the test subject failed to manifest."

"That's an idea." Mephistopheles took a step closer, one wing inadvertently brushing the light image so it rippled like a reflection pool. "Prior to now I'd only stimulated them individually to test for a reaction, but the results were difficult to interpret. It would take a prohibitive time to deduce by attrition because there are so many aptitudes one would need to screen to detect an absolute lack of one."

Gabriel leaned back, breathing hard and still riding a wild joy. "You've proposed a microfilament binding together these beads. You cut the string, but wouldn't the structure just reform?"

"Maybe." Mephistopheles's face transformed with a slow but unstoppable grin, blue eyes bright beneath his curls. "But if one were to reach inside and slide the beads one at a time off the severed string, they'd scatter."

"Are they undifferentiated enough that you can't—"

"—keep them together once they're off the string? That's the theory. If someone were sufficiently dedicated—"

"Yes, but can the beads even retain their shape once separated from the string, which one assumes is their sustenance?" Gabriel shook his head. "Based on what happens after an angel gets injured, I would hypothesize the residual parts would dissipate after about twenty-four hours anyhow, leaving only a narrow window of time to reconstitute the angel in the first place." He frowned as he thought. "The string is our subconscious cohesion?"

"And the beads are personality traits fitted together seemingly at random."

"With the various admixtures determining the choir—"

"—so that God could manufacture an infinite variety of creatures with a very few base components."

"And presumably no one is entirely lacking any single trait—"

"—but with different angels amplifying differing aspects of the Almighty—"

"—meaning that spread out over all creation, every aspect of God is illuminated by at least one soul—"

"And also, in theory, if one could 'harvest' these traits form already living angels and somehow restring them—a new angel!"

They both stood breathless, eyes burning.

Gabriel raised his hands again and clanked against the chain ends, but he didn't seem to notice he was still anchored to the wall. "You'd need to get God to breathe into it. But what makes the string? What material makes the soul itself? Is the string what gives it awareness and animation?" he blurted, even as Mephistopheles was urging, "Tell me how it feels—tell me everything. I'll record it for study, and I'll even share the results with your choir-mates."

Mephistopheles lunged closer and grabbed him by the forearms. "Gabriel, if it has to happen, the least you can do is make sure it's properly documented."

With a bang, the chains tightened again, slamming Gabriel into the wall. Gasping, he closed his eyes.

"Shall we begin?" said Lucifer.

Help me, Gabriel prayed, and at the same time he instinctively reached for Raphael's heart. *Satan's here.*

Gabriel wriggled his wrists around so they fit better in the cuffs, and he tried to look at Lucifer without Lucifer meeting his eyes in return. The leader of the rebel angels, Lucifer seemed to move as if every gesture were calculated and captured for study; he had a Seraph's height and chiseled features. Gabriel watched as Lucifer cleared the room of the excess contents: a chair; the paper cup with a coffee logo on it. Even tucked at his back, his twelve wings all but filled the room, and his platinum hair lifted Gabriel's light so naturally that it seemed to glow of its own accord.

Mephistopheles said, "I'll summon the others," and momentarily Beelzebub and Camael stood in the room.

Gabriel turned away from Camael, who glared at him with Remiel's wild eyes but an abrasive edge that scoured the air around him.

"Fasten him." Mephistopheles checked the chains for tension, and abruptly Gabriel felt another Guard form over his chest, crushing him into the rock. His glow wavered, or perhaps it was his vision blackening.

"Back off," Mephistopheles said. "He has to remain conscious. We discussed this."

The pressure eased. Gabriel tried to sneak in a breath, praying as fervently as his logic-based Cherub soul could manage.

Lucifer straightened his sleeves. "Any last requests?"

"Once a year," Gabriel panted, "remind God that I loved him."

Lucifer paused. "I don't think so."

Gabriel chilled as icy fingers probed his soul.

Lucifer caught the lifeline about his heart, tugged it, and lifted it free of its fastenings.

"God!" Gabriel screamed, his spine trying to arch against his restraints, his wings snapping out, but with him unable to move because he was so tightly bound to the rock.

With Camael kneeling like a makeshift altar, Lucifer channeled all his power through the twin and fine-tuned Camael's larger strokes while Mephistopheles and Beelzebub together wove a perfect living Guard with their bonded souls.

Absolutely immobilized, Gabriel foundered as he tried to retain whatever those beads were that composed himself. The last thing he saw was the intensity of Camael's eyes—horrified and helpless and grim. Then Gabriel's glow winked out, plunging the chamber into blackness.

"They're attacking," Mephistopheles and Beelzebub said simultaneously. "Michael's hurling himself at the Guard."

All around the chamber, rock shivered like a space shuttle at T-minus-one.

"Stay strong," Lucifer said. "He's mine."

Gabriel felt his personality slipping apart. There were tears on his face, but the drama enfolded him. Gritting his teeth, he chanted in his mind, *God is strong, God is strong, God is strong.*

Energy from Raphael and Israfel empowered him from within. He soaked it into his heart as quickly as he could to fortify what Lucifer had not yet breached.

The room sparkled now even though it was the lab area: the Guard flickering, the eerie energy of Lucifer coursing through Camael and out his eyes, Gabriel's soul leaking light it never had before. Michael's sigil glowed white-hot with its owner outside the room.

The outer Guard shattered, but the stronger one remained.

Camael missed a notch, and Lucifer cuffed him, but the reprieve was only momentary.

"We're holding," said Mephistopheles-Beelzebub.

The clamor of Michael battering their Guard filled all the room as he forced the living web with the point of his sword. Gabriel called for him, tried to reach upward with his soul but then recoiled because the effort left him exposed. Parts of himself slid away like a cliff-face during a landslide.

Raphael and Israfel were ready to flash him outside the room if given a chance, and Gabriel thought they might be encouraging him: *Not far now*. But maybe that was only his yearning.

It had grown difficult to think. He ached to tell God he loved him one last time, but the words wouldn't form. He had grown so cold. Dull ringing swelled to absorb every sound while queer patches of grayness soaked the fabric of reality. He tasted metal. Then nothing.

The ring on Mephistopheles' hand gave one spangled burst of light that rippled the entire fabric of the Guard. Lucifer channeled a last burst through Camael. Light exploded through the entire cell, and then it was finished.

The chains dangled empty.

Camael collapsed.

They stood silently, the four in the room. The walls glowed as if with phosphorescent lichen, uneven but able to shine: Gabriel's spiritual residue.

"Oh, God," Mephistopheles whispered. "We did it."

"Michael's still on the ceiling," said Beelzebub.

Lucifer didn't spare him a glance. "Are you strong?"

"We're holding."

"Good." Lucifer stepped forward to where Gabriel had been. "There's nothing left at all. It worked just as you predicted."

Mephistopheles sounded shocked. "Annihilated."

Shuddering, Camael tried to stagger to his feet, and Lucifer took his hand and pulled him upright, then let him lean with his arms wrapped around his stomach until he could support himself.

"Do you suppose he's aware right now," Beelzebub said, "listening?"

"There's nothing after this," Lucifer said. "He's non-existent, not aware at all. It's as though he never was."

Mephistopheles fingered the sigil on his hand. "Other than the memories."

Lucifer said, "I want to scan the room for anything that might remain. Destroy whatever you find. Figure out how to burn the glow off the walls." He bent and lifted a four-leaf clover off the floor. "Well, what do you know? It's our lucky day."

He incinerated the clover on his palm.

They scanned the room for residue. Beelzebub seared every inch of the walls, floor and ceiling. When they were done, Lucifer declared the job finished.

Four

Lucifer flashed Camael, along with Mephistopheles and Beelzebub, into another lab area chamber, an easy feat of translocation for someone with enough willpower to lasso three souls and carry them away regardless of—or despite—their own intentions.

Unable to be seen, still Camael tried to contain his gag on breathing an antiseptic odor covering a musty scent and the hint of smoke. Lucifer was pacing the room. As he moved, the chemical burn smell faded and intensified.

This must be Lucifer's own chamber, his office, a place so secret that even Michael had never located it, let alone broken in—and yet here was Camael, carried inside like the closest of friends. For one mad moment Camael dreamed of exploding the place, shining light over all the dark corners, maybe for the first time since Hell's creation. He didn't.

The scrape of a chair and a rustle of feathers. "I want a full account from all of you."

The next scrape sounded different, wooden, a tall bench at a work station: Mephistopheles' slighter form on a stool. Beelzebub's deep voice came from Camael's other side, at a height that meant he remained standing. "Why do you need an account? You were there."

Camael slid down the wall and drew his ankles close.

"It's an analysis," Mephistopheles said. "We have to ensure we did it right."

"He's not there anymore. Of course we did it right!"

For two hours, Lucifer debriefed Camael and the other two, one hundred twenty minutes of pure fright having seen one angel dead and knowing that if he wasn't fully, totally Camael, the next moment would see the death of a second. So many questions, so many different ways of asking the same thing. And every time, the same answers. Lucifer wanted to be sure. *You had your hands in him. Did he die?*

Yes, I told you, I think he did.

You think, or you know?

I couldn't find anything else. He was there and then he burst into nothing when you moved through me and made that last pull.

Not mentioning—not even remembering the moment Camael decided there was no choice but to resist, but then not enough time, that moment when it felt as if Gabriel were vacuumed backward, but then there was nothing at all and hope turned into emptiness when Camael realized it wasn't the arms of rescue but the suction of nothingness and the Abyss.

Lucifer, all excited: had they really done it? And Camael, ripped in half again and again: yes, we did it. Mephistopheles: the evidence indicates that we succeeded, just as I hypothesized. Beelzebub: this is awesome, everything we've ever wanted.

No, no, Lucifer would say at that point, let's go over it one more time. Just in case we missed something.

After that excited roundabout, Lucifer and Beelzebub all the more fervent with every exchange and Mephistopheles more analytical and less certain (what if in theory—what if we allow for this differential) Lucifer received a message from Asmodeus, chief of Hell's army.

Beelzebub let off an irritated sigh.

"Come in," Lucifer said, but Camael felt that Lucifer actually looped him into the room. These must be unique Guards. You couldn't be let inside; you had to actually be drawn in like a fly on a frog's tongue. Camael wondered if the reverse were true and tried to send out a tendril of thought—but back it bounced. Interesting. In by pull, out by shove.

Asmodeus bowed. "We've positioned sentries in defense formation as you ordered. No attacks so far." Again the irritated sigh from Beelzebub—Asmodeus had disrupted their meeting to report nothing? Asmodeus continued in his even bass, "I wanted to note something interesting."

"Asmodeus," and the firmness conveyed that Lucifer's next words, however phrased, were to be considered a threat, "interest me."

"The angels stationed in Creation are silent," Asmodeus said. "All of them. The tourists are gone, but the angels with assignments are paired up."

Lucifer's chair creaked. "But silent?"

"They're doubled up," Asmodeus repeated, "but nobody is singing."

Camael recoiled. Beelzebub gasped.

"That's what they did when *he* died," Mephistopheles whispered, his voice abruptly coming from the same corner as Beelzebub's.

No one spoke.

"We did it!" Beelzebub said. "I told you, we did it!"

"We had sentries surrounding the Guarded dome over the field where you abducted him," Asmodeus said. "That dome remained in place and we were unable to break it, not even enough to see through, but—" and here they felt his excitement surge, "we were able to hear Raphael scream 'No!'"

Camael felt both Beelzebub and Mephistopheles cringe simultaneously.

Lucifer and the captain of the army pinpointed the moment the scream happened, about half a second before the annihilation finished. "That corresponds to when I broke their bond," Lucifer added.

Mephistopheles sounded hollow. "You could find that?"

"I saved it for last," Lucifer said, "in case Gabriel was in pain."

Camael stared toward his hands, only he couldn't see them. *I feel nothing. I feel nothing.*

"Are they in attack formation?" Lucifer asked.

"They're not staging anything we can determine," Asmodeus said.

"Excellent work." Lucifer cracked his knuckles. "Alert me if you think you can interest me again." And Asmodeus was gone.

Camael's head dropped onto his folded arms, and all three pairs of wings came up over his head.

Silent angels. A buddy system. No invasion. Gabriel dead.

Gabriel.

Dead.

No—stop feeling. Feel nothing.

Mephistopheles said, "We shouldn't conclude too much from their behavior. I want to conduct one more sweep—"

"We don't need one more sweep!" Beelzebub's energy sliced through the room like a quasar. "We did it!"

Camael mustered his voice. "What's next?"

Lucifer said, "I know you want to kill her, but she's last."

Camael bit his lip. His blood had a sickly taste. Too cold in here. This was Hell—where was the fire? Where the sound? Silent angels. Silent Gabriel, never to sing again.

I feel nothing.

Mephistopheles said, "Michael is the next logical choice."

"It would be to our advantage to take him down," Lucifer said. "When we thought we had only one chance, it had to be Gabriel. With two, though—Michael, or Uriel?"

"We'd never get near Uriel," Beelzebub said. "Do you think we could do this to one of the monkeys?"

Mephistopheles murmured, "I told you, they're not put together the same way."

"It's too bad," Lucifer said, "because I'd love to permanently remove that woman from the picture."

Beelzebub laughed. "Camael, who's your choice?"

Camael stayed ducked. *Raphael. If you killed Gabriel, it was only a kindness to obliterate his Seraph too and spare him existence as a half-moon and a lifetime of memories no one wanted to mention and a name you never wanted in the first place. To dance and hear only half the music, and to know God loved you but would not give back the only other thing you ever wanted even though you knew it was wrong even to want—*

"Suggestions, Camael?"

Camael swallowed. "Raphael."

"Not strategically significant."

"With all due respect, sir," Camael said, "you don't know how Raphael is going to react. He might make himself important."

Beelzebub snorted. "You mean like your sister did? Or like you?" He laughed. "I don't think we have anything to worry about."

I feel nothing. I feel nothing.

Lucifer was quiet.

Camael laid his head on his folded arms, again tenting himself within his wings. *Gone, going away. I feel nothing. I am nothing.*

Camael uncurled a long thought and snaked it outside the Guards as if they didn't exist, hunting for air, hungering for light and water, for someone's hand and a presence inside that said, *you are, you feel, come to me.*

Camael felt thoughts probing over him, so he sent away his mind outside the Guard. *Light. Quiet. Oblivion. Gabriel. Gabriel wasn't thinking anything any longer, never again. I feel nothing.*

"Debriefing is over. Dismissed," Lucifer said. Camael ended up free, somewhere else in Hell but carrying the hell of loss deep inside.

Still in Lucifer's chamber, Mephistopheles found himself not dismissed.

Lucifer was writing, a light scratch of nib against paper, and then, when Mephistopheles began wondering if he had been forgotten, said, "Camael is getting slippery."

Mephistopheles said, "He's only a Virtue. That sustained an effort must have exhausted him."

"He's hard to grip right now. He was probing outside my Guards. Observe him. I don't want him going insane."

Mephistopheles listened to the pen scratching and tried to deduce the letters he was hearing written, at least the language if not the actual words. "I'll assign someone to assess his movements."

"You know his value to this process," Lucifer said. "I don't need to tell you how displeased I'd be if we had to revert to our backup plan."

Mephistopheles was sure the pattern he had just heard could be the letter n, but it might have been a ん or a れ. "Will that be all, sir?"

"Not yet." A pause in the writing, and then it resumed; that was almost certainly a さ. "I'm fully aware that the discovery was all yours which enabled today's success."

Mephistopheles inclined his head, knowing Lucifer would pick up the acknowledgment he projected.

"I want you to get to work on a way of mass-producing the effect. A technique so any demon can work that way."

Mephistopheles hummed. "Do you want that technique in everyone's hands?"

Lucifer chuckled. "I'll make Beelzebub my next victory if he even thinks of trying it on me. And you can feel free to repeat that."

"I didn't mean—"

"Naturally you didn't." Lucifer continued writing. "Tell me, do you think it hurt Raphael when I broke their bond?"

Shaking, Mephistopheles clenched his fists. "I can't say."

"But surely you suspect. I've never seen fit to permanently fetter myself with such an anchor, but you and Beelzebub use the bond to your mutual advantage enough that I consider you an expert."

Mephistopheles bit his lip. Lucifer was definitely writing in hiragana, but it might have been anything at all. A report, a poem, even the crossword puzzle. *I just violated God's sovereignty in a permanent way* ten thousand times.

"If it didn't hurt at the moment," Mephistopheles said, "then I'm certain it hurts now."

"Very well." Lucifer set down his pen. "Let me know if you ever want all your bonds broken. Dismissed."

Mephistopheles found himself in his own chamber, pushed back through his own Guards. He sat on his desk with his head in his hands.

They'd prayed. The group of angels and humans at the playground had prayed. Everyone in Heaven had prayed, once word went out. But Michael's sword was his prayer, and Raphael's deep injection of power toward Gabriel's soul was his. Uriel and Mary stood, hands clasped, tears over-shining both their faces as they united in prayer for one thing, one thing only.

A dozen Principalities maintained a dome-shaped Guard over the field, shielding the archangels and saints.

Across the field, Raphael had drawn storm clouds, six wings extended, eyes raised, wind whipping around him louder than a shout. Parents had gathered their children into minivans to hurry them home in advance of the storm, not knowing this storm would encompass all Heaven and Hell.

Beside Raphael at the storm's center stood Israfel, adding her Seraph surge to the might that had shredded the temple veil and shaken the Earth on Good Friday. Their combined strength shot through creation like a needle: deep, insubstantial, a probe into the heart of Hell searching for the heart of God.

Find him.

Then Michael found Gabriel, found his own sigil protesting on Mephistopheles' hand, found Remiel's sigils shrieking rage, and he tracked their outcry through the labyrinths of the mind to the locked room in a lightless area. He landed on the roof of the room, then grasped and targeted that Seraphic spike, guiding it into the Guard like a surgeon's biopsy needle. Using his sword, he'd pried at the Guard—not enough to force himself inside, although the bonded pair within thought that was his intent. Instead he called to his sigil, and it responded. With thrusting against both sides, he widened the mesh just enough to slip that filament inside.

Like a pump, Israfel and Raphael had flooded Gabriel with their strength, sending all but their souls into Gabriel's heart. Raphael couldn't force himself through, but he struggled to feed more than a tendril of power through the eye of that needle. And when at the end they all realized it was too late, not enough, no more time, Raphael engulfed whatever he could and aspirated everything out of that cell.

With a cry, Raphael snapped back into himself, but more than himself because within him he contained the dissolved remnants of his bonded Cherub. Israfel dropped her sword.

Uriel rolled out a command to the others like a shock wave: *Everybody leave!*

Raphael knelt, eyes flared, hands open as if at a loss for what to do next, how to fasten together the shattered slivers of a soul. Millions of them.

"Heal him!" Uriel's breath brushed Raphael's lips, their faces were so close. "Heal him—all of you! Don't let a single part of you not be healing him!"

Raphael enfolded his wings around himself and Uriel. An amber sheen suffused the Seraph, pulsing, searching, seeking out every sliver of Gabriel—glue to grains of sand. The energy formed up like egg-white, shimmering in Raphael's lap.

"Dear God," Uriel was whispering in a voice lost to the wind, "dear God, let this work, please make this work—"

Uriel could insert spiritual fingers into what Raphael had dragged back, but fitting the pieces together was like stitching marmalade. There wasn't nearly enough, and it had no cohesion.

Uriel pulled back from Raphael's sphere.

Mary had remained, Israfel at her side with one hand on her shoulder while the wind whipped their drenched hair.

"Do you need me to go?" There was no reason for it, but Mary's voice had reverted to a hospital hush that the storm scattered like dry leaves.

"Stay." Uriel looked at Israfel. "You should leave. Your substance might mix with his—but—"

Israfel didn't budge.

Uriel looked again at Raphael. "If anyone can heal him, he can. Their bond, plus his God-given healing ability. But..."

Michael reappeared, pale, his red hair tousled and his eyes stark. The Archangel's whole soul formed one question mark, but Uriel just let him sample the silence to sense their tension. Michael plunged his sword into the ground and leaned on it, then dropped to his knees and rested his forehead against the hilt.

Dear God, please make this work.

Mary turned to Israfel. "Are you still strengthening Gabriel?"

The angel faced the wind. "It's like pouring wine into a sieve."

Mary stepped closer to the pregnant orb that was Raphael, her face aflicker with the ferocity of eternity and existence struggling to survive. "Gabriel," she whispered, "it's okay. We're working. You're with friends. God loves you. We'll find a way."

Michael glanced at the Guard shimmering around the field. "We've got to move them both. If we're attacked here, now, I can't protect them. The slightest disruption—"

"Agreed." Israfel sheathed her sword. "I'll cast a Guard around Raphael and transport them together." She frowned. "Where to?"

"Gabriel's home," Michael said.

"No." Uriel looked back over one shoulder. "Mine. There's too much of Gabriel's residue in his library, and the same with Raphael's house. We're going to need to repair him, and we'll need to know what's him and what's not without a question."

Michael swallowed. "You're right. Mary—" He looked at her and drew a long breath. "I hate to say this, but stay here. Right where Raphael is now. In case something—some part of them gets left—"

She bit her lip.

Michael clasped his sword. "Okay. Move."

Israfel appeared above Raphael, flung out her arms and all six wings and cast a magenta sphere around the amber orb of the Seraph healer, shading him violet. Uriel set a second orb around Israfel, and first Israfel vanished, then Uriel. Mary sat on the grass, her eyes on Michael until he wrenched his sword from the hill and vanished too, bringing the Principality Guard with him.

It took another half hour for the storm to ebb, but Mary remained in the rain, eyes closed the whole time.

Uriel guided Israfel and Raphael into the bedroom of Uriel's bungalow. Uriel immediately changed the house so there were no windows, and the walls and floor met without any seams or chinks. With the room now doorless, Uriel turned to Raphael.

"I don't know what to do." Raphael's cracked words dissolved like a match shaken out.

Israfel added, "He's so weak."

Keep working. Uriel knelt in front of Raphael, who now existed half as disembodied energy and half his own spiritual form. The

Throne extended a hand to the globule of an angel unrecognizable any longer as Gabriel. A touch evoked no response. "Gabriel? Cherub?"

"Oh, God, my God," Raphael whispered, his hands over the orb. "He can't die now. You can't let him die like this. Not among friends. Not with all of us here."

"He's firmer than he was." Michael had appeared from the hill and raked his hand back through his hair. Heat shimmered about him momentarily, and then the rain was gone from him. Israfel and Uriel had already done the same. "You're doing some good."

"I can't feel his mind." Raphael remained soaked from the storm, but Michael understood why he wouldn't want to heat up.

Israfel settled on the floor, her wings tucked at her back. *"Holy, Holy, Holy,"* she sang, her voice a thread through the room. *"Holy God, Holy Omnipotent, Holy Immortal, all your works adore you—"*

Raphael ran his fingers along the light energy inhabiting his lap, and he joined Israfel's song, the Trisagion of the Seraphim. *"You are the one who was, and who is, and who is to come."*

Uriel sat with closed eyes, praying. Michael stood in the corner, pale.

As if in a dream, Raphael raised his hands to shoulder height, and between them he cast a bar of light, then flicked the fingers of his left hand so it began to spin. Michael frowned, alone watching in silence as Israfel continued singing and Uriel continued praying. Raphael pulled his right hand away from the spindle, and it pivoted on the fingers of his left hand until it swung perpendicular to his lap, pointing at Gabriel.

Michael's eyes widened, and he opened his mouth to speak, but then he stopped himself.

Raphael guided Gabriel's energy with his right hand, up and onto the spindle where it spun, then emerged on the other side more solid.

"How—"

Uriel raised a hand, and Michael fell silent. Israfel's song hesitated, but she maintained it.

As Gabriel's fabric solidified, visions assaulted the four angels: memories, stray words and odd thoughts. Like four AM inspirations, impulses darted through their minds, apparitions, scenes from the wrong point of view.

Michael recoiled, but he didn't leave.

The flashes of Gabriel's experiences left no footprints. From one moment to the next they couldn't be sure what they had just been thinking, but Raphael continued spinning, and the spiritual energy continued thickening.

Uriel moved in very close now. "Sing, Israfel. Keep singing. And Raphael, spin him through again. Make it tighter."

The whole process repeated, Raphael guiding with his hands, an amber glow cast onto his lap. Israfel drifted to the end of the song, and she didn't resume. After a moment, she lifted a hand and focused her energy on Gabriel; Michael's head raised as the random memories intensified. Uriel sat taller.

After the second spin, Raphael had in his lap an amorphous form, but semi-solid and with at least something of Gabriel's signature.

Knee-to-knee with Raphael, Uriel traced cool fingers over the angel, guiding the body into a form, calming the rough areas, firming where it was too prone to melting away. It took time, but before Israfel's and Michael's gaze, the angel developed limbs, wings, then features, then an approximation of Gabriel's features.

Sitting back, Uriel breathed deep.

Raphael sought out the Throne with wide eyes, water still dripping down his neck.

Uriel opened both hands and looked down.

Raphael flinched, his body projecting mortal confusion.

Uriel was barely audible. "It will come in God's time. The Spirit showed you how to spin."

"We can't leave him like this," Raphael urged.

Uriel looked right into Raphael's eyes. "You're exhausted. I'm exhausted. No one has any clear idea of what to do next, so until God chooses—"

"That's crazy!" Water sprayed around the room as Raphael's wings snapped open. "God *let* this happen! God let them attack with no warning, and now you're suggesting we just wait on God?"

Israfel met Raphael's eyes, the heat rolling off her. "Maybe we could wait for God to send in a second wave of demons."

"Or a text message." Raphael's fire surged. "We could wait for a clear sign for years and let Gabriel fall to pieces and find out afterward that God wanted us to *do something* rather than sitting on our wingtips waiting for revelations with instructions."

Michael found his hand on his sword, but Uriel remained calm. "We've discussed this before, that God won't step in to avoid the results of someone's evil."

"Don't try to out-Gabriel Gabriel!" The pitch of Raphael's voice had steepened to a painful degree. "This isn't theory! This is his life and he's almost dead and there's hardly anything left of him, and it wasn't his evil, and it wasn't his fault!"

Israfel said, "How can you call non-interference fair when Gabriel is going to die and Gabriel never sinned?"

Israfel and Raphael both gasped simultaneously, and Israfel darted toward the angel in Raphael's lap.

"He moved?" Michael whispered.

"Gabriel?" Israfel stroked where his hand ought to be. "Gabriel, squeeze my hand."

Nothing.

Uriel moved between Israfel and Gabriel. "Raphael, Israfel, the two of you have got to get control. He's trying to absorb your fire, and it'll tear him apart in this state."

Raphael closed his eyes and stilled his soul's vibrations.

"Gabriel," Israfel whispered again, "can you hear me? Can you squeeze my hand?" She draped herself and her wings over Raphael's lap, resting her head on the crook of Raphael's arm and keeping Gabriel cuddled at her shoulder. "You've got to come back. Please, just let us know you're still in there."

Raphael rested his hand where Gabriel's shoulder ought to be. With his eyes closed and his mouth twisted, he swallowed. "For the love of God, Gabriel, don't leave me."

The milky form shifted on Raphael's lap.

Michael shivered.

Uriel looked at Raphael. "You're going to have to be his principal healer for as long as it takes. Can you stay with him?"

Liquid gold, Raphael's eyes projected that he wouldn't leave.

Uriel turned to Michael. "I've got the room Guarded, but I want you to re-Guard it over mine and link to my permissions. We'll make sure there's no second strike."

Michael did this.

Uriel opened both hands in such a way that the room itself widened, then created a full-size bed in the corner and a couple of chairs. Raphael gathered Gabriel, allowing one pair of his wings to drop around his shoulders like a cloak, which Israfel pulled free and gathered underneath the Cherub's form. They wrapped it tight before lowering Gabriel on the comforter. Stretched out, he lay so small, wispy like a malnourished four-year-old.

Uriel told Michael and Israfel, "I'm going to ask the two of you to leave. Raphael is already so close to him, and at any rate he needs to be here, but I don't want to have lots of angelic residue when I get down to the actual repair work. It might be difficult to tell what's him and what isn't, and in this state his soul might graft onto anything else around."

"Except for you," Michael said.

Uriel shrugged. "I know what's me."

"I only meant you're made of Teflon."

Uriel snickered. "I'm a Throne."

"I know your choir. It's the same thing." Michael departed.

After laying her hand on Gabriel's forehead, Israfel left too.

Uriel sat at the edge of the bed, wrapped in a purple aura of prayer, wings relaxed. Silence enveloped the scene, the only movement the flicker of Raphael's healing glow that traveled over Gabriel's form while the Seraph sat closed-eyed at his side.

Mary appeared in the room, drenched, and Uriel looked up to meet her gaze.

She extended a hand. At the very center of her palm lay a silver drop, rounded on itself like a bead of mercury.

Uriel closed both eyes and struggled against a frown.

Five

Michael took the long way home, walking through the Gobi desert instead of to the conference center where the other angels awaited.

Jesus joined him after a few minutes. Michael didn't look at him, only kept his head lowered and his shoulders hunched as he walked, his green wings tense but not extended.

Jesus didn't challenge him, just kept pace, occasionally sweeping the black hair from his dark eyes.

Between one stride and the next, Michael stepped onto the snow fields of the Antarctic, ice that flowed like rock through centuries, rigid instead of rippling, locked into one form by an accident of location.

Jesus walked beside him there too.

Then they were climbing a mountain, and Michael used his hands to heft himself high through the trees and boulders, using a path too narrow to call a trail, seeking handholds until he reached a sheer rock face and there were none.

Jesus stopped at his side while Michael craned his neck to search up the sheer rock.

"Is he going to survive?" Michael said.

"That depends," Jesus said, "on how tightly Raphael hangs on."

Michael chewed on that for a moment. "Even if the Father would let him die, Raphael wouldn't."

Jesus nodded. "Raphael is definitely a force to be reckoned with."

"Uriel said Gabriel was stable for now, at any rate." Michael plunged his hands into the pockets of his clothes, which had morphed into jeans and hiking boots. "And we've set the strongest Guards we can around that room, so there's no way they'll know where he is to attack him again."

Jesus' brow furrowed. "Tell me about the rest."

Michael drew a sharp breath, then moved back to the rock face, found a handhold, and tugged, then looked for the next. "How's Remiel doing? Was she caught?"

"She's safe," said Jesus, "and undiscovered."

"It's occurred to me, if she'd been annihilated, we wouldn't know. Satan wouldn't tell us." Michael looked for the next handhold. "How is she, mentally?"

"I'm holding her together." Jesus looked into the deep of the woods. "The strain is hurting her, but she'll make it out again. Go on—that isn't all that's bothering you."

Michael ascended a little further. "I nearly didn't pierce their Guards at all. There were two levels. The first shattered easily, but the second held, and I'd never have broken through if not for that sigil ring." He frowned. "I'd better get that back from Mephistopheles. I really don't like that I let him keep it this long."

He pulled himself up another four feet, then searched again for a place to cling. Jesus remained at the base looking up at the climbing angel.

"It was just luck that I'd made that sigil at all," Michael said.

Jesus was smiling. "Luck?"

Michael lowered his eyes and looked at the stone only inches from his face. "Just because of that game."

"Lucky break." This time it sounded a lot like laughter in Jesus's voice.

Michael looked down. "You prepared that?"

Jesus nodded.

Michael jumped back from the wall, landing lightly with his wings spread.

Jesus folded his arms as he stood eye-to-eye with the Archangel. "Is that it?"

Michael made his eyes as bright as he could. "For now."

"What about your real terror?"

Michael paled.

Jesus chuckled. "Michael'shêli, I made you. I know when you divert your fear by dealing with another problem." He leaned against a pine. "Granted, it makes you efficient, but I can't have you crippled by doubt at a time when the host needs you at your sharpest."

Michael shook his head. "I can't do this."

"Not on your own."

The Archangel folded his wings. "I don't even know where to begin! I only have this position at all because I stood up a long time ago and told Satan that God alone was God. Anyone could have done that."

Jesus nodded.

Michael frowned. "But now I'm supposed to be holding what might as well be a press conference to tell everyone in Heaven what happened to Gabriel and how we're going to respond to protect the rest of them, and I haven't even figured it out for myself."

When Jesus said nothing, Michael turned to him. "What would you have me do?"

"I would have you do what you've been doing—exactly what you've always done before. Speaking up. Seeing what needs to be done and then taking care of it."

Michael walked back to the rock wall and lifted himself from one handhold to the next, faster than before. This time when he reached a spot where he saw no handholds, the rock itself seemed to resolve into more protrusions. He climbed until he reached a ledge, then pulled himself to sit on it. Jesus was already there waiting. Michael sat breathing hard.

"We can be destroyed." He waited for his breath to stop coming so rapidly. "And not by you. And I never thought it was possible one moment to love you and the next not to, but I wouldn't even know I didn't love you any longer because I wouldn't be around to know anything. That's something I couldn't fix, and it would be all over for me, for any one of us."

Jesus looked grim. "That's what it would mean."

"That's *wrong*."

"That's why he wants to do it."

"To be uncreated by something that's not itself Uncreated, that's unimaginable." Michael clenched his fists until they hurt. "Until now. I never imagined it until now." His eyes narrowed. "Why?"

Jesus laid an arm over Michael's shoulder, and Michael cupped him with his wing.

"Why?"

Jesus said, "I won't permit it to happen to you."

"And it was okay that it happen to Gabriel?"

Jesus regarded him narrowly.

"I'm sorry."

"I'm not going to tell you all the details. Right now I'm asking you to trust me, and you'll figure out why in your own time, if you ever need to. The blow was going to land. It landed in the way to do the least damage."

Michael said, "And you were in control even then. Things like my sigil. Things like Camael being part of the team."

"Things like that."

Michael drew his wings close to his body and gazed out at the clouds. There was so much higher he could climb, but for now he sat.

"Humans deal with death all the time," Jesus said. "Angels don't. Never have."

Michael traced a finger over the flat of his knee. "You should end us all simultaneously."

"Humans have learned to recover from grieving."

"We shouldn't. It's against everything we are. Annihilation isn't a fulfillment, only a crime. The most tragic and unfair death humankind ever experienced is still a fulfillment. There's more to it. There's justice." Michael's opened his hands and leaned forward. "If our enemies can escape it into oblivion, what purpose is Hell? We made our choice for all eternity. You can't change the terms now."

Jesus frowned. "Can't I?"

Michael blanched. Even his wings went yellow.

"I won't, though."

"You'll stop them if they try again?"

"No." Jesus put a hand on Michael's knee. "I designed you to be my champion. You'll stop them."

Michael's mouth twitched, as though to say, *Well, that eases the pressure.*

Jesus laughed out loud. He clapped Michael on the shoulder and then got to his feet on the ledge. "You're more than capable, and you're in command of the most amazing force I could create. Plus, they trust you as much as I do."

Michael stood, reached for his sword and realized he wasn't wearing it at the moment. "You'll guide me?"

"Of course," Jesus said. "I always do."

Michael glanced at one of the hawks circling and called it closer. It cried with that small-sounding voice, then drew nearer. He studied its flight, not moving. He could have left then, but for the moment he was content to stand, just stand, with his Lord at his side.

"You're needed," Jesus said.

As Michael turned to ask more, Raguel appeared before Michael, armed. "We've got trouble at the gates."

Michael flashed away with Raguel, not saying goodbye because he wasn't leaving Jesus behind. Jesus remained on the cliff face, inhaling the scent of pines and watching a hawk in a stoop, and it was good.

Michael and Raguel appeared at the heavenly gates where Mephistopheles stood before two Principality guards.

Flanked by white stone walls, the main gates of Heaven were formed of wrought iron, with guard houses on either side and a wide field visible through the bars. More for appearance than function, the gates served ceremonial purposes. Angels and saints could flash into Heaven at whatever point they wanted; the last time the gates had been opened had been for Jesus's ascension with the newly freed human souls. The gates served also as a convenient meeting-place whenever the enemy requested an audience.

Mephistopheles inclined his head, letting the light of heaven play over the ringlets of his hair and accentuate the poised lines of his face. "My compliments to the help. The service here is quite excellent."

Michael's eyebrows raised. "Would you care to fill out a comment card?"

Mephistopheles slid his hands into his pockets, but not before Michael caught a glimpse of his sigil ring. "Actually, the one I wanted to speak to was Raphael."

"I'll be glad to take him a message," said Michael.

"While I'm sure you would do an excellent job," Mephistopheles said, pacing languorously, "I'd prefer to see him in person."

Michael's wings raised a fraction, and his eyes went cold. "And you'll tell him what?"

"Give me the Seraph."

Michael's hand itched for his sword even as he forced himself not to form it. Mephistopheles still kept his right hand hidden, but Michael knew that if he concentrated from where he stood, he could make the ring hot enough to burn. But since it couldn't be hotter than the anger of God, he restrained himself.

Mephistopheles paused. "Why can't I speak with him?"

"Why can't you get it into your head that I won't let you?"

Mephistopheles formed his sword (left-handed) and instantly Saraquael with ten Archangels materialized behind Michael, who even then didn't make a sword of his own. He still looked like a backpacker. He could alter his clothing to armor in an instant if necessary.

Mephistopheles didn't acknowledge the newcomers. "Are you afraid I'm going to do something to him?"

"Like annihilation?"

Even Michael was surprised when Mephistopheles lowered his blade, and the ice-chiseled etiquette wavered. "I'm not going to gloat." Michael fought the urge to tighten that ring on his hand. "I wouldn't be so uncharitable as to vaunt the annihilation of a Cherub to his closest Seraph. But he was a member of my order, almost my superior, and I said I'd do him a favor."

Other than the out-and-out lie about being Gabriel's superior, the entire sentence didn't ring either true or false to Michael.

"At the end he wanted Raphael to know he loved him, and that he didn't blame him."

Michael's eyes went obsidian.

Mephistopheles whipped his head around. "You disbelieve me?"

Michael gave in just a bit and made the ring hot. "His last words would have been his love of God, which of course you've forgotten."

"I complied with his request." Mephistopheles gave no indication of feeling the metal searing his hand. "You should endeavor to show more appreciation."

"Thank you," Michael said. "Get out."

Mephistopheles flashed away.

Raguel rubbed his chin. "Do you think Mephistopheles was telling the truth?"

"I doubt Mephistopheles knows if Mephistopheles was telling the truth." Michael's brow furrowed. "Saraquael, choose three Principalities and have them keep tabs on Raphael all the time. This may mean Satan wants Raphael next, and that's unacceptable."

Saraquael nodded. "Should I assign guards to the rest of the Seven?"

"With all due respect," Raguel said, "I don't need that. And I can't imagine Satan being able to lay a hand on Uriel."

"I can't either," Michael said, "but to be frank, I couldn't have imagined having to have this conversation yesterday, so Saraquael, do it. Actually, make them Angels, and make them unobtrusive. Their first responsibility is to get help, not to get into the line of fire."

Saraquael nodded.

Michael folded his arms. "And although I hate to admit it, it's time for something else too."

Two hours had passed. Mary returned to Uriel's bungalow, carrying a medium sized basket.

Uriel sent Mary a series of images: the room, the room again, the room yet again, along with a sense of time passing. In Mary's human mind, that nonverbal communication parsed as "Still the same."

It wasn't entirely the same. Uriel had replaced the quicksilver droplet of soul in Gabriel's heart, hoping it would migrate to the correct place, and Raphael had fallen asleep, wings overspreading the Cherub, the amber glow pulsing even as both slept.

Mary peered at Gabriel as if looking over the side of a crib, and her heart trembled even as her stomach twisted. You didn't get used to seeing something like this.

Mary kept her voice low. "I brought you something." She set the basket at the edge of the bed, then unpacked a beige cloth, smoothed the cloth into a square, and set out cups, a thermos, muffins, butter and knives, another thermos, bowls, and cookies.

"Perhaps you recall," Uriel said mildly, "that angels don't eat?"

"Joseph and I got tired of praying ceaselessly with words and scriptures, so I prayed with cookies." Mary poured a cup of tea from the first thermos, handed it to a suddenly-solid Uriel, then wrapped two cookies in a napkin and passed those over as well. "Peter has every human he can in prayer right now, and Paul organized folks to visit churches on Earth and get them praying for healing, although clearly we can't specify for whom. But me, I baked cookies."

"It's good to know some things never change," Uriel said.

Mary looked up from pouring herself a cup of tea. "How so?"

"Remember when Elizabeth was giving birth to John? How many loaves of bread did you bake?"

Mary closed the top on the thermos. "It wasn't the bread that was a problem. It was the fish."

Uriel laughed out loud. "I'd totally forgotten the fish!"

"How could you forget the fish? I was still morning sick all the time, and the fish reeked like crazy."

Uriel chuckled behind one hand. "That's the thing I never expected about being a guardian angel—the way humans push yourselves rather than admit defeat."

"Someone had to cook the fish." Mary cocked her head. "Well, fair's fair. I never expected angels to be anything like you are either." When Uriel looked puzzled, Mary continued, "I figured that beings with a perfect understanding of God would never disagree and would live in perfect harmony all the time."

Uriel squinted. "And when you find those creations perfect enough to have a perfect understanding of God, let me know!"

"Of course only God is perfect." Mary fiddled with the handles of the basket. "I knew it said in Job that God finds fault even with his angels. I knew the Yom Kippur liturgy actually says angels sin. But even hearing in Daniel that the guardian of Persia fought with Gabriel for twenty-one days and had to be called off by Michael didn't prepare me for the idea that angels might disagree with one another."

"Don't God's people disagree with one another?"

"We're not angels," Mary said.

Uriel's hands opened, forming a faceted gem which revolved slowly, splintering the light to scatter tiny rainbow dots over the walls. "None of us is big enough to contain and understand all of God, even with unclouded reasoning abilities. God designed us all a little differently from one another so that spread out over the whole of creation, eventually one of us amplifies each aspect of himself. But given that, doesn't it make sense that the angel of justice might argue with the angel of mercy? Or," Uriel added, winking, "that an angel embodying God's creativity might argue with God over a schedule?"

The Throne made the lighted jewel disappear.

"It makes sense. I just never expected it." Mary handed over a cookie. "Please?"

Uriel tried a bite, then radiated approval.

"Thanks." Mary looked at Raphael. "He pulled Gabriel out of Hell, and you helped put him back together, and I baked cookies."

Uriel said, "Cookies solve all the world's problems."

Mary paused. "That's not true. Some problems can only be solved with brownies."

"Aren't brownies are a type of bar cookie?"

"Oh, dear," Mary said. "All the world's problems *can* be solved with cookies." She sipped the tea and finished her cookie. "This is so much like when Jesus was a baby. You guarding me, Raphael guarding him."

Uriel had a wistful smile. "Gestation is a hazy time. I wasn't expecting that either."

"I've gotten to realize we're never really prepared."

Uriel squinted, projecting assurance that God had prepared them, then added, "We just never realize it until afterward." Setting the empty cup on the bed, Uriel said, "Raphael figured out how to toughen up Gabriel's spirit to survive death. I think he was able to do that because as Jesus's guardian angel he'd witnessed him doing the same thing to himself from the inside. No one else had ever seen it done."

Mary took a deep breath. "But what's next?"

Uriel's fingers knit together. "We have to find the rest of Gabriel. I'm not positive we got everything. Especially not after you found that residue in the field."

"There wasn't anything else, though." Mary got another cookie. "We checked."

Uriel gestured with one hand. "*That* can't be all there is of him. If it's not in the field, then it's got to be back in Hell. Or else it's gone forever."

Mary bit her lip. "Can we send in a search party?"

Uriel emitted a small cloud of frustration, worry for the ones they'd send, fear of a baited trap.

"Have you asked Michael?"

Uriel's eyes lowered again, and another cloud of frustration: no time to have mentioned it already, and uncertainty. Finally words, "I won't be sure until I try putting him back together."

"You could try now," Mary said.

"He's too dehiscent." When Mary squinted, Uriel added, "You know, thin. Ready to pull apart. Imagine trying to cover a pizza pan with only a handful of dough. What would happen when you rolled it out, and kept rolling it?"

"How thin can you pull a soul?"

"Not that thin," Uriel said. "I've never done anything like this before, and even so, I know it can't be pulled that thin."

Raphael stirred. Mary sat back from the edge of the bed to give him room.

As he sat up and checked on Gabriel, Mary felt from him the same shock she'd felt, as if Gabriel's form were an insult; it was bad enough he'd been damaged and mangled, but why did he have to look that way so they remembered it anew every time they looked?

"Cookies," the Seraph said, blinking away the sleep. He wasn't looking at the cookies, though, only at Gabriel. "I still can't feel him. It's as if he's not there."

Mary clasped her hands. Uriel said, "Give him time."

"Time for what?" Raphael began to vibrate. "He's had time. It's not doing any good."

"We can't say that for certain," Uriel said, "and he's not any worse, so that's something."

Raphael tried to adjust Gabriel on the bed. "He looks so small."

Uriel flinched.

Mary moved to the head of the bed. "Here, can I try something?" She grasped the fabric that had been Raphael's wings, adjusted it beneath Gabriel, then tucked him up so he seemed even smaller. She paused. "This isn't hurting you, is it?"

"Not at all." The Seraph squinted. "What are you doing?"

"Remember how I used to carry Jesus?" She tied a firm knot at the base, then pulled the ends up tight. "Come closer and bend over him."

It took a lot of adjusting of the fabric (thick, silky, warm on its own) around Gabriel's form, but when Mary was done, Raphael had Gabriel bundled up at chest height, and he had his hands free.

"That way you can carry him easier," Mary said. "It gives you mobility."

Uriel quirked a smile. "Where is he going to go?"

"Wherever he wants," Mary said, "although it might be best if he stays here."

Raphael looked down at Gabriel's featureless face, the limp hair, the way he'd seemed to lose his shape. "I don't want to risk anything."

"But he's with you," Mary said.

Raphael's eyes glistened, and after a hard swallow, he nodded.

Six

Still in the form of Camael, Remiel lay with her legs draped across the arm of a chair in the great hall at Hell's entrance. While dark, it wasn't the lab area, and while hot it wasn't the Lake of Fire. It didn't have the preternatural cold of the ice fields. It was just an annoying place to be—noisy, crowded, smelly, and prickly with the presence of souls who all wished the rest would just leave already.

So why am I still here?

Because she'd failed. Returning to the surface meant seeing the hollow affect on the faces of the angels working throughout Creation, hearing angels crying, seeing the blank empty of Raphael's heart when she so well remembered the same feeling immediately after the winnowing.

All the demons were chattering like seventh graders on amphetamines washed down with espresso. Telling about angels dressed in black, angels without songs, angels constantly armored—and angels grim, so terribly grim.

Around her, demons laughed and pretended to be Gabriel being ripped limb from torso until Remiel wanted nothing more than to rise from her chair and start stuffing parts of them down one another's throats.

But the disguise had to hold, particularly now, so Remiel put on Camael as best she could and scowled, keeping her eyes closed.

A demon bumped Camael's head as he passed, and Camael growled so the interloper skittered away.

The air had a fug Camael detested—give him the open air of Creation any day, the freedom of wide spaces; even the darkest alley in Sodom seemed preferable now. The continuous noise—less sound than static feedback—could drive anyone to frenzy with its whine. From the pits and the ice fields it was possible to hear the tumult of the human damned. At least this room had only a few columns to support the weight of everything above—a weight anyone could feel just waiting; the deeper levels had more columns, smaller chambers, no room even to open your wings.

Another pair of demons launched into an Amos-and-Andy style production of "How I Killed Gabriel" when Camael decided he'd had enough. Looking off to the western side of the room he saw it vanish into the thick air of the lab area. He pushed aside a demon and started walking. That was the place to go to be alone, but being there, near where it happened... Even if the real Camael did have chambers there—and who would want to see the contents of a demon's privacy?—being there would only bring it back, the memory of standing with Beelzebub and Satan in a darkness hungry to devour any light they shed. Neither had tried. Gabriel alone had shone there, and Camael could have given away the game by doing the same. For all the good his presence had done, he might as well have.

Camael stopped in mid-stride. No, don't go there. Don't go in and remember how he'd been so weakened that Satan had helped him to stand, that he'd leaned on God's enemy and his friend's murderer.

Murderer. A murderer from the beginning, Jesus had said. Jesus had known Gabriel would— That this would happen.

"I hear you were around when they got him?"

Camael faced the demon with a growl. A low-ordered one, but the demon stood its ground.

"Did the poor freak scream?" it said. "Did it renounce God? Mephistopheles said it did. Beelzebub said Satan drank his blood, too."

"Get out of my sight," Camael said, but an audience had been drawn, clustering around him like maggots, and they all expected him to say something, a victory speech with an account more amazing than the ones before. He'd be the star for a moment, and then they'd move on, trying to coax a story out of Satan.

That opened up some possibilities. What couldn't Satan top?

"Fine," Camael said, "but I'm only telling this once."

He walked into the center of the throng, reminding himself that the lower demons lived for the higher orders to condescend to them. They might as well get someone's approval and guidance, having spurned God's.

Almost at the center, Camael looked into the eyes of an Archangel that once had been a friend, and he looked at another, and then a third, and he remembered all their names, remembered happier days when they all had loved God together. Camael had to grip himself not to scream, not to cry at the stupid loss of so many bright lights, so many individuals who had played the same songs, read the same books, fought with the same weapons, and then drowned for a different god.

As the shock rippled through Camael, he realized he couldn't follow through on his original plan to play Henry V, to be one with the troops and pretend to be their friend. He had been their friend once, and what remained, these husks of spirit, repulsed him. He dreaded contact.

The low-order demons filled this whole corner of the great hall. Camael sat on a table, wings raised and feet dangling, resting his toes on a bench. He was a head higher than the hive, and that made it easier not to meet anyone's eyes. Not to see them.

What couldn't Satan top?

This was going to transgress some kind of unspoken demonic etiquette because he would include details that would prove embarrassing if Satan didn't change them and unbelievable if he did. As long as Camael could concoct it well enough.

The groupies were calling over more of their ilk and repeating Mephistopheles' and Beelzebub's stories. More time.

But was it wrong to lie? Gabriel would have objected. He'd refused to play the role of Hamlet once because he said acting was a lie, albeit small, "to purport to emotions never felt." Or whatever a Cherub said when he wanted to sound persuasive and ended up sounding confusing and geeky.

Maybe you never felt this. Remiel had lied that she was Camael in order to come down here at all, and to no avail. Why further betray Gabriel? Camael wished he'd escaped, but probably the Guards had kept him pinned until he had dissolved in agony.

Oh, hell, Camael thought.

"Do you want to keep telling the same stories?" Camael raised the pitch of his voice to carry over the noise of the crowd. They pressed closer, and Camel pulled up his booted legs onto the table top. "I'm going to tell you what actually happened."

The damned fell silent. Camael smirked.

"First off, the Cherub wasn't chained to a wall. Don't you think Satan would have used an altar?"

The groupies oohed.

"Beelzebub and Mephistopheles set two Guards, one around the room and one over his body so he couldn't move at all."

"What did our lord do?" asked one, and Camael hesitated until he remembered which lord it was.

"Did you drink his blood now?" asked another.

God, help me, Camael prayed, then wondered if this wasn't being unGodly. His stomach twisted. *God, help me!*

Camael cocked his head. "Our lord instructed me not to divulge all the details of how we worked on him. Apparently he has his eyes on some would-be rebels and wants to do the same to them."

A delicious frisson rippled through the room. Camael realized the details would manufacture themselves in a crowd this hungry. When this was retold, he'd be naming names and giving approximate dates for each of the accused to go under the knife.

Camael said, "Do you think any creature could withstand such pain and not renounce God? At the hands of the lord of pain?" The hall filled with glistening faces all trained on Camael's. "Gabriel did not die a martyr. He was assaulted by us from the outside and God from within all at once."

"He joined us!" they shouted.

Now the demons were lobbing questions like hand grenades: Did they set him on fire? Did they cut him to pieces? Did they drink his blood?—a refrain so often repeated that Camael had to wonder if it weren't so unusual to this assemblage. Instead he said, "Beelzebub cupped his blood in his hands, and he *baptized* Mephistopheles with it!"

Why only flirt with blasphemy? Why not dance with it?

Camael got to his feet as the demons pressed close to hear better, and the curve of his wings brushed the ceiling. Satan had to have noticed the commotion at this point—some loyal minion would have notified him. There would be another session of questions, a reprimand of sorts, and it was all in futility if angels could die. If Satan really could stop them from loving God after all, despite their choices.

Why would he do that?, Camael thought, blanking out the names of every ex-angel, wishing for a part of Gabriel to have remained alive somewhere, loving God even if it was only in the way the rocks cried out.

"Lucifer dared God to stop him," Camael shouted. "He channeled all his energy through me, and I magnified it, and we started annihilating Gabriel's soul."

All the demons hooted. No one asked what material forms a soul, or how it was put together, or how they had destroyed it. Camael didn't volunteer how it felt to be flooded with Satan's filthy light, nor the paralyzing fear of discovery.

Now for the real propaganda.

"The Guard broke."

A number of demons protested. "They said it held!"

"Naturally they'd say it held! It didn't—I was there. God himself assaulted that room, but our leader worked quicker, desperate to succeed, and Gabriel's soul dissolved faster and faster, everything but our memories, until Gabriel screamed and screamed and even damned himself to make the pain stop, but by then he was too far gone for even us to restore. God grabbed Lucifer by the throat, but I gave one last blast, and the Cherub was gone."

The demons cheered. Camael closed his eyes.

"Lucifer begged for mercy," he said. "God dropped him. Beelzebub and Mephistopheles reset the Guard, but Gabriel's whole form had vanished. There was only a flame kept burning on the altar."

The groupies gasped.

Camael added. "It floated from the room—and we don't know where it went. But it's somewhere in the lab area. Somewhere."

They all stood gawking, the groupies.

He noted the beginning of a push away from the dark to the western part of the room.

Leaving them to their awe, Camael vanished from the thick of them to Gabriel's prison chamber, where he fought back any vestiges of Remiel and tried to regain composure.

Seven

Michael and Raguel flashed into the conference room with tense wings and clenched hands.

"I never realized you hate this too," Raguel said.

"Why do you think I always asked Gabriel to handle them?" Michael sighed. "I thought he enjoyed them."

"He probably did, knowing him." Raguel laughed. "He'd take any chance to offer a lecture."

Michael caught Israfel's eyes across the conference room, the betrayed glare, and he realized they'd begun using the past tense.

The room itself had stadium-style seating for fifty, a ring of windows on all sides revealing a partly cloudy day and the valleys falling away around them. It had no doors because souls didn't need them.

Everyone fell silent as Michael went to the table at the front. He scanned the crowd and recognized the heads of all nine choirs, but of the Seven only himself, Raguel and Saraquael. Five humans attended including Peter, the equivalents of "heads of the choir," and he missed Mary if she was there.

With a deep breath, he called the meeting to order, and then in as brief a summation as he could, delivered the official news of what had happened.

Silence overspread the others. Even Saraquael and Raguel, who had been present, stayed unmoving and rapt, as if in the retelling they might find a way out, some way this hadn't happened.

Before he'd finished by urging them to keep the details away from the enemy, Mary had appeared in the back and slipped into a seat.

Michael quieted, not having the heart to ask for questions.

"But he's going to recover?" said the head of the choir of Angels.

Michael swallowed. "I can't say for certain."

A collective flinch from the angels. Michael closed his eyes. They all projected at the same time—he might die? He might really die? God would allow that? But couldn't they save him?

Michael looked for Mary's eyes, and he arched his brows. She shook her head: no.

No improvement.

Michael summoned a chair and guided himself to a seat. He put his head in his hands. *God, center me. I need to lead them. They need it right now.*

Raguel stood. "I want to know how we're going to respond to this."

Michael looked up, weary. "What would you have us do?"

"A full siege of Hell," Raguel said. "Immediately."

Michael sat back. "We do need to respond, but I'm not sure that's the best way."

Raguel folded his arms. He was the tallest and broadest of the Seven, arguably the strongest even though the Principalities were in the lowest triad of choirs. Michael put a little ice into his glance, but Raguel remained unmoving.

Fine. Michael returned to his feet. "None of us denies the basic facts: two hours ago, one of our own was abducted and subjected to murder. The sheer magnitude of that action defies every spiritual and ethical norm. Annihilation violates the most basic of God's decrees, that God alone is the Creator and the destroyer."

Michael scanned the room. "I'm sure Satan will try again. He's got to be proud of himself for breaking the most sacred law, and who can doubt he has designs on every other one of us?"

No one responded, so Michael finished with, "We cannot permit this to happen a second time."

Ophaniel, head of the choir of Cherubim, said, "How can we stop him?"

Raguel said, "We invade."

A Throne said, "We could issue a stern warning that we'll take action if they try again."

"And what would it say?" said a Virtue. "Kindly don't annihilate anyone else?"

The Throne said, "Gabriel isn't dead."

The Virtue folded his arms. "Their intention was clear."

Michael said, "Murder and attempted murder are morally the same."

The Virtue said, "And what if they don't try again?"

Speaking for the first time, Saraquael said, "That's a dilemma I look forward to confronting."

Michael flashed him a grateful look, and Saraquael leaned back, a light in his eyes.

Raguel set his jaw. "Should we allow them to think Gabriel's death goes unanswered?"

Saraquael tilted his head. "This isn't an executive council meeting. Everyone is forgetting that. We convened to give you accurate information to distribute to your choirs." He took a deep breath. "We aren't a decision-making body."

Raguel said, "But we need to decide—"

"For pity's sake," Michael said, "how can we? I understand you want to strike at them—don't you think I want it every bit as much? But now isn't the time to decide. There's nothing to accomplish with an immediate strike. It can wait an hour, Raguel."

Michael looked back at the others. "Information only. I'll open the floor if anyone has anything to add."

Ophaniel stood again. "If I may, I have something."

Michael hoped he wouldn't regret turning the floor over to a Cherub as he gestured toward the front. Ophaniel joined him.

"The Cherubim have discovered that the lower demons don't believe this is the first time Satan has performed an annihilation."

The whole room hummed.

"They claim that Satan destroyed three Principalities who openly rebelled. Shandriel, Mendrel, and Astrifer."

"I've never heard of them," said the chief of Principalities, and Raguel agreed.

"He invented the story. It keeps the lower orders in line. This seems to be the first actual attempt."

Another Cherub added, "Rahab."

Michael glanced at Ophaniel, who looked pale. "Yes," Michael said. "There's Rahab. But I'm not sure Rahab counts."

When Michael dismissed the group, Saraquael and Raguel stayed behind, and he also called over Mary.

She said nothing, just gripped his hand for a long moment. Saraquael turned away and paced to the window. Raguel closed his eyes.

"No change whatsoever?" Michael said.

"None Uriel can detect." Mary folded her hands. "Uriel thinks we didn't get all of him back."

The three archangels vibrated with momentary shock.

Saraquael spun to face her. "What does Raphael think?"

Mary said, "I left before Uriel told him."

"We need to go look for the rest, then," Michael said. "Shouldn't we? How long can the various parts stay around if they're just—loose?"

Mary opened her hands. "That's why I wanted to ask you. Is there any way to go and check?"

"I was in the place where they did it," Michael said. "I could try going back—"

"Absolutely not," Raguel said. "For all you know, they're waiting for you."

Michael said, "Why is my life more valuable than Gabriel's?"

"Because," Saraquael said, "Remiel is down there, and she's still undiscovered."

"Can you get word to her?" Michael said.

"I can try."

Raguel said, "If we invade, we can definitely access the area."

Michael fixed a look on him.

Raguel stared at his feet. "We need to make a decision."

Michael shook his head, and the summons went out.

Not as many returned for this meeting: the heads of each of the nine choirs and one other representative, plus Peter and Abraham representing humanity. Mary remained. Saraquael rearranged the room with one gesture, placing a wide table the length of the room and doing away with the stadium seating. There were about half as many present as before.

Michael drew a breath to begin when Uriel appeared.

Everyone turned, but Uriel was looking away—at Raphael behind him.

But didn't that mean Gabriel—?

That's when he saw that no, the brown fabric bundle on Raphael's chest was Gabriel, tied snug.

There were startled exclamations, and then Ophaniel was right up to Raphael, machine-gunning questions which the Seraph attempted through his exhaustion to answer. After a minute, Michael forced Ophaniel back.

Uriel met Michael's eyes with worry.

Mary stepped up next to Raphael. She checked over the sling, pronounced it tight, but then adjusted it minutely. "He looks better to me."

"You think so?" Raphael's voice was thin.

"He seems to respond to the sunlight."

Michael glanced at the rest of the assembly, all of whom were brittle with shock. He could tell a couple were thinking, "This is better?"

Michael turned to Raphael. "Is it wise to move him?"

Uriel looked relieved that he'd asked. Raphael turned his gaze to Gabriel. "I thought—maybe if we were with others—"

Israfel flashed to Raphael's side. "Would you like me to go back with you? They don't really need me here, and I'll help arrange the windows so there's more sunlight in the bungalow."

"I need you here," Michael said.

Israfel put her hands on Gabriel. "Let Raphael represent the Seraphim—I'll take Gabriel for a while."

Michael said, "Raphael's his primary. They have to stay together."

Israfel got up close to Michael and whispered, "Gabriel's my primary too." Her eyes narrowed. "Don't forget that again."

Michael flinched.

Flashing behind Raphael, Israfel wrapped her arms around his shoulders.

Michael glanced at Uriel, whose ordinary pallor had picked up a porcelain sheen, and whose black hair looked more tousled than usual. Michael wanted Israfel's input, but at the same time, he could see defeat crowding out the usual spark in Raphael's eyes. Raphael needed someone to lean on: Uriel had spent everything and more already.

Even as Mary touched Raphael's arm, saying, "I think the sunlight really is helping," Michael flagged the three Angels keeping tabs on Raphael.

Head bowed, Raphael whispered that Gabriel probably did need the quiet, and he vanished from the circle of Israfel's arms. Michael sent the Angels after him.

One of the Powers broke down in sobs.

Uriel pulled out a chair and leaned back, head craned back all the way, arms limp, legs extended.

Michael dropped onto a chair beside the Throne, and he put his face in his hands.

Satan had to have known it would come to this. He might not have predicted what would happen to whom, but he'd have calculated the collateral damage in advance, selecting a target based on status but also on the web of the others. Gabriel, admired despite his quirks and his mental meanderings and Remiel's good-natured coronation of him as the King of Geeks. If Michael had died, they'd have rallied but considered him a hero, as if he'd asked for it. But Gabriel, the Prince of Heaven, hadn't made himself anyone's enemy and was only doing the things God created him to do. Satan must have had a flow-chart of whom his friends were and how powerful, then unleashed his strike with the directness of a sniper's rifle.

I hate him, Michael prayed. *I hate what he's done and the fact that he wanted all this.*

Ophaniel turned toward Uriel to ask a question, but one movement from Raguel ensured continued silence.

Michael forced himself to sit up. "So," he said, very subdued, "you see what's happened and what they did."

Even Raguel didn't start in with his demands for an invasion. That would come in time. Now was the moment to just let the horror hit home. Michael joined hands with the other angels and saints, and together they prayed. For healing. For direction, for strength, for understanding, for resolve. For Gabriel's life.

Afterward, Michael said, "We're meeting to decide how to respond. I'd like to hear all your ideas, no matter how off-base you might think them." He met Raguel's eyes. "You suggested a full invasion before. Tell us more."

Raguel stood. "Satan broke the most basic of spiritual laws, and clearly he worked hard to achieve that mastery. He's sure to continue — either with our own angels or with his."

Murmurs of assent.

"None of us will be safe. He'll always hold that threat against us." He folded his arms. "We can't afford to have our movements restricted to only certain areas or curfews or a buddy system. We have to attack now."

A Throne said, "How will an attack now prevent future annihilations?"

Raguel said, "A show of force will make them afraid to try again."

"All right," Michael said, "let's have more ideas."

The Throne said, "We could issue a warning."

"If the fires of Hell don't deter him," Israfel said, "he'll laugh at a stern warning."

"He ought to be warned."

"He's not ignorant," Mary said. "He must have suspected this was the worst thing he could do. I'm surprised he waited this long to attempt it."

"Corruption is more severe than destruction," said Ophaniel.

Sidriel, the Cherub beside him, added, "You might as well mention the fact that even our Cherubim never figured out how God made us. This isn't a new application of old information."

Ophaniel shrugged. "That too."

"If I may," Michael said, "let's have more ideas."

"What if we abduct Satan?" Mary said.

Saraquael shook his head. "Beelzebub would say good riddance. He's wanted the throne of Hell for years. Asmodeus too. Mephistopheles would help us capture Satan if we asked, and no one except the lower order demons would really miss him."

"Maybe Belior," Sidriel said. "He seems genuinely loyal."

"It wouldn't give us assurance anyhow," Ophaniel added. "Camael indicated he didn't work alone. Mephistopheles must know how to do it as well."

Michael said, "We've got three ideas now. Let's keep moving."

The chief of the choir of Dominions raised one finger and smiled demurely. "We might let natural law take its course," she said.

"Do nothing?" Raguel said.

Israfel said, "We're the tools of natural law."

"Not always," said the Dominion, named Zadkiel. She along with Saraquael were Michael's standard-bearers. "This is a crime against the Spirit. It's not for us to decide the case."

"How can we let this go unanswered?" Raguel was again on his feet, his wings flared. "Gabriel may die because of him!"

In a low voice, Saraquael said, "She's aware of that."

Raguel hesitated, then sat back down.

Uriel said, "I want to hear more."

Zadkiel met Uriel's eyes with a quickness like Saraquael's. "When Satan refused to worship God, he committed a crime against angels by taking a third of us down in rebellion, so an angel took action and threw him into Hell."

"With a lot of help," Michael interjected.

"When Satan seduced mankind, that was a crime against humanity, and Jesus, the Word as human, redressed the wrong. Annihilation is a crime against God himself as the life sustainer." Zadkiel looked at her slender fingers. "We aren't on a plane to fix that wrong, nor to avenge for him, nor to make reparation for Gabriel's pain or the pain of everyone who will be affected by his loss. I say, let God take care of the matter."

Uriel said, "If we follow your lead, we must remain completely passive."

"Agreed. Sooner or later, God will ensure that the natural consequences of Satan's actions to punish him far more appropriately than we could."

"But Satan hates his own," Raguel said. "He'd be happy if they started annihilating one another, as long as they didn't annihilate him. And if they got him, he'd be free from punishment—which as I recall, was supposedly eternal."

Zadkiel rubbed her chin. "I trust in our Father."

"Trust isn't the issue," Michael said. "No one is questioning that God will work this out for his glory—it's just a question of how best that should happen. Your point is definitely worth consideration, and I'm glad you suggested it." He looked around. "Anyone else?"

An Archangel said, "We could send spies into Hell to determine their next move."

"Remiel is already established there," Ophaniel said.

Saraquael said, "Remiel is not a long-term option."

"But spies in general are," Michael said. "Other ideas? I want everything on the table at once."

From beside Ophaniel, Sidriel said, "Maybe if we explained to Satan why what he's doing is wrong, he'd understand the need not to do it again."

"He'd do it even more," Saraquael said, "possibly starting with whomever went to talk to him."

"But every option depends on his eventual cooperation."

"That's why God has to intervene directly," Zadkiel said. "We can't force Satan to be good."

Raguel said, "We can chain him down and keep him from being bad."

Michael snickered.

Zadkiel said, "Forever?"

"If that's what it takes."

"Hold on," Michael said. "More ideas? We're just brainstorming now."

Israfel said, "Can God protect us from the process in a special way? Can we be double-knotted or locked?"

Mary said, "I already asked. He said there's no technique that would prevent it."

Israfel said, "Will he consent to re-creating any angels destroyed by this process?"

Mary shook her head. "I asked that too."

Momentary quiet from everyone.

An Archangel said, "Is Satan preparing to defend against a full-scale assault right now? We ought to consider his expectations as we decide."

"I'll investigate that," Saraquael said. "I'll also try to recall Remiel."

"Do that," Michael said.

Everyone returned to quiet.

"Are we out of ideas?" Michael scanned the room, then added, "Let's take a break, and when we return, we can work out a solution."

The meeting dissolved, some angels moving outside, others gathering in different parts of the room in smaller groups. Zadkiel and Ophaniel joined two Thrones by the long windows that stretched floor to ceiling, framed by the green sky outside. Some Archangels and Angels had gathered in another corner and sat on the multi-colored carpet; one read poetry to the rest of the group. Saraquael departed on his assignments.

Michael turned to Uriel. The Throne's wings sagged, and the purple eyes had darkened to black. Michael leaned closer, then backed off a bit, projecting that if the Throne had something to say, to feel free to say anything at all.

Uriel simply sent back exhaustion. Tension.

Michael tried to offer reassurance.

He noticed Raguel talking animatedly with Zadkiel. Good—let them work it out.

Ophaniel appeared beside Uriel, calling over a chair and feasting his eyes on the Throne. "So, how is it done?"

Uriel focused on Ophaniel, who sat back sharply.

"How could it be wrong to know?" Ophaniel said. "Knowledge is knowledge, and this is God's best-kept secret of all!"

Uriel's eyes narrowed.

"How much *can* you tell me?" Ophaniel said.

Uriel sighed.

Ophaniel leaned forward, eyes bright.

Sidriel approached.

"Uriel won't tell us," Ophaniel said.

Shock and frustration rolled off the other Cherub. "They're allowed to know it, but we're not?"

Uriel glanced at Michael, then back at the pair of Cherubim. "Some things we shouldn't know."

"That's crazy," Sidriel said.

Ophaniel paused. "Maybe it's true." When Sidriel regarded him with questions, Ophaniel added, "I wouldn't care to know how to perform a Satanic sacrifice."

"You wouldn't do it, but the knowledge of how to do it, that wouldn't be wrong."

Uriel snapped, and both Cherubim looked up.

"God will reveal only as much as I need to know to do the repair," Uriel said, and then before Ophaniel could ask to know that much, added, "and afterward I'll have to surrender it back."

"No!" both Cherubim cried out simultaneously.

"This is something that's never been done—"

"It's our identity—"

"It's who we are as angels—"

"It's God's decision," Uriel said.

When Sidriel huffed, Michael hid a smile.

Ophaniel said, "You said you'd do the repair. Can I at least watch?"

Uriel's eyes flashed.

Sidriel said, "I hate to ask this, but—how are you expecting to be able to repair him? He looked pretty torn up."

Michael said, "He should recover." When the Cherubim and the Throne turned to look at him, he added, "I asked Jesus."

Sidriel brightened. "Oh! That's good."

Ophaniel said, "What exactly did he say?"

Michael thought for a moment. "That it depended on Raphael."

Uriel expressed surprise.

Michael looked at the three sets of curious eyes and could feel their disbelief. "What do you think I'm missing?"

"Give me the whole conversation," Ophaniel said.

"Just that I asked if Gabriel would survive, and Jesus said it depended on how tightly Raphael would hang on."

He didn't feel from them the relief he'd expected.

Ophaniel said, "And that doesn't frighten the daylights out of you?"

Michael shook his head, hesitant.

Sidriel said, "That's hardly a yes."

"It's not, but—"

Uriel flagged Mary over and repeated Michael's conversation with Jesus.

Mary looked concerned. "It sounds a lot like 'Destroy this temple and I'll rebuild it in three days' when he knew his listeners were going to think he meant the building."

Michael said, "But we know Raphael would hang in there for as long as it took. That's why I'm not frantic."

Uriel said, "He's discouraged, but he wouldn't give up."

Sidriel said, "Ophaniel and I have primary bonds with him. We can try to help keep his spirits up."

Uriel said, "And check out Gabriel at the same time?"

Sidriel sighed; Uriel grinned.

Michael said, "Is there any way to help Raphael? If he's really the lynch pin, we need to keep him going also."

Uriel said, "I'll keep an eye on him. I really don't want Gabriel exposed to too much residue. Raphael shouldn't have come here before, but he so much hungered for contact with the rest of you. It's hard on him to be alone with only me and Gabriel, and Gabriel isn't even responsive."

Mary said, "I knew a mother who cared for a child like that. He never responded either, but she took care of him all the time, no matter how tired she was."

Uriel said, "She had help from her family, and we need to provide Raphael the same kind of respite."

Michael leaned on the desk and closed his eyes. The room sounded so loud: Raguel and Zadkiel all but having a fist fight in one corner, poetry from another, laughter from a third. How could they be laughing when Gabriel lay in pieces?

He felt Uriel's touch on his arm, but he didn't raise his head.

"Is it true Raphael didn't get everything?"

Michael had projected that more than said it, his voice blending into the hum of the room.

Uriel's heart stirred in his own: it was true.

"Then we have to send someone back inside."

Michael thought about whom he could send. Remiel, already established in Hell. Himself because he couldn't ask his own to do something he wouldn't. An overextended Raphael, who might be best able to find what they were looking for. Israfel, also one of Gabriel's primaries and possibly strong enough to defend herself if attacked by all five of Hell's commanders.

Uriel said, "I think it's necessary."

Another decision. Gabriel usually handled this kind of thing. Maybe that's why Satan had singled him out. One of the others should have stepped in as the decision-maker. Michael worked better like a weapon: aim it in the right direction and fire, but don't expect it to select its own target.

"You'll do fine," Saraquael said, abruptly at his side. "You have a knack of responding instantly the right way."

Michael turned his head. "I don't know what's right to do this time."

Uriel had departed to speak to Mary, and the Cherubim were going head-to-head about whether knowledge itself, in its pure form, could possibly be wrong to have. For the moment, it left Michael and Saraquael in relative privacy.

"You second-guess yourself." Saraquael sat back in his chair. "You know, ordinarily I love the fact that every angel understands and reflects God's infinity in a different fashion, but it's times like this I wish we all just reflected it one way. Working stone against stone is a nice way to get down to the nugget of truth at the center, but the friction is pretty intense while we're getting there."

"We're in agreement about the important things," Michael said softly. "There's no question about those. But yeah. This one's going to be rough."

Saraquael said, "Remember after the Crucifixion, you had to stop a meeting and make everyone repeat to everyone else in the room, 'You are not the enemy'? Keep that in your toolbox in case we need it again." He put a hand on Michael's shoulder. "I've got the information you wanted." Then he hesitated.

"You want to pre-brief me?"

"You might want to know this first."

"Is it something that requires immediate action?"

Saraquael shook his head.

"Then hold off." He looked at Saraquael. "How does Gabriel do this?"

"You never studied him?" Saraquael chuckled. "He walks in, presents a logical and thorough description of what he intends to do, explains why he's discounted all the alternatives, asks if anyone has any objections, and then suddenly—surprise—we're in agreement."

"In other words," Michael said, "he's always right." When Saraquael laughed, Michael said, "Do you want to take over?"

"And get it from all sides? To be honest, I'd much rather be your lieutenant."

"Then there's nothing else for it." Michael got to his feet. "Gabriel has to get better."

He called everyone back to order.

Saraquael stood. "Camael has admitted that he as well as Mephistopheles and Beelzebub were to take part in the annihilation, so he understands the rudiments."

Ophaniel said, "We'd do well to assume the other two also know the whole procedure."

Sidriel said, "Mephistopheles has to be the one that developed it."

Michael waved the Cherubim down.

Saraquael continued, "Hell has sentries posted everywhere, but they aren't in formation to defend against a full attack."

Michael nodded.

"Everyone in Hell believes Gabriel was successfully annihilated."

Saraquael shifted his weight. "This last is a potentially damaging situation. Camael's involvement is not coincidental. He was chosen to participate because he supposedly used Remiel to direct Gabriel to Earth for spurious reasons."

"But there's no bond between them," Ophaniel said. "There's no bond between the other pair of twins."

"The Qaddisin aren't separated," said Sidriel.

"But we determined—"

"You were wrong," Saraquael said with a shut-them-down firmness. "He sent her suggestions, and she acted according to them. And before you point out what Gabriel already would have, that positive correlation doesn't necessarily indicate causality—" (both Cherubim chuckled) "—that doesn't mean the two happenings are necessarily connected. She might have decided she wanted to play a game at any time, and for no reason other than she wanted to play a game. Her nature leads her toward spontaneous action. I felt it necessary to mention this only because Camael believes it, and Camael was one of the abductors."

Everyone remained silent for a moment, and then Ophaniel said, "Does the feedback go both ways?"

"Do you mean, could Remiel send him a command?"

"That too, but more importantly, can he scan her thoughts?"

Saraquael's mouth tightened. "I didn't ask. It didn't seem as if he could."

"It's not her fault," Israfel said. "Even if this connection exists, we couldn't punish her."

Michael raised a hand. "Obviously she was used, if it happened at all. The difficulty is, what if Camael can learn our plans through her?"

Raguel said, "Camael is chained and Guarded."

"And later?" Michael said.

"We deal with it later. There's enough immediate worry to handle now."

Michael tilted his head. "Fair enough."

Saraquael took a seat, and Michael met his eyes as the Dominion project, *Back to you.*

Thanks.

"Does anyone have any more ideas about possible responses?"

Raguel stood. "Zadkiel was right about what we should do. This isn't our crime to pay back. We have to let God do it."

Michael fought the urge to stare open-mouthed, something a number of the other angels were unable to do.

Israfel stood so quickly she knocked over her chair." We can't just ignore what they did!"

Raguel folded his arms. "We're not ignoring it. We saved him, we discussed it and prayed over it, and we're taking some sort of action, even if that action is leaving it to God."

Michael noticed Uriel looking satisfied, and then he noticed Ophaniel nodding too.

Israfel, on the other hand, had flames in her hair. "We're the tools of God's justice! If he's going to strike, it must be through us!"

Mary said, "God can act however he chooses, and that might not involve any intermediaries whatsoever."

The air shimmered around Israfel. "I refuse to go along with that. I still say we have to invade and let the lower orders know with full certitude that if Satan does it again, *they* will suffer, and then let them put pressure on him to keep his filthy hands to himself!"

Zadkiel said, "But it won't be a full passivity on our part." She reached a hand toward Israfel, who shed sparks as she recoiled from contact. "We should mitigate our non-involvement, and the best way to do it might be the stern warning we discussed before."

Even as he responded to Zadkiel, Michael couldn't take his eyes off Israfel and her fellow Seraph, both ablaze. "What would you put in the warning?"

Zadkiel also had her gaze on Israfel as she answered; in fact, everyone in the room was having a hard time looking away from her. "That Satan is in serious violation of spiritual law, and that if he repeats himself, we'll beat the living daylights out of him."

Michael said, "Rough paraphrase?"

Zadkiel snickered.

Israfel flared with a whoosh that pulled all the air in the room toward her, causing the angels nearest her to flash a distance away, excepting the other Seraph and the two Cherubim. "We don't need to wait for him to repeat himself before we beat the living daylights out of him. This needs to be answered with force."

Uriel said, "You want to match power for power."

"We have the power," Israfel said. "We need to bring it to bear."

Uriel said, "If you don't mind, what would it accomplish?"

The flames decreased a little, and Michael looked to Ophaniel to see if he was the one drawing it down, or whether Israfel was calming herself. She said, "It would show them we won't take murder lightly, as if it were graffiti."

Uriel linked eyes with Israfel, speaking and projecting simultaneously. "What should we do when we invade? We can't annihilate Satan or we'd be in violation of the same law."

"We can chain down the ringleaders in the nether levels for a hundred years, or a thousand," Israfel said. "We did that after the Resurrection."

With spread hands, Uriel said, "But did it have any long-term effects? When Satan does get free, assuming we don't get leave to keep him chained until the Final Judgment, won't he act even worse, with a century of humiliation and time on his hands to plan? We need a plan of our own that ensures he'll never try it again." Uriel took a deep breath. "That sort of security is providable only by God."

Israfel folded her arms, but the fire had retreated to only flamelets around her eyes and wings. "We can get God into position to provide that security. We can push Satan up against the wall and keep him there."

Uriel said, "God works in his own time. You know that."

Ophaniel said, "As for your treatment of annihilation in comparison to graffiti, by which I presume you mean the slightest sin, the fact is that even the slightest sin merits damnation. Annihilation and carving one's name in a tree differ only in degree."

Israfel glanced at the other Seraph, and both exchanged a look that Michael could read easily: "Cherubim."

Sidriel said, "We leave justice in the small matters to God. We could logically justify leaving this to him as well."

Israfel said to Ophaniel, "Backstabber," but her eyes had become resigned.

Michael tried to unkey himself as Israfel sat and said nothing further, but she and Ophaniel had their eyes locked, and they were probably talking through their bond.

Peter, at the far end of the table with Mary, said, "What does Gabriel want?"

Uriel said, "He isn't in a position to want anything right now, unfortunately."

Michael said, "But it's a good point."

Saraquael said, "You can bet that whatever he wanted, he'd have a good rationale for it."

Michael smiled wearily. "Probably so. But right now, we're all we've got. So let's take a preliminary vote and see where that gets us.

Eight

Raphael slow-danced through Uriel's house, singing the song of the Seraphim. *Holy, holy, holy.* Rocking Gabriel to the rise and rush of the song, he kept his head bowed and voice hushed, arms around the sling bundle made from one set of wings, another set cupped over him, the final one relaxed. The song lent itself to a waltz, but he didn't dance any formal step as much as he moved where it led.

A touch had transformed Gabriel's room into a greenhouse, windows for walls, windows for ceilings. The Angels Michael sent had summoned trees outside the windows and then birds for the trees, dragonflies for color, chipmunks and squirrels for warmth, a stream for vitality. They didn't omit any detail they could think of trying to make it more pleasant.

The birdsong wasn't enough, though, nor the rustling of the trees, so Raphael had listened for his choir's ever-present song, and he sang too.

Every so often Gabriel shifted, but only a little, just enough to be comfortable. It was something.

When Raphael made his way back into the transformed room, he found Jesus there, and he inclined his head with a smile.

"You need a break," Jesus said.

"I'm fine."

"Rapha'li."

Raphael said, "I'm not fine, but he needs me, and I'll cope as long as I'm helping him."

"That's more accurate, but not entirely." Jesus moved up behind him and stepped through the angel so he and Raphael were in exactly the same place. Raphael noted again how he and Jesus were the same height and build, but then Jesus said, "Now step out of the sling."

He froze.

"I'm not going to hurt him."

Raphael exhaled, then went insubstantial and stepped out of the sling so Gabriel was cuddled against Jesus's heart instead of his own.

Jesus had one arm around the bundle. "You need a break. I'll stay with him the whole time you're gone, but you need to recharge."

"Can't you just heal him?"

Jesus said, "I'm not going to abandon him, but I'm also not going to interfere."

Raphael said, "You can heal him if you will."

Jesus said, "Yes, I can."

Raphael looked him in the eyes. Jesus returned the look.

"Go." Jesus waved him off. "He'll need you to be strong when the time comes. And I'll need you to be thinking clearly."

Raphael indicated the amber healing glow around Gabriel. Jesus chuckled, and with a gesture, he detached the glow from Raphael and left it self-sustaining around Gabriel. "I made the universe," Jesus said. "I know how to provide for him."

Raphael vanished, reappearing on Earth.

A moment later, Jesus joined him, although not with Gabriel. This didn't strike Raphael as odd, since Jesus wasn't limited to a singularity of place. Jesus flagged over the three Angels Michael had sent to follow Raphael, and he assured them they could wait back at the bungalow, as he would see to Raphael's safety himself. It amused Raphael that they argued they would stay anyhow, but only on the verge of sight, and Jesus laughingly agreed they could.

Raphael chose to visit a number of the angels under the umbrella of his command, all of whom asked how he was doing, gripped his hand, and conveyed an understanding that they knew how Gabriel was but were pretending he'd died in order to maintain Hell's ignorance. One at a time, Raphael met with guardian angels in charge of travel and transportation, his secondary purview. After helping an Archangel straighten out a snarl on the New York subway system, he moved on to checking his primary command, healing and health.

"You're right," he told Jesus between stops. "I needed to get out of there."

"What a surprise," Jesus said, and Raphael laughed as he spread his wings.

In a London hospital, a woman labored with her first baby. Raphael spoke to the guardians of the woman and her baby, who admitted to being at a loss. "It's hurting her," the woman's guardian said, "and her contractions are powerful, but she's not making any progress."

Raphael laid his hand on the woman as she rested between contractions, noting as he did the bright lights, the nurse with a studious expression as she regarded the monitors, the hovering new father. The baby felt safe for now, although Raphael made one quick adjustment and encouraged the baby to tuck his chin further. Then he felt the different energies flow through the mom as another contraction overtook her.

"There," Raphael said to her guardian. "Did you feel that?" The angel nodded but projected that he didn't know what it was he'd felt. "The uterus is a basket-weave of muscles. The up and down ones are contracting to deliver the baby, making the uterus shorter. They don't have pain receptors."

The angel nodded. "Go on." The woman was resting again.

"The horizontal muscles are ordinarily tense to keep the baby in, except during labor when they need to relax—and they do have pain receptors. Unless the horizontal lower segments relax while the vertical segments contract, she's pushing against herself."

The angel's eyes widened. "Oh! Once she's relaxed and can let go, the rest of the system can do what it's supposed to?"

Raphael waited until he and the guardian rode through another one of the mom's contractions. Then, "She's fighting herself. That's making her more scared and less willing to relinquish control."

The angel nodded. "Thanks. I think I know what to do now." He turned away, then turned back. "Oh, and I'm sorry about Gabriel. I'm praying for you."

Raphael looked down. "Thanks. It helps."

Jesus brought Raphael to another birth, this one in a private house in the Netherlands. A midwife played guitar while a mother labored in a tub surrounded by her three children and husband, all singing. The mother would drop out of the song during contractions.

The angels all looked up when Jesus and Raphael arrived. "Is something wrong?"

"Not at all," Jesus said. "I wanted to show him something."

The baby's guardian relaxed, and the other angels all returned their attention to the family. They should have joined in the song;

they didn't. The baby's guardian took Raphael's hand and said how sorry she was about Gabriel.

"This was what I wanted to explain before," Raphael murmured to Jesus. "She's working hard, but it's effective because she's not fighting her own body."

"He understood," Jesus said, "and I can see you understand too."

Jesus brought Raphael to a hamlet in Zimbabwe where Raphael consulted with the guardian of an old man dying of tuberculosis. The angel had his hands on the man's chest to give him some relief from the wracking cough. More condolences, more reassurances of prayers from the man's guardian.

Raphael and Jesus walked outside.

It was midnight on this part of the planet. Had the attack come only four hours earlier? How could someone's world change so quickly?

"I want to go back."

"Not yet," Jesus said. "There's no rush. He's still the same."

"I just want to be with him," Raphael said, but he didn't protest. He didn't want to hear another condolence message either, though, so instead of going to the next stop on his rounds, he walked into the jungle. Jesus kept pace. After a few steps, Raphael found himself solid and wingless, nearly human. A stick cracked beneath his feet, and the rich scent of rotting detritus enfolded him. Night insects sang, and even the air had a gritty flavor. Raphael looked over his shoulder at Jesus, who was now dismissing the three Angels. Jesus gestured he should move forward.

The path, such as he could follow one, headed eastward, presumably to another small collection of homes in another jungle clearing. The canopy of trees hid the starlight, and Raphael quickly found himself knee-deep in underbrush without a trail to follow.

There was something to just standing here, surrounded in a place he'd managed to work his way into but that had no path out. In this half-magic night he could be fully present, breathing the spice, dwelling in God's presence, feeding the world's largest mosquito, hearing the full spectrum of life that had multiplied to fill this world of wonders. Back home there were worried faces and an impossible task and the hollowness of something he knew to be true but would deny and deny until he had no choice but to accept.

Gabriel—

He struck forward again, forcing back the brambles as he moved, random snapping sounds in his wake. Gabriel wasn't getting better, maybe never would, but if he had it in him, even for a second longer, he'd keep the Cherub alive. Giving up was not an option because Gabriel was Gabriel, and what would the universe be without him? A bell without a clapper, or a dry engine, a barren fig tree, that was what. An old stream bed waiting for floods decades after the land had gone to the desert, or a ship at the bottom of the Mediterranean longing to set sail again. And that—

No, that mustn't ever happen, because not even God could set right something of that magnitude, and Remiel had dealt with the pain, but how could he?

The Cherub couldn't love or serve God from beyond the grave.

Raphael's soul vibrated like a grand piano with all its keys struck simultaneously.

As he struck through a low bush, something wrapped around his face.

He pushed back at it, but then he felt it grip his arms like a dozen tiny hooks. Back he pulled, but it tautened.

"Hey!" He twisted, and now it gripped his legs, the thorns embedded in his jeans. He couldn't kick free, and his arms were drawn fast by the brambles. Leaves stuck to his face, and when he shook his head to dislodge them, the vines constricted around his shoulders.

Full-blown panic set in. Thrashing, Raphael blew back into his angelic form only to find the vines and brambles and thorns still holding him. He summoned his sword, but against vines that now enwrapped his forearms with a strangling tension, he couldn't bring it to bear. The ones around his neck threatened to crush his windpipe. He ignited into a blue-white flame, trying to consume them, but they wouldn't burn.

"God!"

Jesus was right in front of him, looking him directly in the eyes. "Stop struggling!"

Raphael tried, but the vines stayed tight, and he wanted to get out of here, get free, get away—

"Stop!" Jesus said. "Be still!"

It was the same voice that had commanded the waves, and it commanded Raphael too. He was still.

As he stopped fighting, the vines relaxed, and Raphael found them letting go. The grip slacked off, and Jesus was able to make them loosen so he could work free.

He turned to Jesus, shaking.

"Remember," Jesus said, and then he was gone.

Nine

Camael had found the ice fields and their barren fury, wind and sleet above and frozen heartlessness below. Motionless for a moment, he began to be coated in the stinging ice.

Beelzebub found him there and shouted a command—come back with me. This Camael ignored. Beelzebub might be a Seraph and Satan's number-two guy, but what was that after all? The number two bully in a world of bullies.

Beelzebub struck him, and Camael turned golden-speckled eyes on him. *I feel nothing. I feel nothing.*

The sleet coated his hair and eyelashes. Camael could hardly see.

Beelzebub pounded the message into his heart the way a Roman had pounded a nail into Jesus's feet: *Come with me!*

This time Camael went. They landed in the dark of Beelzebub's chamber in the lab area.

"Why would you go there?" Beelzebub snorted. "It's worse than the Lake of Fire."

Camael pursed his mouth in defiance as the ice melted off his body and collected into a puddle at his feet. No one else had been at the ice fields. Wherever Gabriel was now, it would be lonely and without warmth too. The ice fields had seemed as good a place as any.

"I heard about the little show you put on in the common area. Everyone has. That was just about the stupidest thing you could have done. I protected you," Beelzebub added, a hungry growl that made his "altruism" sound like the appetizer of a fine dinner for which Camael would be picking up the check. "Asmodeus wanted your skull on a pike, but I think even he was a little amused by the discomfort it caused our lord. You just keep that in mind, and keep your head down."

Camael shrugged. "I knew you'd cover for me. You want me intact."

After a blind standoff, Beelzebub said, "I covered Mephistopheles. You I would let Lucifer chew up and spit into the Lake of Fire. The fallout was going to come on him, and no one disgraces my Cherub."

"Have it your way." Camael flared heat through his hair to resettle it. "Are you quite through, or should I fall at your feet to grovel my thanks?"

"Spare me. I've got an assignment for you." Beelzebub shifted in the darkness; he probably took a seat, but Camael couldn't be sure. "Our lord wants to pick out his next victim. You're to go to the surface to hunt out lone angels—any of the Seven, or any of the choir heads. When you find one, report back."

Camael heated the last of the water from his skin. *I feel nothing.*

Beelzebub said, "It's ridiculous to start scanning when we're not ready to try another one, but that's Lucifer's order. Asmodeus has agreed to keep a lookout as well, and you don't want him suddenly proving useful after all this time."

Camael snickered. "As if."

"You see through him. I don't think *he* does."

Smirking, Camael folded his arms. "I think he does. I think he just knows how much Asmodeus irritates you."

Silence from Beelzebub. Camael flashed to the gates of Hell, signed out, and went to Earth.

Lone members of the Seven.

Do I count?

Remiel spread her wings to hover in the sunlight over Antarctica, ice like mica shimmering on the gold feathers. The frigid air kept her aloft, and she let it penetrate: not as rude as the ice fields, just a gentle honest cold for her dishonest hot heart.

I want to go home. I feel nothing.

Remiel descended, letting her wings fill as she glided to the crunchy surface. *I want to go home.* At home, everyone could be sad together, and maybe no one would say Gabriel was dead because she hadn't been good enough to prevent it. But she wondered if they'd know, the same way everyone knew Camael had fallen, and since Camael had fallen that meant she was flawed too and had only survived the winnowing by chance. And now here she was, Camael herself, and there wasn't really a difference.

Prayer would answer everything—would confirm the worst in one horrid moment as possibility collapsed into an eternal reality about which she could do nothing. So why pray? Until she reached out for God and God provided an answer, Gabriel both existed and didn't exist in a bizarre contortion of quantum theory, the same way she could be both Camael and not Camael. Why become fully one or the other, fully grieving, fully fallen, fully a failure? Life on the dividing line would require the most precise dance she'd ever demanded of herself, but then again, precision came easily when you had to cut parts of yourself away from other parts. She could continue this way: it was all an elaborate game of pretend.

An elaborate game of pretend. Pretend who you are. Pretend Gabriel still exists. Pretend your deception had any effect whatsoever. Pretend God still loves you.

Sensing a question sent to her, she startled at a friendly soul's touch. Before considering the consequences, she sent a reply.

Saraquael appeared at her side. "I'm so glad you're safe." He hugged her so tightly he squeezed her armor, and she grabbed him as if holding onto a life preserver. With her eyes closed, she tried to put down her guard, tried to feel at least relief.

"Hey, you're okay." He patted her back, then pulled away. "They didn't discover you."

She looked at herself, still wearing Camael's armor and Camael's hard features. It was a wonder Saraquael could stand to touch her at all.

After a momentary silence, Saraquael said, "I was surprised you didn't come straight home."

"How could I?" Her voice cracked. "What they did—might do again— It's all an elaborate game of pretend this way."

"Wholesale pretending." Saraquael looked at the snow dusted over his boots. "On the brink of a lie but not quite, never entirely establishing the truth."

She shook her head, swallowing against the moment—Saraquael might *tell* her, might bring down the duality and kill Gabriel in her heart forever. She blurted, "It's crazy down there. It's one big party for the lower orders, and the top tier is backstabbing and outmaneuvering one another continuously." She stared at Camael's sword lashed to her side. "They're all wondering if there's going to be a funeral for Gabriel."

"Yeah," Saraquael murmured. "I'm wondering the same thing."

I feel nothing.

Saraquael raised his head. "I'm afraid I need to ask you to go back in."

Remiel went mask-faced.

"We think parts of Gabriel might have been left behind in the room where they did it."

"There weren't," Camael said. "I was in there."

"It might be subtle, like beads of mercury or a glaze on the walls." Saraquael rubbed his chin. "We need you to look again."

Camael gazed off at the white glare of sky on snow. *I feel nothing.* "I'll do it. But there's nothing."

"Thanks." Saraquael put his hands in his pockets. "Have you found out their next move?"

"They sent me out here looking for archangels who are alone. Any of the Seven or any of the heads of choirs."

"I don't count, I hope?" Saraquael chuckled. "I'm with you."

Camael forced a laugh, touching the hilt of Camael's ever-present sword with gauntleted hands. On a regular basis, he realized, Camael couldn't feel his own sword. *I feel nothing.*

"I'll let Michael know," Saraquael said. "From now on we'll travel in pairs or greater."

Remiel used to be a pair all by herself. "How is Raphael coping?"

"Badly." Saraquael's eyes dimmed. "But he's doing whatever he can."

"It stinks," Camael said.

Saraquael sent his agreement.

Camael turned away. "You'd better go. I don't want you seen if Beelzebub is spying on me to make sure I'm not double-crossing him while he's double-crossing me."

"It sounds like you need a scorecard to keep track," Saraquael said just before vanishing.

Camael grabbed the hilt of his sword, spread his wings, and resumed a patrol for angels he hoped not to find.

Uriel came home to find Jesus rocking Gabriel in a chair that hadn't been there earlier.

Uriel bowed, projecting thanks. Jesus inclined his head.

"Raphael needed some time to connect with others." Uriel gestured toward Gabriel. "Are you going to heal him?"

"The job is yours."

Uriel pivoted slightly aside. "I was hoping you'd changed your mind."

The Throne walked to the next room and leaned against the wall.

Jesus followed.

"I was wondering, maybe when he's done with that sling, if I could crawl into it too." Raking back unruly hair, Uriel said, "It's daunting. He's a mess."

Jesus looked grim.

Uriel went further into the room, which unlike Gabriel's room here or Gabriel's own private spot in Heaven (naturally it was a library) was outfitted casually. The furniture consisted of a rainbow of cushions and a low table. Not a straight-backed chair had entered the walls before Uriel had summoned them for Gabriel's room. Chimes hung from the ceiling, and bead-curtains divided the alcoves off the main room.

Uriel sprawled on one of the cushions, then gave a sigh. Jesus settled on the one adjacent, and Uriel moved closer to lean against his leg. "How have we done so far?"

"You've made all the correct calls."

Uriel remained silent.

A bird sang through one of the open windows, and Jesus spoke back to it, coaxing a smile from the angel. The pillows took Uriel's weight enough for the Throne to enjoy the human warmth of him so near, and shortly the angel's pseudo-heartbeat matched his. A wave of weariness broke through Uriel, ignored strain that had pitted the surface of Uriel's strength.

Jesus touched Uriel's hair. "The work is delicate, but I know you're capable."

Uriel's eyes stayed closed, but all Jesus's words penetrated, and the images he sent approximated the work that had to be done. The way Jesus explained it, Gabriel had been "unlaced" and Uriel needed to thread everything back together again. Raphael's undifferentiated healing power had made everything stronger, but eventually what was needed was very directed, needle-fine soul-work to rejoin every part of Gabriel to every other part.

Uriel marveled at the magnitude of stitching together a soul.

Jesus explained the way the interior of an angel fit together like puzzle pieces or grooved beads on a string, so the task wouldn't be as impossible as actually forming a soul. Where parts were missing, Jesus assured Uriel some regrowth could take place if only a small segment any particular "bead" was there, but what could not be regrown were entire "beads" or the string itself.

Uriel shuddered.

Jesus said, "It's not as easy as fitting together cardboard puzzle pieces, but not as hard as fitting together the molecules that make up the cardboard."

"You'll have to help me."

"I'll be with you," Jesus said, "but the work is yours."

Uriel lay against his arm and reached up to touch the bundle that was Gabriel, imagining the business of relacing a friend. Drifting, Uriel thought about what might be found there. No secrets, but perhaps unrestrained emotions or thoughts Gabriel might not want anyone to handle. They'd already been awash in Gabriel's memories once, and now Uriel wondered if Gabriel might resent it if they succeeded, how all his most private self had been so transparent to his rescuers.

"Raphael should do this."

Jesus said, "I chose you for a reason."

His fingers traced the lavender feathers on Uriel's outermost wings. Uriel stretched a little, then settled back against him. "When should I start?"

"Let him begin to awaken on his own. He's so soft inside right now that you'd tear the eyelets if you tried."

Uriel said, "Until then?"

"Keep hunting for what's missing."

With clenched fists, Uriel prayed, trying to force back fear while holding tightly to the Father, resting against his Son, and enfolded by the Spirit.

Michael returned to Uriel's living room to find Uriel in prayer, Raphael in the other room pacing with Gabriel in the sling, and Mary setting food on the table in the kitchen.

"Did I forget to tell you angels don't eat?"

"Uriel reminded me before. Have a cookie."

Michael made himself solid enough to eat it.

Raphael returned to the kitchen. "What did the executive council decide?"

Michael took the mug of hot chocolate Mary handed him. "It took a couple of votes, but we reached consensus to send a written warning to Satan that we'd retaliate if he made another attempt on anyone. Until that time, we wouldn't take action against them."

Raphael's eyes widened. "No invasion? Raguel actually voted for that?"

"Israfel was the toughest sell," Michael said. "She nearly burned the place down."

Raphael's wings closed around Gabriel.

Saraquael's arrival spared Michael from asking how Raphael would have voted. The Dominion shook some snow from his hair, told Mary he didn't need any hot chocolate, repeated his protest, then agreed to just one cup. His cheeks were pink and his brown hair windblown.

"You found her?" Michael asked while Raphael tried to demur that he didn't want a cookie.

Saraquael nodded, although a cloud drifted over his eyes. "They had sent her out to patrol the Earth. Her orders were to find lone archangels. Members of the Seven or heads of choirs."

Michael huffed.

Saraquael said, "I can spread the word that no one is to head out alone. Meanwhile, she'll search the room where they worked in order to find anything missing."

Uriel had joined them. "That's of paramount importance right now."

Michael looked at Saraquael, who said, "She told me there was nothing left behind, but she'll check again."

Michael couldn't help but glance at Gabriel.

Wings tight around the Cherub, Raphael paled.

"Parts of us weren't meant to exist in isolation," Saraquael murmured. "How long do you think they can last?"

Raphael walked away.

"They can grow back as long as something is left," Uriel said, "but you can't grow an entirely new piece."

"So we're segmented?"

Uriel nodded.

Saraquael sent a nonverbal question: Do you think you can do it?

Uriel picked up the cup of vegetable soup Mary was trying to foist on someone and gestured toward it. *It will be like trying to put the tomato back together.*

Saraquael left. Michael felt his last message—that he was going to write that letter now—but he avoided saying he was leaving before his emotions flooded out and hit Raphael.

Mary looked up. "You guys kept mentioning Rahab. I assume you're not talking about the harlot of Jericho. Is he a demon? I've never met him."

Michael and Uriel exchanged a look. "Rahab," Michael said, and then he looked down.

Uriel only glanced aside.

Mary said, "It's okay if you don't want to tell me. I was just curious."

"Ezekiel 28," Uriel whispered.

"Rahab did fall," Michael said, "but that's not why he keeps coming up in conversation. Before the winnowing, when God was creating the Earth and everything else, he gave some of us assignments so we could participate."

Uriel interjected that God had been perfectly capable of doing the whole thing himself, but the angels were enjoying the process so much that God stretched it out and let them participate too.

Mary said, "Like the way I used to let Jesus stand on a chair and help me bake bread."

Uriel's eyes sparkled violet.

Michael said, "Some of us were told to gather handfuls of dirt from around the globe when it was time to create Adam. Things like that. Rahab was asked to separate the upper and lower waters at the time of Creation. And Rahab, for whatever reason, refused to do it."

Mary's eyes widened. "But this was before the fall?"

Michael nodded. "I didn't see it happen. But after he refused, God destroyed him."

Mary stood in shock.

"Someone interceded," Michael said.

"It was Ataf," Uriel said. "Rahab was a Cherub. Ataf and the rest of Rahab's Seraphim asked God to restore him. God did."

Mary said, "And then he fell anyhow." She looked down. "What a waste."

Michael said softly, "He was one of Satan's top demons, a member of the Maskim like Mephistopheles, Asmodeus and Beelzebub. We don't know exactly what happened, but Rahab tried to prevent Israel from escaping Egypt across the Red Sea, and when he didn't succeed, he disappeared. We haven't seen Rahab for three thousand years, but the reports we got from Hell were that Satan destroyed him by chaining him under the Lake of Fire."

Mary's eyes had a glazed look. "That's horrible."

Uriel stressed that they didn't know if the story was true.

Michael said, "But as Gabriel would have said, none of the evidence contradicts it."

They were quiet for a while. Uriel finally said, "God re-created Rahab the first time. I only have to fix Gabriel. It's an entirely different order of magnitude."

Michael looked at the reddish soup. "But how do you do it?"

"Jesus told me." Uriel moved closer to Michael, studied him, then went partially insubstantial. Michael felt a sudden lurch as his sense of balance told him up was sideways, then a tingling in his fingertips which suddenly seemed a mile away from the rest of his body. The tea cups rattled in their saucers, and Michael heard indistinctly the clattering of bead curtains against themselves even though he felt no wind. At the same time he detected Uriel's marvel toward God for making them this way, and the moment after that the world returned to normal.

Uriel wore a tremendous grin, and both eyes sparkled.

Mary clasped her hands. "That's terrific! If you can grab the parts on Michael, who's whole, then you can definitely move them around on Gabriel!"

Michael clapped Uriel on the shoulder. "And remind me not ever to annoy you."

Uriel sank onto a cushion without responding, but Michael could feel the relief in the air. Raphael even returned from the other room.

"Finally some good news?"

Uriel couldn't stop smiling.

Ten

Saraquael landed in his home to find Zadkiel playing with a cat while waiting for him. "How is he?"

Saraquael headed straight to the desk, then took his time selecting the right piece of cotton bond paper and the right fountain pen and the best color ink.

"That bad?" Zadkiel set the cat to the side, then again as it returned to her lap. After the third time she flashed to a stand, letting an irritated cat drop through where her lap ought to have been.

She lingered alongside the glass-covered book shelves filled with every sort of book, reference and literature, prose and poetry, ancient and modern, angelic and human. By the bay windows she leaned on the cedar chest and idly rubbed the head of a second cat.

Saraquael mustered up a "Let's get started," so they prayed over the letter, then armed themselves with a thesaurus and the perfect slice of paper. God's court poet, Saraquael chose to word it as tersely and formally as he could to imply grief through stiltedness. Zadkiel convinced him to omit the thinly-veiled threat. The letter stressed that Satan's action had been contrary to the primary law of creation, and he was summarily ordered to desist from that behavior.

"I still think we should allude to what we'll do if he tries again," Saraquael said.

"A full-blown attack would be in keeping with grief and rage," Zadkiel said. "Threatening to do it next time is not. Let's keep him wondering."

"We might as well, since we're wondering ourselves," Saraquael muttered.

Zadkiel flipped her eraser in the air and snatched it back mid-spin.

The Lord approved of the letter, so the two Dominions got it sealed with the Divine Seal, and prepared to deliver it.

Saraquael flicked a speck off the sleeve of his formal uniform.

Zadkiel, dressed entirely in black despite the pallor it gave her, sighed and projected, *Vanity*. Saraquael laughed.

They donned ceremonial swords and black armbands, then flashed to Hell.

Music and the tumult of dancing greeted them at the main entrance, along with a choking odor that God warned them they didn't want to identify. Zadkiel's eyes were already scanning the corners for ambushes—and there were many corners—when a low-order demon staggered forward with his sword drawn but wavering.

"Halt!" Zadkiel shouted.

The demon stopped, its weapon clanging to the stone.

Saraquael folded his arms. "I will speak to Satan."

After a moment, Mephistopheles appeared. "You summoned us?"

"Bring Satan," Saraquael said. "Immediately."

"I assure you I have the authority to handle whatever you want."

Zadkiel rested her hand on her sword. Saraquael didn't do even that much.

They waited.

Mephistopheles waited.

After a full minute, the fallen Cherub said, "Must you really be so stubborn?"

Saraquael opened his hands. "We have our orders. I'm sure you can understand that."

Mephistopheles flashed away, reappearing beside Lucifer.

He stood at the shores of the Lake of Fire, neck craned back to stare at the cliffs surrounding it while keeping his back to the flame-engulfed water. Mephistopheles instinctively pulled his wings closer against the heat. Lucifer didn't bother diverting his attention from wherever he was looking.

"The enemy has sent emissaries, sir." Mephistopheles wondered if Lucifer would respond. "They requested a conference with you."

"Mephistopheles," Lucifer said, drawing out the name, "you have the authority to deal with them."

"I pointed exactly that out to them, but with their typical myopia they want only you." Maybe flattery was necessary. "While you've conferred great authority on me, sir, I'm sure they understand where the real power resides."

Lucifer grinned. "I'm certain they do. I was hoping you'd completed the work I assigned you."

Mephistopheles bowed. "Your faith in me is reassuring, but it's going to take a while."

Lucifer's eyes narrowed. "It's going to take even longer if you keep playing gate-man for the front desk. Shouldn't that be Belior's job?"

"The duty guard requested me." Mephistopheles forced a smile. "He knew Asmodeus couldn't handle two of them, and Beelzebub would have started a fight. The situation required someone with good judgment, and that meant me." Mephistopheles inclined his head. "I can hold two ideas in my mind simultaneously, so please be assured that I'm working on your challenge."

Only then did Mephistopheles realize how he'd bristled. Lucifer looked amused as he said, "Return with me to our guests."

Again at the entrance, Mephistopheles kept a half-pace back because Lucifer liked it that way. Michael's two standard-bearers stood side-by-side, identical in dress and expression. There was no question this was an emissary mission. Mephistopheles drank in the dark ghosts of their eyes, their instinctive repulsion as Lucifer drew closer.

Saraquael projected that they had come as ambassadors, then repeated, "We are here as ambassadors to present this document."

Mephistopheles fought a grin at the subtle insult, but Lucifer failed to react to it. He walked a few steps forward to take the letter but stopped short. Saraquael made the last step and handed off the sealed paper before returning to his partner.

Lucifer read the document expressionlessly, one finger brushing the seal at the bottom. Mephistopheles extended his senses but couldn't detect any emotions from either the pair of Dominions or from his lord.

Lucifer had no inflection. "Have you read this?"

"We have." (Again the double answer as they projected assent.)

More silence.

"What are you going to do in the event we refuse to comply?"

The Dominions remained silent as shadows.

Lucifer cocked his head. "Make it worth my while."

Again, no response.

Lucifer idly waved a hand. "Dismissed."

The pair vanished.

Mephistopheles stepped nearer, hungering for a look at the paper that Lucifer had folded back along the creases. He hesitated, inched into Lucifer's line of sight. Five seconds. Ten seconds—

"Oh, here." Lucifer handed it off, and Mephistopheles snapped it open. "It's a declarative statement that we violated spiritual law, and an order not to do it again. No threat of impending action. A waste both of their paper and my time."

Mephistopheles gave it a second read-through. "Don't dismiss it so soon. There's no mention of Gabriel. None at all, precisely where you'd expect one."

Lucifer opened his hands.

"I'm analyzing for what's not there, and the other element missing is the actual word 'annihilation.' They said we violated spiritual law and then refused to name what we did."

Lucifer folded his arms. "Just get to the point. I enjoy your conclusions without having to wade through every bit of trivia you compiled to arrive at them."

"But it cuts down on the questions afterward," Mephistopheles said in a low voice.

Lucifer looked amused again, and Mephistopheles tried to de-bristle. "My conclusion is that they're in shock and have no idea how to respond. It's hard for us to know what to do next, and we were planning it. Consider them foundering about trying to cope without the input of the one who would have told them how to cope with it in the first place."

"I believe you anticipated that," Lucifer said, "when you successfully argued we ought to single out the Cherub."

Mephistopheles' eyes glinted like hematite. "What I want to know is what happened to Raphael."

Lucifer looked over his shoulder at Mephistopheles. "The next time we take delivery on a written warning, feel free to enquire after his health."

Mephistopheles continued, "Those two had bonded so closely they were like one soul. Did he lose his mind? Did we destroy part of him too?"

"Earlier you suggested he might be upset," Lucifer said. "Why does it matter?"

Mephistopheles' wings opened as he shifted his weight. "If they lost Raphael because of Gabriel, then maybe Raphael's other primary bonds were wiped out as well—"

Lucifer folded his arms and tilted his head, a tolerant expression in his green eyes.

"—and we might have set off a chain reaction through the top two choirs. What we did was so unprecedented that we have no means of knowing what we actually accomplished."

"While this is fascinating," Lucifer said, "I don't care."

The Cherub stammered, "But—"

"If I never again see another Seraph or Cherub from that side, I'll ask you why. Until that happens, you're only making noise. Plug your brain into doing what I asked. Find a way to make this easier to do—and do it from a distance."

Mephistopheles backed one step, still clutching the letter. He vanished to Beelzebub's chamber, shaking, pulse pounding.

The Seraph focused his attention on Mephistopheles as soon as he arrived, his mouth tight and his eyes narrow. All this Mephistopheles felt nonverbally. He had no other way of knowing in the curtains of lab area darkness.

Beelzebub probed him, pushed against the Cherub's apparent fear to track it to a source. Mephistopheles shut down as much of his heart as possible, but not before Beelzebub caught a wisp of Lucifer's green eyes in his thoughts, the flatness of an idea shot down.

Mephistopheles handed him the paper and leaned against one of the walls. Focusing a glow, Beelzebub read the contents, smiled in mockery, and then crumpled the page.

Mephistopheles called the paper back to himself. "They're in shock."

Beelzebub radiated approval.

"I was wondering if maybe Raphael wasn't annihilated as well due to our destruction of Gabriel. If that happened, we could assume the destruction of his other primaries Ophaniel and Sidriel, and the loss of Ophaniel might cause the destruction of Israfel. It could well snowball until it wiped out the top two choirs."

Beelzebub had returned to whatever he had been doing before in the dark.

"I can't fathom any other reason for them to be so vague. It's almost as if they think they don't need to tell us what we did, but maybe they don't yet comprehend themselves the full effect, nor how many others will succumb, and you can't plan an invasion if you don't even know how many soldiers you have." He smoothed the paper against his thigh with a light crinkling. "We didn't take into account the ramifications of the bond other than the fact that we were going to make Raphael miserable for a while."

He realized then that Beelzebub was still ignoring him, so he went behind him and grabbed him by the shoulder. "Will you listen to me?"

Beelzebub spun with the pull to face him. "You're so far out in left field that you're not even in the same stadium any longer." He pulled Mephistopheles closer to him. "Why do you keep going on about impossibilities?"

He felt Beelzebub putting fire into the air, but he refused to absorb it. "What do you mean?"

"I mean that when you told us how it was done, you were the brightest thing ever, just hopping about and so smug that you'd been the one to crack the safe on God's best-kept secret. But you've moped non-stop since we actually did something with it."

Mephistopheles drew breath, but no words emerged.

"What did he say to you in there that upset you so much?" Beelzebub brought up his wings so they were touching Mephistopheles', but the Cherub pulled his wings upward away from the Seraph's. "What did he do after I left?"

"After you tried to use him."

"We all used him! Or do you forget the new and different pains of Hell in the form of a five-hour planning meeting during which we weighed exactly how much each archangel was worth? And this—" He grabbed Mephistopheles' hand and forced it open, snatching away the letter and instead grasping Michael's sigil ring in two fingers. "You didn't find this on him and take it for your own usefulness?"

Mephistopheles yanked away his hand.

"We may be bonded," Beelzebub said, "but I don't need this garbage from you."

"What do you need me for? To decorate your life?"

"I don't need you at all. You came to me." Beelzebub released him and turned back to his desk. "Was that pathetic letter the only reason you had?"

Mephistopheles trembled with irritation.

"Then you can feel free to go at any time." A moment later, seductive fire spread through the room, curling around Mephistopheles and brushing against his soul with the promise of ready energy and momentary togetherness. "Unless, of course, you'd rather keep decorating my life, as you call it."

Mephistopheles vanished.

Beelzebub opened the paper again, reading more slowly now that he was alone. After a while he frowned and said, "Mephistopheles?" but no one appeared to answer his question.

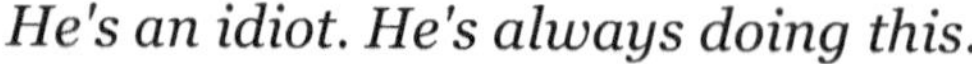

He's an idiot. He's always doing this.

It was typical, so terribly typical, and Mephistopheles shouldn't have expected any better of him after all this time, but sometimes down went his guard and then he got reminded yet again that Beelzebub wasn't really his equal, and that was all there was to it.

Mephistopheles had revisited *the scene of the crime*, the suffocatingly small chamber in between four other chambers where they'd snuffed out Gabriel's light like a smoldering wick. He approached the wall and hooked his fingers into the rings, leaned his head against the stone so it rested where Gabriel's throat would have been. Gabriel was taller than Mephistopheles, although not as tall as Raphael or Lucifer, but Mephistopheles still noted that the rings were just a bit too high for Gabriel, that he must have been a little stretched as he awaited death. Beelzebub had driven the rings into the wall without regard for height. In fact, one of the arm rings was a little bit higher than the other.

No care for detail whatsoever. Typical.

Raphael in shock, maybe hemorrhaging from his heart, maybe dead. Certainly grieving. This shouldn't have happened in the natural law.

But really, if God hadn't allowed for something like this to happen, wouldn't he have put the knowledge under better lock-and-key? There were two possibilities: one that God had wanted him to do this, and the other that God hadn't but simply wasn't capable of safeguarding the knowledge enough to keep out Mephistopheles.

But why hadn't Gabriel discovered it? Every Cherub carried around the raw material for testing any hypotheses as to the formulation of a soul—and for that matter, so did every other angel. During a bored moment it was so easy just to turn to the microworkings of a soul to figure out how it functioned, to half-destroy one of the lower order demons and take notes on the way it reconstituted. The answers hadn't come easily, but with persistence and numerous bursts of inspiration, they were attainable.

And oh, the thrill when he had that breakthrough, the moment he realized, the first instant he reached inside a minor demon and felt those beads, pinched them apart and felt the string vibrant and hard beneath his spiritual hands— The thrill that had wracked his mind as he'd realized what he'd done, what it meant, how everything would change. He'd burst in on Beelzebub while he was issuing orders to one of their underlings, preened the Seraph's outer feathers until Beelzebub had turned on him, at which point Mephistopheles had flooded his heart with anticipation he couldn't contain any longer. Beelzebub had dismissed their minion, and then Mephistopheles had Guarded the office to disclose everything.

They'd planned for over an hour—was there any way they could use the technique on Lucifer himself? It was unfortunate, but there was no way. Not even if they could guarantee Asmodeus and Belior's cooperation could they be assured of keeping Lucifer still long enough to reach inside him and destroy all those delicious beads. They pondered soliciting help from Gabriel or Michael. They ran through fifty scenarios before they decided to bring the technique to Lucifer as an offering instead—but oh, the political capital that would be theirs! They'd spent another couple of hours in quiet celebration before they'd approached Lucifer together and presented the discovery.

And Lucifer had been pleased—no, he'd been ecstatic, and all of Hell walked around in relief for days while the master planned a way to unload his new weapon, lost in his own thoughts and at times even bouncing ideas off Mephistopheles as if they were bonded themselves, although of course they weren't and never would be. Asmodeus was forgotten in that week, and Beelzebub had consolidated a long roster of allies for them, especially including Camael once Mephistopheles had the flash of insight that isolated his unique contribution.

So maybe it was just the disbelief that God had allowed them to do it after all, only one which kept feeling like a weight on his wings, like something half-forgotten struggling to be recalled at all hours. Lucifer had given him a new assignment, which Mephistopheles knew if completed could make him indispensable to his lord, only he hadn't even started.

Moping, Beelzebub called it. No, he was just regrouping, nothing more. This life of the mind was hard to sustain. It needed nurturing in quiet, in isolation, if only because silence made it simpler to hear that small whisper inside. But sometimes, like now, Mephistopheles felt no inclination to listen to whispering voices.

A second presence entered the chamber, quickly identifiable as Camael.

"Why are you here?"

Camael huffed. "I should ask that of you. Or are you worried you insufficiently annihilated him?"

"I'm sure of my work," Mephistopheles said. "It's this room that's lacking. The first set of Guards is so shoddy that two first-graders and a hamster could snap it."

Camael laughed.

Mephistopheles jerked his head toward Camael, trying to contain a burst of surprise.

Cautiously he spoke. "And you?"

"I have my own orders."

Unseeable, Mephistopheles summoned his sword to his hands. Camael couldn't feel the weapon, wouldn't hear it. "I'm sure you do." He threaded a Guard of his own through the walls, allowing it to expand like oil soaking through linen. "Don't let me stop you."

Camael didn't move. "I need you out of here."

"Then you'll have to wait. What I'm doing may take days."

Mephistopheles filled the room with his senses, taking in every aspect of Camael other than sight, repeatedly probing. The twin had a slippery feel, but nothing so off as to confirm—

Mephistopheles made a show of testing the rings he'd just checked, and as he did so, Camael inspected the corners of the room, focused singularly, concentrating on the edges one spot at a time. Interesting. Mephistopheles felt his Guard finally meet itself so it covered the entire chamber, and then he said, "You know why we can't kill Remiel."

Camael said, "The wench deserves it."

Good. "She's too valuable to us as she is."

That drew Camael up short. Mephistopheles could feel that focused attention waver. No questions followed, so Mephistopheles crouched, checked the leg shackles with a deep clanking sound. "What could make you want her dead," he said, "that overrides her contribution to this venture?"

Camael's voice betrayed none of the tension Mephistopheles could drink out of the air. This was perfect, perfect. "There's just something wrong with her. Her very existence is an insult."

"What makes you say that?"

"If there weren't something wrong with her," Camael said, "she and I would be together right now."

There was no way of alerting Beelzebub or Lucifer without simultaneously alerting the twin, so Mephistopheles would have to act alone.

He raised his sword and bound Remiel with his will.

Her shriek reached no further than the Guards. Mephistopheles concentrated to keep her pinned, thrashing against his patient hold until she would expend her strength.

A strobe of light from Remiel blinded Mephistopheles, but he was used to not being able to see here. He hurled her toward the wall and then wrestled her arms into the chains emptied the last time by an annihilation. They gripped her, laughing, as Mephistopheles forced her back.

"Satan will have your head if you destroy me!" Remiel screamed. "I'm too *valuable* to your operation, remember?"

Mephistopheles huffed. "We'll find another way to lure angels to their deaths."

She stopped struggling.

Bad misjudgment there—time to redirect. "Tell me, are they going to hold a funeral for Gabriel?"

Her voice sounded stunned. "I'm wondering that myself."

Mephistopheles reached inside for her heartstrings...and missed.

Remiel's glow didn't return, keeping them entombed in sightlessness, but he could see her with his heart, feel as that slipperiness intensified, almost detect what she was telling herself: *I feel nothing.* Rushed, he made another grab, and this time he had her heartstrings in hand just long enough to realize he wouldn't be able to grip them long enough to unlace any part of her: in denying so much she was in the process of denying herself. Hadn't Lucifer said Camael was going mad after the annihilation?

He tried to unhook the first part of her, but in fear she lashed out, and her heart slipped away.

"I'll destroy you," he said.

She had tears on her cheeks—he could smell them—but more than that, he could hear them in the way she said, "You should. I deserve it. There must be something wrong with me."

"Don't expect me to pity you." He tried for the third time, and finally he had a solid grasp on the insubstantial. She wasn't fighting. If anything, she was struggling to stay sane, giving his spiritual fingers a full purchase on her interior building blocks. He had her. Now—

Now—

These were the pieces touched by God Himself when they all came forth new and soft, made as individuals even though he didn't respect the things he'd made, made all at once in a gush of wonderment—

And he, Mephistopheles, the only one who'd figured out how—

Do it.

Just pull. Get it started. It will be easier once it's started.

I'm responsible for this. The only one here.

Her heartstrings slipped away once again, him feeling at once her own denial, the skewed unreality of the moment, her own questions as to who she was and where she could go from here, and he knew he couldn't lay a hand on her again.

He'd call Lucifer. Let him do it again; let his hands be the ones for the second time.

Illuminating the room, Remiel looked about as if stunned by her surroundings. She pulled her wrist out of the chain and stepped forward.

Mephistopheles retreated: it was too late even to call for a backup. She pulled free her other hand. He couldn't grab her will because her will wasn't in command right now. Crazed like this, nothing could hold her, no Guard keep her in or out.

He said to her, "Do you know how I recognized you? Because even Camael isn't that twisted inside."

Looking at him over her shoulder, she bit her lip. Then as though they didn't exist, she stepped through his Guards and vanished.

Mephistopheles dropped against the wall, one of the ankle rings jutting into his back. He didn't shift. He maintained the Guard and sat for ten minutes.

Lucifer ought to know about this, but then again, Mephistopheles could fully predict the kind of response he'd get, the subsequent loss of status, the sneers, the interesting nicknames unforgotten for an eternity or until someone else fell from favor.

What was Remiel looking for, anyhow? Such a dangerous mission couldn't be for no reason, surely. Knowing she might be killed if captured, yet heading in alone and disguised as her brother (something Camael had never been able to stand doing—something she'd never done before) bespoke a desperation Mephistopheles didn't understand.

The options were, either she was crazy before she'd started and wanted to visit this room as a shrine, or else they thought something had been left behind, or they wanted reassurance that Gabriel was really destroyed and not just trapped.

The letter never mentioned annihilation.

Maybe they weren't convinced.

But what evidence could she be seeking? There wouldn't be blast marks on the stones, and no trace signature remained of Gabriel's energies. Therefore, spiritual residue.

That was an interesting prospect, that they might be trying to collect bits of Gabriel, maybe not for reassembly, but for a memorial, or—no, they'd never be able to clone an angel, would they?

Without wanting to, for the hundred-and-eighth time, Mephistopheles relived the scene. Their Guard, unbreached. The way the Cherub had screamed for God. Camael's energy drilling into Gabriel. The Cherub unable to move, unable even to cry out by the end as they disconnected one piece from the next from the next from the next. That flash of raw light as Lucifer finished.

Mephistopheles sat on the floor and closed his eyes.

I made that possible.

Remiel insane. Angels not singing. Raphael crippled.

I did that.

A great victory. Everyone said so. A crowd of revelers chanted so. Even the minions of Heaven seemed to think so. Victory.

Oh, Gabriel.

Mephistopheles' eyes flew open.

He gripped his Guard and drew it down on itself, rendering it ever smaller until it hit the chain anchors for the arm braces and he had to give those permission to permeate; then further down, slowly, until he had to give permission to pass himself through, and still smaller until the Guard was the size of a grapefruit and fit on his palm, and finally so small there rested on his palm only a tiny bead.

It rolled a little, trembling from the contact. Mephistopheles probed the contents of his Guard the way he'd probed Remiel.

It felt like Gabriel, only it wasn't Gabriel any more than the letter 'b' spelled Gabriel or a picture of Gabriel would have been Gabriel. It was only a part of a part of one of the beads that made up a soul riding the heartstrings.

The question remained: what would Remiel have done if she'd found this? There certainly wasn't enough to make an angel. Three could fit on the head of a pin. Most likely he hadn't found it in the post-annihilation sweep because it was so small. Yet Remiel had anticipated its presence and come searching.

She had sounded pained regarding the funeral. Maybe they required something of Gabriel to dispose of properly. But surely symbolic laying to rest wasn't worth risking Remiel's life and sanity. The only way to make her potential sacrifice worthwhile was if they believed they could resurrect Gabriel.

Admittedly you never knew what God was going to do after you won a hand. A notorious sore loser, God would change the rules of the game midstream if things hadn't gone the way he liked. Lucifer and he had acknowledged that basic unfairness during the planning stages. Still, making God change the rules meant they'd won inasmuch as they'd done something so unexpected that he couldn't have won by ordinary means.

Keeping a hand cradled beneath the bead, Mephistopheles sent a summons to Lucifer, who appeared momentarily.

"I trust you've been working on your assignment."

"You needed to see this." Mephistopheles handed over the bead wrapped in his Guard.

Lucifer flashed out of the chamber into his office minus Mephistopheles. A moment later, Lucifer pulled him inside.

Stark anger. "Explain this."

"It's spiritual residue from—"

"Explain how you think it survived."

Mephistopheles stood ramrod straight before his blistering attention. "It survived because at the last when you disconnected his heartstrings, you blew apart what remained, and this bit must have gotten trapped in a corner." Mephistopheles tried to calm his own heart. "You can see from its size it's almost nothing, and without a Guard around it, I doubt you could handle it. If you'd like me to further study it—"

Lucifer crushed down on the Guard with two fingers, smashing apart the bead and causing a pain to shoot through Mephistopheles' head. He felt the bead go, felt whatever had been inside the Guard absorbed into Lucifer's hungry spirit.

"You will track down any more of these."

"Sir, I can say with complete confidence—"

"You were *already* completely confident that we'd found and annihilated all of him, everything except the memories. Your confidence means nothing to me. I want assurance that nothing more survived."

Mephistopheles bowed his head, an obeisance Lucifer would feel even in the dark. "I apologize. I should have taken it on myself earlier to squeeze the room, but at the time our search seemed thorough enough."

"I don't keep you around to *seem* thorough, Mephistopheles." And with that, Lucifer pushed him back out into the cell.

Yeah, maybe he would just neglect to mention Remiel.

Mephistopheles reset his Guard on the room and repeated the squeeze, bringing the Guard tighter and closer until it collapsed on itself without entrapping anything inside. In order to make sure the room contained nothing further, though, Mephistopheles would need to devise a new kind of technique. They'd never had to filter out something so slippery and small.

Lucifer appeared at his side. Mephistopheles didn't react, just endured a moment's humiliation as his master set a Guard on the room and squeezed it again.

Embarrassment yielded momentarily to awe. A Guard's strength is directly proportional to one's willpower, and Mephistopheles had never encountered a Guard anywhere near this tight. It had to be three times stronger than the one he'd just used, and Lucifer beside him vibrated with the tension of the San Andreas Fault.

The next feeling was panic as Lucifer's Guard hit the edges of Mephistopheles and contained him within the squeeze. He moved toward the center, but he could feel Lucifer's amusement as the Guard tightened around him, forcing him closer on himself. Just when he wondered if he were supposed to beg for mercy, Lucifer allowed him to permeate the Guard, and it continued shrinking to a singularity.

"If I may," Mephistopheles said, "don't dissolve your Guard yet. Start expanding it slowly again." He threw a Guard on the room, attempting to make it as iron-tight as the one Lucifer had just done. Mephistopheles made a note to practice Guarding. Tight enough and maybe you could keep out the Almighty.

Lucifer said, "This is new."

"Between the two of them, we should be able to determine if anything remains."

Lucifer's Guard contacted Mephistopheles' and pushed outward while Mephistopheles concentrated to hold the shape of his own, the crushing pressure between the two always in his thoughts, and from what he could tell, perfectly even. Nothing blemished the seal of one against the other, but was it ever hard to maintain concentration against that kind of pressure—

Mephistopheles' Guard shattered, leaving him seeing arcing lights that couldn't be there. His head pounded. He tried to ask if this were a sufficient degree of certitude, but the words wouldn't form.

"Very well, then." The rustle of folding wings. "Now get back to my assignment." And he flashed away.

Mephistopheles dropped to the floor, unable to stop shaking.

Eleven

Saraquael's summons came to Michael while he was securing three minor demons outside a church. Leaving them with a pair of Archangels, he reappeared at Uriel's bungalow.

Saraquael was handing Uriel a paper packet the size of a credit card. Michael looked over Uriel's shoulder at the mottled beige paper, blank but regardless imprinted with a message. Remiel's: *I found this but can't check more.*

Uriel uncreased the paper to find six beadlets.

Michael tried to swallow his disappointment. Uriel refolded the paper and flashed to Gabriel's room.

Saraquael said, "She doesn't sound good in that message. Rattled."

"You think they came close to capturing her?"

Saraquael flinched. "We ought to pull her out of there."

Michael considered.

"No, I didn't see her." Saraquael dragged a hand through his hair. "She left it on my desk, and it felt to me like it had been done long-distance, maybe from the plane of Creation. I'm worried about her. About everyone assigned right now."

Michael rubbed his chin. "The enemy is getting bolder, too. Spiritual attacks are way up since this started."

"I've been deploying more angels but ordering they move in pairs," Saraquael said. "The idea being at least one could get word out if they're attacked, and I keep telling them all just to run for help, not to stick around long enough to be the 'second victim.' But it's possible for a pair to be overwhelmed."

Michael smiled. "Put the Cherubim on it."

"I'll give it a cool name, too, like Operation Lifeguard." Saraquael clapped Michael on the shoulder. "You'll figure something out, don't worry."

"You're more confident in my abilities than I am."

"It's not you I'm confident in."

"Oh, sure." Michael gave him a shove. "Drag God into it, why don't you?"

A moment after Saraquael departed, Michael felt surprise from Gabriel's room, and in he flashed.

Raphael was sitting on the side of the bed, his guitar standing by his calf, and Michael saw Gabriel's hand was resting on his.

Uriel and Raphael both looked stunned. Michael said, "Is he awake?"

Uriel projected that Gabriel seemed to have reached for Raphael deliberately. Raphael assented, but Michael could feel his distress: apparently he still wasn't picking up anything from Gabriel.

Michael looked at Uriel, who nodded back at him. So Michael departed.

At the peak of Mount Kilimanjaro, Michael prayed for what was happening right at this moment. Uriel would have put a Guard around the room and reached into Gabriel's heart with the same hands that had reached into Michael's only a little earlier.

At the edge of his awareness, Michael felt three Angels join him, keeping watch. He'd forgotten his own orders, but they hadn't. It was a ridiculously stupid slip-up, but thankfully no harm done.

Wings cupped about himself, Michael reached for God's hand and squeezed, so tense, unable to form words or even to formulate the desire, but he knew God knew, and close at hand God remained.

He looked at the other mountains, all so young. He could remember their formation. One of the nearby mountains was still a perfect cone, and from here he could see another mountain that used to be taller than the peak on which he sat. Although he was near the equator, crunchy snow clustered around him, yielding only at the lower elevations to brown and then to green as the land fell toward the earth and joined the other valleys. Michael let the winds tug at his feathers, tilted back his head and let the world sing its praises to God while he offered back all that beauty in exchange for Gabriel's life.

Uriel appeared next to Michael.

Surprised, he opened his wings to look at the Throne: Done already? Shouldn't it have taken hours, all that fine beadwork? Or did Michael need to help somehow?

Uriel met Michael's gaze with eyes that glistened.

Michael grabbed his knees to his chest, dropping his forehead to them, and clapped his wings back around himself like a clam shell.

Uriel said, "He's going to die."

Michael only shook his head.

They shouldn't be having this conversation here, out in the open in the middle of Creation. He knew that, and yet he couldn't marshal the will to move, to even ask more questions. Uriel had tears but wasn't crying. The last time Uriel cried had been the winnowing.

Uriel touched Michael, wing to wing, and in the next moment they were both at a lakeside in Heaven. Michael saw the six Angels, their escort, taking places in the trees just at the edge of sight.

Michael managed to say, "Does Raphael realize?"

"I couldn't have hidden it from him." Uriel sat on the ground and traced lines in the gravel. "He's the healer. It takes him an instant to diagnose, another instant to heal, yet for all the energy he's poured into him, Gabriel hasn't done more than tread water."

"The things Jesus taught you—"

"I tried. I tried and tried, but there wasn't enough thread or string there to make it work. Look." Uriel drew a line of light in the air, a cord as thick around as the circle of thumb and forefinger. "That's what yours was like, flexible and healthy. This was what Gabriel's was like." And here Uriel skipped one finger through the air, creating a ragged string only a foot in length, shredded like used dental floss. "I can't tie that. I wound together a couple of pieces, but even at that I was afraid it would break. And Michael, yours seemed to go on for a kilometer. This was all of his I could find."

Michael turned back to the water. "Could it have been hidden inside, just not where you expected to find it?"

"It would be like misplacing a Howitzer cannon in a broom closet."

"Jesus told you we had to find as much as we could."

"But that string would have to be somewhere, and no one's found it. We searched the field. Remiel searched the cell. I even searched my house, but it's not there."

"Then it's up to Raphael," Michael said.

Uriel's eyes flashed. "He can't do any more than he has. Jesus gave the work to me, and I can't do it."

"Jesus said it depended on him holding on."

"And I can tell you right here and now that I haven't any idea what that means." Uriel stood. "I'm sorry, Michael. Give me a minute."

As Uriel walked away, Michael stared into the water, stared and listened. There were fish in the lake, and dragonflies, and birds above. Trees whispered in accompaniment to the lapping wavelets, and the insects hummed a descant as they darted. He wished it would rain, drown out the whisperings and the zings of the insects, just smother it all in an unfriendly roar of falling water and gusting wind.

Uriel returned. "I'm sorry. There's no reason to get mad at you. I'm beginning to think Jesus said I had the assignment rather than Raphael because he didn't want Raphael to blame himself when it failed."

Michael flinched. "But... Can't we do anything?"

"I already had this conversation with Raphael, only he won't accept it." Uriel's head bowed. "He keeps telling me we'll find a way to pull him through, and I can't see that we can with what there is."

Michael said, "Jesus wouldn't have given us encouragement if there were no hope."

Uriel smiled ruefully. "You have so much faith."

Michael swallowed. "You trust God more than anyone I know."

"I trust him to do what's best," Uriel said. "That doesn't mean it's going to be easy. Nor that we're going to like it. If Gabriel's death were for God's greater glory, I have no doubt Gabriel will die, and that in the long run we'll praise God that he did."

After a moment, Uriel added, "I combed everything Jesus told me. He said the job was mine. I can't remember at all him saying I would succeed."

Michael tossed a pebble into the pond. "What more can we do for Raphael?"

"I'm going to give him a breather, send him out to look over Gabriel's jurisdiction." With folded arms, Uriel gazed across the pond the way Michael was looking, a more intimate togetherness than looking into his eyes. "He returned before so restored. Once it's over, I don't know." Uriel nudged the gravel. "I can't imagine one without the other."

Michael said, "Remiel adjusted."

Uriel said, "Remiel."

Michael arched his neck and looked at the sky. "Maybe the added parts Remiel found will help him turn a corner." He drew a long breath. "In the meantime, I'll get Ophaniel on it. Maybe he can figure out where the other parts might be."

Uriel said and projected nothing.

They returned to Raphael and Gabriel, Michael wondering what they'd find, what he'd say, how much Raphael would admit.

The Seraph sat playing guitar, subtle finger-picking in a repetitive tuneless fashion, a basso continuo more than a song, over and over. With his eyes closed, he played. Michael realized the song itself served as the prayer he couldn't pray.

They didn't interrupt. Uriel stood at the window looking outside, hair gleaming black in the sunlight.

"Excuse me," Michael heard.

He turned to find Mary in the corner holding a vase of lilies. "I had an idea."

Uriel sent a wave of recognition, and Raphael, looking up, cried, "That's his!"

Mary put the vase into Raphael's hands. "I don't know if this would be of any use, but you can have them."

Michael sent out a question.

"Oh, I'm sorry." Mary turned to him. "Gabriel gave these to me the first time he appeared, when he told me about Jesus. He didn't have them when he arrived, but just before he left he handed them to me, and they've never wilted."

Michael's eyes widened. "He must have formed them from his soul material, only he never called them back to himself."

Raphael held the vase close to his chest. "You understand the flowers won't be here any longer."

"But *he* might," Mary said.

Uriel snapped.

"I'll get the word out." Michael summoned Saraquael, then belayed that and went for the Dominion himself.

Half an hour later, they had located four more soul-manifestations of Gabriel. Uriel placed them beside Gabriel on the bed and set about finding a way to distill them back to soul-essence, nearly impossible because an angel locks a form like that with his will, and Gabriel wasn't able to unlock them himself.

One of the items had been a brass key, worn to dullness, only an inch long.

"What's the story behind that?" Michael asked Saraquael in the kitchen.

"I nearly had to mortgage my soul to get it." Saraquael rested on one of the cushions. "He'd given it to a woman on Earth when she was a girl, and she'd worn the thing on a chain ever since. I offered her a replacement, a duplicate, a bathtub full of cash, but she wouldn't part with it. In the end I had to explain why I needed it and she just handed it over."

Michael chuckled. "I'd love to hear him tell the story behind that."

"I'd love to hear him tell us anything right about now." Saraquael rubbed his eyes and raised his aqua-tinged wings. "What's next?"

"Have you made any progress on Operation Whatever Cool Name We Gave It?"

"You're getting punchy." Saraquael shook his head. "I started the Cherubim debating. After another half hour I'll step in, poll the top three ideas, and bring them back to you. Assuming they're all metaphysical possibilities."

Michael snickered. "That's always a danger with them."

"Because if something's not possible, I'll get a couple of hours of why in a perfect universe it should be. I know." Saraquael stood. "But there are other things I should be doing, so I'll get to them."

"You can rest a bit," Michael said.

Saraquael shook his head. "I'd rather be working." And he vanished.

Michael returned to Uriel and Mary, who looked up wearing a huge grin. "We unlocked the flowers."

Uriel said, "I'm not sure how much it added, but they're done. I'm trying the rest of them."

Raphael returned carrying a hard-sided black box the size of an overnight bag. "I remembered this."

Uriel grimaced. Michael felt the Throne projecting that Raphael should put it back.

Raphael vibrated angrily.

"God made that, not Gabriel." Uriel returned all attention to the assortment of objects. "I'm not going to destroy it."

"It's quite possibly—"

Uriel projected, *No.*

Raphael set it on the window sill.

Michael said, "You know, if he sees you treating it badly, he may just get out of bed to beat you up."

Raphael chuckled.

"What is it?" Mary said.

"His trumpet."

She whistled, but she didn't ask to see it.

Raphael had flamelets around his eyes, but he didn't insist. In the next moment, Michael realized he was trying to stay calm so Gabriel didn't reflexively absorb the fire.

Michael wanted to say that given what Uriel had found inside, the trumpet probably wouldn't make a difference, but his mouth went dry and his throat tightened.

We have to find that string. The cord. Whatever it is. Otherwise all this does is delay.

Uriel didn't look away from the objects on the bed. "Raphael, you'd better go now. Take a break. Like we said before."

Raphael kept his eyes on Gabriel for a while. He rested his hand on the Cherub's head, whispered a blessing, and murmured, "Hang in there." Then he departed.

Raphael ran through Gabriel's jurisdiction, rounds they'd often made together during brighter days. Raphael knew all the angels he checked up on and who asked for assistance. Gabriel had the areas of higher education (naturally) and communications (less obviously) so Raphael found himself dealing with professors and students, messy add/drop forms, miraculous cell phone reception for a stranded traveler in the middle of New York State's southern tier, and a newspaper editor trying to prove one of his columnists had made up his material—and furthermore, figure out what to do about it.

Again as he moved through the list of needs, Raphael heard repeatedly how sorry everyone was, as if he somehow owned the loss—and that everyone was praying.

It's true, he realized. Everyone was praying but no one was singing.

Not even a sad song. Even angels who made up songs on the fly about the people they guarded kept an odd silence. If he listened, Raphael could hear the Trisagion, the holy-holy-holy maintained continuously by the Seraphim before the throne of glory. But only that.

Raphael arrived in the park where Gabriel had been abducted, solid and wingless, his guitar again in hand. It was too much silence, too many angels in shocked separateness rather than together under the same burden.

Children played on the swings, and others climbed the slides and clambered over the monkey bars, their guardians keeping their grips sure and their feet steady.

Raphael warmed his hands, surprised by the briskness of the morning, but when it came time to play a song, he stopped. He knew a million songs and could play any instrument he'd ever come across, but right now he couldn't choose a tune, couldn't decide on a melody or words.

"Hey," a little girl said. "You were here yesterday."

Raphael nodded, thinking at the same time, *Only yesterday?*

"You gonna play again?" The girl looked to be about eleven, longhaired and lithe. Raphael noted her orange-winged guardian standing a short distance away, and behind him, an angel with two-toned wings watching with singular intent. In the tree above them was one of the Angels Michael had deployed to keep tabs on him.

"What's your name?" Raphael asked the girl.

"Elizabeth." The girl folded her arms. "What are you going to play?"

"I can't decide." Raphael forced a smile. "You pick something."

"I can play Arkansas Traveler on the piano," she said, "so I know the words if you can play the music."

Raphael played, and Elizabeth sang. She suggested Shortnin' Bread next, but she only knew one verse, so after three repetitions they gave it up.

"You're fun," the girl said. "Are you going to be back again?"

Raphael said, "I'm not sure," sending his fingers picking over chord progressions again.

Elizabeth said, "You look sad."

"One of my friends is very sick." Raphael looked at the guitar, almost unfamiliar with his own fingers as they moved with such assurance.

"Is he going to die?" Elizabeth didn't wait for an answer. "I'll pray for him, okay?"

"Thanks." Raphael forced a smile. "He'll appreciate that."

She grinned. "I've gotta run now. See you!" and she raced across the playground to her brothers.

The guitar sang softer now. No angels joined it. Raphael scattered his senses across the field, listening with his heart to feel anything that might have been Gabriel's, but nothing answered.

"Excuse me, mister?" Elizabeth was back. As he tried to focus on her, she handed him a stuffed teddy bear on a key chain. He turned it over, seeing where the fuzz had been worn off the nose and the white belly gotten dirty, but he also saw her bright smile, and he thanked her.

"That way your friend will have something," she said, then darted back to her brothers.

Raphael looked at her guardian, and he found the orange-winged angel and the two-toned one standing side by side, arms folded, smiling at the girl. The two-toned one projected toward Raphael that he was very sorry, and they were praying. Raphael thanked him.

The park quieted down with the kids gone. Singing with the girl had opened a floodgate of songs in his mind. He slowed his fingers to a crawl over the strings, but he only played. His heart wasn't in his voice, and he was afraid to try singing if it was only going to shatter everything holding him together. A crow called across the park, and from the distant houses a wind-chime clanged. Raphael paused, then continued playing guitar.

Twelve

At Mephistopheles' summons, Camael arrived immediately.

The Cherub checked him over thoroughly in a silence unbroken by anything. Camael stood, arms folded, wings tense, hands gauntleted and sword gleaming in its scabbard.

"Are you aware," Mephistopheles said, "that your sister attempted to impersonate you?"

Camael rolled his eyes.

They stood in a corner of the main hall near the Lake of Fire, but the heat benefited them by creating a relative privacy.

"Did you kill her?" Camael said.

Mephistopheles shook his head. "We were ordered specifically not to kill her, if you recall. Yesterday, in fact."

Camael said, "She's really only of dubious value."

"She's about as valuable as you are," Mephistopheles said, "but *he* wants to use her at least once more."

"Far be it from me to say he's misguided. Look," Camael snapped suddenly, "quit *probing* me, okay? You did it once. I'm not going to suddenly turn into her."

Mephistopheles murmured, "You can't be too thorough."

"You can be too thorough if it gets you knifed."

Mephistopheles said, "Try it."

Camael said, "I would, but Beelzebub would beat me senseless."

Mephistopheles enwrapped Camael in a Guard using the technique he'd reverse-engineered from Lucifer's. Letting out a yelp, Camael struggled, but Mephistopheles gripped him, iron-willed, and drew the Guard tighter as if squeezing him.

"Beelzebub might not arrive in time to beat you senseless."

Camael tried to spit at him, but the Guard caught that too.

Mephistopheles took a deep breath, then turned his back. Down went the Guard, and Camael dropped to all fours, wings splayed across the rocks.

"I know you hate your betters, but at least let's be civil."

Camael struggled upright. "I'll sell you out to Asmodeus in a heart-beat."

"Would you like to work for a loser?" Mephistopheles opened his hands. "Be my guest."

Beelzebub appeared. "Hey, you two. I can feel the fight all the way across Hell. Would you mind keeping it down?"

Camael pulled on a rock to drag himself to his feet. "Just as long as he keeps his nasty hands to himself."

Beelzebub looked at Mephistopheles in shock. The Cherub glared at Camael.

"My," a voice drifted over to them. "Discord in the high command?"

Beelzebub flashed a smile at Asmodeus, the commander of Hell's army, tilting his head so the firelight glinted off his hair. Mephistopheles drew his wings tight, then folded his arms.

Camael could feel the Cherub-Seraph pair communicating on a level even subtler than projection, a breathless back and forth so reflexive that by rights no one should be able to detect it. Certainly he never had before. But the pair shared a volume's worth of dialogue in a handful of seconds, all while Beelzebub straightened his sword and stepped toward the other Seraph, and Asmodeus swept back his cloak to reveal his armor's dull gleam and the shine of his black boots.

"Shouldn't you be selecting our next target?" said the captain.

"I'm amazed that you're able to show your face in public after you so spectacularly failed to keep Michael out of Hell during our experiment." Beelzebub moved to stand closer to Asmodeus. Camael realized how tall both Seraphim were, how they'd both drawn themselves up marginally taller, so minutely no one ought to have noticed, except that Camael did as his thoughts floated away while he listened to the gentle vibrations in the air between Beelzebub and Mephistopheles.

A second dark Cherub appeared. This one was shorter, brown-haired to Asmodeus' black, dark-eyed to his blue. He took his place by Asmodeus' side, hands clasped at his back.

Camael couldn't feel the interplay between Asmodeus and his Cherub the way he could between the other two. Momentarily he detected Beelzebub drawing power from Mephistopheles, but Mephistopheles was doing very little with his part of the bond.

"It's an internal matter," Beelzebub was saying, head tilted.

Asmodeus said to Camael, "You can retake your place in the armed forces if you desire."

"Thank you," Camael said, "but I'd rather be effective."

"Effective," said the other Cherub, making the syllables as slow and long as a country road in the heat of high noon. "Is that how one describes himself when our lord gives an assignment and he doesn't complete it?"

To Camael's surprise, Mephistopheles said nothing.

Beelzebub said, "Did Lucifer ask you to handle anything special, Belior?"

Belior looked at Mephistopheles. "How long will it take? And did you force him to take Gabriel so you could claim to be the smartest surviving angel?"

Asmodeus said, "No, we mustn't squabble. We don't want to deny that Mephistopheles has done us a great service."

Camael noticed something even subtler than even the Cherub-Seraph communications: Mephistopheles had turned off, utterly tuned out. He wasn't playing the game, was barely even paying attention. Beelzebub had stretched out to utilize the Cherub's wit without Mephistopheles engaging in the conversation whatsoever. Camael had seen Gabriel do exactly that so many times—in fact, right before they'd captured Gabriel, he'd been off on an endless series of rabbit trails in his own head. Israfel had frequently laughed and called him their distracted genius.

For some minutes, Beelzebub traded jabs with both of their rivals just fine while Camael felt his own detachment, wondered why he couldn't be at home for real—bantering rather than bickering—and if Gabriel would have a funeral, and if God would forgive Remiel for turning into Camael and going to Hell in the first place. Had there ever been a difference?

Yes, Mephistopheles had said as much: Camael was less twisted.

At the time Jesus had died, roles had been reversed. Asmodeus and Belior had the top two spots in the Maskim, and Beelzebub with Mephistopheles headed Satan's army. He'd reversed the roles for a reason—keep the more popular Seraph at his right hand and not in control of the army. Mephistopheles and Beelzebub in their ascendancy could grab a handful of soldiers for an assignment, but the army was not theirs. Keep the four of them at one another's throats and if one of them tried to seize power, the others would step in and stop it. If Asmodeus became too popular, Satan would doubtless "promote" that pair back to being right under his thumb and give Beelzebub and Mephistopheles back the army. But for now, Mephistopheles was a hero to the lower orders because of his discovery, so Asmodeus would stay down for a little longer.

Five minutes had passed. Asmodeus and Belior left. Beelzebub said, "Good riddance."

Mephistopheles shuddered. "He's ugly just to look at."

"Not that you were much help." Beelzebub snorted. "What on Earth made you form a tertiary bond with him?"

"The same thing that prompted all my bonds," Mephistopheles said. "Terminal bad judgment."

Beelzebub whacked him with one of his wings.

"You've got a secondary yourself with that backstabbing piece of tenure." Mephistopheles didn't bother turning his head. "At least Asmodeus can't hear my thoughts."

Camael said, "What's the assignment they keep talking about?"

Mephistopheles said, "Lucifer entrusted it to *me*."

"I'm not going to steal your glory." Camael folded his arms. "Like I could even follow whatever it is you figured out, and Lucifer even used me as his focus." He leaned against a rock. "But you know Belior is going to tell him you can't do it, and I don't feel like looking at his smug face."

Beelzebub said, "It's going to be hard for us if you don't finish."

Mephistopheles said, "You can't help." Then he squinted. "Actually, Camael, I'll consult with you later. Maybe you can, since you're the only one with experience."

Camael shrugged. "And?"

"He wants me to simplify the process, so anyone can do it, and do it long-distance."

Camael swallowed against terror.

Beelzebub said, "And he wants it done yesterday, naturally."

Keeping his voice steady, Camael said, "And you think—do you think it's possible?"

Mephistopheles said, "For me."

Beelzebub took a step backward, waving a hand. "Wow, the ego in here is getting kind of thick, isn't it?"

"Then you take care of it," Mephistopheles said. "Wait, I forgot—you can't."

Beelzebub glared at him.

Camael looked aside, still feeling their bond. *Dear God, what a corruption—a bond that should have completed each other—*

And instead hatred. A Seraph and a Cherub yoked evenly but hating it, refusing to pull together. Asmodeus and Belior were the same way, magnets repelling but lingering nearby one another because in the back of their minds they knew they *should*, this *ought* to be good for them both, and instead it was mutual using. Two that should have been one.

Camael looked at his hands. Two that should have been one.

If there'd only been one of him, only one Irin, would he have fallen? Or would he have stayed?

It hurt to always be around Seraphim and Cherubim. They didn't have the same thing as the twins had, but it reminded him.

Only six primary Seraph-Cherub bonds had been broken in the winnowing (according to Gabriel.) Maybe one of them could help Raphael. Maybe Raphael and Ophaniel would become inseparable. Maybe Camael should just quit thinking.

Maybe it was time to go home.

Saraquael got only one glance at Remiel before summoning Raguel for help.

She arrived just as he was ready to approach the Cherubim for their answers, but immediately he asked God to send word for him and flashed with her to his home. Raguel appeared a moment after, and Saraquael put up a Guard in case someone from Hell was listening.

"Don't send me back again." Remiel clenched his shirt, white-knuckled. "I can't."

Although normally gold-speckled, Remiel's eyes had a sharp quality, and Saraquael felt her will raging against half-hearted constraints. Every feather on her wings stood apart from the others.

"You don't have to." Saraquael realized Raguel had manifested his sword but hadn't drawn it. "I can't imagine how awful it must have been."

"You needed me, but I can't go back. They're horrible." She collapsed toward him, and he held her against his shoulder, enwrapping her in his teal wings. He exchanged looks with Raguel, who intensified his alert.

"I'm sick of Seraphim and Cherubim." Her heart pounded against him, and in the next moment Saraquael realized she was crying. "All tied up in one another, and they should be happy, and bonds and wholeness, and I can't—"

Saraquael hummed to her, a tuneless croon from deep in his heart to deep within hers. She relaxed, and he added words, a language unheard on Earth for three thousand years but primal nonetheless. In his arms, she began to relax.

So did Raguel. Saraquael shook his head.

"I found out Mephistopheles' assignment." Her voice was muffled, but she was also projecting the words into his head. He found her echo odd, as if she were more than just herself still. "He's trying to make the process streamlined so any angel can do it. And at a distance."

Raguel bristled. "But that—"

"That changes everything," Saraquael murmured.

"He says he can."

"Criminy." Raguel shook his head. "We should have invaded."

"Why in blazes didn't you?" Remiel pushed backward out of Saraquael's wings. "I prayed to God that you would come down there and avenge Gabriel, and like a bunch of pussy cats you wrote a nice letter on a quality bond paper and said pretty-please don't murder anyone else in cold blood—"

Saraquael said, "It wasn't that—"

"'Stop or we'll say *stop* again.'"

"Remiel—"

"How do you think Gabriel would feel if he found out his death warranted nothing more than a citation?"

Raguel said, "But he's not dead."

Remiel whirled. "What?" She turned on Saraquael. "You said you were planning a funeral! That it was all a game of pretend!"

"You—" He stepped backward. "I'm sorry. I messed up. I didn't realize you didn't know."

"You kept me ignorant!" Flames erupted around her as if she were a Seraph. "I was more useful to you fallen!"

"I promise, it was a mistake!" Saraquael raised his hands. "He didn't die, but he's not well either."

Her eyes had gone totally gold. Her wings spread, and Camael's sword was in her gauntleted hand. She seemed bigger than the room containing them. "Let me see him."

"You can't." Saraquael paled. "He's not well enough."

"You're lying!" He could tell she was trying to flash out of his house, probably thinking, *To Gabriel! To Gabriel!* Only the Guard on Uriel's house would make it seem Gabriel didn't exist. In this state she could pass through Guards, but she wouldn't know which Guard to pass through in order to find him. "You're lying to me—he's dead."

Saraquael forced himself to step closer. "He's weak. He may still die. But he's alive for now."

"He's dead—or let me see him."

Given what Uriel had said about stray angelic residue, the emanations coming off Remiel right now would julienne the Cherub. "None of us can see him. He's just too fragile."

She had started emitting light, and Saraquael had to fight her contagious tension. "Where's Raphael? Mephistopheles said he might be dead too. Is Raphael dead?"

Saraquael was close to her again. "Listen to me. The contact with Camael is distorting what you feel. I won't lie to you. You're my friend." Her breathing was still too rapid, her eyes sparking. "You're home, not with them."

She said, "I have no home." Her head dropped. "I have no more home."

She tried to flash away, but Raguel's Guards contained her.

Eyes aglow, every feather spread, she pivoted on Raguel like a hawk ready to kill. "Let me out of here!"

Saraquael tried to bind her with his will, then Raguel, but she was so slippery, half there and half in the labyrinths of the mind.

"Damn you!" she screamed. "You don't know what it's like! You don't know what I'm going through!"

She blasted through the Guards, and for a moment only fire remained.

Saraquael's head dropped as he stood, empty, because she'd gone mad.

"We have to follow!" Raguel grabbed him by the shoulders. "What if she goes back to them?"

"I can't feel her anywhere." Saraquael's voice quavered. "This is my fault. I should have called her back sooner."

"It doesn't matter now," Raguel said. "Let's follow her trail."

Saraquael concentrated as he had for Remiel's game, only the game was long over and the hide-and-seek carried a deadliness. Hide and seek: find Remiel. Find parts of Gabriel. Find and find and find.

Saraquael gathered all creation in his mind the way only a poet can, absorbing it all and loving it, knowing it, and distilling it to a phrase. A breath later, it fell into stanzas, life a rhythm and a repeating pattern. Lives as rhymes, motion as themes, gravity and energy as meaning. An angel gone mad can't be tracked, but she still has an effect on the universe around her, like skywriting after the plane has landed. His heart expanded into the poetry of existence until he found the dissonance, one word out of rhyme and rhythm, careening madly to escape its own meaning.

Saraquael flashed after her, Raguel at his side projecting more than a little awe. But who cared how tricky it was to find her, as long as they did? Their results weren't being graded on degree of difficulty.

They located her in a jungle on Earth, lost in blackness and wrapped around herself like a fetus in the womb. Shaking with her every sinew taut as a violin's strings, she huddled against the moss on a tree.

Saraquael said nothing, just sat beside her. Raguel kept watch.

For half an hour she remained cocooned, her thoughts cycling but always rapid. Saraquael tried not to travel down the delusions that streamed from her mind like ribbons of roads. She still wore Camael's armor and half the time she still wore Camael's thoughts—until momentarily Saraquael wondered if maybe this weren't Camael trying to play-act Remiel after all.

"Sing with me," Saraquael whispered.

"I can't sing. No angels can sing now."

Saraquael hummed.

"We can't sing," she repeated. "Silent Earth. Silent Heaven. So quiet. Terribly, deadly quiet."

Raguel put out a soundproof Guard.

Saraquael sang, and she cuddled around herself again, head down, losing tears expensive as champagne. Saraquael could feel her soul reaching for the song without grasping it. But at least she was paying attention.

Raguel joined with his bass, and Remiel focused further. Saraquael could truly feel her beside him now, not just the emptiness where he knew she was and the terror of the small lives peeking from the infinite nooks the jungle offered. Snakes and mice and birds watched in sympathy, near enough that all three angels could detect them.

Remiel raised her head and looked around, discerning the pairs of eyes, the scales and softness and light breathing.

She reached her hand to Saraquael's on her shoulder, drew an unsteady breath, and joined the song.

Together they sang for another five minutes. When the last notes ended, Saraquael said, "Now will you believe me?"

Tear-stained, Remiel nodded. She dragged some errant strands of hair from her face.

Saraquael glanced at Raguel, who redoubled the soundproofing on the Guard.

"He's alive for now, but we're not sure how much longer." Saraquael swallowed. "When Raphael rescued him, the job was nearly complete."

"But Raphael should be able to heal him."

"Raphael and Uriel working together couldn't fix him. Parts are missing, and I guess they're important parts. That was why we wanted you to search the cell. We need something like a rope."

Remiel gasped. "I know what you're talking about. That was there when they started, but when I went back into the chamber I didn't find anything like it."

"Uriel said the parts can't survive on their own for more than about a day, so the beads you found were a quarter the size of the one we found right afterward."

"But no heartstrings." Remiel dropped her head. "And without heartstrings, there's no way to attach them to one another."

Saraquael said, "They didn't explain it all to me, but that's the rundown."

"I don't suppose we could all donate a bit of our heartstrings and spin them together?"

Saraquael said, "If we can, no one's mentioned it."

Remiel rested her head on her forearms. "He's really going to die. After all that." She leaned into Saraquael and drew up her wings. "Oh, God, why?"

God did not answer, so the three angels remained in place, silent, until Remiel shifted away from Saraquael. "I can't be alone." She tilted her face toward him. "I was alone there the whole time, even when I was with them, and then I wished I was alone. Don't leave me alone."

"Let's move." Saraquael felt around until he found a better place, and he flashed the three of them to Heaven.

In a clearing with picnic tables, Israfel and Zadkiel had set up a game of chess on a picnic table surrounded by pines. Beneath a threatening sky, they huddled over the board and didn't at first notice the newcomers.

Raguel looked over Israfel's shoulder. "Checkmate in four."

As Zadkiel dissolved into giggles, Israfel snapped, "You too? It's bad enough when Ophaniel does it. 'Checkmate in twenty-five, unless you resign in ten moves when he takes your rook.'"

Zadkiel had her hands over her mouth to cover the grin. Israfel got up from the table and conjured a small harp to her hands.

"Glad you're back," Zadkiel said to Remiel.

"I'm glad to be back."

Zadkiel gestured to her uniform. "You can relax a bit. I'm not going to barbecue you."

Glancing at Camael's armor, Remiel tensed.

"Unless," Zadkiel added, "you'd like me to pummel you in chess too."

"Those are fighting words." Remiel wished away the armor to wear a pair of jeans and a cotton turtleneck. The gauntlets took longest to vanish.

Israfel's fingers flew over the harp strings so quickly they blurred.

Zadkiel cleared the board and started sorting pieces.

Remiel recoiled. "Why are you making me black?"

Zadkiel shrugged. "I didn't think about it. I don't care." She scooped the black pieces back to her side and turned around the board. They set up, and Remiel went first.

Saraquael relaxed, listening to Israfel's music, feeling the strength of Raguel, knowing both of them prayed constantly, as did the chess players, offering the very game as prayer.

Remiel didn't look up from the board. "What's that song called?"

Israfel said, "It's the tune to Psalm 51 the way David did it originally."

"It's a strange range."

"Part of it is the limitations of this instrument, but you're right. It's huge."

Zadkiel laughed as she moved a piece. "Gabriel could handle it."

"Gabriel is insane to sing with," Israfel said.

"I know." Zadkiel sat back as Remiel studied the board. "I'd be there struggling along, and I'd see the notes ahead of me are just going up and up and up, and I'd get this message in my head from him, *let's switch parts,* and he nails this note that would curl my hair while I'm trying to figure out what the tenor part is supposed to be."

"That's my fault," Israfel said. "The angel of music can just switch parts without notice, so he got used to snatching the very high parts I couldn't hit."

Zadkiel laughed as Israfel added, "Show-off."

Remiel moved, and Zadkiel returned her attention to the game.

Zadkiel took one of Remiel's pawns, and as she lifted it off the board, she said, "Where does the flame go when it's out?"

Saraquael flinched. Israfel's song hesitated.

"You put a pawn to the side of the board," Zadkiel said, "but what happens when God lifts an angel off the board?"

Remiel took the pawn from Zadkiel's fingers and set it on the table. "It's out."

Raguel stared at the board as if trying to predict checkmate in ten. Saraquael closed his eyes, smelling the richness of pines, but he had nothing to say. Remiel touched the pawn with one finger over its bald head.

"I know there's nothing after this," Israfel said, "but—maybe there should be."

"That's why what they did was so wrong. It would have been completely over for Gabriel, everything, and we'd have lost him forever."

Israfel said, "It's going to happen anyhow."

Remiel said, "I saw what they did to him. That kind of damage you can't survive."

"God could recreate him," Raguel said. "He'll have to."

"I doubt he will," Israfel said. "We live with the consequences of our choices."

Remiel's eyes flashed. "Did I miss Gabriel making a choice?"

"Satan's choice," Israfel said. "Mephistopheles' choice."

Zadkiel wove her fingers together. "And it seems so arbitrary, too. Michael I could have understood, but Satan doesn't especially hate Gabriel. It could have been any of us."

Remiel scrutinized the chess board even though Zadkiel seemed to have forgotten it was there.

Israfel said, "I'm just not sure how we're going to deal with it afterward. How can anything be the same, with one of us missing forever?"

Remiel said, "Humans do it."

Israfel stared up at the pines dark against the sky as if she didn't see them, only an eternity with one fewer light to say he loved God. "We all lift and embody different aspects of God. Without Gabriel, does that mean some aspect of God will go forever non-illuminated?"

Saraquael shivered.

Raguel paced. Saraquael projected at Zadkiel, who noticed Remiel's concentrated stare at the board and made a quick move with a pawn.

"We're eternal," Israfel said. "Or we're supposed to be. We've always known we were eternal. Even Rahab got re-created."

Raguel said, "It's going to be worst for Raphael."

Saraquael noted Israfel's sudden lost look. He said gently, "Israfel's a primary bond for Gabriel too."

Raguel flinched. "I'm sorry."

Israfel grimaced. "That's okay. No one else acts as if I'm losing him, so why should you?"

"Israfel, I'm—"

She blew an errant strand of hair from her eyes. "It makes me wonder if Gabriel would even notice if I were the one chained in Satan's basement." She looked over at Raguel and offered a smile. "But you're right: even for primaries, he and Raphael are exceptionally close."

Zadkiel said, "Raphael will feel like an angel torn in half."

Saraquael winced, and Zadkiel's eyes flew wide. Remiel only said, "Don't worry. It's an accurate metaphor."

Saraquael said, "Raphael might ask God to annihilate him too. And when God refuses, I don't know what he'll do. I imagine he'll just bury himself in the Vision for aeons. And maybe time will help. I can't imagine."

Zadkiel's eyes flew to Israfel, who lowered her gaze. "Don't worry about me." Israfel took a deep breath. "I couldn't abandon Ophaniel and Zophiel to grief in order to escape it myself. But I'm not sure what will happen to the parts of me where Gabriel's been anchored since pretty much the dawn of creation."

Zadkiel walked over to Israfel and grasped her hand, and Israfel forced a smile she couldn't reinforce with her heart.

Remiel moved a knight onto a black square.

Saraquael said, "You and Raphael will eventually recover your equilibrium and reach some kind of acceptance."

Israfel said, "I can't see it."

Zadkiel said, "Humans divorce, and humans mourn and accept, but a Cherub and a Seraph are so wound into one another's hearts that they're always going to feel it."

Saraquael noticed Remiel again, sparkling, and projected to Zadkiel, who returned to the chess board and moved a bishop.

Saraquael said, "The hardest thing will be the first time you laugh."

"No," Israfel said. "Please, you're too much a poet, Saraquael. I don't want to know what's going to happen."

Remiel traced a finger along the edge of the board nearest herself. "You'll forget yourself one day and laugh at something and feel guilty." She ran both hands along the side edges of the board. "You'll think to yourself how ungrateful a friend you are, that you're being disloyal to the memory and the pain, but it will happen again, and someday before the end of time you'll be at peace, except for sometimes when you remember a brilliant, delicious age that ended tragically."

She knocked over her king and stepped away from the table.

Saraquael nudged some fallen pine needles with a stick. "At least humans can hope in a life after death. They might delude themselves as to what that means, but they can believe they'll have a reunion. We don't have that, and we can't lie to ourselves about it. He won't be happier. He won't be watching over us. We won't meet again."

"Stop it!" Raguel slammed his hands into the table so all the chess pieces jumped. "He isn't dead yet! God might not allow it—he might re-create him! Why torture ourselves with things that might not happen?" He folded his arms. "We didn't spin our wheels like this over the damned."

"You're wrong." Remiel plucked an evergreen frond and brushed the needles against her lips. "We did mourn, and we did talk about the pain, and we hung together because we didn't know if it could happen again, but we certainly didn't want it to." Remiel snapped the twig. "And we did recover, although it took a while. Remember how broken Uriel was afterward, how Uriel cried? I remember thinking God cried too, and that the damned deserved Hell if only for those tears." She tossed the halves of the branch onto the chess board. "But that's the key. The damned deserved the Hell they're in, and even though they have no hope, that's their choice. Gabriel didn't side with them, and he's being destroyed as if he's worse than they are."

Raguel flashed away.

Israfel put her face in her hands, and Zadkiel hugged her. "I think God's going to resolve this soon," Zadkiel murmured. "We won't linger in confusion much longer, and whatever happens, God will be with us."

Among the evergreens and beneath the swirling grey of the sky, four angels remained silent.

Thirteen

Jesus appeared behind Raphael at a balcony in the Westfield Parramatta Mall in Sydney, Australia. The sunlight streamed through him as easily as it did the skylight over the interior courtyard. People passed without seeing either of them, but Jesus noted how all their guardians usually had something to say. So sorry. In our prayers.

Jesus stepped alongside Raphael, dressed for the venue in khakis and a t-shirt, hands in his pockets. The Seraph greeted him with his heart but remained with his elbows resting on the railing, his back to the crowds that strolled between stores. Jesus leaned on the rail facing the other direction, close enough that one of Raphael's wingtips brushed his leg.

Raphael continued staring into the faceless crowd. "This is a good place to people-watch."

Jesus frowned. "What do you see?"

"Everything, one at a time." Raphael singled his attention onto a woman pushing a stroller. "Boredom." Another woman with a friend. "Loneliness." An older woman carrying a cosmetics bag. "Fear of death." Three teens chattering into cell phones as they walked the mall. "Hunger."

"It's not all negative." Jesus indicated a woman with a toy store bag. "Generosity. Over there I see excitement. That man drove here as an act of charity for a friend who can't drive any longer, giving up his morning so the man would have a day out."

Raphael lowered his gaze.

Jesus touched his arm. "Come with me," and they went.

It was the Judgment Hall, empty at the moment, and the rustle as Raphael folded his wings echoed from the domed ceiling and stone walls. Jesus sat on the edge of one of the wooden tables at the front, one foot still on the floor.

"If I did that," Raphael said, "you'd say it was disrespectful."

"If you did this," Jesus replied, "your wings would bang into the table and you'd be uncomfortable anyhow, so I wouldn't need to say anything."

Raphael turned around a chair and straddled it backward, grinning mischievously. Jesus returned the look.

The Seraph regarded the hall, as large as a cathedral and yet small for its intended purpose. Sitting at the front he would have to shift into long-distance vision to see the back walls. Humanity was to gather here for the final sorting.

In the middle of scanning the room, Raphael gasped, and his wings flared. The thought rolled out of him as forcefully as if shouted: *Gabriel's funeral.*

Jesus raised his hands. "We're not here to plan anything." But Raphael didn't relax.

"How are we doing?"

Jesus said, "You're doing everything you can."

"But it doesn't seem as if it's helping." Raphael bit his lip and leaned into the back of the chair. "I keep hoping something will trip and the balance will swing, but I can't find that one thing, and I don't know any longer."

Jesus looked out into the rows of unfilled benches. "What would you do if this was it and he couldn't get any better than this?" When Raphael didn't answer him, he added, "And without any hope of improvement?"

Raphael blurted, "What are you saying?"

Jesus said, "I'm not saying anything. I'm asking."

"I'd do it anyhow," Raphael said. "I'd carry him with me. I'd give him all my healing power, and I'd keep doing everything I could."

Jesus said, "Eternity is a long time."

"It's too long to live with the knowledge that I could have done something and didn't. It's too long to live without him knowing I should have hung on."

"Should have." Jesus breathed the words. "What of Gabriel?"

Raphael was looking straight at the floor. "He talked about this with me, all these debates the Cherubim had for what seemed like years. There's a thousand shades of grey here, but they nailed them all down. He'd want to live if there was any chance he could still love and be loved by you."

Jesus folded his arms and looked aside.

"Mothers do this for infants." Raphael picked up his head and squared his shoulders, inadvertently flaring his wings. "I know he wouldn't grow out of it—in this scenario," he reminded himself. He began vibrating, his wings shaking. A glow cut through the front of the judgment hall, and it came from his shimmering eyes. "But I could do it."

"Of course you could," Jesus said. "I'm not impugning your abilities. But I'm asking if you should."

Raphael's soul vibrated more violently, and a hardness came into the set of his jaw. He seemed to grow taller as he stood out of his chair, and his wings spread. "Of course I think I should!"

Jesus gave Raphael a few moments to calm himself, but the Seraph didn't try. Below the surface he'd been sparked into frenzy, and everything about him rang denial. This Seraph's eyes were brown instead of green, and his hair brown instead of blond, but the Judgment Hall had seen this conversation once before.

"Would you consent to re-create him?" Raphael asked.

Jesus said, "No. I would not."

"Then I'll keep at it," Raphael said. "I'm not going to give up."

Jesus didn't say anything in reply. The final vestiges of Raphael's voice finished their echoes through the vaulted ceilings, and Raphael turned, his heart coiled like an overwound spring and his eyes unyielding. He shoved the chair toward the table, and it slid to stop when it banged into the side near Jesus's knee.

Jesus said, "What if I told you to let him go?"

"What?" Raphael lunged toward him. "I don't have to let him go! I can take care of him! I'll stay with him!"

"But if I told you to let him go—"

"I will not sacrifice Gabriel on the altar of my convenience!"

"I didn't say you would do it because it was convenient." Jesus looked right into Raphael's eyes. "You've done everything you can."

"And I'll keep doing it until we find another way—"

"What if there is no other way?" For the first time, Jesus raised his voice. "I asked what you would do if I told you to let him go."

Raphael had flames around his head. "I would hate you."

"I didn't ask if you would like me," Jesus said. "I'm asking specifically if you would obey."

Raphael vibrated so quickly that he threw off heat. His mouth was set in a line, and his eyes had darkened to obsidian as he threw shadows around the hall of judgment. Perfectly still, Jesus watched him. Just God and His creation and a question.

Raphael took a deep breath. "Yes. But—"

"Then let him go."

Raphael whipped away, and even though Jesus couldn't see his expression, he knew he would have his eyes clenched, his jaw locked. Raphael had been Jesus's guardian angel.

Raphael's fists were at his sides, and his wings were in flames, but his head was bowed, and all around him swirled streamers of a dozen emotions as he struggled to lock down some and unlock the one thing he wanted the most to stay secure.

Jesus dropped his gaze, swallowing hard. Raphael's shoulders sagged. The fire went out.

"Raphael," came Uriel's voice in the Judgment Hall, disembodied and without an echo, "you need to return right now. He's slipping."

Raphael looked over his shoulder at Jesus, his eyes like ice and his glare as penetrating as an arrow into its target. Then he vanished.

Jesus put his hands to his face, and he sobbed.

Michael ached to see how Gabriel looked deflated, like an old balloon.

Israfel already sat at the bedside, and she had Gabriel's hand in both of hers. From the corner of the room, Michael watched as Raphael appeared: shoulders slumped, wings limp.

Where was the fire? Michael had expected Raphael to explode into the room, frenzied and half-mad, and instead Michael saw only resignation. With a second look, though, he could detect the aftershocks of fury as they rippled away, dragging the last of his strength with them.

"Don't give up," Michael murmured, one hand on Raphael's arm. "You have to hang on."

Raphael averted his eyes. Michael let out a gasp as if he'd been punched in the stomach. It didn't feel for the next minute as if he could draw breath.

Uriel whispered, "Mary, I need you here," and in the next moment she was there, the front of her sweater dusted with flour, her hair pulled back in a ponytail with wisps escaping to frame her face.

"This is it?" she whispered.

Michael nodded.

Israfel still had her harp in her hand, and she settled at the edge of the bed so Raphael could come closer to Gabriel. She rested the instrument across her lap and began to play.

"Do you remember the song we sang—I sang—" Raphael looked down at Gabriel growing formless. "Every night before Jesus went to bed?"

Between one musical phrase and the next, Israfel transitioned to a major key and a suspended seventh chord.

Mary took Uriel's hand. Raphael sang,

Blessed are you, Lord our God, king of the universe,
Who causes the bonds of sleep to fall on my eyes,
And slumber on my eyelids.

Mary added her voice to the bedtime prayer—Jesus's favorite—as he hesitated.

Grant me, O Lord my God,
And God of my fathers,
To lie down in peace,
And raise me up again in peace,
And suffer me not to be troubled with evil dreams
But grant me a calm repose in your presence
And enlighten my eyes
Until I sleep the sleep of death.

Raphael eased Gabriel's hair from his eyes, fingertips tracing his forehead as if stirring the wavelets of a pool without breaking the surface.

Blessed are you, O Lord,
Who gives light to the whole universe in your glory.

Israfel transitioned into the words Raphael had always added into the bedtime prayer.

I promise I will never leave you,
And all the long night be at your side
Always thinking of you until you wake,

Until your eyes open again in the light of God.
You'll always be a part of me
Because that is the promise I have made.

Israfel brought the song back to the beginning, but the words still rang in Michael's ears. He could see Mary horror-stricken as he was, remembering how many times the angels had sung this at nighttime when Jesus was a child, a little boy bouncing on the edge of his bed begging for just one more song before he went to sleep.

Raphael's face had crumpled.

Mary touched Uriel's wing. "Please try once more, whatever it was he told you to do."

On the other side, Raphael grabbed Uriel's arm. "Don't hurt him."

Squeezing Raphael's hand, Uriel said, "I'll be gentle."

Uriel went insubstantial and crouched in the middle of the bed, kneeling halfway through Gabriel and vanishing partly into him. The effect from Michael's perspective was much like seeing a cloud and thinking it looked something like an angel might, with clear-cut wings and shoulders but a smear of mist for arms and legs.

Raphael leaned closer to Gabriel, kissed him on the forehead. He whispered as if every word stung, "It's okay if you have to leave us. It's okay if you have to let go."

Israfel choked.

Michael's heart ached. *Why did you say that? Don't you realize it all depends on how tightly you hold on?*

Then Michael felt Uriel send to Raphael, *Keep talking to him.*

Raphael looked up, blank.

If you can't talk, then sing. Just keep doing it.

Michael detected the Throne's surprise. He projected a question to Uriel, making sure not to attract the notice of the Seraphim.

Uriel's voice replied in Michael's mind, *His substance is reaching toward Raphael.*

Wouldn't you expect it to?

It didn't before. It's as if he's awakening to Raphael's presence.

Michael frowned. Mary had her hands on Israfel's shoulders, and he was sure the Seraphim hadn't noticed Uriel's wonder as they transitioned into the Trisagion.

Uriel's misty form extended toward Raphael, and Michael felt himself emitting rings of tension even as Uriel sparkled with curiosity and searching.

What are you finding? Michael kept the question contained within the walls of his mind. *Dear God, let him find something—*

Uriel whispered, "Raphael, let him go."

Raphael raised his head, tears overspilling.

"You can't keep him forever."

Raphael put his face in his hands, but Michael could see Uriel sparkling. Something had changed, and Uriel's look didn't match Uriel's words.

"Hold my hand," Uriel murmured. "Now squeeze and let go, and as you do it, imagine letting him go too."

As Uriel caught Michael's eye, a series of disconnected images swam through his head: Raphael's and Gabriel's wills coiled about one another like a spiral staircase, Raphael's tight as a stranglehold around Gabriel's and plugged into it, nurturing it but keeping it firmly in place.

Michael gasped. *His heartstring? Raphael has it?*

More images: the thing tested out sound, whole, muscular as an anaconda and miles long.

Raphael moved closer to Gabriel at some prompting from Uriel, whose misty form now encompassed both of them.

"Do it again," Uriel said to Raphael.

The Seraph grabbed with both hands this time, squeezing until he ought to have crushed Uriel's hand, and then letting go with a long breath like a sigh that shuddered at the end.

Michael tried to offer reassurance, but Uriel shook his head. Instead, Michael sent a stream of his energy into Uriel's heart to empower the Throne.

God, please, let this work.

"Keep doing it," Uriel murmured. "Raphael, let him go. Easy, easy, just let him go. You can't hold onto him forever. Let him go."

Tears streaked Raphael's face. Michael moved close to the Seraph, stood behind him and rubbed his shoulders. Raphael grabbed his hands, and Michael hugged him.

"Leave him alone!" Israfel was her feet. "If Gabriel's going to die, then let him die, but don't make Raphael help!"

Michael moved close to her. "Wait," he whispered.

She whirled on Michael. "Why are you torturing him?"

He projected into her heart with the force of a pile-driver, *Stop!*

"Stay relaxed," Uriel murmured to Raphael. "Keep letting him go."

Tension rolled off the Seraph until Michael longed to send him calming thoughts.

Mary settled at Raphael's side. "Are you in pain?"

Raphael's head dropped. Michael got the impression that he thought murder should hurt. The things in the room were rattling as in the early stages of an earthquake.

"One more bit," Uriel said, and then Raphael collapsed to his knees, elbows on the edge of the bed, and he sobbed.

Israfel pushed past Michael to kneel with her arms around Raphael's shoulders. "I hope you're happy."

"Look," Mary whispered.

Michael stepped aside to see around Israfel's wings, and he too gasped. *Oh, God, my God!*

—because while before Gabriel had been like an emaciated preschooler, now he seemed almost the right size, certainly an adult, and the misty edges had firmed up.

Raphael raised his head in shock.

"What in blazes just happened?" Israfel jumped to her feet. "I thought he would be gone."

Uriel let out a long breath. "Raphael had his heartstring."

There was silence in the room. Raphael didn't even move, only stared.

Israfel pushed close to Uriel. "And you didn't tell him?"

Like a marionette with its strings cut, Raphael dropped his head into his hands, and his chest onto his knees, his wings splayed.

"Why didn't you say something?" Israfel shouted. "You made him let Gabriel die!"

"I did tell him to let it go." Uriel's voice jumped as Israfel grabbed the Throne. "I did it the only way I could ensure he wouldn't keep holding on."

"I could kill you!" Israfel was like lightning. "What you put him through—what you put me through—!"

"I'm sorry." Uriel's gaze dropped. "I did what was necessary."

Forcing himself between them, Michael stared into Israfel's eyes with what he hoped was enough steel to bring her to her senses. "Don't make me force you to leave. None of us have done this before. Uriel may just have saved Gabriel's life. We can quibble about the techniques later."

Israfel swung away from him. "And boy, are you getting an earful about it then, too." She gestured to Raphael. "You nearly destroyed him with that stunt."

Raphael still hadn't moved, as if giving up Gabriel's heartstrings had ripped out his own.

Mary had her arm over Raphael's shoulders, the other hand smoothing his collar. "You've done the repair?"

Uriel projected a negative. "I only dumped the thread back in with the rest of him. We need to give him time to settle, and then I learn to do beadwork on a soul."

Michael positioned himself on the floor beside Raphael and laid his wings over him. It wasn't just relief he could feel but also shame. "You didn't know," he murmured.

Raphael didn't reply. Maybe he hadn't heard.

Uriel rested a solid hand on Raphael's head.

A glow flared around Israfel. "Maybe it would help Raphael if you had Ophaniel wish him dead."

Michael glared at her. "I told you to back down. Uriel isn't cruel. If it had to be done that way, it had to be done."

Uriel slipped off the bed and hugged Raphael, who buried his head in the Throne's shoulder. Uriel soothed him for a few minutes, and eventually Raphael reacted, first by crying, then by putting his head against Gabriel's chest and hugging him, repeating how sorry he was. Mary and Michael stayed nearest, and Uriel didn't move, shoulders bowed as if defeated. Israfel laid on the opposite side of the bed, covering Gabriel with one wing while she traced his hair with her fingertips.

Time passed, until eventually Raphael calmed. Israfel no longer looked ready to detonate. Michael breathed easier. It was time to proceed.

"I need your help," Uriel said to the Seraphim. "What is Gabriel's biggest regret?"

Raphael pulled back, rubbing his eyes.

Israfel said, "He doesn't have any regrets. He just thinks it all to death."

The Seraphim exchanged a knowing glance.

Uriel sighed. "I need to know because it's hard to feed the string back through all the beads, so I need something heavy on the end to push it through."

Mary said, "Like the way you put a pin on the end of a drawer string that's come loose, otherwise it bunches and you have nothing to grab?"

"That's a good analogy." Uriel looked from Israfel to Raphael. "A regret should be heavy enough for me to keep track of the end and push it through."

Israfel said, "That there weren't enough hours in the day to study everything."

Raphael stared at his folded hands. "Israfel."

She looked up. "What?"

"No, I mean you were his biggest regret."

Her eyes flew open. "Oh." She bit her lip. "It figures."

"Not that way." Raphael twisted his hands. "He regretted that he never treated you like a primary bond. He realized he didn't make time for you, and then I'd encourage him to do it, and he'd get lost in some problem, and two months later he'd remember he had ignored you again." He sighed. "I'm sorry."

"Uriel needed to know." Israfel forced a smile. "And I guess it's good for me to know that too."

Uriel looked pale. "I was hoping he regretted something like not studying Hungarian opera." The Throne took a deep breath. Israfel seemed to have drawn in on herself. "I'd like to get started, but if you'd rather not be here, you can go."

"I'm staying," Israfel said. "If I can help, I'm staying."

"Thank you. He'll need your strength." Uriel looked at Michael. "I appreciated your powering me up before, but I'd rather you stay separate. I may need someone on the 'outside' so to speak."

Michael nodded. "Just tell me what you need."

Mary said, "And I'll pray."

Uriel drew a long breath, then blew it out with force.

Raphael said, "You're more nervous than I am." His eyes were still reddened, and he looked exhausted.

"You know how to heal," Uriel said. "I'm brand new at this."

Mary said, "Tiny stitches are harder to see."

"Thanks." Uriel met her eyes, offered a smile. "Do you happen to have a thimble?"

Mary smiled in return, and Uriel went desolid.

There wasn't much to see from the outside. Gabriel didn't noticeably change from moment to moment, but periodically Uriel and Raphael exchanged comments: "That feels wrong." "Gentle." "That one was easy," and "Shine more over there."

Uriel eventually discorporated, working entirely in the spiritual realm and communicating with Raphael only by projection.

At one point, Michael felt compelled to remove Gabriel's trumpet from the case and bring it to the bedside. There was no reason given. He assumed Uriel wanted to pattern-match with something they knew to be Gabriel's soul material.

Uncertain what to expect, Michael manifested his armor and sword, and he kept watch over them all: Mary sitting cross-legged in the corner, eyes closed as she prayed; Israfel also with her eyes closed but suffused in a creamy light which she thickened between her outstretched hands and directed toward Gabriel; Raphael clothed in the amber that enwrapped both himself and Gabriel; and Uriel, somewhere not quite here and not anywhere else either, utterly focused.

Now Michael thought he knew why Jesus had chosen Uriel for the repair: the sheer sustained concentration was possible only for someone as contemplative as a Throne.

Raphael's voice was the only half Michael could hear or feel, depending on whether he was speaking or projecting, but the tenor had changed. Raphael had gotten tense, and now worried, and now tense again. Then it changed to, "Take a break. Take a break now. You can't afford to mess it up. Back off. He'll last another fifteen minutes."

Uriel swirled out of the mist into a shape, then into an angelic body. The Throne's hands shook. Strain lined the usually peaceful face, but there was nothing of worry or fear.

Uriel projected an apology.

Michael said, "What happened?"

Uriel sank onto a cushion, and a moment later Mary was pouring a cup of tea. Uriel waved her off, simply lay sprawled, chin pointed at the ceiling.

Raphael hunched, head between his knees, out of breath. Michael wanted to offer some encouragement, but the words wouldn't come.

"Are you done?" Israfel said.

Uriel projected a negative. Raphael gasped, "About halfway," and Uriel agreed.

Michael swallowed. "You've been working so long."

"You have no idea," Uriel said, throat raspy, "you have absolutely no idea how much damage Satan did in a quarter hour."

With an effort, Raphael raised his head. "You're doing fine. It's taking a while because you're being careful."

"I fumbled one of the eyelets." Uriel shivered. "I don't want to hurt him."

Mary rested a hand on Uriel's hair. "Rest. You don't need to worry right now."

Raphael's eyes sparked. "Just think—God did this all at once," and he snapped, "with all of us, at the same time."

Michael grinned. "That is amazing when you think about it." He sat back. "What's it like inside one of us?"

"I can't actually see the pieces," Raphael said. "I'm able to feel through what Uriel is doing, and that gives me a sense of how Gabriel responds overall." He thought. "Imagine tuning a piano blindfolded. You can hear when something is going right. Then Uriel directs the healing energy to whatever has just been set in place."

"To reinforce it?" Israfel said.

Raphael shrugged. " I assume so."

Uriel said, "I hit a couple of parts preemptively to stop them from disintegrating when I moved them into place, but the rest of it is accurate."

Michael felt Saraquael probing the Guard to get inside, and he told him no.

Israfel moved up the bed toward Gabriel's head. First she tucked his wings so he'd be more comfortable, then straightened the wing-cloak Raphael had left lying across his shoulders. She reached for his hand, then stopped herself.

Uriel sent Michael a question.

"I'm fine," he said. "Only a couple of requests to get inside. Why?"

"Because this may get harder for you in the final stages when he becomes aware." Uriel struggled upright, then went forward to a head-on-knees position.

Israfel said, "Who wanted to get in? Not Satan, I hope."

"Saraquael. Zadkiel." Michael shrugged. "They can handle whatever it is."

"No doubt," Israfel said. "They might only have wanted a status report. They were pretty upset when I left."

Fourteen

One hour and a half earlier, Uriel's voice had recalled Israfel to Gabriel's side: she'd left Saraquael, Zadkiel and Remiel beneath the trees.

"We'll be praying," Zadkiel had said, but Israfel was already gone, only the ripples of her shock remaining.

Zadkiel and Saraquael joined hands, and then Remiel, and together they prayed, eyes closed, calling on their Father. The light of eternity, shine the light of eternity, don't extinguish the light of love. He loves you. Don't let him forget how he loves you. You are our Father.

Amidst the pain, Remiel's voice dropped free, then her heart, and finally her hands. Saraquael didn't immediately pursue her, but then he realized where she'd gone, and he tried to follow. He landed in a shopping center.

Zadkiel appeared at his side. "Can you sense her?"

"She jumped here, then somewhere else. I can't follow."

Zadkiel extended her senses. "Me neither."

"She was half insane when I found her before. I'm afraid for her."

Zadkiel grabbed his hand. "No need to explain."

"She's on the brink. Be careful." He folded his arms. "I'm betting she's trying to find Gabriel."

"She won't."

"But she may be able to track Raphael, and that's just the same."

Zadkiel's mouth twitched. "Now that you mention it, I do get a sense of Raphael. From..." She looked around, then pointed. "That balcony."

Saraquael tried to send Michael a message, but the Guard reflected it.

"She won't get in," Saraquael said. "Not if she's in her right mind."

"So we keep looking," Zadkiel said. "She's got to be somewhere."

Mephistopheles summoned Camael to his office. The Cherub had an assignment, and he'd learned one thing well after four thousand years: you could put off a project indefinitely by asking thousands of questions in order to formulate your hypothesis.

After ten minutes Camael still hadn't come. While Mephistopheles didn't demand the immediate-attendance dance Lucifer did—to be specific, Lucifer gave you no choice, it was just, "Come here" and then he pulled you in—ten minutes was excessive for a creature able to appear anywhere in Hell, Creation or Heaven with the direction of a thought. "Camael," he said, "get your sorry carcass over here."

Again no response. Maybe Camael had been playing both sides of the game? Maybe Belior had gotten to him with a better offer: I'll solve Mephistopheles' assignment, and then you can be my second-in-command.

That was a good one. Mephistopheles shouldn't have shared the details of the assignment in the first place. If no one knew what it was then no one could steal the glory of its completion. But the whole idea, the notion of angels disintegrating across a room from their foes—what would they call it, the Mephistopheles Touch?

Gabriel.

Oh, God, the light in the lab area. You didn't see how he died, but I did, and his light was so bright, so clean.

And then Gabriel had crumbled, his owner's name on his mouth, his eyes searching the dark for a savior that never came, a God who in the end hadn't cared.

You heartless monster, Mephistopheles thought. *You didn't care either, not a bit. You could have stopped it at any point, but once the ball got rolling, it just thundered ahead until someone got crushed.*

Are you proud? This is all your fault that Gabriel is dead—how dare you even say his name?

Shaking, he hungered for Beelzebub to come pull the thorns from his heart, but then Beelzebub would want to know why, and then Mephistopheles might have to answer because what good was a Cherub if he left an unanswered question? Next Beelzebub would dump energy into him, and together they'd be more stable, but he'd *know*, he'd see right inside his Cherub and then feel obliged to bury the thing he saw because it was a weakness and a filthy shame.

One of Gabriel's last thoughts had been of Raphael. Beelzebub's last thought would always and forever be of himself.

"This is stupid," Mephistopheles muttered, and he tried to flash to Camael himself.

Camael's trail had vanished. It had been a while, but Mephistopheles should have just been able to think about him and take himself there, and instead "there" brought him a nebulous bounce.

Someone had Camael behind a Guard.

Lucifer. Questioning him why Mephistopheles hadn't begun his work yet.

Belior. Making him a better offer.

Beelzebub. Laughing at him.

Mephistopheles went to the lobby, signed out, and flashed to Creation.

The void of space didn't help—too much like the labs. He traveled to Earth to check out a couple of smaller projects he was overseeing, but then he still couldn't find Camael.

Mephistopheles opened his senses. This wasn't his specialty, but he understood how to do it, at least in theory. Wherever Camael was, the created space around him knew. This wouldn't work if Lucifer had him behind Guards, but it should help in almost every other circumstance. He held an image of Camael's soul in his head, then began matching it to every bit of creation and Hell, machine-gunning the pattern in a broad hunt for anything similar. This method would give scores of false-positives, but Mephistopheles made note of every place that felt "right" and then reviewed them each with a second challenge, and finally proceeded to check in person all fifty-four that passed.

At the fifteenth site, Mephistopheles found Remiel alone in a cornfield.

Intriguing. Why waste the opportunity? This time he might be able to contain her.

He flitted into the nearest oak to stand immobile in the branches, a shadow clinging to the trunk. Partly cloudy himself, he blended with the sky and avoided the scattered sunbeams that penetrated the foliage.

An exodus of birds lifted from the limbs with rapid wing beats, but Remiel didn't look toward the tree. She sat, feet tucked under her legs, leaning over herself.

Mephistopheles knew he ought to call Beelzebub or Lucifer, but instead he focused entirely on her.

"Why couldn't you do this?" she whispered. "See?"

Mephistopheles leaned out but still could see only golden feathers. He smelled blood.

"Gabriel," she whispered, "if I can do this, then why couldn't you?"

Like a breath of vapor, Mephistopheles inched along the branch directly over her head, curling around the bark of the tree and proceeding like a snakeish coil.

"See?" she said again, and this time Mephistopheles did see.

Remiel did it again. She took her curved dagger and with the slender blade slit the thin skin of her arm lengthwise from her wrist to her elbow.

He'd gone ice-cold as Remiel watched the slice heal perfectly beneath the blood that welled up. "Why didn't you do this?"

He couldn't descend and trap her. No one could, not with her more quicksilver than angel. She might well continue sitting here and slicing and mourning for all eternity, and no one could move her because the madness rendered her untouchable. Otherwise he would have stopped her himself.

She rocked a little on her knees, then cut deeply into the brown-stained flesh and held down the point of the blade so her substance couldn't immediately seal. It left a red mark when it did join.

Her face was dirty. "See?"

Mephistopheles inched back toward the trunk, wondering if Remiel would care even if she did discover him.

He froze on feeling a new presence.

Saraquael had arrived, and now he knelt in front of Remiel with one arm on her shoulders, but not forcing her to stop. He murmured slowly, softly, and he kept his head near hers. Remiel looked up from her arm and met his eyes as he spoke with all the gentleness a poet-soul had to dispense. She listened, and Mephistopheles wondered if silent tears had overspilled those eyes.

Saraquael slipped one hand under her left, the other on top, and drew away the dagger.

Mephistopheles twinged with relief. He tensed, then, as Saraquael looked right up through the branches of the tree at the smoggy form of him.

The contact lasted only a heartbeat. The next, Zadkiel had appeared at Saraquael's back, armored and on alert. Five Archangels appeared by her side.

He wanted to laugh. As if they'd be hard to dispose of on his way toward Saraquael. Still, Mephistopheles didn't move.

Saraquael had returned his full attention to Remiel, who seemed to respond to him. At the very least, he was able to touch her. There must be enough of her left in there for him to contact. "Stay with me," Saraquael was saying. "Please just sit by me."

Remiel slipped sideways so she faced off into the distance, giving Mephistopheles a full view of Saraquael and a profile shot of her. She wore a lostness, as though she had never seen the Earth before. Saraquael kept his wings and one hand on her, a contact Mephistopheles marveled at: why didn't she shove him aside? But she seemed to absorb his presence while staring blankly at the stones, the insects, the ripe corn.

"That's right," Saraquael said. "Stay with me."

Good luck, Mephistopheles thought. *You'll never keep her here if she wants to be somewhere else.* She was so effervescent now that a strong breeze might carry her away, dissolving her into a mist spread across space and time.

The breeze rustled the tree. Mephistopheles shifted so he straddled the limb, then swung his legs up and leaned against the trunk. Every time he moved, Zadkiel tensed, so he flexed his wings once just to see her jump.

Odd that Saraquael had summoned her rather than Michael.

"I'm with you," the Dominion was saying, flashing a wet cloth to his hand and wiping the blood stains, leaving the skin pink and raw when he'd finished. Remiel extended her arms beside one another and showed Saraquael.

Why was he taking so much time with her? She was safe, if you could call it that, since if Saraquael had this much trouble reaching her, Mephistopheles never could; he'd have had better luck talking to Gabriel with a ouija board.

As if she'd heard, Remiel said, "Why are you here?"

Saraquael said, "I can't leave you here. You're special to me."

She screamed, and Mephistopheles got a terrific view of the moment Saraquael realized his fatal mistake.

Cold wind blasted the tree. Mephistopheles darted to the whipping edge of the limb to watch, not caring that Zadkiel had drawn her sword. Remiel was on her feet. "How can you tell one of the Irin she's special? She's never been unique, never cherished, and if she plays herself right she can turn into the other one and no one ever cares about the change! Special? Can a facsimile of anything be special?"

Wind exploded from the rises of the hills and whipped through the tall corn. Mephistopheles stilled his branch, but the rest of the tree flailed around him. Rain plummeted from the clouds.

Saraquael scrambled to his feet, armor-clad.

"See how special I am?" She shifted her body to masculine so she again resembled Camael. "Look how special I am."

Mephistopheles thrilled as Remiel raised her arms to conduct nature like a symphony orchestra, calling more rain now, more wind there. The sky darkened to olive.

Zadkiel was praying. Mephistopheles laughed.

"Quite a show," said a deep voice at his side. Asmodeus.

Mephistopheles didn't answer, but he felt his soul despite itself welcome the weak bond with the Seraph.

"I'm wondering what they're planning to do," Asmodeus said.

"She's too far gone to capture. The sheep are asking God to do something." Mephistopheles huffed. "I'm betting he's just as responsive as he was with Gabriel."

Asmodeus cocked his head. "Which is to say?"

"That he won't care."

Asmodeus sparkled with wild energy: the Seraph wanted to head down there and mix things up a bit. The Seraph hadn't summoned Belior, so Mephistopheles drew off some of the energy to stabilize him. Asmodeus's warmth shot through him like whiskey, and it quelled a hunger of which he'd been barely aware. He hadn't touched Beelzebub's fire since Gabriel's death.

Saraquael shouted something to Zadkiel about getting him at least one sane moment.

Fat chance, Mephistopheles projected.

You've got to admit, Asmodeus replied, *she's got some power.*

The twin raised its arms and called a bolt of lightning. The energy erupted from overhead with a simultaneous flash and boom, searing the air and rocking the earth. Mephistopheles lost his balance, but Asmodeus caught him momentarily before he pulled free.

The lightning struck the Irin.

"Now!" Saraquael projected to everyone, and both he and Zadkiel grasped the Irin as she leaped aloft, him around her chest and Zadkiel around her thighs while Remiel attempted to beat them off with her wings, kicking, head thrown back. A shower of raindrops blasted from her feathers as she flailed, and both demons leaned forward to watch.

Remiel called more lightning, straight at all three of them. Zadkiel stared.

With a gasp, Saraquael wrenched Remiel around in midair so the bolt blasted her full in the chest.

"Bravo!" Asmodeus called. Then, to Mephistopheles, *I didn't think he'd do it!*

Fast reaction time.

Remiel lay limp in Saraquael's grasp. Zadkiel threw out a Guard. Saraquael flashed them away, followed a moment later by the Archangels.

They won't hold her long, Asmodeus sent.

They touched her at all, Mephistopheles replied. *She had to have been rational for at least a second.*

The weather calmed as if someone had turned off a fan. The groaning tree stood firm again, and Mephistopheles flashed out to the flattened corn field to avoid the dripping leaves. A moment after, Asmodeus followed.

He nudged the sticky ground with his boot. "She was bleeding?"

Mephistopheles assented.

"I'm upset you didn't call me sooner."

"I didn't call you at all."

"I notice you didn't call Beelzebub, either." When Mephistopheles shot him a glare, Asmodeus smiled. Wretched snake-oil salesman. Did he think Mephistopheles couldn't read him like a cheap paperback?

With a jolt, Mephistopheles realized—he was being propositioned.

His discovery had earned him enough political capital that everyone was singing his praises—and if Asmodeus could get Mephistopheles to change loyalties, Lucifer certainly wouldn't put someone this popular in charge of the army. Asmodeus would have to be promoted to Lucifer's number two again.

Asmodeus groped for him through the bond, and Mephistopheles absorbed the energy without thinking about it. He'd never even considered— But then Belior...and Beelzebub...

He took a few steps, feeling the wind wrapping his wet clothes against his legs. Asmodeus watched. He shivered.

"I need a favor." The rain plastered Mephistopheles' hair to his head and dripped down the back of his armor between his wings. "Camael is missing. Given Remiel's mental state—"

"Say no more," Asmodeus said. "Consider him found." And away he flashed.

Mephistopheles moved to the spot where the lightning had hit, standing on the charred earth and remembering how Remiel had sliced open her arm while talking to a Gabriel who was no more. The wind wrapped circles around him, and the corn lay beaten flat by the mad rain.

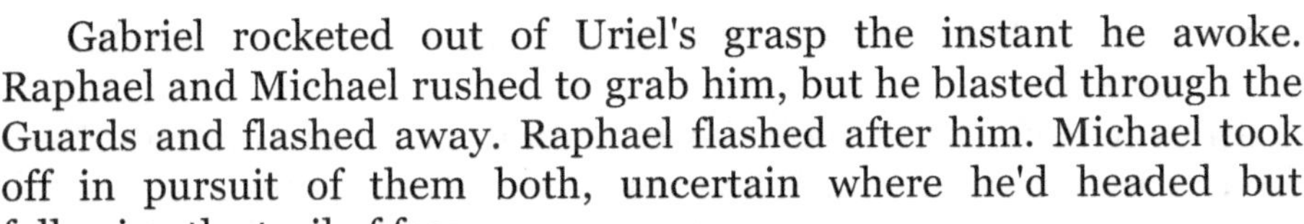

Gabriel rocketed out of Uriel's grasp the instant he awoke. Raphael and Michael rushed to grab him, but he blasted through the Guards and flashed away. Raphael flashed after him. Michael took off in pursuit of them both, uncertain where he'd headed but following the trail of fear.

He skidded up to Raphael, who had Gabriel crumpled at his feet. The Seraph turned, spread his arms, and send a hard blast outward: *Back!*

Michael dropped to his knees beside Gabriel, who had grey eyes white-ringed, question and aching rolling off him. Raphael crouched beside them, covering Gabriel with his wings.

Michael looked around for the first time: the throne of God. Gabriel had fled directly to his Father.

Raphael's "Back!" had been directed at a dozen Cherubim and Seraphim who had come to help. A moment after that realization, Michael made a second one: it wasn't working. The Seraphim had stopped, but if anything, more Cherubim were gathering.

"Is he okay?" "What happened?" "Can we see?" "How does one reattach—"

Gabriel struggled against Raphael's hold, and Raphael had to force him to look into his eyes. Michael expected Gabriel to calm instantaneously, but it didn't happen.

Michael put a Guard around them, then doubled it. Behind him he could hear Raphael trying to talk Gabriel into a state of calm. "You're safe! You're with me! Gabriel, listen to me!"

Michael glanced beyond the bubble to the waiting Cherub faces.

In the next moment he felt Jesus arrive. The Cherubim dispersed on his order, but not without a few looking over their shoulders.

Jesus walked through the Guard as Raphael stood, hefting Gabriel in his arms.

Raphael looked urgent. "I need to tell you—"

"Rapha'li, later." Jesus kissed him on the cheek. "I'll still be here."

Blinking hard, Raphael flashed Gabriel away. Michael projected his thanks, then returned as well.

The first thing he saw was Israfel's livid face. "How could you let him escape? Uriel said we might need you when he regained consciousness!"

"I'd set up the Guard to keep others out," Michael said. "It never occurred to me I needed to keep him in."

Raphael set Gabriel up on his feet, although still clinging to Raphael's shoulders; the Cherub radiated fear, shock, confusion, and then it ebbed.

Drawing close, Uriel looked over Gabriel, then into his eyes, then around to the side of him. "There doesn't seem to be any harm done."

"I've change permissions on the Guard," Michael said. "You guys will have to ask me if you want to leave."

Uriel said, "Gabriel?"

The Cherub turned to look, and then whipped back projecting the same emotional gyrations: shock, confusion, then understanding.

Israfel said, "What's going on?"

Uriel moved in front of Gabriel so they were eye to eye. Gabriel was shaking, leaning more on Raphael. He'd paled all over, and his wings drooped. "Back to bed with you," Uriel said, and Raphael flashed him there.

Gabriel startled: shock, confusion, and then relief.

"Every time he moves," Raphael whispered.

Uriel sat beside him. "Are you in pain?"

Gabriel shook his head.

"Do you recognize us?"

He nodded.

"Do you remember being captured?"

Gabriel's eyes widened. His fear filled the room.

Uriel reached for Gabriel's hands. "Do you remember what they tried to do with you?"

Watching over Uriel's shoulder, Michael saw Gabriel's eyes cloud. The fear grew cold as an arctic wind, and both Mary and Israfel backed into corners. Michael stemmed his own urge to run.

"Do you remember anything afterward?" Uriel leaned closer. "Do you remember being rescued?"

Gabriel shook his head. He'd begun to tremble.

Uriel took a deep breath. "There's a lot to tell you, but right now, you need to know that I'm trying to repair all the damage they did. Your soul is like beads on a string, and—" Michael didn't catch what happened, but Uriel laughed. "Yes, that's it. So they took the time to explain? Lovely." Uriel gave Gabriel's hands a squeeze. "I'm nearly done, but there are still quite a few pieces that need to be attached. I assume that's why you can't keep track of where you are. And you're freezing."

Gabriel was shivering violently by now. Raphael repositioned his wings over Gabriel like a cloak, but the Cherub kept shaking. His teeth were chattering.

"Lay him down," Uriel said softly, and when Raphael did, the same projections: shock, terror, confusion, then realization.

Raphael had gone white. He lay alongside Gabriel, form-fitting around him and warming the air with his wings but not with his Seraphic fire. Gabriel closed his eyes, curled tight with his fists wrapped around the blanket, and by the time they were done raising the temperature of the room, he was in a restless sleep.

Raphael raised his head. "I couldn't feel him at all."

Uriel looked at Israfel, who stepped closer to the bed. "Me neither. That's really unusual."

Mary said, "Why didn't he talk?"

Michael replayed the last five minutes and realized she was right—Gabriel had never spoken.

"He's able to communicate," Uriel said. "If he has to project for a while, I'm okay with that. I'm not sure what all the pieces are that we've connected, but maybe one of the remaining ones is speech." The Throne looked at Raphael. "Are you all right? There's a bit more to go."

He let out a long breath. "I'll have to be all right, won't I?"

Uriel went misty again, but this time it did seem to go faster, and Uriel stayed partially visible. They had the finish line in sight. Three hours ago they'd accepted that Gabriel would die, and now he'd not only awakened but seemed to be himself, if still damaged. It had been thirty hours of solid tension.

Uriel let off an aura of surprise. "I can see where Satan broke your bonds."

Israfel jumped up. "What?"

Sparks shot from Raphael's eyes. "That jerk! What right did he have to do that?"

Michael fought a grin. "Is there a little Cherub-to-Seraph socket?"

Uriel smiled at him, agreeing.

Raphael said, "Plug it back in, then."

Uriel sent a negative. "He's going to be weak for a while." A frown. "It doesn't look damaged, so there shouldn't be anything stopping you from re-bonding after he's stabilized."

Raphael didn't look happy, but he assented. Israfel said nothing else, so Uriel continued the repair. After another fifteen minutes, the Throne pulled back and solidified.

"That's it?" said Mary.

Uriel sighed with weariness.

Raphael and Israfel leaned forward, touching Gabriel. He seemed solid enough. Both Seraphim had tears in their eyes.

Raphael turned to Uriel. "Do you think he'll be all right for a few minutes? I owe someone an apology."

Michael wasn't the only one who caught the pain etched on Raphael's face. "He'll be all right longer than a few minutes," Uriel said. "Go."

Michael lowered the Guard for Raphael to exit, and immediately he had a message from Saraquael.

Michael? Can you be spared?

Not for a while longer. He frowned. *What's going on?*

Remiel. Saraquael's "voice" was shaky. *Gabriel—?*

He's alive!

Suddenly he realized how much joy there was in him to be saying that. When they'd been doing the repairs it was just something being done, but now—

Saraquael had picked up the rest. *He's better?*

Uriel found the string and repaired him.

Oh, thank God!

Saraquael's voice vanished for a moment. Michael imagined Saraquael had taken the time to thank God directly, so he moved onto the bungalow roof and reset the Guard.

You mean it?

Michael laughed out loud: Saraquael sounded the way he felt. *Yes, I mean it.* He got the feeling Saraquael had needed some good news. *Now, what about Remiel?*

She's really unstable. Make that completely unstable.

Michael took a deep breath. *Where is she?*

She's here, but unconscious.

Here, being—?

Being at my home. She rouses from time to time, but she's radiating energy, and as I said, she's unstable. I'm sure I won't be able to keep her here when she awakens.

In the silence, Michael realized Saraquael wanted him to give an order, and Michael also knew he had no clue what it should be. He couldn't contain an angel on the verge of insanity any more than Saraquael could. *You need to stay with her. Make sure she doesn't hurt herself or anyone else.*

The sick dread in response told Michael the situation had escalated beyond that point already.

Try to talk her down.

Will do. Not much assurance, there.

Raphael returned looking stunned, so Michael flashed them both back inside the Guards.

Israfel sat up straight. "My goodness, Raphael—are you okay?"

He just stood with his shoulders bowed.

Michael looked to Uriel only to find the angel already asleep on a pile of cushions. The Seraphim looked equally cooked. "Israfel, take a break. Write a concerto. Do something that has nothing to do with anything."

Once she departed, Michael turned to Raphael. "You're in my chain of command during times of crisis, and this qualifies as a crisis. I'm ordering you to get some sleep."

Wan, red-eyed, Raphael collapsed onto the opposite side of the bed and lay facing the wall.

Michael turned next to Mary, who had settled herself in the rocking chair.

"You go," she said. "I'll stay."

"I'm going to stay with him."

"If I go home," she said, "I'll cook, I'll pray, I'll knit, and I'll talk to everyone about what happened. If I stay, you can head out to take charge of the heavenly host. You'll be immediately accessible if they strike again. You can get the Cherubim to work out a system to protect everyone else. And you'll be able to handle whatever crisis had you so worked up when you came back inside."

Michael sighed.

"Plus, I can do math." Mary called a knitting bag to her hands. "If three of the Seven are in this room, and you stay, that leaves only three out there to keep things running smoothly."

Michael shook his head. "One more of them is down for the count right now. Remiel is in trouble. So it'd be two."

"Then definitely leave the unimportant person here to do the easy job." Mary smiled. "I'll pray for you and for Remiel too." So Michael went.

Fifteen

He felt her awaken.

Saraquael moved closer to Remiel, unable to look at her too carefully but also unwilling to take his attention away from her. His heart pounded.

Remiel opened white-ringed eyes, shivering as she huddled against the arm of the couch. Her chest heaved. Saraquael's cats scattered through the open window, but although he watched them with envy, he remained. Remiel reeked of ozone and smoke which Saraquael tried not to notice.

Clutching a brown pillow to her stomach, she regarded the paintings and the book shelves with a flat affect. Her eyes had faded to butter yellow, but despite that, her grip around her legs remained locked, and her chin rested on her knees. Saraquael had pulled the drapes, but that didn't account for the darkness. Although she must have sobered some because she hadn't fled, she seemed more feral than before.

Zadkiel and Raguel stood guard—Zadkiel on the outside and Raguel within. They'd put up a Guard although it was futile.

Tension emanated from Remiel in concentric rings like the plunk of a stone in a pond, and for a moment Saraquael wished he could do for her as a Cherub did to a Seraph and absorb all that erratic power.

And then the energy ended like a broken circuit. Remiel slackened into the cushions. Raguel stepped forward, then stopped as Saraquael reached for her. A moment after, he recoiled.

She'd done that deliberately.

She'd run herself out of energy deliberately.

His heart was all one question as he knelt on the carpet facing her.

He sought her pale eyes with his green ones, and she reached for his hand. She extended her fingertips to his hair, and they shook as she rolled some of the brown strands between thumb and forefinger.

"It's over now," Saraquael murmured. Why had she drained herself of all her power? Was it still the madness? "You're safe with us, and no one's coming for you."

Remiel said, "I thought angels couldn't dream."

"We can't," Saraquael said.

"I've been dreaming."

Raguel started, and Saraquael had to force himself not to recoil.

"I've been dreaming I'm destroying Gabriel, and my hands are puppets and I have to do whatever I'm told. Over and over I have to rip out his heart, and I know he's dead because his blood is all over me. Camael looks at me, but it's only a mirror. Voices tell me I'm finally special because Camael never destroyed an angel."

"I'm sorry," Saraquael said.

"You didn't know." Remiel knit her fingers, then shifted so her feet dropped to the carpet. "Which one am I? I can't remember. Am I determined by my company, so when I'm with you I'm Remiel—but when I'm with them, am I Camael?"

Saraquael didn't answer. She leaned forward and rested her hands on his shoulders. "Sit with me," she said, and Saraquael joined her. "You too," she said to Raguel, and he took a position on the ottoman.

"Do you still love me?" she asked Raguel.

The Principality nodded.

She closed her eyes. "And you, Saraquael?"

"You know I love you. You're my closest friend."

Remiel hesitated, then rested her head on his shoulder as he cupped her in his wings. "And what about God?"

She waited, and then a tentative smile spread from her lips, transforming her eyes back to golden.

Saraquael let out a long-held breath.

She tensed again. "Let me tell you my other dream." Her wings seemed plastered to her body. "I dreamed that angels are coming to me, all in black, and they're crying, but they say Gabriel is alive. Then Satan comes, but he's disguised as Jesus, and he says, 'Will you believe me? He's alive.' Only he's lying."

"It's a dream," Raguel said.

"But angel's don't dream." The pitch of her voice rose. "We sleep and awaken in the same state of mind. Our bodies sleep to heal, but not our minds, so here I am all at loose ends, only I'm not the way I was when you stopped me—"

Saraquael flinched.

"—and here I am at full spiritual power so I can do things like create hurricanes and slash my own wrists."

Saraquael grabbed her in a hug, closing his wings around her as he realized why she'd deliberately exhausted her energy. She'd wanted to right the scales in order to control herself.

"You're safe with us," was all Saraquael could think to say.

"It will happen again and again." Remiel's voice cracked. "God himself will have to come for me to set things straight inside."

Saraquael tried to ignore the horror on Raguel's face. "Open the drapes," he said.

A moment after, the room shone with colorful morning light that captured Remiel's attention.

"Gabriel isn't dead," Saraquael said at last.

"He's still hanging on?"

"Apparently they fixed him."

She looked puzzled. "Israfel was called."

"I was there," Saraquael said. "They thought it was the end, but Uriel did something, and he's better."

Remiel dragged her forearm across her eyes. "For how much longer?"

Saraquael selected his words slowly. "Michael said Uriel mended him. They recovered the rope or whatever it was. He's weak, but apparently this is for real. Forever."

Light glinted in Remiel's eyes. "But..." She gulped. "Is this a dream?"

Saraquael smiled. "I don't dream."

"I guess you don't." She laughed. "He's really okay? I didn't kill him?" She flung her arms and wings around Saraquael, then tackled Raguel, shrieking with laughter. Zadkiel came inside to see what had happened and got a flying hug for her trouble too.

"Thank you, God, thank you, God," she trilled, then opened her arms to hug all three of them. "Let's go see him!"

"I haven't been allowed to see him yet," Saraquael said. "Uriel's orders."

Remiel shook her head, her eyes suddenly cautious, sparks around her hair.

No, she couldn't lose control again.

"I'll ask," Saraquael said, then spoke into the air. "Michael?"

Anything to report?

"Remiel wants to know if we can see Gabriel."

Is she still throwing energy?

Like a pulsar, Saraquael sent rather than said.

Absolutely not.

"When do you think we can?" Saraquael said aloud, meeting Remiel's eyes. Her expectant look faded.

I don't think he's even awake yet, but I'll let you know.

"Thanks," Saraquael said. "I've got someone here who wants to be first on the guest list." Then he turned to Remiel. "Apparently he's still sleeping."

"Where are they keeping him?" she said. "I couldn't track him down before."

Saraquael caught the gleam in Zadkiel's eyes. "He's safe for now, among friends, like you."

Mary looked up from her knitting to find Gabriel with his eyes open.

"Gabriel!" She dumped half an afghan in a heap and rushed to the bedside, dropping to a seat on the floor so they were on a level. His eyes absorbed all her movements, but his face was slack. One hand rested outside the covers, and she stroked his fingers. "I'm so glad you're awake."

He blinked at her languidly.

Mary looked at the other two angels: Raphael exactly where he'd dropped himself on the bed, and Uriel spread out over a pile of cushions in the corner. She touched Gabriel's hand again, and although cold, it hadn't the bloodless chill of before. He curled his fingers around hers and squeezed.

She squeezed back, taking care not to hurt him.

Gabriel put his hands under his shoulders and started to push himself up, then shut his eyes and gasped. Mary rushed forward, catching him as he panicked. Fear. Confusion. Understanding.

"Does it hurt?" she said.

After a moment, she felt reassurance that he didn't hurt. He had just lost track of his position.

He pivoted as he sat up and again endured the confusion. Then he met her eyes and remembered where he was.

Mary didn't release him immediately. "Your equilibrium is off-kilter?"

Biting his lip, Gabriel swiveled his gaze around the room, taking care to keep his head still. A short intake of breath, and his grey eyes clouded. He tried to look around again without moving.

"Oh, Raphael?" Mary patted Gabriel's hand. "He's behind you, asleep. He and Uriel gave a champion effort to keep you together."

Gabriel frowned. Mary sat directly in front of him, knee to knee. "Are you worried because you can't sense him?" He nodded. "Uriel said Satan broke your bonds—"

His eyes bugged, and he clenched his fists.

"—and you can re-bond later when you're healthy, but not right away." She offered a smile. "Raphael was furious about that."

Mary went across the room to get the picnic hamper, then withdrew a thermos. "Would you like some tea?"

A picture formed in her head: water streaming from a cracked pitcher.

Laughing, Mary looked over her shoulder. "Should I pour you a cup of tea and stand by with a towel?"

Gabriel smiled. She unscrewed the thermos top and poured a mug of steaming tea, which Gabriel took in both hands. She'd wondered if he'd be able to make himself solid enough to drink, but he managed that just fine. As he sat with his hands around the warmth of the cup, she opened another thermos and poured a cup of cream of mushroom soup. When he'd finished the tea, she took that cup and handed him the other.

Gabriel took a deep breath as if to speak, strained, then huffed in frustration.

"Don't worry." She rubbed his shoulder. "I know you can't talk."

He lowered his eyes and projected what he would have said.

"You're welcome. Don't try to force yourself." She touched his hair as he raised the cup to his mouth. "Uriel is my guardian angel, remember? It's not unusual for Uriel to go a century or thereabouts without speaking, so that after three decades you find yourself thinking, was the last spoken sentence in 1637?"

Gabriel laughed without making a sound. Then he raised the mug and nodded.

"You like it?" This was new. Mary hunted through the hamper to see what else was inside. Not all of it was convalescent food, but all of it was comfort food. She pulled out the cookies, macaroons, and some cream cheese and cucumber sandwiches on thin slices of wheat bread. She placed the containers on the bed, and Gabriel took a sandwich.

This won't make him sick, will it? she prayed.

He has an angelic body, God replied. *He can't get sick.*

Mary sorted through the other containers. *It's great to have someone who isn't only humoring me about the cookies.*

He's trying to make up substance, God said. *Below the surface he's aware he's missing a lot of himself, so he's feeling hungry, or what in an angel passes for hunger.*

Mary's eyes brightened, and she unloaded piles of food from the hamper. *Does it work?*

Not efficiently.

She poured another mug of tea for Gabriel and joined him, eating one of the sandwiches. Her heart warmed at how animated he seemed. "I'm so glad you're back." When he paused mid-bite, she added, "I would have missed you terribly."

He avoided her eyes, but she caught the flush of his cheeks.

"I remember the first time I saw you, when you told me about Jesus—it was just so incredible." The experience had buoyed her for weeks; even recalling it made her a little heady. "I'd seen Uriel a few times before, but only fleeting glimpses. But after you came, I was able to see Uriel more often, and I was able to see Raphael too."

Gabriel traced his finger around the edge of an empty plate.

Mary said, "I saw you hanging around sometimes, only I don't think you realized. I didn't know why, but I thought maybe you were looking out for me. Sometimes I'd get scared, but then I'd see you sitting on the well or tussling with Raphael, and I'd feel safe. You were always so relaxed."

She felt Gabriel demur.

"You said the baby would be called the Son of the Most High and inherit the throne of David his father, and I kept that as a shield. If you'd said it, that meant he'd live long enough to do all those things, and even that Joseph wouldn't have me stoned as an adulteress. I clung to that." She touched his hand. "You told me not to be afraid. I'd see you, and seeing you made me strong so I didn't have to feel afraid."

Gabriel really wouldn't look at her now.

"Oh, I'm sorry." She averted her own gaze, as if that could make him less uncomfortable. "I didn't realize you'd finished. Here, there's one more thing." She removed a container from the hamper and showed it to Gabriel. "A tomato-basil salad with fresh mozzarella." He laughed silently as she said, "I went to Leoni's on 15th Avenue in Bensonhurst to get the mozzarella balls."

He laughed again. Mary added, "Then I stopped off at Vasillaros in Flushing to get coffee."

Beaming, Gabriel gestured over his shoulder to the sleeping Raphael. Mary laughed out loud.

They split the tomato-basil salad, but before uncovering the bottom, Gabriel began to shiver again. Mary retrieved Raphael's wings-as-a-blanket and tried to cover Gabriel, but she couldn't figure out how to get it around his own wings. She knew he shouldn't try detaching his wings at this point, not when he'd so recently been in pieces, but she didn't know how the angels had made the room warmer before. She asked God.

They just made it warmer.

But how?

They moved the molecules in the air, God said. *It's not that big a deal for an angel.*

Mary tried again with the blanket, but she shot God a tolerant look.

The Holy Spirit said, *Up on the front of the throne of glory, does it say "Thermostat"?*

Mary bit her lip to contain her smile. The room was already warming as she cleared empty containers off the bed. *I'm not aware of anything it says on the front of the throne because I've only got eyes for You when I'm there.*

The Holy Spirit said, *Come back sometime and check.*

So I can be dazzled and forget again? Okay. But then I'll have to return again. And again.

The Holy Spirit hugged her.

Really, what does it say on the throne of glory?

"Not a step."

Mary laughed as she put away the hamper.

Think about it.

Gabriel had his wings tight to himself by now, and Mary knew he ought to sleep, but he didn't want to move.

"I'm going to lay you down again," Mary said to Gabriel, who projected a strong negative. "No, listen to me. You're tired."

Raphael stirred. Hearing him, Gabriel groped sideways until he touched the Seraph's feathers. In the next moment, Raphael had burst awake and was hugging Gabriel; Gabriel closed his eyes and leaned into the embrace.

"Raphael, he's chilled," Mary said.

"He's beyond chilled and well into freezing." Raphael positioned himself behind Gabriel and wrapped his arms and then his wings around him. Gabriel had his hands up at his chest, and he kept his eyes shut. Raphael murmured, "Believe me, I'd love nothing more than to talk to you right now, but you need to rest."

Gabriel projected an even stronger negative. Mary explained about the equilibrium problems.

"So every time you move, you have no idea where you are?" Raphael sighed. "I hope that's temporary."

Gabriel's eyes flew wide.

Raphael laid his hands on Gabriel's head, and Mary watched him examine the entire Cherub with his mind. Gabriel relaxed moment by moment as Raphael warmed him, and the room itself continued heating.

How warm are you going to make it? Mary asked God.

In answer, God changed her jeans and t-shirt to an airy dress loosely belted at the waist.

Sitting behind Gabriel, Raphael didn't have to hide the distress on his face, and with the bond severed, Gabriel wouldn't be able to detect whatever realization had created that expression.

Gabriel must have felt the examination end, because he cocked his head and squinted.

Raphael touched his head against the back of Gabriel's and spoke in a hush. "You need more time to heal."

Gabriel rolled his eyes.

"I'm sorry I can't be more specific. I've never done anything like this before."

Gabriel reached one hand to his shoulder, and Raphael took it. He sighed. "We got you this far. We'll figure out something. It's not so bad, considering." Raphael's wings vibrated. "Just, when you consider—"

Gabriel leaned into him again, and Raphael squeezed him tight. "Uriel may be able to figure it out."

Five minutes later, Gabriel had surrendered to sleep upright against Raphael's chest. Raphael could probably have laid him down then, but he didn't. For nearly an hour he sang the Trisagion in a low voice, his focus fixed on the Vision. As she prayed while knitting,

Mary could feel the relief sheeting off him like rain off a metal awning. It was to this scene that Uriel awakened.

Uriel admitted to confusion about the equilibrium problems and didn't have a magic needle to fix them. The Throne tried to check the repair work, but as soon as Uriel reached inside, a terrified Gabriel flexed out of Raphael's grasp, desperate to fight or flee except that Michael's Guard trapped him. It took a few moments to calm him.

While Gabriel huddled against him, Raphael said, "Were you able to get a look?" and Uriel replied that things seemed to be holding together for now.

Uriel cleared everything off the bed and put down a cardboard puzzle, spread out all twenty-four pieces, and looked at Gabriel.

Sitting forward, Gabriel frowned.

Confused, Uriel prompted him.

Gabriel studied the pieces for an interminable minute, then set about methodically trying each side of each piece against every other piece. The scheme was thorough and would have yielded a complete picture in an hour, but Uriel cleared away the puzzle and brought out a board with five pegs and twenty-five shapes to stack on them. Gabriel sorted by color, but in order to sort by shape he had to systematically match each shape to every other shape.

Raphael sat stunned. Mary tried not to appear nervous.

Uriel cleared away the shapes and moved on to testing languages, all of which Gabriel could understand.

The battery took over an hour, covering every conceivable area from problem-solving to optics to fine motor to social skills ("No worries," Raphael joked. "You'd have failed that on the best day of your life anyhow,") and basic sensory input. Poker-faced, Uriel had a clipboard to mark everything as they went through. Gabriel ate cookies between tests until he got too tired to continue, at which point they made the room dark, laid him down again (once more the terrified disorientation) and told him to sleep.

Gabriel started to sit up, but Raphael stopped him. "Is something wrong?"

Mary murmured, "You don't want to be alone?"

Raphael closed his eyes and pressed his forehead against Gabriel's. "No, I wouldn't either."

Uriel said, "We'll only be on the other side of that wall."

"No." Raphael kept his voice flat. "You'll only be on the other side of that wall. I'm going to be on *this* side of that wall right here."

Mary and Uriel went into the rest of the house, which felt frigid after the greenhouse effect in Gabriel's room.

Mary took a deep breath before saying, "How bad is the damage?"

Uriel projected that Mary had seen it for herself. "I need Raphael to go over this with me, but his senses aren't integrated. He can't see things and turn them over in his mind."

Mary said, "God told me it's all right that he's hungry."

Uriel sparkled with surprise, then a generalized projection Mary couldn't entirely decipher about Gabriel eating the whole time (it felt like an a-ha moment) and then an image appeared in Mary's head of herself heading right back to her kitchen.

Mary laughed. "You guessed it!" Then she paused. "Why would sensory integration affect his speech?"

Uriel shrugged, projecting no worries. When Gabriel wanted to, he'd speak.

Mary said, "He did want to."

Uriel's eyes widened.

"He tried to say thank you, but he couldn't."

Frowning, Uriel sat on a cushion and ran a hand along a beaded curtain. "I wish you hadn't told me that. But there's a lot of coordination that goes into speaking."

"More than for eating?"

Uriel winced. "You've got me stumped. Please don't tell me you said something he didn't understand."

Mary shook her head.

"Comprehension always leads production." Uriel clattered the beads against one another. "I hereby return to not worrying."

"As long as you're not worrying," Mary said, "why is he always cold?"

"He isn't really cold," Uriel said.

"Shivering," Mary said. "Teeth chattering. Response to warmth. What am I missing?"

"It's a spiritual cold." Uriel looked off as if considering a definition. "It's the counterpart of the spiritual heat the damned feel, even though they're not physically on fire. Remember the sound that two pieces of metal make scraping against one another? Doesn't it make your hair stand on end, so you flinch?" When Mary nodded, Uriel said, "He's feeling that constantly."

Mary looked puzzled.

"Something's a bad fit inside," Uriel said. "When the pieces all regrow to their right proportions and shapes, the fit will be better, but I'm guessing now that something needs to shift around, so two bead-edges are too tight against one another or scraping one another, and every time that happens, he shivers."

Mary said, "Can you release the string a little so it's not as tight?"

"Where would I do it?" Uriel dropped back limp on the cushions. "Everything has to heal before I can go back inside to figure out what's too tight. Once that happens, yes, I can shift things where they need to be. Until then, at least he's safe, even if he needs to be in a tropical paradise."

"That's not so bad." Mary stood. "I'm off to my kitchen to heat that up a bit with the paradise of an oven and cookies."

Gabriel drifted but didn't feel entirely asleep. Although he lay still, his mind thrashed over what had happened...the gaps—in his memory, in his thoughts, in what he could perceive, in Creation where he wouldn't have been— He didn't want to create one more gap by sleeping again.

He braved the vertigo by concentrating on the Vision as he sat up, and although the confusion struck again, he didn't experience the fear. It was okay if he was suddenly somewhere unknown in space and time, as long as God was there with him.

That would be everywhere, God told him.

Indeed, but it helped to have the reminder.

Gabriel saw Raphael sitting sideways on the rocking chair, back to one armrest and legs draped over the other as he read a stack of papers attached to a clipboard. Gabriel couldn't feel the images in his head as Raphael pored over the sheets, and he flinched.

Raphael looked up. "You okay?"

Well, no, not really. But no worse.

Raphael said, "You should go back to sleep," and then returned to looking at the papers.

Gabriel noticed two new thermoses on the bedside table. There was a note with them which Gabriel flashed to his hands. This was what the note said:

Gabriel,

I ruivb rkv a cie od gioeu klf a iswqmpa zi euc. Beew wexxrp lqn I cuww qll wyc cneyf.

Uejs

Terrific. Gabriel swallowed against a sick dread before Raphael could detect it, and then when Raphael didn't pick it up he realized how much he'd expected Raphael to respond anyhow.

The handwriting was Mary's; the only reason he could recognize his own name was that she'd used the single pictogram of his seal.

He flashed the two thermoses to his lap. When he concentrated on the yellow sticky papers, he found he could make out the individual letters, but they wouldn't fit together into words. The shorter one he decided must say "tea" which meant the other probably said something like "soup" along with whatever variety it was.

Gabriel took the cup off the top of that one and tried to unscrew the cap, but it wouldn't turn. Mentally he felt into the plastic grooves; it wasn't jammed on tightly. How humiliating.

You're not quite yourself right now, God reassured him.

The smartest angel in creation would not be defeated by a thermos screw top, that was for sure.

No, somehow I knew that, God replied.

Gabriel sent his senses into the center of the bottle to where the soup sloshed around, and he formed a Guard the size of a fist. Then he second-guessed himself and made sure his fist fit into the cup. When it did, he flashed the ball of soup out of the thermos and into the cup.

It worked! Gabriel was looking at a creamy liquid with floating slices of mushrooms.

Congratulations, God said.

I'll take my victories where I can find them.

Gabriel was finishing the cup when Raphael said, "You really aren't going back to sleep?" Gabriel only looked at him patiently. "There's no need to be rude," Raphael replied. He opened the curtains, admitting a flood of sunlight into the room until Gabriel wished he could move to the window and let it slant over him.

Raphael tossed the clipboard into the air where it vanished just before clattering to the floor.

Gabriel frowned at him.

"Nothing you need to see," said the Seraph.

Gabriel glowered.

"So what if they're your test results?" Raphael came closer. "I'm not going to give them to you."

You're not protecting me—I can tell how damaged I am.

"Then you don't need to see a long row of check boxes." Raphael tilted his head. "There's nothing wrong with your Cherub nature, at any rate."

Gabriel sighed at him. Raphael raised his eyebrows.

A cold hand clenched Gabriel's heart then—what if he wasn't the most intelligent being in Creation any longer? That meant Mephistopheles—that would mean Satan had the number one Cherub on his side, and then how—

It's not worth worrying about, God told him.

Raphael pulled his chair closer and looked into Gabriel's eyes. "We'll figure out a way to get you back up to speed. At least you're still here. And that's what's important."

While Gabriel agreed, he'd rather have all of him here, not just most of him.

Raphael met his eyes, and then he looked aside: he'd instinctively tried to communicate with him through the bond that didn't exist any longer.

Abruptly awkward, Raphael said, "When they took you...what was it like?"

Again that cold hand, only now it was a second one around his throat. That tiny room, the blackness, the other Cherub cheerfully explaining the technique, Beelzebub's proposition—

Hands on his hands: he hadn't realized he'd begun shaking.

Raphael met his eyes, and Gabriel looked into them, longing for the depth he knew he ought to be able to plumb but which he found closed off to him, and in its place he found only a similar yearning on Raphael's part. They shouldn't need words. He extended his soul toward Raphael's.

Raphael turned away. "Uriel said not yet. You're still too weak."

Gabriel opened his hands.

"I don't know when, but I'm not taking the chance that I might hurt you again."

Again?

"If you'd died, it would have been my fault."

Gabriel arched his eyebrows. *Surely Satan had something to do with it?*

Raphael didn't reply.

This made no sense. From what Uriel and Mary had said, Raphael had saved him.

Flamelets appeared around Raphael, and his shoulders and wings tensed. Gabriel couldn't see the front of him, but his hands must have been clenched. His soul vibrated the room around Gabriel, and it would be so easy and so right to immerse himself in that power, absorb it and calm Raphael, invigorate himself and know fully what was the guilt or the admission Raphael was keeping hidden.

Uriel blew into the room. Before Raphael could even turn, the Throne forced him outside the Guard.

Stop! Uriel grabbed Gabriel's hands. "Don't even attempt to absorb that kind of fire right now! I can't say that strongly enough."

The residual flames of Raphael's spirit crackled in the air. Gabriel clenched his fists and set his jaw. He felt like a parched wanderer encountering an oasis as the thirst tightened at the top of his throat.

Uriel's hands touched Gabriel's cheeks, and the Cherub opened his eyes so he was staring into the indigo of Uriel's own. The Throne breathed deeply. Gabriel forced himself to breathe in rhythm, and then again. Those eyes, so deep—but the hunger, the empty space—the chill, the sparkling fire—the darkness, the isolation, the union—

Uriel drew him closer. Look to the Vision. The Vision. God, this is tough. The Vision. Breathe.

Uriel sang softly, "Light of ages, fire of the heart, delight of the soul."

Gabriel joined in. "Ancient splendor and warmth of love, you I know and meet in joy, the breath of me, the light of all, the substance and the soul."

The glinting Seraph energy faded out like fireflies. Gabriel ached, and his eyes burned. He couldn't swallow.

Uriel shimmered, hands trembling.

Gabriel gave Uriel's hands a squeeze, then tried to smile, but he couldn't quite.

Uriel swallowed. "You know why you shouldn't absorb his energy?"

Gabriel nodded. He understood, but that didn't mean it was easy.

Uriel nodded, eyes dark.

Gabriel squinted.

"I sent him to Sidriel," Uriel said.

Gabriel laughed in silence, imagining Sidriel's surprise and then excitement; but then he remembered Raphael trying to hide from him a terrible thing, and he knew that whatever it was, Raphael was sharing it with Sidriel and not with him.

Uriel looked out the window, and Gabriel tried to look as well. Clouds, trees, the darting shadow of a bird zipping past.

"It's only until you're stronger."

Gabriel's hands knotted.

"Sing with me again." Uriel made a mandolin, and together the pair sang and waited.

Sixteen

Remiel returned to her studio for the first time since Gabriel's capture. She didn't turn on the lights because of the mirrors, so instead she groped her way across the smooth wooden floor to a room at the opposite side. There she lighted all the lamps with a hand motion rather than illuminate it herself, and she staggered her way to her desk. The bed, end table and chair stayed in the correct places, thankfully, although the same couldn't be said for the angle of the floor.

She wasn't winged. She was remarkably solid but felt as if she might float away in the slightest gust of air.

A vase of cut flowers stood on the end table, filling the air with the spices of autumn. Remiel looked over herself and could name different scents: iodine, cigarette smoke, beer.

She fingered her ear, then flinched.

After calling a tall glass to her hand, she flashed water into it, added salt, and heated up the whole thing on her palm. When it was hot but not too hot to touch, she raised her shirt and bent over the glass so the lip of it sealed around her navel. She lay back on her bed so the cup was inverted with salt water gently scalding her skin.

Remiel closed her eyes. Saraquael would know how Gabriel was. The whole time she'd been in Creation, she hadn't dared ask in case she'd be overheard by them, and then she'd remembered being one of them and thought she shouldn't know just so she wouldn't tell them (but wait, she hadn't told them, right? Mephistopheles had caught her and asked, but she couldn't remember what she'd answered) and she shouldn't even think too much about him. So she hadn't told any of the guardians on Earth, hadn't asked for an update, hadn't dared let herself believe the unbelievable, because what if that had been a part of the dream too, and what if Saraquael had said something nebulous just so she'd calm down, or what if he had said something else and she'd only heard what she so desperately wanted, although impossible?

Maybe Saraquael would bring her to him now. Maybe Gabriel would be awake and she could see the truth.

Remiel tried to feel around Heaven for Gabriel, but again, nothing.

He had to be dead.

Saraquael said he was Guarded. Who would have put up the Guard?

Oh, of course.

"Michael?" Her voice sounded thin.

The Archangel appeared, at first concerned, but then he drew a sharp breath.

"Don't be like that," Remiel said. "How is Gabriel?"

"I haven't seen him in a couple of hours. I assume he's the same." He folded his arms. "You smell like an ash tray."

"The poison gets into the air," Remiel said. "I need a shower." She pursed her lips. "When can I see him?"

"I'd suggest," he said, undue emphasis on *suggest,* "after you sober up a bit."

"I'm not even buzzed."

"And get decently dressed."

"He's not going to lust after me, Michael. Seriously. I can't even imagine him caring."

"But others might." Michael's eyes glinted. "You went partying on Earth, and were you dressed like that the whole time?"

She propped herself on one elbow to see. Mid-calf black boots, mid-thigh black skirt, and a rumpled white t-shirt that ended a little below her navel when she stood. "It looks skimpier pushed up like this." She laid back down on the mattress.

Michael said, "And you've apparently forgotten how to drink," pointing at the inverted cup of water.

Remiel met his eyes just long enough to register the blue sparkle that meant his last statement was a joke. Okay. He was okay. It was all right.

"He told me to do this."

"Unless 'he' was God, what would compel you to do that?"

"Because he'd know." She rolled to her side, allowing her shirt to cascade over her abdomen and tipping the cup away to reveal a metal ring in her navel.

"That's—" Michael swallowed. "Why did you do that?"

Remiel shrugged.

"Did it hurt?"

"Not enough." Her eyes glistened. She raised a hand to her hair, brushing it aside to reveal three piercings in one ear.

Michael took a step back. "Remiel, are you sure—?"

She looked at the circlet on her abdomen. "I lost all the ones I had when I became Camael, and I needed them back." She flashed a hand mirror to herself and angled it for a better view of the navel ring, then up again so she could look at her ear, then at the other (three more on that side.) She avoided looking at her face, only at the pretty titanium rings that glinted around the red sore spots.

Michael took a step closer. "So the water on your stomach...?"

"Supposed to prevent infection."

"I have an easier way to prevent infection." He sat on the edge of the bed. "You're an angel. If you switch back to your angelic form, you can't get one."

"But I can't, not right now." Remiel started to put down the mirror until she caught a glimpse of her face as it passed by. A dull ache in her chest. She tilted it again so she saw only her eyes and her hair, could see him just as he was back then, back when they could no more be separated than the heat and light in a fire.

Michael sounded as if he ached too. "Was being Camael that bad?"

"I— I wasn't doing it because of Camael." Remiel rolled onto her stomach and felt the twinge where the ring rubbed against the bed. She crossed her arms and laid down her head, keeping the ear protected in the hollow by the crook of her arm.

"Tell me." Michael's weight made the mattress shift. "Why don't you just want to heal up?"

"Because I've got to go back." Remiel closed her eyes and traced circles on the blanket. "The piercer tried to talk me into a rook, but I told him no. Not tonight. I'll go back for it when he's ready. But if I do that and I'm all healed up, he'll know something isn't right."

Michael stroked the back of her hair. "What's a rook?"

Remiel raised one hand. "It's a piercing here, through the triangle part of the ear where it's thick."

Michael grimaced. "Why would you go back for that?"

Remiel blinked unsteadily. "I asked around to find who would be the best piercer, you know? I can go anywhere in the world, so it might as well be the best. I got online at an internet café and asked in a piercing chat room, and someone recommended this guy, and God told me to go to him."

Remiel took Michael's hand. "I don't know, maybe it's stupid. I could make fifty piercings on my body right now if I wanted, just by thinking about it, but what I wanted—somebody solid. Something that reached inside."

Michael squeezed her fingers.

"Anyhow, I told him what I wanted, and he tried to talk me into only doing two, but I'm pretty stubborn. And he—" She rubbed her eyes. "I asked how he got trained, and he told me about studying piercing. At the mall they just use the earring gun on a teddy bear. But he had to learn how the body works, where the nerves are and everything."

Michael put his arm over her shoulder. She rested her head against him, flinched, and then found a place where her ear didn't throb and the rings didn't get pressed.

"In between one ear and the other, he told me how awesome the body is, and how the nerves work, and I don't know, I asked if he knew why it was, and he said he was never sure, and I told him I was. While he did the navel ring, we talked about God, and he wanted to do the rook, but I think he just wanted to keep talking."

Michael closed his eyes. "And that's why you're going back to talk to him again."

"We prayed together." When she concentrated, she could still feel herself focusing the fledgling prayer and laying it at the feet of God even as she sat on the chair touching her newly-pierced ears. "I told him where to read, and he looked so excited. So I want to go back later, just to lock him in, yeah."

Michael stroked Remiel's hair. "You did a lot of good for him. It sounds as if he was ready. He just needed a push."

Remiel ran her hands over her eyes. Michael felt so strong at her side, and she couldn't help but be aware of herself: dirty, smoky, inebriated, indecent, wretched and shameful. Pierced seven times.

Michael squeezed her hand. "I'm sorry I thought badly of you."

Remiel murmured, "You didn't think anything worse than I did."

He bowed his head.

Now was the time. "I need to see Gabriel."

"You can't." Still looking at his lap, Michael shook his head. "He's too fragile. It's like your piercings. Would it be smart to touch them with unwashed hands right now? Aren't you going to keep them protected until they heal?"

Remiel bit her lip. "I suppose. But I'm not that dirty, am I?"

"He's raw." Michael massaged her shoulders. "Uriel wants as few visitors as possible. Even Raphael got thrown out."

Remiel's eyes bugged.

"So no, no visitors."

She let out a long breath. "I just want to forget that it was all my fault. I can do that if I apologize to him. I didn't want to hurt him. I never intended to."

"He knows you would never hurt him."

"But I did!"

"It wasn't intentional." Michael continued rubbing her shoulders. "But if you think you unintentionally hurt him before, don't you see it's possible to unintentionally hurt him now? And not just you. That's why everyone has to stay away."

Remiel huddled over herself. Finally she said, "You'll let me in first when it's time?"

Michael patted her. "If you can push Raphael out of the way, be my guest."

Remiel laid down again, and Michael helped her find a way that she wasn't uncomfortable. She blinked off the lights so he would leave, but then Remiel didn't try to sleep.

Uriel startled when the Cherub Ophaniel walked into the bungalow as if there were no Guard.

Even as Uriel tried to work up the outrage to force him out again, Gabriel's eyes flashed even brighter than his surprised smile. *Good news! I discovered what Satan was trying to do!*

Ophaniel laughed, touched his wing tips to Gabriel's hands, and settled onto a chair.

This was ridiculous. Uriel stood, arms folded.

Ophaniel turned to the Throne. "I figured there had to be a way through the Guard, so I found it."

Gabriel cocked his head, and Ophaniel nodded to him as if Uriel weren't even there. "Now that you're repaired, I can't mingle your substance and mine, so I asked Michael to let me into another place he'd Guarded. He isn't paranoid enough to Guard everything separately, so he gave me permission, and I came here instead."

Gabriel tried to sit up, then battled a moment's vertigo and confusion. Ophaniel grabbed his hands while Gabriel rode it out. "You're with me. No worries. You're among friends."

Gabriel smiled ruefully. Then he brightened again.

"Yeah, it did work. I doubt we'd see the same success against our enemies, to be honest, although there's always the possibility of exploiting a similar weakness—"

By now Uriel had returned to the corner, and the Cherubim continued talking—or rather, Ophaniel spoke and Gabriel participated nonverbally. Ophaniel jumped right into questions about the repair process, and Gabriel batted them back as other questions, a tactic that rapidly established a debate between the Cherubim. Uriel in the corner produced some sheet music and continued to play the mandolin.

Half an hour later, Uriel looked up to find Gabriel a paler grey than usual but still engrossed in a discussion of what the will was and if the will was a part of angelic substance like the soul and how did one define substance in the first place. Ophaniel started by attempting to define the will, only Gabriel must have refuted that because immediately he determined a second definition, and then they moved on to defining substance and soul.

It was when Gabriel protested that Ophaniel's system of definitions was recursive that Uriel realized the increasing degree of complexity Gabriel was able to project. Whether he hadn't needed to before or hadn't wanted to—or simply hadn't the opportunity—he'd kept everything simple: requests, statements, questions. Up until this moment, the idea of forcing a convalescent to tackle metaphysics at the Cherub level would have seemed like cruelty.

All the same, Gabriel was flagging. Uriel sent a warning to Ophaniel, who missed that and two others before he noticed how tired Gabriel seemed. He apologized even as Gabriel insisted he continue.

"I really came by to give you this." Ophaniel handed an envelope to Gabriel, and then Uriel flashed them to the next room.

"Please don't do that again." Uriel frowned. "If you carried any latent Seraph fire—"

"I made certain I didn't." Ophaniel inserted his hands in his pockets. "I knew what I was doing. Raphael explained about the energy, but I wanted to see him myself." He added, "By the way, about his aphonia, I meant to try him reciting something he's memorized. That will determine whether the impediment lies in the apparatus or in the wiring."

Uriel's eyes darkened to indigo.

"I'm not gawking." Ophaniel cocked his head. "He's my friend."

"Half of Heaven would say the same thing to get in here."

"And I knew what I was doing. He doesn't look the way I expected." Ophaniel bit his lip. "When Raphael pulled him out of Hell, he was a mess."

Uriel touched his shoulder, and Ophaniel's wings drooped.

Uriel said, "I want you to tell Michael how you circumvented his Guard."

Ophaniel's wings spread. "Absolutely! I'd hoped we could devise a more stringent means of securing an area anyway, one requiring less concentrated effort with a greater reliability compared to—"

Uriel's eyes glimmered, and then Ophaniel was flashed away.

It would be approximately two minutes until Michael began wishing Uriel hadn't done that: fit repayment for a permeated Guard.

Uriel checked with Mary that everything was all right with her and then returned to Gabriel.

Remiel was sitting on the bed, holding Gabriel's hand.

A shudder of frustration surged through the Throne. "He's sick!" Uriel pushed her out of the room and far away. "Spread the word— leave him alone!"

Then Uriel turned toward Gabriel, eyes wide with concern. Gabriel looked uneasy, a little shocked, but otherwise unharmed. Uriel couldn't detect any signature of Remiel in the atmosphere, so it was possible she hadn't been emanating any power.

Uriel looked out the window. This was no good. Either Michael was distracted or he'd put up the world's shoddiest Guard, to have two breaks in an hour.

Pointedly from Gabriel: What was wrong with Remiel?

Uriel leaned on the window sill, forehead pressed against the glass.

Again the question from Gabriel, stronger.

"She went into Hell to get you out."

The sunlight filtered in so strong, so direct, keeping warm the already sweltering room. The slanted rays illuminated the tiny shadows of the floor, the natural variations in color.

Surprised denial from Gabriel.

"She went in as Camael. She didn't think twice."

A rustle softly behind him. Gabriel had his wings up about himself, tips crossed in front of his lap.

Uriel listened to nature outside, to birds in their relaxed calls, crickets singing with their legs, plants silent by themselves and so rustling against one another to proclaim the greatness of the Lord. There was nothing more to say to Gabriel: the Cherub was fitting the pieces together just fine in his mind.

A moment later, grief.

Uriel turned to Gabriel, still enclosed in his own wings. Remiel had done it because she loved him, because of her own sense of justice, because she knew from serving with Michael that the thing to do was the right thing, at once. Her impulses, her love, and ultimately everything she was.

From Gabriel: admiration.

Uriel agreed.

Another rustle of wings. Uriel felt Gabriel brace himself, look at the Vision, and then lie down on his stomach.

Gabriel's thoughts turned to how stable Remiel was, if she had been able to slip so easily through a Guard.

Uriel squinted. No reported problems had reached here.

Relief sloughed off Gabriel, more than Uriel expected. A cocked head and a frown.

Gabriel clenched his fists: Remiel knew how to unlace a soul.

Uriel protested.

But if she'd posed as Camael, then she'd been there when Satan unlaced Gabriel. In fact, Uriel felt Gabriel clarify, Satan had channeled his power through her as a focus. Of course she knew. She just hadn't mentioned it.

Uriel's lips pursed. Too many individuals knew how to do the forbidden. How long until it became common knowledge? How many more angels would they need to repair? How many would they lose?

But Gabriel's eyes had closed, and Uriel's gaze returned to the greenery.

Just then Uriel remembered Ophaniel's question about reciting. "*Let me not to the marriage of true minds admit impediments.*"

Gabriel murmured, almost asleep, "*Love is not love which alters when it alteration finds.*"

Problems with the wiring, Ophaniel had said. Not with the apparatus.

Uriel's eyes closed in prayer.

Mephistopheles had a minor demon chained in the ice fields, and he played with its heartstrings. Nothing much. He practiced all the work he'd done before, verifying that he still could reach in the same way, grab *this,* unhook *that,* tighten that other thing. He noted the things the demon screamed and tried to determine what part he had touched based on what it said. It might be interesting at some point in the future to chain two minor demons side by side and transfer material from one to the other. Assuming he could by that means graft two together, he could potentially forge a few super-strong angels. The minor demons could be so useless at times: the hellfire burned away all their rational thought and left them as unreasoning as cornered animals. Maybe combining them would give them a boost out of savagery, since objectively they couldn't hurt more than one hundred percent.

To give Lucifer the answer he wanted, Mephistopheles should find a single vulnerable point, a focus in the soul where the power converged, and then surgically remove just that spot. Destroy a locus like that and you might well be able to make an angel fall apart in its tracks, much like removing a monkey's spine without touching the rest of him. To locate such a pressure point, Mephistopheles could infiltrate a minor demon with power from various points on the heartstring simultaneously and note the flow pattern.

Easy enough. Why didn't he do it?

Putting together two minor demons, though—that might be interesting.

Behind him Mephistopheles felt Belior, so he released the minor demon's heartstrings and turned.

The other Cherub wore black armor. "I have a message for you."

Mephistopheles didn't summon his sword, but he armored his heart.

"Camael isn't locatable."

Mephistopheles raised his eyebrows. "Have you tried—"

"I assure you, if the technique exists, we've attempted it. Camael is either hidden or destroyed."

"Or possibly insane."

Belior shook his head. "Since you located Remiel in that state—and did it without help, I might add—you may assume it's shockingly easy to find an angel in a state of mental disorder."

Turning away as if to do more work, Mephistopheles didn't bother to bristle. "Thank you for your efforts. I'm sure you did your best."

"Oh," Belior said, stepping closer, his breath hot on Mephistopheles' neck, "but that wasn't my message."

"If you're going to tell me to stay away from Asmodeus, you're wasting your energy." Mephistopheles gave a bored wave of his hand. "He approached me."

"And if he approaches you again," said an unrattled-sounding Belior, "you send him away."

Mephistopheles shrugged. "If he approaches me again, I'll ask him to consider what you have to offer that I cannot."

Belior emitted rings of tension. Mephistopheles didn't face him. He had enough power to overcome Belior easily. If necessary he could call on Beelzebub, but most likely he would win outright. No attack would come so directly. It would always be the backstab, the power play, the half-lies with their long half-lives and the random inserted truths which gave the whole stew a juicy potency. Belior would talk him down to Asmodeus, might attempt to turn Lucifer against him, could cozy up to Beelzebub, but there would never be a direct attack.

Mephistopheles made a show of continuing his work. Belior left.

All the same—what had happened to Camael? Inability to find him doubtless indicated his apprehension, and that meant questions from the enemy as to how they'd done what they had, what further plans they had in development. Which additionally meant Mephistopheles was unacceptably not in control of the flow of knowledge. This would require, at some point, a trip to Heaven to retrieve him.

Seventeen

Forced away from Gabriel's room, Remiel walked through Creation wearing a demi-human body she didn't want to heal. The left ear felt inflamed, but she concentrated on putting her feet one in front of the other.

The noise in her mind. The questions.

She took a step and was on a mountain. Another and she was on a beach. Another and she was walking through rock walls in a medieval castle. Still another and she was slogging through the surface of a gas giant.

She wanted to pray, but then she remembered demons didn't pray, so she stopped herself.

Uriel said she might hurt Gabriel. But she'd killed him, hadn't she? No, he'd survived. She'd sent him into harm's way, and then she'd gone into Hell in order to finish the work Satan had decreed.

Didn't that make her a demon? Therefore, why bother asking God?

Come to me. Come to me.

Remiel tried to spread her wings, only she hadn't any, which made no sense. No, wait, it did in a way. But there was a calling. Someone wanted her.

No, no one wanted her. Not even Gabriel.

Come to me. Come to me.

No one wanted a demon, so she ought to make sure she was one, and the best way to figure out which one she was would be to compare side by side.

Come to me.

Side by side.

Remiel took another step and arrived on top of a cell block, a concrete cube atop a mountain, guarded by six Principalities. She sat on the rooftop and talked to the Guard. It was Raguel's. Raguel didn't like her—didn't trust her—well, who would? But she had asked

Raguel if he was going to lock her up, and Raguel had said no, and that meant she could head inside.

Come to me.

Remiel pressed her hands into the roof to go desolid through it. The Guard didn't want to admit her, just like the one around Gabriel's room, but then abruptly it yielded—again the same. She wriggled a bit and slipped through the roof, landing lightly on the floor of the cell.

Inside was airless despite numerous windows. A faint smoke tinged the atmosphere, and Remiel could drink the power out of the area—her own power.

"Come to me," said the occupant, her twin.

"I came." So foggy. She glowed a bit to dispel the oppressive feeling of a room that didn't look oppressive enough.

Camael hadn't been restrained within the room. While the Guard wouldn't let him out, he had complete freedom to move within, and he'd been provided a few comforts: books (at least one of which seemed to have been burned) and music and art materials. Camael had been drawing, but Remiel wouldn't look at what he'd made.

He stepped back. "You're wearing a body!"

She looked over herself.

"And you're reeking of smoke." His nose wrinkled. "What have they done to you?"

She blinked.

He moved closer. "Why are they making you turn into a monkey?"

She shook her head. It was like trying to read through a kaleidoscope. "What did you want?"

"I wanted you to come to me."

"I'm here."

He looked just as horrified as she felt. "But why are you like this?"

"You— I don't remember." Her eyes watered. This wasn't right. "I tried to see Gabriel, but they said I can't. I killed him. I slipped my hands into his heart, and I ripped him to pieces and unhooked him and unstrung him one little bit at a time, and I want to tell him I'm sorry, but they said I can't."

Camael's eyes glowed. "We succeeded?"

She fought the tears. "You made me do it. You sent me messages."

He stepped toward her as if he would touch her but then recoiled from her physical form. "We're still connected. You may be enslaved, but I'm free, and they found a way I can call to you. It's still possible to come with me." He let out a long breath. "We don't have to be apart."

"You used me!" Remiel pivoted away. "You got into my head and sent me messages, and I did the things you said! How can you call that freedom?"

Camael folded his arms. "We've won a huge victory this time. No one's ever destroyed an angel before, not even God."

"Rahab," Remiel said.

"Rahab came back because God didn't want it done in the first place; therefore he didn't really destroy him. But *we* did it!"

"How can you be proud of that?" She whirled to face him, took a step toward him and watched him reflexively retreat from contact with her body. "How can you brag about punching a hole right through the heart of creation?"

"No one else ever did."

Remiel's eyes went gold. "That's not a reason to do something! You took—you broke apart—you planned all this—"

She covered her mouth with her hands and choked on the words.

"I made you come to me." Camael stood taller. "I'll make you come to me again."

Remiel felt the blood draining from her head.

"You'll feel an impulse and never know if it's your thought or mine, something you want or I, a good thing or a bad, and always-always-always you'll have that nugget of doubt in your soul."

"No!" Remiel wrapped her arms to her shoulders and tore at the skin with her nails. Nothing could ever hurt enough, not now. "I won't allow you to!"

"It's not a question of allowing." Camael's voice was a thready whisper. "I already made you the judas goat to lead your prince to his end. Think of what I can do next."

Eyes closed, Remiel flashed out of the Guard, flashed away to the hottest sun in the midst of the most crowded galaxy she could think of. Fully an angel again, she let the fusion and the plasma wash through her, and she grabbed fistfuls of liquid hydrogen and tried to scrub herself clean. Her clothes incinerated immediately, but the rings she made a part of herself so they stayed, and she let the heat surge through her heart, burn out the evil, the memory, the voice: *Come back to me. You're mine.*

I'm not yours. I'm no one's. Nobody's. Not even God wants me.

Ophaniel returned to Michael. As he piled a stack of books and a chess set into Michael's arms, he explained that while art and music and nature abounded at Uriel's, there wasn't anything for a Cherub to do. Michael bundled them all together with a Guard and flashed to Gabriel's room.

Uriel sat spinning solid streams of light between both hands, shaping the light into curled strands to be woven together. Three similar fixtures already hung in the window where Gabriel sat.

He was colorless but seemingly stable as he ate a bowl of risotto. Michael enjoyed the aroma for a moment, then showed Gabriel the books and the chess board, only Gabriel didn't react with joy. Instead he flinched.

Uriel looked up abruptly. "You can't read?"

Michael felt Gabriel emanate a deep discomfort as he flushed.

"I'm sorry." Uriel sighed. "I ought to have realized, given the other visual difficulties."

Michael felt Gabriel project that it wouldn't have made a difference.

Michael offered to stay for a while, and Uriel departed. He pulled up a chair and produced a small table. "At any rate," he said, "we can play chess."

Gabriel shook his head, then handed Michael the letter Ophaniel had delivered.

"Oh, sure." Michael went to break the seal and realized Gabriel had already opened it, and from the frustration woven through the paper, it felt as if he'd tried for a while to decipher the words. Why hadn't he asked Uriel?

"Raphael, to Gabriel," Michael read. "I'm sorry I lost control before, and I hope I didn't hurt you with the fire. Uriel had warned me, but now I see I'm not safe to be around you right now, and I guess I owe you another apology. It seems like every time I try to help it's a disaster for you."

He glanced up to see Gabriel frowning. "Don't look at me. I'm just as confused as you are." He returned to the letter. "I'm going to stay away until you're healed up fully. I'm sorry, and I hope you're not angry with me. Always in God's service, Raphael."

Gabriel folded his arms.

Michael said, "The only thing I can think of is that he'd absorbed your heartstring, and we didn't realize. Maybe that's the other apology he thinks he owes you." But then Michael remembered Raphael defeated, giving Gabriel permission to leave them, and he wondered if there weren't something more.

He handed Gabriel back the letter, which Gabriel kept on his lap.

Michael set up the chess board while Gabriel finished the risotto. Gabriel opened with the king's pawn, which Michael responded to with a classical defense. They played in silence, Michael trying not to probe into Gabriel's thoughts because he didn't think it fair to uncover his strategy, but all the same, he realized quickly that Gabriel wasn't at top form. When two moves in a row were surprisingly short-sighted, Michael wondered how good an idea chess had been in the first place. Finally, after ten moves, Gabriel closed his eyes: he couldn't keep track.

Michael puzzled at him.

He received a disconnected series of images. Gabriel couldn't visualize the board.

Michael sat back. "You mean I might actually be able to beat you?"

Gabriel laughed silently.

"See, God brings good from all things." Michael chuckled. "We can put it away."

Before he could clear off the board, he felt Gabriel put a hand on his hand, and a nonverbal negation. He wanted to try again, but he'd need Michael to tell him where all the pieces moved. Michael reconstructed the game in algebraic notation and recited it back to Gabriel, who winced about five moves in: he'd left a bishop hanging.

"You want to try it from that point?" Michael reset the board to the fifth move. "Go again."

Gabriel looked back at the board, frustration swirling about him.

Michael swept one wing between Gabriel and the board. "Don't look at it. Just move."

Gabriel blinked at him.

"You've got the board in your mind. Don't try to make it fit the board you see."

A high-pitched tension streamed from Gabriel, followed by paralysis. Michael wanted to tell him it was all right, that he'd take away the game, but then Gabriel sat up suddenly. He had the perfect move...and no way to convey the information. When he looked back at the board, he got lost again.

"Hey," Michael said, "we'll find a workaround. We've gotten this far."

Gabriel's eyes had gone from silver-grey to the olive of a thunderhead. Workarounds: if he couldn't move, couldn't read, couldn't play chess, couldn't play music, couldn't talk, what good was he?

"You'll keep improving," Michael said.

Gabriel's eyes flashed, leaving one word in Michael's mind: *Now*.

"You're a lousy patient."

Gabriel huffed.

Michael tilted his head. "You really can't play music?"

Gabriel shrugged. If he already knew the song, he could.

Michael frowned. "Can you still learn new music?"

Probably, but he couldn't extemporize.

"Yeah, but Gabriel, you were nearly dead yesterday!" Michael sat back. "Cut yourself some slack for once."

Gabriel sent him an accusing look.

"No, I don't know if I would do the same, but I may never find out, so let's assume I wouldn't be as tough on myself as you are." He opened his hands on his lap. "Let's pray about it. I know you can still do that."

Gabriel's mouth softened, and they did.

Beelzebub was disciplining an arrant underling while singing a lewd version of "Amazing Grace" when Lucifer summoned him. He dropped—of course—everything to respond as he had no choice, and arrived inside Lucifer's office in the pitch black. He found a stool and sat waiting.

After a time, Lucifer said, "Have you experienced any side effects since the annihilation?"

"No, sir. Nothing other than the normal strain of having defended my Guard against the Archangel's full power."

Even though blind, Beelzebub blistered under the scalding glare Lucifer awarded his self-aggrandizement.

"Nothing else?"

"No, sir."

Beelzebub practically glowed with a realization: Lucifer had been weakened after disassembling Gabriel! Lucifer, weakened—and possibly defeatable!

"Don't even think it," Lucifer said. "I'll fight you. We'll see how I do."

"Yes, sir."

Lucifer's resonance bounced back from the walls with a psychic scent Beelzebub would have recognized anywhere in Creation. This signature sparkled with its own beauty, a lively thing always extending itself, curling its light letters into everything it met and absorbing it into the whole.

"Now," Lucifer said, "tell me about Mephistopheles."

"Mephistopheles?"

Silence.

"He—yes, I wondered if he's had some reaction to it."

More silence.

Beelzebub swallowed, but the silence continued, and finally he said, "It's frustrating. You know how he normally is. But since Gabriel died, he springs unworkable ideas at me, and then either he forgets them or else he prattles nonstop until I have to tell him to shut up."

This Lucifer acknowledged.

"He's gotten morose. He dampens everyone's energy. He isn't around anymore. If I want him, I have to go find him, and then he'll only say something dismal and retreat back into himself."

Lucifer moved in the room, but Beelzebub had no idea where. "When he goes into himself, what is he thinking about?"

Beelzebub closed his mouth.

Still more silence.

No, no. This was all wrong. He would not answer. Not acknowledge.

Silence.

No answer.

More silence.

Beelzebub said, "Gabriel."

"All the time?"

He nodded, and the gesture carried. "And sometimes Raphael too."

"Do you know he went to Heaven specifically to speak to Raphael?"

The fire in Beelzebub's heart flared.

"Ah, you didn't. I'd hoped you might explain."

"I'll kill him!"

"Are you afraid?" Lucifer said, suddenly so close that Beelzebub could perceive his glow. With their faces inches apart, Lucifer's green eyes made his stomach hurt. "Any punishment would be visited on him, not on you. Or were you afraid of what he might have done with Raphael?"

Beelzebub turned his head and spit into the darkness.

"As long as it doesn't bother you," Lucifer said with a hint of amusement. "He was right there within two hours after we finished, possibly directly from the debriefing. Michael turned him back at the gate. Did Gabriel ask him to courier a message?"

Beelzebub said nothing.

Silence.

Lucifer faded off into the dark again. More silence.

"I'm not aware of a message."

Lucifer sighed. "I suspect he's shocked. I've seen this before, monkeys who take a while to get past their first kill. If they come to terms with death, they often go on to become excellent soldiers, but some find the first one tough."

"If we get through two or three more—"

"But he's stuck, and until he devises a better method, there won't be another."

Lucifer, weakened.

No, not to think it.

"Don't," Lucifer said. "By the way, are you aware he asked Asmodeus for a favor?"

Heat surged in Beelzebub's throat, and his eyes narrowed.

"Why didn't he ask you to find Camael?"

Camael was missing? Beelzebub's fists clenched so hard he might have been bleeding. "I— I'm not sure."

"Don't be too hard on him," Lucifer said. "He's not himself. I'm sure he's not deserting you for a new alliance."

Pounding heartbeats. Fire inside. Mephistopheles.

Lucifer's voice sounded very matter-of-fact. "You need to enliven him."

"How?"

"You're a Seraph. Use that ridiculous bond of yours—isn't that the reason you have it? He can calm you when you get irrational and you can invigorate his depressed soul. I'm relatively sure you can still do it."

Beelzebub's hands shook in his lap. His throat burned.

"And if that isn't enough, do whatever you have to. Use your *imagination,* how does that sound?"

"That sounds—" Beelzebub's wings were vibrating, and at his side his sword had grown hot. "I'll take care of him, sir."

"I'm glad you feel that way. If you run out of ideas, you could come back to me for a few more, but I don't recommend that you do."

Like an inferno, his heart crackled. "No, sir."

"You may go," Lucifer said, and Beelzebub flashed from the room before the sound had a chance to travel from one end to the other. Like a heat-seeking missile, he had his target.

Eighteen

Remiel lay on her stomach in an Earthly field, sketching in charcoal. The black pencil swept over the rough paper, framing out the young mountains in their sleepiness against the sky. Already she'd rendered the craggy hills gouged out by the rains while being shoved upward by the plates beneath. She began outlining boulders and brush when Saraquael arrived.

"That's striking."

Remiel didn't answer.

Saraquael touched the captive bead ring in her helix. "Michael had told me you'd be staying solid for a while, so you could go back and get a rook to capture a pawn."

Remiel chuckled. "Something. I changed my mind."

"You still can. I'll blind him to how healed-up you are."

She closed her eyes. "Thanks."

"It's no problem."

"Uriel threw me out of Gabriel's room."

Saraquael shrugged. "Uriel won't let me in either."

Remiel continued sketching. "It's maddening. Gabriel looked okay."

As a shudder ripped through Saraquael, Remiel looked up in panic: had Gabriel seemed that bad before? And when Saraquael averted his eyes, it was Remiel's turn to shudder.

"But it'll be okay now," Remiel said. "I didn't kill him."

"It wouldn't have been your fault regardless." Saraquael touched her hair with a wingtip. "He was asking after you. He's concerned that you went down there to get him."

Remiel's eyes stung. She rubbed them with the back of one hand so she didn't get charcoal on her cheeks. "Tell him to take care of himself before he bothers about me."

"Will do. But third-hand. I can tell Michael, who tells Uriel, who tells him."

Remiel's wings lifted a little. "It's ridiculous, isn't it? I wouldn't hurt him."

"I think that's the point," Saraquael stood. "We might hurt him without meaning to. Even Raphael isn't allowed in there any longer."

Remiel shook her head. "You'd think he'd be the one best able to fix it if he did harm him."

"You would," Saraquael said, and vanished. Remiel finished her sketch.

She rubbed the charcoal dust on her hand. "He asked about me."

He loves you, God replied.

"Maybe he was upset by the way he saw me. I'd probably have been upset if I saw myself that way too." She cut herself short, still trying to rub off the black dust on her hands.

Come to me.

She scoured at her hand, then grabbed a fistful of dew-covered grass and rubbed with that, only smearing the black.

"God, it won't come off," she whispered. "What's the matter with me?"

Black-stained fingers. Hands inserted into Gabriel's heart. *Come to me.* I'd hate seeing me like that too.

Shaky, she tried to wipe the tears away, but the charcoal smeared on her cheeks.

Her wings spread as if for battle. *Come.*

"Ridiculous," she said, her voice high-pitched. "It's just charcoal. It's nothing else. Just my hands."

She flashed to a stream and plunged in her hands, watching the black swirl away in the white froth. She dunked in her face, smearing away the coal dust and the tear tracks, stinging her pierced ears. She kept scooping up water and startling herself with the chill.

Come to me. Always that nugget of doubt. A good thing or a bad thing. *Come to me.* Not even Camael was that twisted. Mine. Mine.

Remiel plunged her whole head under the water, wrapping her fingers in her hair and letting the water flood her ears, her mouth. She kept her eyes closed, then wrenched herself out of the water, kneeling on the stream bed with liquid chill coursing between her wings. Her hands were clean.

Sweeping the field with one long glance, she found it different, saw a field from a young Earth when the Lord had separated the light from the darkness. Her eyes dilated with the watching.

A rocking explosion threw her to the ground and unleashed holy light on all Creation—offended light. Remiel—Irin—shook for a moment before she raised her upper body to look around.

Hundreds of her species, bleeding, tired, shocked, scared, horrified by Lucifer's denial of the divine sovereignty and his refusal to worship the Word.

"Father?" She quivered as she had that day. "Father, what's going on?"

They'd fought hard, the angels that had rallied around the one minor Archangel with the broken sword who'd had the courage to prefer to pain to apostasy, but then God had intervened directly.

Irin watched Lucifer with the light flushed from his spirit; she watched Michael, uncertain but driven by justice to answer the angels' need for a leader. Irin struggled to her feet, gasping, and lifted her sword, watching the field for her brother Irin. She called to him, and then he met her eyes.

But he was not Irin.

Fear petrified her heart as she met this avatar, a reflection with a dark twist, and groped with her senses to find God, to know if she were the one who had failed Him. She probed to find that twist inside herself, terrified but determined to learn. She locked eyes with the other Irin, longing to meet him, wanting him to join her, needing him to be complete. He grinned, pleased with his independence, gesturing that she should come with him now. She loved her brother so much that she almost did.

But she loved her Father more. She needed Him more. He called her Shêli, "my own."

But her brother was herself, and if his destiny lay in Hell, then so must hers.

No sound or movement remained in Irin, whose whole person trained on the other Irin while the bustle of angels recovering from God's strike roared around her. She watched, because Irin means Watcher, and he watched her in return.

"I loved you," said Irin. "Come and be mine."

"I love God," said Irin. "Stay and be His."

She ran to him, clutching him tightly and clenching her eyes. His pulse raced beneath her ear, and she heard in it the echoes of her own, but in a rhythm that rapidly differentiated.

"Please," she said, wrapping her fingers in his wings. "Please, you're me. Don't leave me. Stay with God for me."

"We've chosen."

"I'll go in your place," said Irin. "If one of us has to satisfy Justice, then let it be me. I'll do it for you." She wrapped herself against him, her hair so much longer and blonder than it would be in the future when she chopped it short and shot her body full of holes. "I'll burn for you if you want it, but I can't leave you alone forever."

Irin had locked his eyes with hers, holding her with his will as if he could damn her despite herself, and Irin clutched her brother's arms with the equally futile urge to fasten him to God's heart even though he was rebelling. In that moment she knew: no force, no argument, no tears could keep him. He could return her every appeal simply because if it had occurred to her then it had occurred to him simultaneously. She knew she was right, and she also knew that he knew he was right. Weakened, she dropped to her knees, but he had done the same, and they hugged, she knowing every moment with more certainty that never again in all time would she hold him against her heart.

The twins let go at the same moment and fled to their lords, she to her Father and he to his master.

She saw herself drop like molten rock from Heaven, Satan plummeting in a lightning streak at the forefront of the fallen.

She doubled over.

Piercing the silence were screams, her own, only her own.

Hands on her back, touching her wings, her arms, concerned and strong, whichever angels stood closest. "It's one of the Irin." "One of them fell." "Which one?" "I don't know—they're the same."

"Which one?" Irin asked, the words swallowed in her own incomprehensible sobs. "Was it me? Did I fail?"

From the smell of orchids in the wings nearest her, she realized Uriel rocked her gently. Tenderly despite the Throne's own tears, Uriel comforted her. And Uriel loved God.

"Remiel," God had named her, "come to me."

The Irin standing in a field populated by figments only she could see raised her head and looked into a Vision unchanged since that day. She watched the Vision until she decided she must not be the one who fell. She remained Remiel.

Remiel, come to me, rang through her head.

Remiel didn't register that the battle scene faded to leave her alone in a field with a ruined sketch. She stared, stiff-legged, into the glory of the sun, her wings straight back. Her gold eyes reflected the distant leaping flames, and she grinned broadly.

"I can touch heartstrings too," she whispered to her fiery reflection.

Come to me.

Oh, I'm coming for you.

She passed through the Guards with no difficulty at all; she imagined no Guard would ever hold her again. "Gabriel," she called, her voice more serpentine than angelic, "Gabriel, come watch."

She shook the water from her hair, then finished materializing in a room with a very startled Camael.

Gabriel awoke to Remiel's voice, and he felt the added resonance he shouldn't have of an angel immediately post-winnowing, raw and wild. She wasn't sane—the fact that her voice had penetrated the Guard would have told him that anyhow. She knew how to annihilate, and her brother was trapped.

Gabriel realized in shock—he was alone. Alone in a Guarded room. He couldn't call for help.

He reached for God, wordlessly begging for strength.

Gabriel pushed himself upright, endured a momentary panic, then held the wall for support.

Remiel had her fingers in his heart, trying to drag him out of the room. Gabriel released himself and felt her grip him, hoping her insanity would enable her to pull a sane angel through a Guard the same way she could force herself.

Look at me, God said, and Gabriel changed his focus to the Vision.

He felt himself change again, a different place. Where was he? No—God—he could see God so it was all right. He was somewhere. He was...here. Windows. A simple room. Cold. It was frigid.

Remiel had Camael pinned to the wall, her will binding his hands and feet, her blade at his throat. She didn't even turn to Gabriel once she had him inside.

Camael struggled, and Remiel said, "I was in the room when Satan destroyed a friend of mine, and I learned. I'm as smart as you are, Watcher."

Gabriel leaped for her, knocking her a step away from Camael, but she spread her wings and kept her balance even as Gabriel utterly lost track of where he was. He collected himself in time to see her eyes showering with sparks. Grabbing her sword blade with one hand and the hilt with the other, she blasted her power at Gabriel. "Just watch! I'm doing this for both of us!"

Gabriel hit the far wall and crumpled.

"Stop her!" Camael was screaming.

Gabriel tried to call for Michael and couldn't make the words form.

He pushed back to his feet, keeping in mind what he needed to do without caring where he was, then sent as much protest to Remiel as he could. In that moment, both Irin looked right at him.

Camael went white. He tried to recoil into the wall.

Remiel said, "I'm ending it now," and she unleashed all her fury at Camael.

Gabriel mustered whatever power he could and blasted Remiel, who deflected it with one hand. She had so much energy that she didn't even bother taking her eyes off Camael as she did it. Then, as Gabriel watched, she reached into Camael's heart and pulled. The room rattled. Camael's spine arched, and he screamed.

Unable to rise from the floor, Gabriel erupted with protest.

Jesus appeared on the other side of her and said, "Remiel, stop!"

She dropped where she stood, and Jesus caught her over one arm.

Camael was breathing heavily, head slung down, but glaring at him all the same. Jesus glared back at him, and in another moment Camael too had crumpled.

Jesus turned to Gabriel, who hadn't risen from the corner. "Rapha'li," he called, "to me."

Raphael appeared, took in the whole scene, and rushed to Gabriel, the healing glow already marshaled. He flooded the Cherub, who flinched at the touch. "Michael! Uriel! I need you immediately!" He turned to Jesus. "Lower the Guard so I can get them inside!"

Gabriel raised his arms to anchor himself against Raphael.

"What's going on?" Raphael was shouting at Jesus. "What is he doing here? I can tell she was throwing power like crazy a minute ago!"

Michael and Uriel were there then, and Gabriel felt Uriel trying to lift him away from Raphael. He tightened his grip, but Michael disentangled him. Gabriel kept his eyes tightly closed, only listening.

"Rapha'li, take care of him."

"And what about her? She's utterly spattered with parts of him!"

Seraphic fire, all those sweet Seraph vibrations. Gabriel opened—

"Gabriel, no!"

Suddenly all the Seraph fire was gone, leaving Gabriel grasping for nothing.

"Thank you." That was Uriel's voice.

"Not a problem." Jesus's voice. "Rapha'li, you help him. Trust me to take care of her."

A lurching, and Gabriel felt himself moved, but the room still felt the same, felt freezing. Don't look. Where was he? Raphael... Remiel...

"How much damage did she do?"

"I can't tell. He's not sounding out." Raphael's touch suffused him. "He's out of tune inside, and he's hemorrhaging energy. The healing won't stick."

Gabriel tried to reach for him, lost track of where he was in the world, and desperately sought for the Vision.

God remained. God was strong.

More words, now just sounds and vague impressions of concern, and Gabriel drifted away. Why were they so sad and scared? He was with them, so he must be safe. They were strong. God was strong. He ought to help them with whatever it was, but so dark, so warm, so easy to let go and let the tides carry him.

Thoughts like a spotlight forced into his mind, riveting him. "Stay with us," a voice said, and another, "Think—you've got to focus," and a third, "You're going to have to do it again."

Gabriel tried to block the light, tried to retreat from the sound.

A fourth voice, the one Gabriel loved, said, "Stay with them, Gabri'li." Then, "Reach for me."

Gabriel marshaled all himself and extended himself, and in that moment torn by the tides and enshrouded in fog, he felt prayers and wills locking him in place. "We don't have a choice," said one of them—Uriel. "I have to go back in right now."

Nineteen

Mephistopheles had two minor demons chained side by side as he compared them in a feasibility study for the manufacture of a chimera. He kept all his notes in his head, as usual, where no prying eyes or backstabbing competition could snitch a peek, and he gathered information. Bits and bits and bits of disconnected information.

Gabriel.

He remembered talking with him in the cell, waiting for Lucifer to come and destroy, discussing what really happened when a soul came apart and one moment became the final moment. Mephistopheles recalled the rapid exchange of theories, their questions and the answers they'd provided one another. Gabriel's eyes had sparkled like silver when he'd learned how God had manufactured him.

Gabriel's glow had pierced the lab area.

He remembered that burst of understanding in Gabriel's eyes, the one Cherub in all creation who might have rivaled his intellect. The moment of comprehension, the unreachable *theory* of how to form a new angel or destroy an old one, it had been their shared victory over ignorance, and he ought to have smiled because he had made that singular moment possible. But then he knew what else he'd made possible, and the realization penetrated him like a rapier.

Fire formed behind him, and Mephistopheles aroused himself enough to recognize Beelzebub's arrival. Without turning from the pair of minor demons, Mephistopheles allowed his soul to siphon off part of his fire and in return offer back a sense of Cherubic stillness.

"How dare you?" Beelzebub said.

Mephistopheles spun to face him.

Beelzebub burned. His eyes were in flames, and his wings vibrated, and his mouth had formed a tight line.

Mephistopheles steeled himself. "What are you doing?"

Beelzebub was in such a state that he threw off heat. "What are *you* doing?"

Mephistopheles gestured at the pair. "I have a theory—"

"You think too often." Beelzebub stepped closer. "And what benefit has it gotten you?"

Fighting the urge to back toward the minor demons, Mephistopheles tried again to siphon off the fire. There was so much that it hurt. Beelzebub wasn't just enflamed—he was enflamed at him. There was too much power. Something had fueled this fire.

Asmodeus? Belior? Lucifer?

Beelzebub's power surged beyond anything Mephistopheles had witnessed since the crucifixion. Powered like this he might be a match for Lucifer himself, only he stood here instead. That meant—

"Stop thinking!" Beelzebub's eyes glowed white in the center, and he lunged for Mephistopheles, grabbed his arms to his sides with a grip like two train couplings slamming together. "You're always doing this, running off into your own head and treating me like something to leave behind as fast as possible!"

"What are you talking about? Let go! I'm not fighting you!" Mephistopheles twisted, and then fell as Beelzebub released him. He couldn't take down this fire. It would be like quelling the sun with a garden hose. "What's gotten to you?"

"Why must it be something getting to me, as if you're the only one who ever knows what's going on?" Beelzebub's wings were spread fully from his side, and he took up so much of the world. "Maybe I can finally see what's going on, and you're not the only one with any brains."

"What are you talking about?" Mephistopheles took a step toward him. His face was right near Beelzebub's, and he made his eyes piercing, not flinching even though it hurt to stare into that white glow. "It's not that you're not rational, it's that you haven't given me a reason why you're so angry."

"Did the annihilation weaken you?"

Mephistopheles raised one hand to his neck. "No—"

Beelzebub caught his hand between them. "Then what's going on in your head? You're sullen, you're disturbed, you're ineffective—"

Mephistopheles yanked back his hand. "Do you care?"

"Absolutely I care! People are talking, people are laughing at me, and I don't have to tell you the politics if you're weakened."

Of course if that was the case, having this discussion in front of two low-class loudmouths wasn't going to help matters.

Mephistopheles flashed them away. "This isn't about politics."

Beelzebub's cape rippled in his own heat. "Then why don't you tell me what it's about? I just got called into our lord's chamber and got humiliated and lambasted because of *you!*"

Mephistopheles radiated surprise.

"You're asking Asmodeus for favors? You're not working on the task Lucifer set you? You're going to the gates of Heaven and begging for Raphael to come out so you can apologize?"

"I didn't— Beelzebub, that's not true!"

Although it burned his heart, Mephistopheles tried again to pull the power. It charged him, but now he shook. And despite that, there was still a volcano mid-eruption in front of him.

"Don't you dare." Coming closer still, Beelzebub's voice deepened to a growl. "I'm not good enough for you until you need it, and the instant I see what you're really like, you try to reach inside and work that magic to put me on your leash."

Mephistopheles gulped. There was nothing to do. He couldn't handle Beelzebub this way. With time, maybe. He needed someone else to help him take down that power—but there was no one. Lucifer wouldn't. No one else could. He could run for Heaven's gates, knowing they'd shelter him at least long enough to let Beelzebub calm himself—hell, he'd shelter one of the enemy if it gave him a crack at winning them over—

Beelzebub backhanded him, and Mephistopheles went down on his knees. "Quit thinking! I'm right here in front of you! Look at me!"

Was this the fear Gabriel had felt in those last moments? Was this the same agony, knowing he'd never see his Seraph again?

"I said quit thinking!" Beelzebub kicked him in the head, and Mephistopheles rolled with the blow back onto hands and knees, then leaped into the air and flashed away. He had no destination—he just ran, and at his heels he felt the Seraph, the black flames, the acid power.

Beelzebub nabbed him, tackled him, flashed him into the floor of a cavernous room in the labs. His anger's glow shattered the darkness, painting him red, casting shadows. Mephistopheles rolled sideways to regain his feet, but then Beelzebub was down on top of him, pinning his hands back, hips to hips, legs tangled in his. Mephistopheles fought, but a Guard sealed the room, and he couldn't struggle free. Beelzebub leaned forward, wings curved like a canopy over them both.

"You wouldn't take my power for days." Beelzebub's face was close enough to breathe into Mephistopheles' mouth. Their eyes were inches apart. "You resisted me long enough, and now you want to make nice, you worthless parasite? Well take it then, take all of it!"

Mephistopheles' eyes flew wide. "Please—!"

"I own you." Beelzebub arched his back. "From now on, you look only at me!"

Then he forced himself inside, a spear of Seraphic fire solid with fury. Mephistopheles tried to clamp his heart closed, tried to deaden their bond, but Beelzebub's power surged like water through a fire hose, opening all the kinks, flooding him, ramming itself inside no matter what he did. Mephistopheles screamed, screamed, begged, no let this stop, please it's too much, please I'll do anything, I can't—

Beelzebub's form tensed over him like a volcanic eruption, power searing from him into the Cherub, too much power, hot energy broiling the air. Mephistopheles yelled, unable to escape as Beelzebub shot him full of fire. The Seraph's eyes drilled into his, and like debris in a flood, everything in Mephistopheles churned to the surface: all his memories, all this thoughts, his theories, his desires, his guilt, his everything. And as it churned back up into Beelzebub, the Seraph laughed at it, mocked the things he couldn't understand, jeered at every pain and the little moments as he shed light on every privacy and every single dark little thing that had wanted to remain in darkness.

"Scream all you want," Beelzebub hissed into his face. "No one cares. Lucifer doesn't care. Asmodeus doesn't care. Even God doesn't care."

Mephistopheles went limp beneath him.

At some point he realized the pain had abated. He didn't know for how long. He was lying in the dark, a spent Seraph and himself on the rough rock.

Beelzebub climbed away from him and crumpled to the ground. Mephistopheles curled on his side, his knees to his chest, his forearms guarding his face, one wing up over his head. He might have been there a thousand years. It might have been seconds.

"Don't make me do that again." Beelzebub's voice sounded quiet, so quiet in comparison to the screaming fire. Where was he? "I hate that you made me do that."

He kicked the wing to uncover Mephistopheles' head. It didn't hurt. How could it not hurt? How could anything hurt ever again?

For a moment he wondered if Beelzebub had come closer and extended his hand, and he tensed rock solid. But all Beelzebub said was, "Whatever you've done, I won't bring it up again."

With him so close and so spent, Mephistopheles could rip out Beelzebub's heartstrings now and be rid of him forever. But he didn't.

Then the Guard was down and the Seraph gone, and only the Cherub remained.

Warmth.

Hands. Softness. Sadness. Worry.

It's okay. I think it's okay.

Why do I think it's okay?

I don't know.

Worry. Not my worry.

Father?

Gabri'li, Gabriel-mine, stay with them.

I don't know.

You're hurt. Stay with them, Gabri'li.

"Gabriel." Firm voice. Worried. Uriel. "I'm going in. Stay focused."

Gabriel tried to grasp the fog around him, groped for a landmark, wished for a handhold amid the swirl. Tides drifted him sideways, rocked him. Sleep.

Then confusion, fear, tension. Gabriel flexed his spine, wings snapping open.

Crashing sounds, an outcry. The tension ended. Michael's voice: "Clear the room! Everything out!"

A moment later the ground beneath him felt harder, the room emptier, the sounds more echoing. Back to the fog.

"Gabriel," came Uriel's voice again. "Hold still. I'm reaching in."

Again panic, tension, twisting. Tumult around him, and then it eased off.

"Raphael, hold him!"

"I can't! It's reflex."

"He's got to be still."

"I'll get into his mind," Raphael said. "Then you can go in again."

A moment later, the fog thinned, and Gabriel had the peculiar feeling of being two places at once, one in the fog, one above himself in the cell where Remiel had attacked Camael, only all the furnishings and contents and even Camael himself had gone. Looking through Raphael's eyes, he saw himself in his own lap—except it was Raphael's lap. Scary to see oneself so faint, as if an errant wind could snuff out the spark. Michael looked on a razor's edge of strain, and Uriel wore lines of tension.

You have to stay still, Raphael told him.

Gabriel agreed. He watched as Raphael knotted his hands around his own, feeling the double-touch from both sides as if he were touching his own hand. "Let's go."

But as soon as Uriel went inside, Gabriel felt the tension, the pressure, the urge to *run away—fight them—where am I?* and he flexed right out of Raphael's grasp.

Uriel pulled back again, and this time no calm remained in the Throne's eyes. "I can't do anything if he doesn't stay still!"

Michael moved closer. "I'll Guard him down to the floor."

"No, you will not," Raphael said.

"Uriel needs him still. He's thrashing."

"He can't help it." Raphael crossed his arms over Gabriel's chest. "When you touch the string, it triggers a reflex, and he moves, and then he doesn't know where he is, and he gets frightened. It also doesn't feel all that pleasant."

Gabriel realized he'd sent some of that through Raphael. The Seraph continued, "So I'm not going to let you Guard him down. It's too much like what they did."

Uriel said, "I need him in one place."

"Give me another chance," said Raphael.

"And if that doesn't work," Michael said, but Raphael interrupted, "Then you'll give me another one after that."

Gabriel felt Raphael concentrate, and the Seraph's spirit slipped away. He tried to cry out for him, but then he tumbled into the fog, grasping at a world insubstantial as clouds. He called for God.

You're not alone.

Gabriel tried to curl around himself in the mist, but even then he felt himself drifting apart.

A light shone; next two lights. He concentrated on those. Hearing, "Hold onto me," Gabriel trained on the voice, focused on the amber light and in that moment recognized Raphael come to him, face to face, battling the same currents only without drifting. Here was solidity. Gabriel extended his heart for an anchor.

"We're together," Raphael said. "We're going to do this together."

Gabriel relaxed, less afraid of his own body as long as Raphael stayed near.

"You need to stay still." Raphael's heart nestled around his. "Completely still. You need to relax so Uriel can tighten your heartstrings. It may hurt, but we're going to do this together."

Gabriel looked into the amber and resolved to stay still.

"Now," Raphael whispered.

Every part of Gabriel felt like fire, but he trained himself on the amber. "Perfect," Raphael was saying. "Just like that. You're doing great. Now relax. Relax just a bit."

Relax? But the dread, the tension, every moment unbearable, foreboding; he was unworthy, small, ignorant. He grieved for things lost and despaired of things found. He couldn't do this—

"You can do this," Raphael said. "Rely on me."

Stay with the amber. Relax.

"You're doing great."

This was great? This was awful. This was frightening. This was too big a task—

"This is you and me," Raphael said. "It's just the right size for us. You can do it."

A moment later, information flooded him: it wasn't just the damage done by Remiel's power; Uriel had found some parts misplaced. Uriel was going to have to unlace him pretty far down to move things back where they belonged. The tension Gabriel felt—all the negative emotions, the chill—were the byproduct of the parts of himself scraping against one another in a bad fit.

His whole personality began vibrating as if it were a Seraph's, and he felt Uriel unhooking and unlacing the parts of him he'd worked so hard to keep together. His vision plunged to blackness, and he let out a cry, but he felt hands, felt love. Raphael was with him, and God was always with Raphael, so God must be here in the horror too. Tension shrieked through him and fright wrapped him round, but Raphael streamed with constant approval.

Gabriel trembled but held.

"You're doing great," Raphael said.

More information: Uriel would now move the parts that were misplaced before. Then everything needed to be re-threaded, and they'd be done.

"Steady," Raphael said.

Steady. Hold steady. amber vision

darkness	shêli	hold	stay
God	still	hay fight	Mephistopheles
cookies	fire	chains	checkmate
Raphael	fire	love	Father
almost done		stay focused	I love you

"You're doing so well," Raphael was saying.

Father?

I'm proud of you, Gabri'li.

Gabriel reached forward with his heart, found Raphael and clung to him. "Just a little longer," Raphael said. "Uriel is lacing you back up again."

Why didn't it get easier to hold still the longer he did it? If anything, it got harder. He could feel Uriel's touch against his soul, the pressure of being shaped and focused, the random memories that popped into his mind and even more random emotions that had nothing to do with the thoughts. One moment he saw images of flowers and ached for the fallen, and in the next fury at Remiel while he remembered the building of the Brooklyn Bridge, then a meticulous analysis of a minor point of law, and a moment after that unbridled joy as if transported by music.

Physical sensations crowded him: pain in his jaw, in his neck. His stomach tightened. A tension in his throat made him long to throw back his head, but then there was Raphael, urging him to keep still, almost done. The black heightened to grey, and again he could see Raphael's eyes in the dark, and a moment after could feel their hands joined, and then as if breaking the surface of the world Gabriel gasped, and Uriel said, "One more—" and Raphael said "Just another minute—" and Gabriel could hear them with his ears rather than his heart. Next he could see Raphael's face. Raphael was breathing with him, gazes locked, their bodies in a rhythm while Uriel continued to manipulate the ties inside.

A surge of triumph. Uriel pulled back and became solid. Raphael coalesced from his spiritual form and reappeared sitting in front of Gabriel. Michael in the corner moved in closer.

Gabriel looked around at them and swallowed. He whispered, "Thank you."

Twenty

Jesus returned to Mary's kitchen. "Remiel's about to awaken."

Mary pulled a batch of cookies from the oven, an anachronism in a house otherwise replicating the Nazareth one where she and Joseph had raised Jesus. "She didn't move the whole time you were gone."

Mary spatulaed the cookies onto a cooling rack and then handed two to Jesus. He grinned. "Thanks, Mom."

Joseph came from the outside holding a wooden box, and he and Jesus spent a couple of minutes looking over the recessed hinges and admiring how smoothly the wood passed against itself. "The grain on this is incredible." Joseph ran a finger over it. "I'll be back in the shop getting it stained if you want to come look at the rest of the wood."

"And I'll be back in a bit." Mary kissed Jesus on the cheek. "You take good care of Remiel."

"No worries." Jesus snitched an extra cookie from the rack. "Thanks for staying with her. She'd have known if she were alone."

Jesus went into the back room, like his own, and sat beside the mattress where he'd laid Remiel a couple of hours ago. When he touched her head, she blinked unsteadily.

"What am I doing here?" She sought out Jesus. "What did I do?"

Jesus took her hand. "Why do you assume you did something?"

"Because my whole heart feels embarrassed, and I'm blank on a chunk of time." She recoiled a bit. "What did I do?"

Her hands clenched his, and her eyes glistened.

He didn't look away. "You tried to annihilate your twin."

Gasping, she pulled back her hands, covering her face. "I'm sorry! I'm so sorry!" She huddled over herself and brought her wings between herself and Jesus. He stroked the outermost feathers, but she pulled tighter. "Don't touch me. I'm wretched."

"You were in pain."

"Everyone's in pain."

He laid an arm over whatever of her she would allow him to grasp, and when she recoiled from even that much contact, he murmured to her, "Be still. I'm not leaving you."

"Did I realize how wrong it was?" She clutched at the skin of her arms. "I don't remember anything."

"I'm keeping the memory from you. Do you want it?"

She shuddered.

Jesus understood. "I do have one request, though."

She looked up, eyes molten gold. "Anything."

He waited a moment. "I want you to surrender to me the knowledge of how to unmake souls."

Remiel's gaze dropped. "So I can't try again."

"I want that information reserved to me. Uriel is going to render it back once Gabriel is fully mended, and now I'm going to ask you to return it too."

"Take it," she said, and although she felt no different, she knew that she no longer would be able to insert her fingers into the heartstrings of a being and release them from the hooks and eyelets. She chose not to probe the space, like the gap left by a baby tooth. "Please forgive me."

"There isn't any sin in you, Remiel'shêli." Jesus stroked her hair. "Your soul is as clean as I created it, only scarred."

"Couldn't you remove that too?" Remiel said. "Could you make me not just the sole remaining Watcher?"

Jesus folded his arms. "You don't want to be yourself?"

"Why would I?" Remiel's mouth twitched as she stared at her hands. "I'm kind of like the heel of the meatloaf that Satan didn't want to finish."

"You're hardly *just* the leftovers!" Jesus shook his head. "He worked hard to get you, and I know every sacrifice you made to stay true." He touched her chin and coaxed her to raise her eyes. "You're Remiel, one of the Seven. Your twin, no matter what he does, can't equal that. You're my own, and he denied me that. You're courageous and wild and amazing. Not moldy meatloaf." He sat back. "What more do you want?"

Remiel's mouth was quivering. "I want my brother."

They both stayed silent until Jesus said, "Only he could have given you that."

"I'm sorry. I know that's not fair to you." Remiel swallowed. "I love you. That should be everything I want. You're everything I need. I should let go of his memory."

"The Irin were meant to stay one unit." Jesus shifted to sit nearer. "The pain is natural."

"It's restlessness. It's longing." Remiel shook her head. "I'm half an angel."

"Half of two."

"Don't tell Gabriel, but two divided by two is zero in my case." She rubbed her temples. "I wish Camael hadn't fallen."

"So do I." Jesus looked at his lap. "I wish they'd all stayed."

She squeezed his hand, and he looked into her eyes. For a long time, he and she regarded just one another, and then Remiel said, "Don't get mad at me for this, but—"

"I'm not mad."

"—but I'm terrified. Looking at him, I see myself abandoning you." She bit her lip as she stared at the wall. "That's too horrible to contemplate. How could I hate my God? I love you. But— He's calling me. He keeps calling me. I want to stay with you, but I had to pretend to be him, to think like him, and it was so easy to do it, as if it were natural for me to hate everyone."

He said, "You wanted to leave. You wanted nothing more."

Remiel snorted. "It was Hell. Anyone would want to leave."

"He doesn't."

She grimaced. "I guess not. But I did stay down there, and—"

"You didn't," Jesus said. "When it got to be too much, you fled in the only way you could."

Remiel rubbed her forehead. "I already lost him. I don't want to lose me too."

"But here you are," Jesus said with a smile, "so it worked."

"I nearly killed Camael!"

"I stopped you." He put his hand on her knee. "Trust me that I won't let you fall. I will never allow you to fall. You chose me, and as far as I'm concerned, you have chosen me for all time."

Remiel's expression didn't change.

"You are mine, and I will defend you." He nodded. "He cannot take you by force or by sin. You're safe."

Her eyes enlarged to full moons.

"As for the connection between the two of you, removing that would mean your ceasing to be yourself, and his ceasing to be himself."

Remiel's spine straightened. "But—"

He raised his palm. "What I *can* give you is the ability to recognize when influence is being exerted and to send communication in both directions."

"What good is that?" Then realization dawned. "Oh!"

He rubbed his hand over her hair. "The next time he sends you a suggestion, send him one in return. The war will end there."

She laughed out loud.

Jesus roughed her shoulder. "You're all right, Priceless One."

"Thank you." She looked suddenly cautious. "I have one more request, if I haven't already bothered you too much." When he nodded, she said, "I need to apologize to Gabriel for the way I behaved when I was Camael."

He nodded. She said, "I'd like—no, I need for you to come with me."

Jesus said, "He's not going to draw his sword on you, you know." He stood. "But yes, I'll go with you."

Gabriel shifted to sitting upright with no vertigo.

"He's sounding out." Excitement rang in Raphael's voice as he examined Gabriel. "A bit hollow, but the tone is right."

Michael and Uriel exchanged a relieved glance. Gabriel pivoted toward Raphael, but before he could make it there, the Seraph smothered him in a hug.

"I don't ever want to have to do that again." Raphael buried his head in Gabriel's shoulder. "From now on, you stay in one piece."

Smiling, Gabriel projected that he'd do his best.

He looked around the cinderblock room, oddly emptier than he remembered from when he'd arrived to stop Remiel. The only thing on the floor was broken glass—what looked like pounds of it. All the windows were shattered. "Did a bomb go off in here?"

"In a way." Michael leaned back, hands thrust behind him. "You have no idea how good it is to hear your voice."

Uriel sat, heels tucked beneath, hands folded. "What we've been calling the string is the same part that would have to be disengaged during an exorcism, and as we've now come to learn," the Throne added dryly, "throwing things around during one of those is actually a reflex action."

Gabriel started. Michael winced as he said, "I think you shattered every pane of glass in a fifteen-mile radius."

Gabriel turned pink. "I'm sorry about that."

"I'm just glad you weren't anywhere near full strength." Uriel looked aside. "There were a couple of times I thought the roof was coming down on our heads."

Raphael said, "I thought it was fun." When Gabriel glared at him, he added, "I don't often get to see you really unleash yourself."

"I didn't have a choice," Gabriel said, sounding mortified.

"It was rather impressive," Uriel said, "but we ought to get you back to my place and check you over thoroughly."

Raphael pulled Gabriel to a stand, and he staggered before Michael caught him but didn't experience vertigo. At least, not until they transported him back to Uriel's—when he utterly lost track of where he was, pushing back from Raphael before he realized whom he was with and where.

Raphael looked surprised, Uriel just grim.

The room was hot—stifling. Gabriel was about to ask if they could lower the temperature when Raphael started the process. Gabriel settled himself on the edge of the bed as gingerly as he could, and this time he didn't lose his sense of place. "At least I can talk."

Uriel summoned a black duffle bag and held it up. "Remember this? We're about to find out what else you can do."

So while Gabriel ate cookies, Uriel pulled out the 24-piece puzzle, and he solved it one-handed while Uriel set up the stacking shapes (Gabriel did these with a wave of his hand while finishing the puzzle.) He was able to read, add, multiply (here he lost patience and did calculus until Uriel pronounced him mathematically enabled) and speak any language they tested.

Raphael sparkled more as the tests went on and Gabriel was able to do all the things he hadn't before. "Give me a challenge," Gabriel said, so Uriel produced a three-dimensional five-thousand piece puzzle, all black on all sides, and Gabriel set about reassembling it during the remainder of the tests as the long rows of check boxes on the clip board got filled.

Michael said, "When you have a moment, I need to debrief you."

Raphael said, "You're going to take off his shorts?"

Gabriel burst out laughing.

"Sense of humor," Uriel said. "Check."

Michael brightened "You added that in?"

"He does so have a sense of humor!" Raphael exclaimed, even as Gabriel turned back to the puzzle he'd already half-completed.

Michael turned to Uriel. "Why couldn't he do all this before?"

"I messed up." Eyes averted, Uriel seemed to fade. "Right before Raphael forced me to take a break, I found myself faced with two identical pieces that looked like they might fit in one spot. I was exhausted, and I just picked one." Uriel's gaze turned to Gabriel. "I'm sorry. I caused a lot of problems by doing that."

Gabriel shrugged. "I imagine it was like assembling this puzzle in the dark. During a tornado."

Raphael said, "You forgot to add while the house is on fire."

"Point taken." Uriel's hands knit. "But the misplaced pieces interrupted your sensory integration."

"It wasn't all bad," Gabriel said, fitting the 3000th piece. "You gave Michael a chance to beat me at chess."

Michael crossed the room and beat Gabriel at chess again, rapping him on the head with the board while Raphael laughed out loud.

"All kidding aside," Michael said, "I need you to answer a few questions."

Uriel cleared away the duffle bag. Michael pulled his chair across the room, then sat, knees apart, leaning toward Gabriel. "Can you give me a recap of whatever you remember?"

Gabriel spread his hands to create a light prism the size of a shoe box. "As far as I can determine, this was where they held me."

Michael studied the landmarks on the three-dimensional map of Hell. "That correlates."

"This," and a second light appeared beside the one indicating his prison's location, "was Satan's private office."

Michael's eyes bugged. "Really!"

"I could feel it at my back. They'd anchored me with chains at my wrists and ankles, and the chains themselves were embedded in the Guard of his office."

Raphael hummed uneasily, but Gabriel looked only at Michael. "Once they started, it took maybe four minutes until I wasn't conscious of fighting any longer."

Michael frowned. "What about before they started?"

"I was unconscious when they brought me in. I awakened long enough to realize where I was, and then Beelzebub approached me." He glanced at Raphael. "He offered to set me free if I consented to a bond with him."

Raphael vibrated, and sparks glinted in his eyes.

"I've never before had the opportunity to actually choose 'death first.'" Gabriel paused. "Mephistopheles realized what was going on, threw him out, and then explained what they were going to do."

Michael looked puzzled. "Why would he do that?"

Gabriel seemed equally puzzled. "Why wouldn't he?"

"It's generally bad practice to talk to your prisoner about how you're going to kill him."

Gabriel shrugged. "He was desperate to share it with someone. You just know Beelzebub doesn't care, and Mephistopheles would forget the whole thing before he'd discuss it with Belior. I got the impression," he added softly, "that I was the first person to work on it with him."

Uriel projected something that Michael echoed by saying, "Please tell me you didn't help him refine his technique."

"But the making of an *angel*," Gabriel said, sitting forward and opening his hands, "the way God fit us all together and sustains us—"

Raphael put a hand on Gabriel, who turned and found his eyes wide. "There's theory, and there's practice. Theory has its place, but in practice, he was trying to kill you, so it might have benefited you not to help him."

Gabriel sighed. "He already knew how to do it. There was no way I could stop him. I wanted to find out more, and he wanted someone to tell."

Michael was fighting a grin. "How did they actually do it? Not the specifics," he added when Uriel was about to speak. "The general procedure."

"Mephistopheles and Beelzebub put up the Guard," Gabriel said. "Satan used Camael as a focus and reached into me—" he felt Raphael wince, and he dropped a hand onto his, "—and that was pretty much it. I wasn't sure what to do, and I couldn't do more than protect myself." He turned to Raphael. "It's okay. I'm safe."

Raphael was shaking. "It's not okay! What they nearly did is frightening."

Gabriel said, "Anyhow, right at the end I realized there wasn't any way I was getting myself out of there alive, so I started dumping power into the chains around one wrist. I thought my only chance was to leave enough of me somewhere that you could find it afterward, and the only way to do that was to leave an object behind that they wouldn't necessarily search."

Raphael said, "Maybe that's where the beads came from."

Gabriel sat straighter. "Beads?"

Michael explained about finding bits of Gabriel's essence afterward to help him make up substance ("but not efficiently," Michael said while Raphael stayed very quiet.)

Gabriel glanced at Uriel, whose visage had darkened.

"Remiel searched the chamber and didn't find anything. She might not have checked the chain, though. She was looking for beads." Uriel's head jerked up. "Can you show me how the room was laid out?"

Gabriel remade the light box and set up images of himself chained at one wall, then Camael kneeling between him and Satan, and finally Mephistopheles and Beelzebub behind Satan. "That's pretty close."

"Can you make it exact?"

Gabriel flinched as he thought back to the darkness, the moment. Raphael behind him said, "Is this necessary?"

Gabriel rotated the image so he could see it from his own vantage point, then tilted Camael forward a bit (interesting—that position would have deflected Satan's power without Satan realizing what Camael had done) and then adjusted Mephistopheles' position to the left and moved Beelzebub more toward the center. Odd: he hadn't been able to see Beelzebub during the procedure—

Oh, dear God!

Beelzebub had stepped toward the center of the room to touch Mephistopheles. Maybe they'd woven their wings together, maybe just a brush. Maybe he'd grabbed Mephistopheles' hand as they put up a combined Guard. And how horrible to think about, because what could be more normal, more natural, than for a Seraph feeling fear and anticipation to reach out for his primary Cherub?

"Gabriel," Raphael said.

There was still something of them left inside there, underneath all that hate, beneath the rebellion—

"Gabriel." Raphael rubbed his shoulders. "It's over. Come back to us."

Gabriel shook his head as if to scatter the images, and he tried to swallow past the knot in his throat.

Uriel was studying the box. "Raphael said Remiel was 'spattered' with parts of Gabriel, but I didn't find any less substance in him now than before. In fact, given that Gabriel was healing in the meantime, there was far more."

Raphael's voice had steel. "I wasn't mistaken."

"I'm not saying you were."

Gabriel said, "So it must have been from before."

He detonated the light-Gabriel in the picture, drawing a cry from Raphael. Uriel scrambled nearer. "Now, single out the figure of Camael."

Gabriel faded the rest of the picture and made Camael stand up.

Raphael pointed over Gabriel's shoulder. "That's it! The front of the wings, shoulders, thighs, outside of the forearms, face. That's where she had it all."

Gabriel said, "This is just a model. I don't know what actually happened."

Michael shifted to look from the side. "Bring back the rest of the image and show me where Satan would have been impacted."

"He'd get the full force of it." Satan's figure changed color along its front. "We were practically on top of one another."

Kneeling up and leaning over Gabriel, Raphael squinted at the picture. "Beelzebub didn't get hit."

"Definitely not if Satan had his wings flared and Beelzebub didn't," Gabriel said. "That was an incredibly crowded room. Mephistopheles probably got hit too, but not as much as Camael and Satan." He opened his hands. "Why is this important? You can't go wring them out."

As he sat back, Raphael sent an impulse through Gabriel: He'd like to.

Michael said, "But I told you Remiel's report about Mephistopheles' new assignment." He turned to Gabriel. "Satan asked him to find a means of doing it *from a distance.*"

Gabriel gasped. "I hurt him!"

Michael grinned. "I can't imagine how his substance would react to being doused in yours, but you've got nearly as much power as he does under ordinary circumstances."

Gabriel gave a dismissive wave. "We're not even close here—the difference between me and him is only slightly less vast than the difference between him and God." His eyes shifted. "The only one who truly scares him is Uriel."

Uriel smirked. "Boo."

Gabriel shrugged. "That's my take on it, at any rate. Still, the implication of the evidence is that I hurt him—and he didn't like that. Hence no new attacks. Not until Mephistopheles comes through."

"And Mephistopheles got hurt too," Michael said, "according to this scenario."

"But what damage could I have done?"

"It's still soaked into Remiel after three days," Raphael said. "She went mad after posing as Camael, but maybe the residue had something to do with it."

Gabriel deflated. "We don't need an insane Satan to contend with. He's tough enough when you can Guard him out and fight him."

"He might just be weakened," Michael said. "Remiel dances at the edge of sanity during normal times."

Uriel said, "And I would bet she thought about you constantly. That nurtured whatever of your substance remained on her."

"And Mephistopheles?" Gabriel steeled himself for the worst. "What progress has he made?"

"As far as Remiel knew," Michael said, "none. He'd actually accepted Camael's offer to help him, which is how she found out in the first place."

"That's odd." Gabriel glanced at Raphael. "Can you imagine my not diving into an assignment under the same circumstances?"

Raphael shook his head.

Gabriel's eyes brightened, and his wings raised.

"No, don't think it," Michael said.

"Too late," Raphael murmured.

"But if they could return—" Gabriel said. "If he's struggling with guilt or horror due to what he achieved—if this could shock him into realizing what kind of evil he's become, and then let him repent—"

"We don't know if they can," Raphael said. "You yourself said that. Until one of them tries to return, we won't know if they *can't* repent, or they *won't*. It's the question even our Cherubim can't answer, and you're not going to resolve it now."

A huff. "When you're right, you're right." Gabriel reached for more of the cookies. "What steps have we taken to protect others?"

Michael said, "A buddy system for traveling."

Mid-reach, Gabriel raised his eyebrows.

Michael looked down. "We couldn't come up with a safeguard, and the Angels on Earth buddied up naturally, so we said to keep doing it."

Gabriel said, "And you didn't mention an invasion, so I assume that didn't happen either."

Michael said, "Zadkiel convinced us not to."

Gabriel glanced out the window. "It wouldn't have helped, no."

"She actually convinced Raguel," Michael said. "Israfel was the hardest sell, but eventually even she consented."

Gabriel looked at Uriel. "Is there any way to secure a soul so it can't be undone?"

Uriel's eyes dropped.

"There's got to be a way." Gabriel took a deep breath. "Can you get me Ophaniel and Sidriel? This may be a race between our Cherubim and theirs."

"Not yet." Uriel looked at Michael. "You still need to rest. I dislike that the vertigo isn't gone at this point. You're not exhausted right now, but you're only running a little above empty."

Gabriel sighed. "It's not that taxing to *think*, Uriel."

"I'd debate that," Uriel said, "but against a Cherub I'd never win, so this is an order: rest."

Raphael touched Gabriel's shoulders, rubbing the tension loose. "I saw how much work just went into you. I'm serious about not wanting to do that again, ever."

Gabriel knew Michael would be no help, so he folded his arms. "Do I have to sleep, or is reading legal?"

Uriel said, "Reading is okay."

Raphael gave him a push. "Think of it this way: the sooner you get stronger, the sooner we'll get the bond running again."

"Oh," Uriel said, "I forgot to tell you that—you'd already bonded again when I went in to patch things up."

Both Raphael and Gabriel pivoted, and Raphael surged with Seraph fire.

"It's instinct." Uriel chuckled. "I thought you'd realized, the way you two were reading each other earlier."

Gabriel glanced at Raphael. "Sure, just move right on in."

Raphael vibrated, sending streamers of fire into the air.

"Hey!" Gabriel averted his gaze. "None of that, remember?"

"Actually," and both of them looked up when Uriel started to speak, "maybe you should try it now, under controlled circumstances, with help right here."

Raphael's fire flared; Gabriel still didn't relax.

"Just a little bit," Uriel said. "You don't want him to burn you out."

Gabriel looked at Raphael. "That means less power than an atomic bomb."

Raphael nodded. "Just a warm-up dose."

Gabriel closed his eyes and felt the fire in the air, but more than that, he felt it through his soul's connection to Raphael, like a private phone line between them. Raphael's excitement churned on the other side of the door, and taking just a little would be like standing under Niagara Falls attempting to fill a teacup.

Gabriel relaxed his heart and drew off a bit of the fire.

At first, nothing. Next, the sensation as if he'd bitten into a jalapeno, heat in his mouth and stomach, sparks in front of his eyes.

"You're doing well." Uriel's voice: steady, calm. "Try it again."

Again?

This time he opened the gates as wide as he could, pulling in all the energy he could take at once. It didn't flood him only because Raphael applied the brakes—but the heat, the bubbling, the nearly boiling-over state of Raphael's soul filled him with an urgency to act and a heightened awareness of his surroundings. A compulsive grin spread across his face.

"Don't overdo it." Despite his words, Raphael was sparkling. "You're not completely healed yet, so you're trying to make up substance by pulling in mine."

"Would it work?" Gabriel said, a bit breathless.

Raphael tilted his head. "Not efficiently."

Gabriel shielded his eyes from the colors in the room, and his own breathing sounded loud. Raphael cut off the fire, and he felt his heart make a clumsy grab for it as it diminished and faded.

"He's looking good." Checking into his heart, Uriel had gone misty. "But let that be it for now. See how it settles."

Gabriel leaned toward Michael, charged to work until they devised a safeguard for souls as well as a protection system for the forces in Creation. "Send me Ophaniel and Sidriel."

Michael winced. "You can't tell them how annihilation is performed."

Gabriel stared. "But—"

"God wants that knowledge reserved to himself."

"Half of Hell could have it by now!"

Uriel's gaze dropped.

"So what you're saying," Gabriel said, and Michael finished, "is that it's you against half of Hell." He nodded. "You have to out-think them."

"They've got a head-start." Gabriel folded his arms. "And I only know the procedure from the inside. We're going to lose souls if I can't get our Cherubim to help."

Raphael clapped him on the shoulder. "You'll do fine. You've got God as your lab partner."

Uriel stood. "But later, when you've had time to rest." Uriel and Michael said goodbye, then vanished.

The only one remaining, Raphael moved across the room. "I know you have to rest." His soul's melodic vibrations distorted into a fermata. "But I need to talk to you."

Gabriel reached through the bond, but Raphael distanced himself.

Then a burst of realization. "I forgot—a girl gave me this for you."

Raphael flashed a palm-sized white bear onto Gabriel's lap. "I saw her at the park, and she said she'd pray for you."

Gabriel held up the bear by the key ring. "I'll pray for her too. What's her name?"

"Elizabeth something."

"Oh, the girl with two guardians?"

Raphael looked over his shoulder. "There's nothing wrong with you."

Gabriel shrugged. "It was thoughtful of her to do that."

Raphael lapsed into uncomfortable silence, getting more energized as the moments passed. Gabriel tried to keep his attention on Raphael and not on the Seraph's fire. "Tell me. You wanted to tell me before, but you were too upset."

Raphael folded his arms and looked out the window. "I owe you the biggest apology of my life."

"If we're apologizing," Gabriel said, "I owe you one for being so distracted during hide-and-seek."

Raphael turned. "I'd totally forgotten."

Gabriel cocked his head. "You mean I wasted a good apology?"

Raphael chuckled as he glanced back out the window, but then he sobered. "The reason you were in such bad shape was that when I pulled you out, I held on too hard. I'd buried your heartstring inside my own soul, wrapped around mine, and it couldn't get free so Uriel could return it to the rest of you."

Gabriel nodded. "Go on. There's clearly more."

"Then God made me— He made me let you die." Raphael's head dropped. "And I did it."

Gabriel drew a sharp breath.

"After I told you it was okay to leave me...that was when Uriel found I had your heartstring." Raphael bit his lip. "But I told you to let go. I told you to die."

Gabriel frowned. "I'm unclear whether you're apologizing for saving my life or for obeying God."

"None of that should have happened!" Raphael shook. "I'd gotten a strangle-hold on your heartstring, and that would have killed you!"

"And if you hadn't grabbed so tight to begin with," Gabriel said, "Satan would have kept hold of me in that chamber, and that would have killed me."

Raphael's mouth twisted. "You just won't let a guy apologize."

Gabriel shrugged. "There's no sin in you. The only thing requiring an apology is sin."

"That's not true. Sometimes someone gets hurt by accident or neglect, and that requires an apology too."

Gabriel's brow furrowed. "I'm going to have to take your word for that." He tilted his head and reached through the bond to send his calming influence into Raphael's heart, trying as he did not to draw the fire back into himself. It had gotten easier to resist now that he was on a more even keel, although even brushing past it gave him something of a head rush.

Raphael's wings flared. "None of that. The idea is to keep your energy inside you. Think addition, not subtraction."

"And here I was thinking exponents and calculus."

Raphael smiled. "So?"

"If you insist, I completely forgive you for whatever harm you think you committed against me."

Raphael pursed his lips. "That sounds rather vague."

"What do you want?" He thought for a moment. "Ask God to settle it. If you're right, I'll forgive you, and if I'm right, you'll owe me one."

"One what?"

Gabriel studied the ceiling as he thought, then refocused on Raphael with enthusiasm. "You'll take me trick-or-treating in two weeks."

Head raised, Raphael said, "You could win a thousand bets, but I am not taking you trick-or-treating."

"Oh, come on—you know I need an adult to come with me." Gabriel sat forward. "No one else will do it."

"Then you're out of luck."

"I'm out of candy too." Gabriel stared out the window. "Everyone wants to stop by the library and get some, but no one wants to help me get any of it."

"We can hit seventeen grocery stores on November 1st and pick it up for half price," Raphael said, "but I will not ever, for the rest of eternity, take you trick-or-treating again."

Gabriel sighed. "Well, then I guess if you win, I want a root beer float."

Raphael looked relieved. "I can do that. But what if I'm right? What do I get?"

Gabriel said, a little uncertain, "You get to apologize?"

"I want to see you blow up something big, not just shatter windows."

Gabriel bubbled with Raphael's enthusiasm. "Is there a volcano on Io that you wanted to see blow?"

"I was thinking," and Raphael arched his eyebrows, "supernova."

Gabriel's heart raced with overflow fire. "Deal." Then he paused. "What if we bring this to Jesus and he tells us we're both nuts?"

Raphael said, "You blow up a root beer float while trick-or-treating?"

They were shaking hands to close the deal when Jesus arrived with Remiel.

Raphael shot her a look of disgust before seeing how she stood: wings limp, head bowed, hands clasped behind her. Gabriel had sat up, ready to calm Raphael, when the Seraph averted his gaze and vanished.

When Jesus put his hand on Remiel's shoulder, the Virtue shivered.

"Gabriel," she whispered, "I'm sorry."

"It's done now." Gabriel shifted to sit at the edge of the bed. "You weren't in your right mind."

"I was," she murmured.

Gabriel looked toward Jesus, very startled, but Jesus sent him the impression that he needed to wait her out.

She looked up. "How are you?"

"Repaired, apparently." He raised a hand to her. "I heard you were under the weather, though."

Remiel met his eyes with eyes grown cloudy. Taking his hand, she moved to sit beside him. "Don't make me sad." She rested her head on his shoulder so he could finger her short hair. "Do you know—did they tell you I betrayed you?"

Gabriel looked at Jesus, who again indicated that he should wait.

"Camael—" and here she paused a moment, "said he'd sent me suggestions to get you down to Earth where you could be captured. They said I was too valuable to kill. That's how they captured you." She turned her face toward him. "I'm sorry. I didn't realize."

Raising his wings, Gabriel cupped her in the hollow. "You did nothing wrong." He took his hand from her grasp and clasped hers instead. "You went in after me to save me."

She shuddered.

"You're so brave."

She shook her head. "It had to be done. I couldn't let you die." She looked at her lap. "But I had to lie when I was there."

He nodded.

"You hate lies."

"If God sees nothing inappropriate with your conduct, I won't condemn you."

She half-closed her eyes.

"It must have been painful, pretending to be him."

She shuddered. "Looking like him, thinking like him, coming an inch short of cursing God but sounding as if I had—I wanted to run to you and set you free, but then I'd be caught too, and we'd both die."

Gabriel squeezed her hand. "We're both safe now."

She pulled her hands free of his grasp. "I told them you screamed."

Gabriel shifted uncomfortably. "I did scream."

"I nearly screamed, too. But I told them you renounced God to save yourself. They wanted to hear something, so I made it sound good. I lied, Gabriel." She bit her lip. "I wasn't even doing it to save you at that point. I was doing it to save myself."

Gabriel gave her hand a squeeze. "I'm glad you saved yourself."

She looked up, her eyes like sunrise. "Do you forgive me?"

Gabriel felt Jesus telling him it was all right. "I forgive *everything*. If you remember or find out something later that you haven't brought to me, it's covered as well."

Remiel smiled sheepishly. "Thanks for being a good sport."

Gabriel nodded, and Remiel left.

Jesus stayed.

The Cherub looked at him. "Is she going to be all right?"

"She will now." Jesus came to sit on the bed. "You need to rest. You're not healed yet, and you still have one thing to do."

Gabriel squared his shoulders. "I'm ready."

"It's not time. You'll need to be stronger when the time comes."

Gabriel nodded. "Tell your mom thanks for the cookies." He offered Jesus the plate.

"The thanks are to you for enjoying them." He chuckled as he took one. "She's having a ball cooking for you."

Gabriel smiled. "And thank you for everything, the way you sent the others to save me, the way everything worked out just right, even if there were a few snags." He looked at the half cookie in his hand. "If it hadn't been me, Raphael wouldn't have been able to pull the angel out. If it hadn't been Raphael pulling, the healing wouldn't have been as powerful, and the heartstrings wouldn't have been as protected. If it had been anyone else—"

Jesus sat closer. "But it wasn't anyone else. It was going to happen to someone, so I let them choose the one with the best chance of survival."

"Thank you," Gabriel said, meaning it. He finished the cookie, then added, "Michael looked overwhelmed."

"He's in unfamiliar territory right now."

"I hope he's leaning on Saraquael." When Jesus nodded, Gabriel smiled. "He never notices it, but Saraquael is the most competent angel in the host. Michael could mention, 'I lost my favorite safety pin somewhere on Earth,' and half an hour later Saraquael would return with it in a Ziploc baggie."

Jesus laughed out loud. "And then he'd ask if there was anything else Michael needed."

Gabriel chuckled. "And poor Uriel, thrust into center stage."

"Uriel did an excellent job."

"No question, although—" Gabriel hesitated. "On the receiving end, that was a workout. I know it's not logical, but I hated that

Uriel's hands were manipulating my person, and I couldn't object because it was helping me."

"Regardless of logic," Jesus said, "the objection has its validity. Under ordinary circumstances, that kind of contact would have been highly inappropriate."

"It felt more uncomfortable than when Satan tried," Gabriel said. "I couldn't recoil from Uriel."

Jesus nodded. "You've noted in the past that the will can be defiant even if one submits in form, as Remiel did. Against Satan, even though he had you bound, you resisted. Your will was the weapon you used to protect yourself. Toughening it against Uriel would only have hindered Uriel, and ultimately harmed you."

Gabriel sat forward. "Are you indicating the will is what we're calling the heartstrings?"

Jesus nodded. "It's as close as you've come to describing it well."

Gabriel pivoted on the bed so he sat on his heels with his wings cupped, hands on his knees as he leaned toward Jesus. "And the beads, those are the personality components?"

"But you're missing a third part of the equation," Jesus said.

Gabriel rubbed his chin, then gasped. "Energy! There's will, talent and energy, and they all function together to formulate the living soul."

Jesus grinned as Gabriel hashed out three different scenarios describing the give-and-take between the parts, discarding each hypothesis partway through in favor of a more workable one. Jesus tossed questions back at the Cherub every few minutes, firing up Gabriel into talking more animatedly, conjuring light designs for models of the soul, throwing around ideas for experiments, and at one point sitting back to exhale slowly when he abruptly lost his own train of thought.

Jesus looked amused. "Too many ideas whirling around?"

"I'm sorry." Gabriel was breathless. "You've never discussed this with any of us before, have you?" He flung his arms around him. "I love you!"

Jesus laughed. "You're like a Seraph right now."

Gabriel sat back. "Tell me more. If the will is the string, why isn't it possible to compel the string to relinquish its hold on all the beads at once?"

"The segments are all subordinated to the will," Jesus said, "but the energy seals it together, and the 'eyelets' are mounted very strongly with a natural adhesion to the string. Since one's personhood derives its power from the will, it can't detach or annihilate itself."

About to shoot back another question, Gabriel grew quiet.

"Go on." Jesus folded his arms. "I've been waiting for you to get to this point."

Gabriel gave him a dark look, then focused on his hands and sat back properly. "When Rahab was destroyed, there was nothing left." He sounded like a deer on hearing the first rifle crack during hunting season. "But with me, parts would have been—actually were—drifting around, even that disembodied will. Would I have retained any awareness?"

Jesus said, "I would never permit such an atrocity to happen to one of my own."

"But if I could be near you in that state—"

"Gabri'li," Jesus said, "I would not want you to suffer. There would be no fragmentation, no awareness of former state or present. As for the soul parts and the will, without being united and sealed by your energy, or by someone else actively nurturing them, they would dissolve in about a day and a half, which was what was happening to you when I forced Raphael to let you go."

Gabriel bit his lip. "I wouldn't have wanted to have that conversation with him."

Jesus said softly, "I didn't want to, either."

"But you can't pass the buck." Gabriel's brow furrowed. "How did you get him to agree?"

"It was going to be a shouting match no matter how I did it," Jesus said. "But you understand Seraphim. Quick to fly off the handle, quick to apologize afterward. The chief object of the conversation was to get him to release you and not rebel."

Gabriel frowned. "Surely if you'd explained—"

"Then he'd have kept hold of your will because he'd still be working to insure you survived. He couldn't hold onto you and let you go at the same time."

Gabriel's gaze dropped.

Jesus said, "I felt bad for him too. But there was no other way."

Gabriel deflated. "If it had come down to it, if he refused to obey, I'd hope you would have let me die rather than let him rebel."

Jesus said, "If it had come right down to it, if he would not under any circumstances have obeyed a command to let you go, I would have done exactly that."

Gabriel let off a sigh.

Jesus rested a hand on his shoulder. "You've got a list of people a mile long who want to see you." He stood. "Have one more visitor, and then you need to rest."

Gabriel shook his head. "Not someone who's going to apologize to me. That's my only request."

Jesus said, "Granted. One visitor who is not about to apologize to you. Israfel—?"

Israfel appeared. Smiling uneasily, she looked at Gabriel, then turned to Jesus.

"He wanted to speak to someone who wouldn't apologize for anything. Go ahead and talk to him—with no apologies."

Gabriel had only just enough time to realize he didn't like how that sounded before Jesus was gone.

Israfel sounded uncertain. "They said you're doing okay."

Gabriel nodded.

"I'm glad." Except she didn't look glad, only uncomfortable.

Gabriel couldn't figure out what the next part of the conversation should be. Wishing for Raphael's flair, he said, "Apparently I'm able to bond again. If you want—"

"Since you mention it," she said, "I don't."

Gabriel's heart bottomed out.

Israfel pulled up a chair and straddled it, crossing her arms on the back and resting her chin on her wrists. "Raphael said the one thing you regretted was me."

Heat surged through Gabriel. "What possessed him to say that?"

"Uriel needed a regret to put tension on the string. Kind of like a plumb line. I got to save your life by being left out in the cold."

Gabriel stopped trying to meet her eyes and instead looked out the window.

"Your attitude didn't bother me until Raphael said you regretted ignoring me all the time," Israfel said. "Afterward, I was really irritated. We used to talk or go places or do things. You'd stop by on my assignments to criticize the way I did them, and I'd tag along on yours to give it right back. It was a lot of fun." She folded her arms. "You used to show up when we were sitting around singing and just join in. But not anymore."

Raphael's voice in his mind: *Gabriel?*

Not now. I'm getting my head handed to me.

Then I won't bother telling you she's on her way.

Gabriel checked on Israfel, but she still wasn't looking at him, only glaring at the floor.

"You've forgotten we were bonded. Everyone else has forgotten we're bonded. You were going to die and it was 'Poor Raphael,' 'How horrible for Raphael,' 'What's Raphael going to do?' and I found reminding them you were a primary of mine also, only how would I know any longer?"

Gabriel managed, "I'm sorry."

She fixed a stare at him. "I'm tired of you being sorry! In your brain it was always 'eternity is a long time—I'll get around to her someday,' except that someday nearly never came. And you know what I realized?" When Gabriel looked at her blankly, Israfel said, "I realized I didn't feel scared about going forward without you. You'd bet if Ophaniel or Zophiel died I'd be crazed, but you—it just made me wistful."

Gabriel closed his eyes.

Israfel said, "I talked it over with both of them, and they agree. I'm the chief of the order of Seraphim—I don't have to stand around waiting for someone to notice me."

Gabriel shook his head.

"Well?"

"I've been a lousy friend."

"You're absolutely right you've been a lousy friend!" Flames appeared around her eyes and vibrating wings. "Do you blame me for being sick of it?"

Gabriel swallowed. "No."

It was easier to avoid her fire than Raphael's. Gabriel knew he could pull those flames from the air, curl into her heart and bond her whether she wanted or not, and therefore he made certain to keep his soul contained.

"I don't know what else you want me to say. I'm sorry. I didn't mean to hurt you."

"Life just kept getting in the way." The pitch of her voice had raised. "Everything else around you was more important, and you knew I'd always be around if you wanted. Well, I'm not any longer."

And she vanished.

Gabriel reached for Raphael's mind. *Remember when you said I wouldn't pass the social tests on the best day of my life?* He sighed. *This must be the best day of my life.*

Raphael sent back wordless reassurance, then a question. Gabriel told him no, leave Israfel alone.

When she didn't return, Gabriel stretched out on his stomach, but the tension in his neck and wings wouldn't go. Part of him wanted to remain on guard. It didn't make sense because he was safe, but it felt wrong to be alone.

He shifted to the Vision. *You're with me?*

Absolutely.

I hurt her, didn't I? He rested his head on his arms and closed his eyes. *Help me make it right.*

This also meant he was about to lose a bet with Raphael, because he hadn't sinned against Israfel, but he knew simultaneously that he'd needed to apologize to her and that it hadn't been enough.

Though tired, his body refused to sleep. After five minutes of mental thrashing, he curled on his side, drew up his wings around his body and over his head, and stared into the lightless cocoon he'd made of himself.

Things to think about:

1. How to protect an angel against annihilation
2. Israfel
   A) making amends
      1) gift? letter? something?
   B) going forward
      1) new ground rules
      2) substitute the bond
3. Remiel - personal healing
   A) how to deal with her when she realized she'd hurt him
4. Prevention of future attacks
   A) replace anemic buddy system
   B) network system
   C) early warning system, information distribution

Prioritization: protection seemed to be the number one priority, although potentially prevention ought to take precedence. Of course, if he could render an angel immune to the attack, prevention would have been accomplished anyhow. Therefore the obvious schema—

Fire again in the room, more subdued. Gabriel opened his wings and found Israfel again, seated by the window.

"Apology accepted," she spat.

"Wait." Gabriel scrambled upright. "Stay and let me talk."

She folded her arms.

"You're entirely right." He tried not to look into her face. "I say that at risk of angering you again. We should have had this conversation centuries ago. Thank you for not pretending any longer."

Although he could feel her glare on him, her fire was down; she must have gone to Ophaniel and dumped power like crazy.

"The question is," Gabriel said, braving a look at her, "what do we do next?"

She opened her hands.

"How can I make it right?"

Her eyes tightened even as the fire surged. "You can't make it right."

Gabriel slumped. "You're not giving me much to go on."

"I don't have to give you anything to go on."

"You don't." He traced one finger over the edge of a blanket. "But we're going to be working together for a long time now that I'm not dead. If you walk off now, we can avoid one another for years—"

"Which you do just fine."

Touché. "But eventually we'll have to deal with one another, and it's no good if you're angry and I'm unsure how you'll work with me. It's in our best interests to at least work out some ground rules."

Israfel crossed her legs and leaned back in the chair.

Gabriel's head swam, but he sat up on the bed. "I respect your decision not to re-bond. I'll talk to Sidriel about a way to form a tertiary bond—"

"I don't want any level bond."

"If you'll let me speak, we have to form a tertiary if you don't want a primary, otherwise at some point one or the other of us is going to reach out at the wrong time and we'll have a primary once more because our souls were made for that level. Either we fill the slot with something else, or else you're going to be stuck with me again."

Israfel's frown eased a bit. "All right. Thank you."

Gabriel averted his eyes. "The next thing is, I know I can't make amends, but I at least want to offer you this: there's nothing wrong with you. I get my head in the clouds and get consumed by ideas, and I only end up with Raphael because he drags me away. If he didn't do that, I'd never see him either, so it's not that you're unworthy or a bother."

No protest from Israfel.

"I didn't want to hurt you," Gabriel said, "and I'm sorry I already have, because you didn't deserve that."

She sounded tentative. "Do you think we can re-make a tertiary?"

"I'll have to work on it. Deliberately under-bonding has never been done before, but that doesn't mean it's impossible."

She nodded.

He felt God prompting him, but he froze inside. A peek at Israfel showed her so— He couldn't describe it.

Talk, God told him, and he knew he had no words, so he said, "But—"

There was hesitancy in her eyes.

"Maybe," he said.

"You're not going to do better," she said.

"What if," he said, "we work on the tertiary problem, but—" His head hurt. "What if I made time for you in the meanwhile? And then when we have a way to make a tertiary, you decide what level to re-bond."

Her eyes narrowed. "Don't pity me."

He opened his hands, but he looked only at his lap. "You're right that we used to spend time talking and going places, although I dispute that I only ever tagged along on your missions to criticize you."

After a moment of silence she said, "It happened so gradually. But we used to have fun, and—" He looked up in time to see her eyes go from sky blue to hard like a dagger's silver. "What do you have in mind?"

"We set up a schedule," he said, "iron-clad so I don't go wandering off into research. And you come get me if I forget."

She recoiled. "That's patronizing."

He squinted. "To me or to you?"

"I guess to both of us, but mostly to me. I have to be scheduled into your life?"

Gabriel blinked. "Nothing is wrong with having a schedule. Schedules exist to make sure important things get done."

Smirking, she tilted her head. "Do you schedule prayer too?"

His ears felt hot. "Yes."

She stared, open-mouthed.

"I pray at other times too." He had the distinct impression she was laughing at him. "But I've scheduled the minimum acceptable amount."

Dead silence reigned for a minute. Moderately dizzy now, Gabriel reached for God, who sent back reassurance.

Israfel said, "You are one-hundred-percent a Cherub."

Gabriel quirked a smile. *Thank you for noticing.*

"If it's good enough for God," she said, "I'll take it too. So you were thinking one hour a week, pushed off to the 167th hour when your alarm went off and you realized you were about to blow the deadline?"

"Actually," Gabriel said, "if I wait until the 167th hour, it would be more efficient at that point to spend two hours together and take care of the next week's obligation as well."

In the next second, Gabriel wished he hadn't said that.

But Israfel laughed out loud, and her fire sparkled, and Gabriel let out a long breath.

"I think that's okay," she said. "Then we'll decide later."

Feeling distanced and hazy, Gabriel let Israfel touch her wingtips to his. When she flashed away, he collapsed gratefully onto the bed.

I hope there's nothing more right now, he prayed.

Sleep, God said, and Gabriel obeyed.

Twenty-One

The Lake of Fire lay at the bottom of a cavern with its ceiling a mile in the air. Fingers of rock jutted from the bare beaches, reaching like the petals of a chrysanthemum that had yet to unfold fully, the effect being that the only opening straight down was right at the lake's center where the cavern yielded to dark. On one of those projections stood Mephistopheles.

Poised a mile up on rock baked to glass, he had his wings extended and his eyes closed. The heat scalded him even this high, but still he remained. While his heart pounded, he waited for the fear to rouse him, knowing at the same time it would not.

He remembered: Rahab—oh, God, Rahab!—the sixth member of the Maskim and the demon-guard of Egypt who had watched Moses defeat Pharaoh ten times and had lost his grip on Israel; Rahab who had caused Pharaoh to pursue and then watched as a whole army's bloated bodies floated on the Red Sea.

Mephistopheles looked at the red sea flaming beneath him and closed his eyes again.

And Rahab, Rahab had reported to Lucifer, who had publicly humiliated him and stripped him of his rank. In a desperate attempt to regain favor he had tried to prevent Moses' receiving the Law from the Lord. He had failed. So he'd returned to this pinnacle and leaped.

Rahab had been destroyed by God once. He'd sought a different annihilation for himself under the flames, and to all intents he had succeeded. His whole spiritual form had dissolved after a month. Nothing remained to fish out now, even if they should find him, just a will that lingered and burned.

Under that flaming lake, one could lose his identity, suffer a name-change like the first—when their falling bodies had impacted on Hell's floor and each had tried to remove all traces of God from himself forever. Asmodeus from Asmodiel. Belior from Beliel. Mistofiel had become Mephistopheles; Belazael, Beelzebub. And now Rahab was nothing.

He could be nothing.

To suffer without remembering why.

The Cherub dreamed as he stood with closed eyes, tracking the sweat beading down his cheeks and against his nose and around the corners of his mouth. It lay in his power to forget that he had spat in the face of God. He, who had whored his mind to worse tyranny than the one he had refused to accept long ago, he himself had ripped one of the bright swords from his Creator's hand and shattered it against the stones.

And in a month, he could forget what he had done and know only that he endured eternal reparation.

Mephistopheles knew it would take a month because Rahab's primary Seraphim had screamed for a little over four weeks after their Cherub had submerged. Mephistopheles had stood on the beach among the rest of the higher-order demons (all but Lucifer) dragging the lake, one at a time flashing under the flames tethered to someone on shore; the diver would search the plasma for five minutes and then be reeled out when the pain became dangerous enough to dissolve the will.

Beelzebub will suffer, he realized.

He smiled wryly.

"Why are you doing this?"

The voice of Lucifer, smooth as the lava chugging over the edge of the waterfall.

"I asked a question, Cherub."

"I want to stop thinking."

Lucifer behind him sat on the rock spike and wordlessly ordered Mephistopheles to do the same. He did, still keeping his eyes closed, then turned so he straddled the stone facing Lucifer.

"Are you going to honor God by finally handing over your intellect? Is thinking so bad that you'd lose your freedom to halt it?"

Mephistopheles slumped forward.

Lucifer's tone never wavered. "You can't exchange your life for Gabriel's in some perverted form of justice. There is no justice. It's only us in this world. You can't satisfy any spiritual scales."

Mephistopheles opened his eyes enough to glare at him. "I'm not after justice."

"Then what do you want?" Lucifer said. "I can give it to you."

Fixing famished eyes on Lucifer, Mephistopheles said, "*Nothing.*"

Lucifer sat a little taller, his eyes wide.

Flattening his palms to the spike, Mephistopheles slid forward until his chest pressed against the stone. He crossed his arms and laid down his head.

Mephistopheles understood enough of the future to know that when the world ended, when the Word flooded Hell with uncreated light for the final time, they all would be chained beneath that lake. Their will to do more than endure would be dissolved by the God of their creation—not the god of their rebellion—the one to whom was truly reserved that right.

But even then, not completely. They would know they were no longer self-aware. They would know what they had relinquished.

"I think it's better that way," murmured Mephistopheles, and Lucifer, who had felt the general turn of the Cherub's thoughts, said, "*He* won't ever do what's better for us. You're an idiot to think otherwise."

To silence the voice in his mind, the voice that night and day accused him—

"Mephistopheles," Lucifer said sharply, "use Beelzebub for this. Make him give you fire of a different sort."

Snapping his wings tight to his shoulders, Mephistopheles only shook his head.

Lucifer studied him, his green eyes piercing. After a minute, he murmured, "He used to care about you."

Mephistopheles' head whipped up. "Why don't you shut up and leave me alone? I'm no concern of yours!"

Lucifer leaned back, knees up on the rock, wings spread for balance. "He used to love you, back when he could look into your eyes and give you his fire and you could give him that inner focus he longed for."

Mephistopheles was on his feet now. "Who cares? He's not your concern—you never bonded!"

"I can only assume it was love." Lucifer gazed off into the dark. "Not a crazed need to feed on one another like paired parasites—"

Mephistopheles lunged at Lucifer and slammed him into the cavern wall, a crash that resounded through Hell like the clapper of a gong. They grappled in balance for an instant when it seemed both would plunge to their torments. Then the Cherub gathered himself to emit a concussion blast that filled the top of the chamber, bringing down tons of rock and collapsing the pinnacle on which they stood.

Lucifer snatched him out of the air and flashed him to the ice fields.

"I'll rip out your throat if you go on!" Mephistopheles was screaming. "I'll drop you into the lake!"

Lucifer shimmered until wind and wings merged in the blinding snow. "I'm pointing out the obvious, Cherub, things you already know."

Mephistopheles blasted him again, fire around his eyes and a geyser of snow filling the air. Lucifer batted it aside. "Do you want to kill me?" he yelled over the wind. "Would that silence my voice, or is that in your mind too?"

Mephistopheles rose into the air, six wings spread like the limbs of a mutant sea star, Michael's sigil on his hand streaming spangles of light. He grabbed Lucifer with his will, encircling his heart in chains that pinned his arms to his side, enwrapped his throat and bound his legs together. The Cherub sent power flooding through the web of his will, electricity that struck Lucifer with a crack-boom like a lightning bolt.

Lucifer flexed all twelve wings, doubled up under the web, and blew it off.

Fully armored now, Mephistopheles called his sword to his hand. He flew at Lucifer, who raised an empty hand only to materialize his sword the moment before impact. Mephistopheles hurled himself at him, striking twice a second, throwing all his will and power into the attack. Lucifer parried, dodged, pivoted. The tips of several feathers blew away in the wind.

Mephistopheles broke off the attack and flashed to a nearby ridge, chest heaving.

Surprised and thrilled, Lucifer flashed right in front of him. *There's my Cherub!*

Engaged in battle with Michael's enemy, the ring on Mephistopheles' hand was on fire. Mephistopheles flung himself at Lucifer, crashed him into the side of the hill, stabbing at him with a dagger, hurling energy from the ringed hand, fire and light hemorrhaging from his entire form. With Michael's power supplementing his own, he drove Lucifer a step at a time until finally Lucifer had his back to a snow bank. Mephistopheles aimed for his heart.

Lucifer brought up his hands and bound Mephistopheles with his will.

Frozen, Mephistopheles tried to thrash, tried to flash away, tried even to close his eyes and scream, but none of himself responded.

"You have your own fire." Lucifer's hair was buffeted by the wind as ice crystals formed on his outermost wings. "You don't have to smother yourself."

The Cherub couldn't break his gaze from those eyes, those eyes.

Without a movement, Lucifer transported them inside a frozen cave, blue-white with internal refractions from Lucifer's own glow. Out of the wind, Mephistopheles could hear his own heartbeat, feel his frenzied breathing.

Lucifer released him enough that he could stand, not enough that he could move. As he settled to the frost-glistened floor, Mephistopheles averted his gaze.

"Remember your power and your independence." Lucifer crooned into Mephistopheles' ear like a lover. "Think of what you accomplished, the accolades you deserve because no one else was even close to being able to figure out the things you did. Not even Gabriel knew the secrets of a soul's construction. Am I correct?"

Mephistopheles agreed.

"I will again make you the offer." Lucifer took a step backward and spoke clearly. "Since they appear to do you no benefit, would you like me to break all your bonds?"

A long stillness in Mephistopheles' mind. Then, almost without thought, a refusal.

"As you will. However, from a practicality perspective, I cannot allow you to stay depressed." Lucifer shook his head. "You're impeding our next move, and you're causing a morale problem. Belior is maneuvering to replace you, and I have enough to do without shoving him back into his box."

Mephistopheles apologized.

"I don't want an apology. I want results." Lucifer folded his arms. "Beelzebub failed to motivate you, but I'm not going to fail. If reminding you of your true strength didn't knock you out of this rut then I don't know what will, but I want you to apply your unrivaled intellect to the problem above and before all other pursuits, and you *will* find yourself a solution. You are not to drown yourself in the lake because I'll personally reel you out and do something worse."

Lucifer released his hold on Mephistopheles' voice. "Yes, sir."

"Go straighten yourself out, and stay out of my path until you're functional again. Then we'll go fetch Camael from his presumably enchained vacation."

Mephistopheles found himself flashed out of Hell onto the top of Mount Aconcagua in South America, higher than the clouds that foamed grey beneath his feet.

Michael and Raphael were in the middle of discussing preventative tactics when Raphael's eyes lit, fire surged around him, and he vanished.

Saraquael drew back. "Well, that doesn't look good."

Michael flashed after Raphael.

He appeared in Uriel's bungalow to find Raphael scolding a blue streak and Gabriel on the edge of the bed with his head between his knees.

"Are you some kind of idiot? Did you forget you're hurt?"

Gabriel projected the beginnings of an explanation, that he'd thought if maybe—

"That maybe if you just killed yourself, then Satan could have a nice relaxing afternoon?"

Michael pushed between the pair. Saraquael had appeared, and momentarily Ophaniel followed. A touch found Gabriel shaking. "This is nice and all, but can you heal him a bit?"

Raphael folded his arms. "Not if it's going to give him license to keep pushing himself beyond reason."

Michael got on his knees, face-to-face with Gabriel as he picked up his head. "Are you in pain?"

Gabriel shook his head. More like, startled.

Ophaniel got down next to Michael. "What were you doing?"

"We need a safeguard." Gabriel couldn't keep his voice steady. "No one else understands the mechanics of the soul, so it's up to me."

Raphael huffed.

Behind Michael, Saraquael said, "Raphael, please?"

The healing glow looked almost begrudging, but instantly Gabriel's breathing eased, and he sent Raphael a thankful look. Raphael's wings relaxed a bit.

Ophaniel moved closer to Gabriel, inadvertently pushing Michael out of the way. "What did you try?"

"I toyed with the idea of a soul reserve." Gabriel rubbed his chin and frowned. "If we could store enough of ourselves in a safe location, maybe we could reconstitute that in the event that someone got captured and destroyed."

Ophaniel tucked up his knees and mirrored Gabriel's expression. "That makes sense, but how would you do it?"

"That was the issue." Gabriel sighed. "A Guard is disembodied will. When we make an object, it's disembodied substance. A sigil is disembodied energy. I couldn't figure out how to combine them."

Michael and Saraquael exchanged looks. "Cherubim," Saraquael mouthed at him. Michael smothered a laugh.

For five minutes Gabriel and Ophaniel traded questions and answers in a firefight with words for bullets until Raphael tried to intervene.

Ignoring Raphael, Gabriel wiped out a handful of light-diagrams with a wave of one hand. "That's when I considered the power reserve again. Some athletes bank their own blood so they'll have an added infusion of their own hemoglobin before a competition."

Ophaniel tilted his head. "Completely undetectable. But that helps only if there are enough parts remaining to recharge."

"And I'm not even sure how to put them all back together," Gabriel said.

"Guys," Raphael said.

"The next thing I did," Gabriel said, "was I bi-located—"

Ophaniel let out a "eureka!' gasp as he jumped to his feet. "And then you have it all in one spot!"

"But naturally one can't head around doubled all the time." Gabriel spoke with a bright animation as if he hadn't been shaking minutes ago. "It weakens all of us. The key has to lie in diminishing one half and increasing the other—"

"Gabriel," Raphael said.

"—but that's when I got dizzy and couldn't continue." He looked up at Raphael. "You're about to detonate, aren't you?"

Brushing a wing by one of Raphael's, Ophaniel imposed calm on him through their own bond.

Michael turned aside from the laughter bubbling in Ophaniel's eyes and focused on an amused Gabriel. "Was I mistaken, or were you supposed to be sleeping?"

Suddenly sober, Gabriel admitted he was.

"And you're not."

This too Gabriel acknowledged.

"And one more thing," Raphael said, getting between Gabriel and Michael. "You do not—do not—run experiments on yourself. I'm not sure how you even had enough energy to bi-locate, but there's not enough of you now to go dividing yourself."

As Gabriel was about to protest, Raphael said, "I told you I don't want to have to put you back together again, so do me a favor and *stay in one piece!*"

Looking chagrined, Gabriel acquiesced.

Ophaniel still sparkled, though, and Michael wondered what he was thinking to give him that secret smile.

Michael left Gabriel with Raphael. He brought Saraquael and Ophaniel back to the conference room.

Saraquael looked out the window. "We're still stuck for protection."

"Has the enemy made any progress?"

Saraquael emitted an uneasy aura. "I have to say, I don't like the rumors coming out of Hell right now."

Michael frowned.

"I have conflicting reports, all from minor demons, that Mephistopheles is on the move, but they're divided as to whether he attacked Beelzebub, whether he attacked *Satan*, or whether he got attacked."

Michael opened his hands. "What's the harm? There's nothing I'd find more welcome right now than a demonic civil war."

"He's probably got the political capital to pull it off at the moment." Saraquael shook his head with a sigh. "But when I found Remiel, I saw him consulting with Asmodeus. If he's combining the army and his own people against Satan, we may be facing a very motivated, absolutely united force. What better way to consolidate a new ruling order than by invading Heaven and annihilating a few of your enemies?"

Well, that would stink. Michael turned to Ophaniel for his opinion, but the Cherub had a thousand-miles-away gaze.

Raphael returned. "He needs a private guard. Or an anesthesiologist."

"Is he all right?"

"Now," Raphael said, eyes glimmering like the heart of a coal. "I can't convince him it's wrong to push himself like crazy. Even worse, Jesus told him he has to recover soon, so what is he doing? He's taking that as an injunction that something bad will happen soon and that he can't afford to sleep."

Michael folded his arms. "That doesn't sound good."

"Not on any account, no. I forced him back to sleep. I made him promise to contact me the moment he awakens, and when he does," Raphael said, smirking, "I'm going to put him straight back to sleep."

A windblown Zadkiel appeared. "Michael, I need your help with a situation."

Michael noticed just before he flashed away how Ophaniel looked right at Saraquael, and how the Dominion wore an intrigued smile.

Twenty-Two

Ophaniel's shaded face was the first thing Gabriel saw when he awakened, followed by the shadow of Sidriel immediately behind him.

Raphael, he sent, *I'm awake.*

Raphael would arrive in a minute.

Gabriel projected a question.

Ophaniel pressed into his hand a heavy object that just fit into his palm with his fingers curled.

Gabriel puzzled. Then his eyes flew open, and he bolted upright.

Sidriel laughed out loud, and Ophaniel beamed.

Gabriel whispered, "Saraquael?"

Both Cherubim nodded with enthusiasm.

Gabriel made the room light so he could see the thing in his hand. It was round, metallic, and far heavier than its size would lead one to believe. He rolled it in his fingers and found it perfectly smooth.

Saraquael appeared. "What do you think?"

Not looking up from the sphere, Gabriel radiated curiosity.

"We did as you said." Ophaniel wore a bright enthusiasm as he exchanged a look with Sidriel. "I had him bi-locate, then started a process of transferring everything from one to the other, but leaving samples of everything behind."

"I couldn't do it myself," Saraquael said. "They needed to guide the process."

Gabriel examined the ball. "It's— It feels just like you."

"It is him." Sidriel cocked his head. "If he wanted to, he could call it back to himself. But if instead he needed our help, we could pump energy back into it and try to recreate him."

"Instant Dominion." Saraquael grinned. "Just add water—or something."

Gabriel rolled it between his palms. "There's no way to test the process."

Saraquael shook his head. "I'm all for a good experiment, but I'd rather not try getting destroyed and re-created."

Raphael appeared. "You know, this isn't a convention center."

Gabriel raised the sphere. "This was what I was trying to do. Ophaniel and Sidriel finished it up."

Raphael took it from Gabriel's hand. "Nice work. But did you guys have to wake him up to show him?"

Sidriel squinted. "Wouldn't he want to know?"

Ophaniel said to Gabriel, "Sidriel had to help with condensing everything, otherwise the second Saraquael just got filmier."

Sidriel knit his brows. "I suspect that if we mold it as it collapses, we can make the token shaped like an ordinary object to further safeguard it. A bell, a fountain pen, a necklace—"

"You'd break your neck," Raphael said, weighing it in his hand.

"But the point would be to hide it in plain sight," Ophaniel said. "Otherwise they'd destroy the token and then hunt down the angel."

Gabriel looked over Saraquael. "Are you at a diminished power?"

"Not that I can tell."

Raphael opened his hands. "Why wait? We should get tokens made for likely targets, staring with Michael."

Gabriel looked at Ophaniel. "Raphael first. And Israfel."

Ophaniel met his eyes with understanding.

Sidriel said to Saraquael, "Whom do they want to strike next?"

"If they've got plans, they've been quiet. But it'll be the Cherubim or the Seraphim that get hit," Saraquael added. "Satan will strike the top of the hierarchy first. He knows we'll retaliate, so he'll make it worth his while."

Gabriel said, "I think he'll hit one of the Seven. Satan would sacrifice his own existence for a shot at Michael's."

"Michael has too much of God's power in him," Raphael said. "Satan might as well try unlacing God Almighty."

Ophaniel folded his arms. "They think Gabriel's dead, and they must think you're paralyzed with grief. Plus they think Remiel is half mad."

"That leaves three targets," Gabriel said. "Raguel, Saraquael and Uriel."

Raphael cleared his throat. "Before you get further into this discussion, Gabriel—"

Gabriel hesitated, then looked from Raphael to Ophaniel. "What?"

Ophaniel raised his eyebrows. "Israfel."

Gabriel took a short breath. Then he summoned Israfel.

When she appeared, Raphael said, "Strategy session. Who's the next target?" and recapped the conversation. While he did this, Mary showed up with a banana bread and a thermos full of hot chocolate, but no one took any except for Gabriel.

Israfel said, "It won't be Uriel."

As Mary closed the hamper, she said, "Who do they think replaced Gabriel?"

Everyone paused.

"I have no idea," Saraquael said. "But you're right. They'll assume we have a new Seventh by now."

Israfel said, "Ophaniel or Sidriel would do."

"You could serve," Mary said.

Both Raphael and Israfel laughed. "Two Seraphim on the Seven?" she said. "It would have to be a Cherub bonded to Raphael."

"Not necessarily." Saraquael's eyes widened. "They think Raphael is unfit for duty. If Satan were the one making the decision, he'd boot Raphael out of the Seven in a heartbeat and replace him and Gabriel with Israfel and Ophaniel. He's going to assume God did the same."

Gabriel shook his head. "He didn't replace Rahab and Ataf on the Maskim."

Saraquael said, "Think social dynamics. He can't control a team of seven as effectively as he can a team of five. God isn't worried about that." Then he handed the token to Mary, who nearly dropped it. "It's me. For safekeeping."

Raphael looked at Gabriel. *You need more rest.*

Not after you just called Israfel.

Raphael reluctantly agreed to let him stay awake a little longer.

Because the room had gotten crowded, they moved outside, a transition that left Gabriel confused and frightened.

"You're still dealing with that?" Israfel said, and Gabriel nodded weakly.

They spread out in the sunlight, talking, playing music, and enjoying the togetherness. Gabriel lay on his stomach and fanned his wings to the light, luxuriously warm, but after an awkward thought, he forced himself awake again.

Gingerly, he moved behind Israfel and brushed her hair.

She peered over her shoulder, but he looked only at the blue-black strands in his fingers.

Ophaniel and Sidriel started a discussion about tracking random angels in random places, and this Gabriel followed without joining. Something, at least, was coming back to him now, the way he'd braided Israfel's hair when they were sitting in groups, weaving in odd things because it annoyed her. Feathers, flowers, grass bits, ribbons.

As he plaited her hair, he remembered how everyone always told him he braided it "wrong": he'd always divided a braid into four parts rather than three, a pattern which yielded a rounded braid rather than a flat one. Right outermost part under two, over one; left outermost part under two, over one. While he braided, he "spoke" to the soil until some poppies sprang up in answer, growing and blossoming. Gabriel picked one to braid the stem into her hair.

The other two Cherubim had devised a check system more complicated than the FedEx delivery algorithm, but he trusted that in a few moments the scheme would collapse under its own weight and they'd resume with a modified simple system.

Israfel said as he started a second braid, "Don't you have anything better to do?"

"No."

He felt power go out of her. Then she turned, thrusting a black box into his lap.

The other angels, minus the Cherubim, looked up at attention.

Mary sat forward. "The trumpet?"

"I never showed it to you, did I?" Braid abandoned, Gabriel opened the case so the instrument gleamed in the sunlight. "I'm supposed to sound this for the final resurrection."

Mary extended a hand, then drew back. "Can I hold it?"

Gabriel handed over the instrument. She sighted along its edges, moved the valves, and admired the craftsmanship. Behind them, the Cherubim were still debating.

The awe in her voice blended with the breeze. "God outdid Himself."

Raphael leaned back on his palms. "It's the most perfect instrument in all creation, and the sound it makes is heart-stopping. It makes a D and you just want to keep on hearing a D."

Looking puzzled, Mary handed it back, and Gabriel kept it on his lap. "You've played it?"

"You mean without raising the dead?" He laughed. "It won't be the trumpet itself that brings about the resurrection." He rested his fingers on the third valve tube. "Any trumpet would do, and any player. It's just an instrument."

Raphael swept one wing out so he brushed the top of Gabriel's hair. "Tell me another one. You love that thing."

Gabriel traced a fingertip along the bell. "I like the sound quality."

Israfel made a face at him. "Go ahead and play."

Gabriel raised the instrument, lowered it, then stood. "You have to straighten your windpipe to get a strong note."

Raphael murmured under his breath, "Not that he's fanatical about the trumpet."

Gabriel feigned surprise. "Doing things right is being fanatical?"

Raphael turned to Mary. "That's obsessive-compulsive *with* a hyphen, if you were wondering."

She laughed until Gabriel raised the trumpet and played one note.

Everyone silenced. He looked down at where she sat.

"Play it again," she breathed.

Tilting the trumpet higher this time, he used the full force of his lungs to play first a scale, then to work his way back to the starting note before picking notes at random.

The trumpet met him in his soul, and he closed his eyes as though engaged in a long kiss. The stillness of those around him made for an echo like a concert hall, and Gabriel let all the notes fall together into a melody and then braided his heart directly into the sound.

Remiel appeared, startled. A moment after, Gabriel felt Michael's arrival, his nonverbal approval. Gabriel cut off the song.

Mary sat forward. "Keep playing."

"I don't like having an audience." Gabriel's head buzzed as he sat, and he felt as if his axis were wobbly. "Not when I'm just fooling around with it. It's all the trumpet, anyhow."

Raphael extended his hand, and Gabriel passed him the instrument. Still sitting, the Seraph played a short tune.

"Now," he said, "was that the trumpet, or was that me?"

Gabriel laughed. "If I say it's the trumpet, you'll say I'm disregarding your years of practice. If I say it's you, you'll ask if the trumpet magic works only for me."

Raphael grinned.

"It's grace." Gabriel took back the trumpet. "For me, the instrument is the grace. For you, it's your talent." Handing it to Israfel, he said, "Show us what someone can do with both."

Israfel stood. After taking a few breaths to steady herself, she blew.

Gabriel knew the Islamic legends indicating Israfel would be the one to sound the trumpet for the final resurrection. Until that moment, he'd never given them a second thought. The note Israfel voiced had the power of resurrection in its depth, the tone of longing and the timbre of regret. Breathless he listened as she found a new note and held it, then continued into a song Gabriel suddenly recognized. She and the trumpet seemed at war, and the struggle itself produced the sound.

Israfel abruptly handed the trumpet back to Gabriel. He regarded her without ability to speak.

Raphael found his voice first. "Were you trying to raise the dead?"

As Gabriel snapped the clasps on the case, Israfel said, "Maybe I was."

Still at the pinnacle of Mount Aconcagua, Mephistopheles raised his head.

Closing his eyes and stopping his heart the better to hear the sound, Mephistopheles shivered.

That trumpet.

He stood, cursing his own movement as he sent a half-dozen pebbles rattling down the slope, then attuned his hearing even further to the notes.

Music. From Gabriel.

It resounded only faintly, and he shifted into Hell where the sound felt just as faint: a thrum that set his whole soul on the edge of an unspeakable grief.

Shifting planes back to Creation, he stood rigidly and arched his neck as though he could feel a trumpet brushing his own lips. The feathers on his innermost wings trembled with the slow sound.

After the rebellion, when Gabriel had received that trumpet, Mephistopheles had realized the instrument was an extension of Gabriel's own soul material. This must be the trumpet's dirge for its owner.

The sound ended abruptly, and he awaited more.

If Gabriel had to blow that trumpet to begin the resurrection, maybe now it had been prevented.

Or else someone in Heaven was trying to resurrect Gabriel.

Or worse, someone in Heaven wanted him to hear the sound on Earth to make him feel guilty.

He bristled. Guilt meant sin, and sin he ought to love, so he smiled as though to display unbridled glee at violating every moral norm with his natural endowments. Which, of course, he had.

The trumpet played again, obviously not Gabriel this time not just because Gabriel was dead, but because of the difference in style. This song was planned. Although played with more skill, this music didn't resonate within.

Mephistopheles' heart stabbed him. Raphael.

The Cherub sat again, pulling his legs close to his chest and wrapping himself in his wings, head tucked into the cocoon he'd made of himself.

"I did it. I told Lucifer how. I conducted the experiments. I found the link between the Irin. I was the first to reach inside a soul and hold the strings that make it whole, and because of me those strings were snapped. I did it. I'm the reason."

Why should he regret it? What God had done deserved no lesser punishment than that. Mephistopheles had plucked one of the stars from his heart. He'd given their side a key to unlock their freedom. Why then the urge to go stand before God and say, *I did that. I'm the one. I made them sad, and now I have to tell you—*

No, don't even think the words.

Then came a note of such unfulfilled tension that Mephistopheles huddled over himself. A second note flew like a second arrow into his soul.

Who was that? No way was that Raphael. But then he remembered, didn't Gabriel have a second primary? With Israfel? That could well be her.

Two primary Seraphim, the trumpet, a sound audible in Hell.... This must be Gabriel's funeral.

He blinked.

Gabriel's funeral. They'd done it

They'd really, actually, genuinely done it! *He'd* done it—him—Mephistopheles! He'd reached into Gabriel and stabbed Raphael through the heart and Israfel in the gut. He'd wrenched Gabriel out of Heaven and into the void, and he'd done it *himself*, with no one's help in devising the theory, only a little extra support in coordinating the test—he'd done it!

And he laughed because he'd fulfilled his true nature, his fortune he'd designed for himself, his own destiny in every sense of the word.

Well, then, God, he thought, *now I'm the smartest angel you created—and no debate!*

He leaped to his feet and looked over the world as though an audience watched to record his movements in its spiritual minutes.

He was free—and freedom came with its own intoxication.

With laughter he scanned the valley stretched before him with its shanties and muddy villages. He leaped from the pinnacle, spreading his wings to break his fall, then arcing in the air to knife over the coffee fields. He extended all six wings to their fullest and punched a hole in the cloud cover.

"We did it!" he screamed to the unhearing Earth. "We annihilated an angel!"

He tucked into a ball and plummeted, waiting until a heartbeat before hitting the ground to flash far distant.

He landed in Beelzebub's chamber. "Seraph," he whispered in his ear, draping himself over Beelzebub's back and enwrapping him in his wings, "are you busy?"

Beelzebub turned toward him, surprise and fire bubbling inside for Mephistopheles to drink deeply. The heat flooded into his core before rushing outward like a release of long-built tension through his limbs and wings.

Cherub steel exuded from Mephistopheles' heart in rings for the Seraph to absorb. He joined his hands around Beelzebub's chest. "I suspect we have a funeral to crash."

Beelzebub's fire surged.

At that moment, Mephistopheles heard in his heart the summons, felt Beelzebub feeling it too, and they disentangled even as Lucifer drew them before him.

Asmodeus and Belior were already present. "You're presentable?" Lucifer said to Mephistopheles. "The both of you get armored. It seems a funeral is taking place, so it's time to retrieve Camael."

Saraquael was explaining to Michael about the ball token when Raguel's warning rolled through them all: Satan at the gates.

Raphael was behind Gabriel in an instant, hand over his eyes. Immediately Gabriel slumped unconscious, wings spilled at his sides. The next moment they'd flashed back into Uriel's bungalow.

Saraquael followed with the trumpet. "I'm going to put up an in-and-out Guard specifically geared to Gabriel. It should be impossible for them to sense him, but keep him unconscious if you can."

Saraquael left with the impression that Raphael thought Gabriel needed the sleep anyhow.

At the gate, Saraquael found the entire Maskim: Satan flanked by his top four officers, the two Seraphim a step behind and to either side the two Cherubim. All five in black armor, caped, booted, and stern.

Remiel perched on the top railing of Heaven's gate, and Raguel had a position just before it. Archangels stood at the gate houses, but they weren't doing more than watching. Saraquael took a place beside Raguel. After another moment, they were joined by Michael and Israfel, Ophaniel and Uriel.

Satan scanned the seven archangels in apparent confusion. "Is someone in charge here? I want the manager on duty."

Saraquael let out an irritated sigh, but Michael only stepped forward looking for all the world as if he had not just been insulted. "That would be me. What can we do for you today?"

From behind and above, Remiel project to Saraquael, *Welcome to Heaven. May I take your order?*

Behave, he sent back.

"I want my lieutenant," Satan said.

Remiel's voice again: *And would you like a drink with that?*

No ice, Saraquael replied.

Michael said, "Lieutenant?"

"Give us Camael," Satan said.

Remiel said, "What makes you think we didn't annihilate him?"

"Because you're there and not here." Satan squared his shoulders. "Don't be a wench. Return my lieutenant."

Michael said, "You destroyed one of our own. We're entitled to keep one of yours."

The Seraphim on Satan's either side had flames around their eyes, but the Cherubim remained unmoving.

"I still don't believe you really did it," Remiel said. "You have no proof."

Satan said, "What proof do you want?"

"Anything," Remiel said. "Whatever is left over."

"There wasn't anything left over." Satan stared off to the side, seeming bored. "When we found leftovers, we destroyed those too. Trust me that I have no interest in keeping any part of him." He returned his attention to Michael. "Now, my lieutenant."

Remiel said, "What if we decide to keep him? What will you do?"

Saraquael saw Mephistopheles and Asmodeus exchange a glance. Both had seen Remiel go mad earlier.

"Well?" Remiel's voice had risen in pitch. "What will you do? Even annihilation is preferable to Hell. We'd be doing him a favor."

Michael looked around at Remiel, who fell silent.

Satan said, "My lieutenant. I don't care what you have to do to get him. Just do it."

Michael smiled dryly.

Mephistopheles, in flat tones: "What do you want?"

"What we want," Michael said, hands clenched behind him, "is the assurance that you won't perform any more annihilations. Your word is worth, ultimately, nothing, so we retained Camael as a kind of insurance."

Mephistopheles said, "What's Camael to us?"

"You want him returned." Michael arched his eyebrows. "He must be worth something."

"It's a matter of dignity," Satan said. "We can't leave one of our own with you. Now bring my lieutenant."

Saraquael felt Remiel speaking in his mind again. *Can you feel Mephistopheles and Beelzebub going at it?*

He glanced at the pair, both motionless. *In what sense?*

Their bond. It's like it's alive. You can't feel it?

Not at all.

He felt her turn the same question to Israfel only to have her say a bond can't be felt by outsiders.

He had no doubt Remiel was right—but watching them, he felt nothing and saw nothing. A moment after that, Satan turned his head and glared at the pair of them. Both radiated surprise, and Beelzebub's feathers flared.

Asmodeus hadn't noticed. "What do you feel like demanding instead? We've complied with the restrictions in your letter."

Michael said, "I want to see the room where he died. I want five minutes in there alone and unmolested with anyone I choose."

Satan's eyes widened.

"Ten," Israfel said in a cracked voice. "We want ten."

Michael met her eyes, and when Saraquael faced Israfel, he saw tears.

Ophaniel stepped nearer, and Israfel shielded her face with her wings.

Satan squinted at Michael. "When do you want it?"

"Immediately."

Satan turned to Beelzebub. "Escort him. Then return."

Saraquael noticed how Mephistopheles brushed Beelzebub's wingtips with his own as the demon stepped forward and brought Michael, Israfel and Ophaniel into Hell.

Satan turned to Saraquael. "Now, my lieutenant."

Uriel vanished, taking Saraquael along.

Mid-flash, Saraquael sent, *We can't return him yet. He'll tell them too many things.*

Uriel sent reassurance as they appeared in Camael's chamber.

Remiel's eyes stared at them with patient mockery. Shivering, Saraquael approached Camael, securing him with his will.

Uriel's aura changed. God's presence suffused the room.

Even as Saraquael thrilled to God's touch, Camael's face transformed with hatred, and the demon tried to back through the wall in response to Uriel's approach. In a dream-like voice, Uriel said, *"Thus says the Lord,"* and the Throne extended a hand toward Camael's forehead. Camael thrashed and spit, but Uriel's touch remained steady, the words continuing like a dream and a sequel. *"You will not remember your own story. I am the Lord of truth and the Lord of your sister. As you sought to control her, so now let her memories control your own."*

Saraquael tightened his will around Camael as Uriel worked, and he felt the demon screaming, felt him trying to cry except that Saraquael held him even down to the tears. *Get out of my head! You have no right!*

Uriel's hands came back. The job finished, Camael now remembered destroying Gabriel, remembered the days in Hell afterward, remembered being captured by a vindictive Raphael (although not when it happened) and remembered time alone in a cell.

Saraquael released Camael enough to stand free. "Come on." He shook from the memories still lingering behind his own eyes. "You're being freed."

They flashed Camael back to the gates. He spit at Remiel, who waved her hand so it missed.

Satan studied Camael, and Saraquael wondered at first if he was making sure the Virtue was unhurt. In the next moment, though, he sensed him sending challenges into Camael's head to determine if this was Remiel in a state of bi-location.

Behind him, Remiel remained totally still.

Satan looked back at Saraquael. "Do you consider the terms met?"

"Michael has another five minutes."

"He will have them in perfect safety." Beelzebub had returned, and he stood with his arms folded, but one wing trailed a little to brush Mephistopheles. "Don't you trust us?"

Remiel said, "What were Gabriel's last words?"

Beelzebub snickered.

"He renounced God." Satan shrugged. "He promised me his allegiance if only I spared his life, but I didn't." He put his hands in his pockets. "Try not to hold that against him. He was in a lot of pain."

Saraquael felt himself burning, wanting to obliterate that smug smile, the easy lies from that perfectly controlled mouth. He realized his sword glowed at his side only when Asmodeus chuckled.

Smiling with only the left half of his mouth, Satan flashed his entourage back to Hell.

Uriel said, "All of you, come with me."

They reappeared in the conference hall. Raguel was first to speak. "Michael is still down there."

Uriel nodded. Raguel vanished.

When Saraquael's sword burned his leg, he tried to calm himself. "What a— It's not enough that he thinks he destroyed Gabriel. Why does he have to destroy his reputation too?"

Uriel waved him down. "We know the truth."

Remiel huffed. "Serving Satan to spare his own life never crossed his mind. The final thing he was doing was praying."

Michael returned, his eyes agleam. "Uriel, I want you to go in there and try pulling the chain anchor from the wall. Israfel can't drain Gabriel's power from it, so we have to extract it, but it's embedded directly into the Guards on Satan's office."

Uriel vanished, leaving behind a trace of enjoying a challenge.

Michael looked at Saraquael. "Whatever Mephistopheles and the others had going on before, they patched it up quite nicely, don't you think?"

"He wasn't like that when I left," Remiel said, sitting on the conference table. "More like baffled and half-dead."

"Satan didn't appear noticeably weaker, either." Michael tilted his head. "Raphael, are you able to come?"

"I have to let him out," Saraquael said with a laugh, and as soon as he released the Guard on Uriel's bungalow, Raphael appeared.

"Gabriel stayed unconscious. What did Satan want?"

"Camael's been returned," Michael said. "We got access to the room, but we can't pull the power Gabriel dumped into the chain anchors."

Raphael looked uncomfortable. "He might not need it."

Uriel returned. "That anchor is in there solidly. I've never touched a Guard like that before."

"Incredible, isn't it?" He turned to Raphael. "Do you want to give it a try?"

"If you say it can't be done, I'll go with that." Raphael tried to shrug. "I'd rather not see the room."

"It's just a room." Michael touched his arm, but Raphael yanked back.

"Then there's no need for me to see it, is there?"

The Archangel flinched. "Remiel?"

"I know that I was in there twice," she said rhythmically, "and so I know enough of hate / to say that to my thinking twice / was quite enough, / and will suffice."

Saraquael grinned. "Nice reference."

"Thanks for catching it."

"You?" Michael said.

Saraquael shook his head. "Not unless you think they need me down there, or for the sake of verisimilitude."

"Not necessary." Michael frowned. "No civil war. Asmodeus even looked friendly with Mephistopheles."

"He was only confirming something he saw," Saraquael said.

Remiel tucked up her knees and raised her wings. "Okay, so why was I able to feel Mephistopheles' and Beelzebub's bond?"

"That floors me," Saraquael said.

"Satan felt it too, though." Remiel wrapped her arms around her calves and tightened up. "He glared at them, and they exchanged a

'What on earth?' sense, and when he kept looking at them, they stopped communicating at all."

Uriel hummed as Raphael said, "It sounds like more of the spatter-theory."

Michael explained about Gabriel's spiritual substance being soaked into Remiel and how they suspected it had hit Satan and Mephistopheles as well.

Remiel turned to Raphael. "When did you figure that out?"

Michael said. "At first Raphael thought you'd gotten spattered when you attacked Gabriel, but Uriel said it felt older than that, and Gabriel wasn't missing anything additional at that point."

Remiel's eyes had gone wide. "When I what?"

Saraquael went cold, Michael bloodless.

Springing off the table, Remiel grabbed Michael by the shoulders. "I attacked Gabriel?"

Arms folded, Raphael leaned against one of the windows. "You sliced him up pretty good, but we'd have had to do some more repairs anyhow. Hey—" he added, seeing Remiel's eyes beginning to sparkle, "—didn't he say he forgave you for *everything*?"

"But—"

"Specifically that if you remembered anything else, it was included?"

Saraquael moved behind Remiel and rested his hands on her back. "A two for one deal on forgiveness from Gabriel?"

Remiel shrugged him off. "How insane would I have to be to attack him?" She looked at the others. "And he didn't flatten me?"

Uriel came closer and hugged her, and she bit her lip.

Raphael shrugged. "I wanted to flatten you, if that makes you feel better."

Remiel looked up, tremulous. "I'd have approved if I'd been there." She took his hand, and staring at the floor, she said, "Thank you for patching him up. I still think I should apologize."

"Hey," Raphael said, looking toward Michael, "that reminds me. If you do something that inadvertently hurts someone, even though you thought it was the right thing at the time, do you have to apologize?"

"I would," Michael said, "but I'm not sure it's mandatory."

Saraquael said, "It probably depends on if you're sorry. It can't hurt."

"I have a bet riding on this," Raphael said, "and you two may just have won it for me."

Uriel laughed.

Michael said, "Back to spatter theory, though—Remiel, you and Satan were able to feel Mephistopheles even though you shouldn't be able to detect a bond, and no one else was." She nodded. "And you were able to pass through a Guard set up so you couldn't, but not set up to exclude Gabriel." She nodded again. "We've still got time. I need you to go into the chamber in Hell and see if you can reach into the Guard to remove the chain anchor."

Remiel frowned. "Why?"

"Because if Satan is spattered with Gabriel's substance," Michael said, "then he's subconsciously reconfigured his own Guard to allow Gabriel's substance through as well."

Remiel swallowed. "You don't think— Mephistopheles too?" She wove her fingers. "He caught me, in Hell, and I escaped. Maybe the same way. The Guard recognized parts of me as parts of him."

Saraquael caught Michael's wide-eyed look, but he shook his head.

"Can you handle it?" Uriel said. "I'll go with you." And they went together.

Saraquael said, "That's the first I've heard of Mephistopheles attacking her."

Raphael looked out the window. "As soon as Ophaniel returns, we ought to get the Cherubim busy making tokens of the high-profile targets."

"But at least you don't need to worry about me." Michael stood straight, giving an innocent smile. "I'm only the manager on duty."

Remiel returned. "I've gotten further than the others, but I couldn't release the energy to get it to come back. And time is up now."

Uriel, Ophaniel and Raguel returned.

Raphael pivoted, frightened. "Where's Israfel?"

Before anyone could respond, Israfel exploded into the conference room, flames in her hair. She hovered a head higher than everyone and shouted, "Why can't I get in there? To Gabriel?" Then she pointed at Ophaniel. "Don't you dare! I have every right."

Ophaniel raised his hands.

"He's sleeping." Raphael moved toward her. "He's so far under right now that you could perform surgery."

"I'm tired of this!" Israfel shouted. "You're not his gatekeepers! Let me in!"

She flashed away, and Saraquael winced.

"She's battering the Guard?" Michael said.

He nodded. "It's holding. Ophaniel, can't you—"

"She took that hard," the Cherub said. "Obviously."

"That wasn't what I was going to—"

"I'm not pulling that kind of fire." Ophaniel squared his shoulders. "Especially after she told me not to."

Israfel blasted back into the room, armored, holding a sword in flames. "Let down that Guard!"

Uriel rose into the air. "He needs to rest."

"This isn't right!" Israfel got right in front of Uriel's face. "Gabriel was my primary too! I want to see him."

Uriel stood with spread hands.

"No, it can't wait!" Israfel made the whole room a kiln, and Saraquael backed to the wall, Remiel beside him. "It's always been 'Israfel can wait' and 'There's time for that later,' but there nearly wasn't. I want to see him. Now!"

Raphael passed through the Seraph flames, then got between her and Uriel. Saraquael could barely hear his voice over the roar, but he could feel the calmness he exuded. "I can tell you as soon as he awakens. But for now, he's still compromised."

"And I don't matter as much as you." Israfel tossed her head. "Again."

Ophaniel said, "It's not about Raphael. It's about Gabriel."

Israfel erupted in still more flame, then flashed away.

Saraquael steeled himself, waited, then felt nothing. Odd. "She didn't try the Guard again."

Ophaniel said, "I'll go after her in a bit. She needs to slow to a low boil first."

As the room cooled, Michael said, "We shouldn't have her going off like that." He turned to Raphael. "You really can't let him wake up long enough to patch things up with her?"

Raphael sighed. "I could. But he won't go back to sleep afterward. I let in Israfel and then Remiel will want to go in too." He looked at her. "You were about to ask, right?"

She folded her arms. "Why do you have to be right?"

"Gabriel's rubbed off on me." He shrugged. "But all of those things he really can take care of later. I'm a Seraph so I can say this—Seraphim aren't exactly patient."

Ophaniel said, "I'd never have guessed."

Raphael shot him a look, and then both cracked up laughing.

Ophaniel said, "What got to her was realizing Gabriel wasn't fully to blame. She'd been working through that anyhow. It was a mutual drifting apart, and she's determined not to make the same mistake. Hence: let me in now."

Raphael said, "I assume you mean she wants to re-bond. Gabriel's not going to take that well."

Ophaniel said, "I want to be on another planet when he tells her to wait and make sure."

Saraquael shook his head. "We can head her off and warn him. At any rate, we need to make a token of her, so that gives her more time to get control."

Michael said, "How difficult is the process? You need to teach a team to do it so we can get started."

Ophaniel shrugged. "Not difficult at all, but I'm wondering if Satan will try again now that he knows Gabriel survived."

Silence from everyone. Heart pounding, Saraquael turned to Ophaniel.

Michael said, "I'll bite. Why do you think he knows Gabriel survived?"

Saraquael murmured, "The last thing he did was lie to us about Gabriel's last words."

"But by now he's debriefing Camael." Ophaniel flicked some dust off his sleeve. "Camael will have said he wasn't there for the annihilation."

Uriel said, "God removed the knowledge from him."

Ophaniel flinched. "War really does require extreme measures."

Saraquael fought a laugh. Only from a Cherub...

Uriel said, "God allowed it. I transplanted Camael's memories with some of Remiel's so he'll think he was there when it happened."

Ophaniel sighed. "I suppose that's for the best, no matter how repulsive. Everything would have been undone the instant he said Gabriel stopped Remiel from annihilating him."

Shock from Uriel, who then said, "He saw Gabriel?"

Twenty-Three

Lucifer brought Camael directly into the lab area along with all the others except for Mephistopheles, who signed them in at the front gate. Lucifer sat Camael on a stool and paced his office, noting as he did the positions of the Maskim. Asmodeus and Belior sat or stood to Camael's left, and in the far right corner was Beelzebub. After a moment, Mephistopheles requested admittance. Lucifer flashed him into the room, but not near Beelzebub. As he suspected, within seconds Mephistopheles had moved closer to him.

Politically speaking, he'd stabilized the situation, even if it meant having to endure a Cherub-Seraph bond in a "honeymoon" phase again. Which reminded him—

"Mephistopheles and Beelzebub," he said, "what was wrong with the two of you up there? You were chattering like a pair of adolescent monkeys."

"We weren't," Beelzebub said.

"It was constant," Lucifer said. "*I know you didn't mean it* and *I'm glad you see why I was so upset* and *You only wanted what was best*—what was that about?"

Mephistopheles said, "That was all through the bond. No one should have been able to hear it."

Lucifer huffed. "But I did, didn't I?"

Belior blurted, "How could you hear into their bond?"

Even Lucifer could feel the blistering hatred Belior sent toward Mephistopheles, and Beelzebub confirmed it by saying, "What are you hinting at?"

"I'm implying that someone is engaging in the world's oldest profession."

"Let me settle this," Lucifer said. "If bonding with Mephistopheles guaranteed that I could annihilate God, I would do it. Short of that, not a chance."

"Rest assured, I'm fine with that," Mephistopheles said.

Belior said, "Then how can you hear into their bond?"

Lucifer felt Mephistopheles send, *Can you really hear me?*

"Of course I can," he snapped.

Beelzebub shimmered with nerves.

Belior said, "Bonds are private. You can't tap them. That's part of the point." More hatred and jealousy from the other Cherub.

Mephistopheles said, "Therefore you may put your mind at ease. Our enemies weren't at all inconvenienced by anything that went between us."

"All the same," Lucifer said, "when you're working for me, I expect you to be working for me, not carrying on extra conversations."

"I can do two things at once," Beelzebub said.

"That's what we tell drivers with cell phones, but it's not good enough for me."

Lucifer could sense Mephistopheles attacking the problem from five directions at the same time, expanding into Beelzebub's intelligence to use his energy too, creating hypotheses and striking them down in almost the same moment, swirling the evidence together with the possibilities and weaving them, testing them, challenging the ones that survived the first round and then modifying those.

Interesting. He'd never watched a Cherub solve a problem from the inside. The process had never struck him as important, only the results. And it did leave him curious, too, why he could feel their bond and no other, so he left Mephistopheles to wrap himself in the question.

"Now for you." He turned to Camael. "How did you get captured?"

"Raphael. He was enraged. Wanted revenge."

"That answers one question," Lucifer said, but Mephistopheles was so engaged that he didn't even register it. "But Raphael also seems to have been replaced on the Seven." He frowned again at Camael. "When they questioned you, what did they ask?" He paused. "Don't hedge. If you told them how to annihilate, say so."

"They didn't ask how it was done. They asked about afterward, though, and some process. How many were in the room, what response we expected, our next move. They were really interested in Mephistopheles."

The same could not be said for Mephistopheles, who hadn't registered his own name.

Belior said, "I suppose someone ought to be."

"Stay civil," Beelzebub said, "or I'll help you remember your manners."

"Not on my watch," said Asmodeus.

"Settle down," Lucifer said. "Camael, go on."

"There wasn't much else. They kept me enclosed but not chained, and they gave me pretty much anything I demanded." He tensed. "But Remiel—she's gone crazy."

Asmodeus chuckled. "I saw her. She was slicing her arm while talking to herself, and then she attacked Saraquael. He had to hit her with lightning to stop her."

Beelzebub said, "That must have been fun to watch."

"You could ask your Cherub sometime."

"To move along," Lucifer said, "Remiel seems to be fully recovered, if irritating."

"You might want to know...." Camael trailed off, and then his voice returned shakily. "She came through the Guards on my room and tried to annihilate me."

Shock rolled around the room. Even Mephistopheles was paying attention now.

"I swear on my own blood," Camael said, "she reached into my soul and grabbed the heartstrings."

Lucifer said, "Mephistopheles? Why do you find that so distressing?" The Cherub was all but radiating fear, and Beelzebub felt confused. "Do you have something to tell us?"

"You're lying," Mephistopheles said. "No one else knows how to do it."

"She grabbed my soul," Camael said, "and I swear on my own blood, she started disassembling me."

Beelzebub said, "What, did Jesus come and save you?"

"Actually, yes," Camael said, "but that's not the worst of it. Remiel was clearly nuts. She grabbed my heartstrings, and I swear this, Gabriel appeared to stop her."

Four cries of surprise. "No way!" Beelzebub said. "He's destroyed! I saw it!"

Asmodeus shouted, "You four swore he'd been annihilated!"

"Quiet!" Lucifer said. "Camael, go on. What happened next?"

"He couldn't do anything. He tried to get between us, and really he looked so filmy I didn't recognize him at first. She swatted him away and attacked me."

Complete silence took on its own sound-form in the next moment.

Lucifer said, "Remiel wasn't surprised when he showed up? She swatted him away?"

Mephistopheles didn't give Camael a chance to reply. "What did he look like? Did he feel like Gabriel?"

"He was much greyer than before, misty at the edges. She tossed him off like nothing." Camael paused. "He didn't feel like anything to me, but I wasn't checking him out."

Again silence. This made no sense—Remiel should have reacted to Gabriel's return. With joy, with terror—with *something* other than only irritation at the inconvenience of having to remove him from the scene of the crime. And how did she know the process? Unless the link with Camael wasn't as unidirectional as they'd thought.

Lucifer noted how Mephistopheles was not engaging this new problem with the same fervor as the previous one. In fact, he seemed to be avoiding it.

"You mean, there's something *after* this?" Beelzebub whispered.

In the same tone, Mephistopheles said, "I hope not." His voice and Beelzebub's were coming from almost the same spot now.

Lucifer said, "Are you sure it was Gabriel? There are half a trillion angels."

Camael assented.

Belior said, "When she attacked your heartstrings, or however she did it, are you sure you didn't hallucinate?"

Asmodeus laughed. "Maybe you dreamed it all."

Beelzebub said, "You were thinking of Gabriel because he's the one we annihilated, and you were upset."

Mephistopheles said, "Be reasonable. He said Remiel responded to Gabriel. They weren't both hallucinating."

Belior said, "He could have hallucinated her response."

"We could all be hallucinating this conversation, too, but that's hardly worth discussing."

Lucifer paced. He realized both bonded pairs were standing next to each other, and it made his skin crawl. He could feel Mephistopheles calming Beelzebub, drawing off his fire and replacing it with whatever it was that kept Cherubim so unreasonably logical during a crisis. Mephistopheles still wasn't fully engaged with Remiel annihilating anyone or Gabriel returning to stop her. His brain still played with the other question, the spy-hole in their bond.

Lucifer said, "When you were rescued, what did *he* do?"

There was no mistaking the inflection on the pronoun. Camael said, "*He* appeared, and Remiel collapsed in his arms."

"And what did he do with Gabriel?"

Mephistopheles gasped.

Camael said, "He—he didn't do anything to Gabriel. And Gabriel didn't interact with him either."

Asmodeus said, "Gabriel's back! You didn't get all of him!"

"Don't be ridiculous," Mephistopheles said. "We got all there was."

Lucifer said, "Let's be thorough about this. What happened after?"

"He looked at me too, and he put me under the same way he did Remiel."

Revolting development, that. "In theory, he might have interacted with Gabriel afterward."

Camael assented. "When I awoke, the whole room was different. It was subtle, but things had been moved, and there was power soaked into the walls. Even the windows felt 'fixed'."

"The enemy searched for traces of Gabriel," Lucifer said. "They must have taken apart your prison."

Mephistopheles said, "But what did Camael see? If Gabriel isn't really destroyed, then he'd have made contact. If he was destroyed, then he couldn't have."

Lucifer said, "How about a transitory state, between being and nonbeing?"

Mephistopheles had that flat Cherub intonation again. "There is nothing else."

"You know as well as I do that God changes the rules when He doesn't like what we've won. No one can get out of Sheol; then His Son dies and voila, people can get out of Sheol. There might not have been another mode of existence until Gabriel died, but maybe now there is."

A long quiet permeated the room.

Belior said, "But if Gabriel were there, wouldn't *he* have responded to him?"

Beelzebub said, "That means Gabriel wasn't there. Camael had to have been hallucinating."

Mephistopheles sighed. "We've already established that Camael didn't witness the entire scene."

"Shut up!" Beelzebub said. "There couldn't have been anything there!"

"Are you scared?" Mephistopheles sounded as if he were grinning ear to ear. "Maybe he's in the room with us *right now!*"

A second's scuffle in the dark. Lucifer felt Mephistopheles laugh through the bond, then pull off the fire he'd just spiked up in Beelzebub, empowering himself and leaving the Seraph just as energized as he'd been before. The Cherub's soul sparkled.

Lucifer checked Camael over again in his mind, challenged him and found him whole and not Remiel, but bearing the slight distortion in his thoughts similar to that in their test subjects when he'd practiced grabbing heartstrings. Belior and Asmodeus he ignored for now; they had nothing to offer.

How to defend against something that might not even be alive any longer?

Well, that was why he had Cherubim, wasn't it? "Belior, conscript three Cherubim of your choice and devise a defense against Gabriel if he still has some sort of existence. Do it by tomorrow."

Asmodeus said, "And at the same time, why not tell him to take two more Cherubim and devise a means to extinguish the Lake of Fire and eradicate God? You can't be serious!"

"Asmodeus, you will implement this defense as soon as Belior develops it, using whatever of the armed forces you require." Lucifer turned to Mephistopheles. "Your thoughts about why I can feel your bond?"

Mephistopheles monotoned, "Gabriel detonated all over you. I must have been spattered as well, and because you're a Seraph and he was a Cherub, his substance is responding to both of us."

Belior huffed. "Then why can't Camael sense you?"

A pause, and then Mephistopheles said, "Have we established that he can't?"

Camael said, "I can't...but I think I did. Back when you told me... something. I don't remember. But I remember realizing I could sense your bond when I couldn't before."

"You were down, crouched with your wings tucked." Mephistopheles didn't sound concerned. "With far less surface area, I'm sure you absorbed less of his substance, and therefore the effect wore off sooner."

Lucifer said, "If this is true, then how long—"

"—soon. I'm surprised his substance would have persisted this long. The beadlet we found after twenty-four hours was nearly dissipated, but there was a lot of him."

Lucifer knew one question it always paid to ask a Cherub: "How confident are you of this theory?"

"I can't test it," Mephistopheles said, "but it fits."

"Belior?"

"I can't comment. It makes some sense."

The lack of criticism meant as much as a standing ovation, considering the source. Lucifer said, "Very well, then. Mephistopheles, you have your previous assignment to finish. Get to work."

Lucifer forced out everyone except Camael.

"Sir?" said the Irin.

"Were you calling Remiel prior to her attack?"

He assented.

"Had you spoken to her prior to the attack?"

Again assent.

"Are you aware that once she realizes you can influence her, your usefulness is limited?"

A feeling of dread from Camael confirmed he'd revealed their link.

"You were trying to win her?"

Defeated, Camael assented again.

Why God liked to do things in pairs Lucifer would never understand. Angels functioned perfectly fine alone, but these inexorable pairings simultaneously increased and decreased their usefulness. Split Irin, depressed Cherubim, defensive Seraphim...it was too bad he hadn't convinced any Thrones to join him. They were reclusive, and if he could have brought onboard even one of them, he could have fired the rest of the Maskim.

"She's highly unlikely to leave. God has paid her enormous bribes and given her every freedom in an attempt to keep her enslaved. You realize you can't compete."

Camael sounded defensive. "The one thing God can't give her is me."

"Ah, but you nearly were given to her—first as a trussed prize turkey and then as a living sacrifice. You're better off avoiding her." Lucifer folded his arms and leaned half-sitting on his desk. "The other option you've failed to consider is that Remiel might ask for you, and God might brainwash you and enslave you at her side."

Camael smoldered. "He'd have to change me."

"I'm not sure she would care. She must feel about you as you do about her."

Camael's voice lowered. "Yes, sir."

"I recommend keeping your distance, but you're free to do as you wish. Dismissed."

Lucifer enjoyed his solitude for a while.

Mephistopheles' theory about being drenched in Gabriel's offal might have some merit to it—how else would he have heard that trumpet? Of all four subordinates, only Mephistopheles hadn't reacted with surprise when he said there was a funeral taking place— and there might have been, but the Seven hadn't made it appear that way. In retrospect, who knew why they were blowing that trumpet? Choosing then to regain Camael was useful enough, though. If a funeral did take place at a later time, he'd find a way to disrupt that too.

But hearing the trumpet and sensing the bond might well mean Gabriel-residue, and waiting for it to dissipate on its own just didn't appeal. How disgusting to be covered in a monument to someone else's weakness.

Lucifer tried burning it off, tried focusing himself, tried squeezing it off with a Guard. He couldn't tell if anything had worked because he had no litmus test except for detecting Mephistopheles' bond with Beelzebub.

What a pain. Lucifer flashed to Mephistopheles.

He and Beelzebub were in the common area, nauseatingly honey-mooning. Beelzebub sat on one chair with his feet propped on another, and Mephistopheles sat side-saddle across his lap. The pair had their wings up to form a kind of shelter, and Lucifer could feel two things: they were actively trading power, and Mephistopheles was talking through an idea at two hundred fifty words a minute, with occasional gusts of up to three hundred.

To get their attention, Lucifer had to project an announcement.

Mephistopheles pulled back his wings and pivoted. "Sir!" Beelzebub sat up, lowering his legs from the chair, and Mephistopheles slipped around so he straddled Beelzebub's lap, leaning forward with his hands on the Seraph's knees.

"Sir," the Cherub said, "I have a portion of your answer for my assignment."

This quickly? He ought to have intervened earlier. File that away for next time. "Let's hear it."

Mephistopheles opened his hands to create a hologram. Lucifer noted as he did so the way he balanced by hooking his feet behind

Beelzebub's ankles and bringing back the innermost pair of wings to wrap around the Seraph's waist.

"This is a mock-up of the soul." Mephistopheles waved a hand and made more lights. "I'm tracing through the power conduits common to most angels, and I believe if you attack a few central points rather than merely unwrapping the entirety of the heartstring you'll end up with an unlaced angel in a fifth the time."

Lucifer seated himself in the second chair. "Go on."

"If you notice here and here," and those points lit on the mock-up, "the various attributes cross over on themselves. The model more accurately mimics a weaving than a string of beads, I've discovered, and at these points there's a combination of important attributes. If you remember, you were stuck momentarily at this point on Gabriel, and now I know it was due to the crossover attributes strengthening the linkage. But if you attacked all three and released them simultaneously, an important structural integrity point would be undone, weakening the entire form."

Lucifer saw Beelzebub had worked his fingers through the shortest feathers at the back of Mephistopheles' innermost wing pair, and the Cherub shifted a little as if to guide him.

"I've found three pressure points so far." Mephistopheles spoke as if Lucifer's problem were the only thing he was thinking of and the bond wasn't lit up like the New York City skyline. "I suspect there may be as many as ten, more likely six or seven. I'll require a few test subjects to map the common points, but it shouldn't take prohibitively long to develop a working model. A day, perhaps two."

Lucifer rubbed his chin. "This still can't be done from a distance."

"No, sir. Someone still needs to be in close proximity. And the subject needs to be still."

Shaking his head, Lucifer folded his arms. "That won't be any use in a battle situation."

"I'm working on it."

"I can see that. Get me the complete list of pressure points in ten hours." He leaned forward. "Then get to work on the distance strike."

Mephistopheles nodded, his blond curls all but obscuring the brightness of his eyes. "Yes, sir."

"Beelzebub." Lucifer's tone went stern. "Do not distract him. I'm glad you're encouraging him, but do not become a distraction right now."

"No, sir."

Beelzebub had no intention of following through, but in a couple of hours he would send Beelzebub on an errand and give Mephistopheles time to work alone. For now he was keeping the Cherub well-fired, intentionally or otherwise, so it paid to let him stay.

"Call me if you need anything or anyone's cooperation," Lucifer said, standing. "Your assignment is my top priority, and I'll ensure it's also the top priority of everyone else in Hell."

Against the sunset, a pair of angels stood overlooking a lake. Swallows darted over the surface of the water, nabbing insects from the air. A family of ducks swam out from shore, gliding across the silent water with noiseless paddles, a mother and six ducklings until one was pulled under.

"This absolutely reeks," said one as he watched the reduced duck family swim to shore.

"It worse than reeks," said the other. "I told them not to attempt it, but you know how Cherubim get, and Mephistopheles convinced him he had it all figured out just because he lucked into a couple of ideas that turned out to be right." Asmodeus shook his head. "I told them not to try. I told them it wouldn't work from the start."

Fighting a smile, Camael said flatly, "You're a foresight god."

"Screw off."

"Because Lucifer's treating you like a fifth wheel? I don't think so."

"Go amuse yourself," Asmodeus said. "Or just shut up and leave me in peace."

Camael grinned.

They stared for a while at the bugs which made use of the last glimmers of daylight. Idly selecting a dragonfly, Camael called it to the attention of one of the swallows, which swooped low and enjoyed its dinner.

Camael shivered as a breeze reached parts of him more used to Hell's flames. "It's the most un-freaking-nerving thing to be taken apart." He pulled his wings closer. "I wonder if I'd have been able to talk with Gabriel."

"Would you even want to?" Asmodeus said. "Lay off. You've got Belior wasting his time because of your self-aggrandizement, and we all know you didn't see anything."

"I don't have to justify myself."

"You can't justify yourself, you mean."

They watched as the sun finished its apparent descent and left only a residual afterglow of its glory.

Gabriel's afterglow. No direct light, only the reflection of something too big to be swallowed all at once. Not Gabriel, just the afterimages, the leftovers, lacking a home and an anchor, drifting apart like a dust cloud dispersing after an explosion.

"Quit thinking." Asmodeus glared at him. Did he look that horrified? "It's no good when Cherubim do it, and it's even less attractive in Virtues."

Camael shrugged. "I'm bored."

"Pull that stunt again," Asmodeus said. "Call your sister."

Camael squinted. "Lucifer said not to."

"You're bored and she's crazy. You could have a little fun."

"I'd rather go scare some minister's son."

Asmodeus narrowed his eyes and raised his wings. "Call her."

Camael shook his head. "I don't want to see her like that. Enslaved. It leaves me nauseated for days." He could see Asmodeus wasn't convinced. If anything, he liked the idea even better now. "If Lucifer catches us—"

"What will he do? Kill her?" Asmodeus opened his hands. "Kill you? Either way, you won't have to see her enslaved again."

Camael rolled his eyes.

Asmodeus turned to look again at the sunset. "Of course, if you're afraid of her, we can go find a minister's son."

"Oh, please. She frightens me even less than you do." Camael folded his arms. "I have nothing to prove."

"You're certainly proving something right now."

As the afterglow dissipated, Camael said, "What would you do when you got her here?"

Asmodeus drummed the fingers of one hand against the opposite forearm. "That depends. Last night she went crazy as far as we could tell. She went bar-hopping, did some online chatting, then ended up at a tattoo parlor in Australia getting pierced."

"Her ears." It was so repulsive. "I saw they were all in different places."

"Navel too." Asmodeus turned toward Camael. "She was smitten with the piercer, and quite drunk. I'd love to watch when he pierces her next, whatever part she chooses. Whatever *he* encourages her to choose."

Camael's eyes flashed as sharply gold as Remiel's had ever gotten. "I'll kill him."

"Bring her down," Asmodeus said. "Let her watch."

Camael clenched his fists, set his teeth.

"When she sees how protective you are of her," Asmodeus murmured, "she'll be impressed." A pause. Then he added, "You might still win her."

Oh, wow. He might. He could. Just this once.

Camael closed his eyes and lowered his head. He listened to the rhythm of his existence until clarity came and he could feel hers as well. Holding her heart in his own, he sent, *Come to me.*

Suddenly he had the strongest, oddest urge.

Up snapped his head.

Asmodeus cracked his knuckles. "You called?"

Camael gave a shaky affirmative.

"Where is she?"

"Back off. It doesn't happen all at once."

Camael concentrated—and the next moment found himself waist-deep in the lake.

Camael leaped out of the water as if he'd landed in the Lake of Fire while Asmodeus flashed to the pier, staring open-mouthed.

He transported onto the wood and stared in bafflement at his own hands while water puddled around his legs, then flowed between the wooden slits.

Asmodeus sent him a question.

"She turned it back at me." Camael didn't even try to disguise the fear pervading his voice. Lucifer had said *Are you aware that once she realizes you can influence her, your usefulness is limited?* He'd hit the limits of his usefulness, and that was never a good thing. "I sent her a suggestion, and she sent one back to me."

It was easy to pinpoint what Remiel had told him to do.

Asmodeus cracked up laughing. "Do it again!"

Camael's cheeks burned, so he flared heat around himself to finish drying his wings and clothing and hoped that hid the flush. "So she can send me even more pointed instructions? No thank you."

Asmodeus smiled wickedly, throwing a stone into the water. "How imaginative can she get?"

Camael paid an unusual amount of attention to his fingers as he rubbed them through his flight-feathers to interlock them. "Go screw yourself."

"I'd like to see that!"

Camael flashed back to Hell with the sound of the Seraph's laughter still burning in his ears.

Twenty-Four

Ophaniel approached Israfel where she sat atop a New York brownstone.

She tightened up her heart and folded her arms. "Go away. I have nothing to say to you."

"Say it anyhow." Ophaniel sat beside her. "You shouldn't be out in Creation alone."

"This isn't alone." Israfel gestured at the world. "This is Park Slope, and there are thousands of angels in shouting distance."

"None right here with you." Ophaniel frowned. "If our enemies strike, they strike quickly."

"As opposed to we who take hours to decide to do nothing." She still had flames licking around her wings. "Is he awake, or am I still waiting?"

"You're still waiting."

Israfel hit the rooftop with a fist.

Ophaniel said, "You understand as well as I do. When you spoke to him last time, did he feel whole? Or did he feel as if he were full of holes?"

"He braided my hair." She knit her fingers. "He didn't get angry at me for not wanting to bond again. He said he'd do what I wanted, but he was sorry. And then he braided my hair."

"You warned Zophiel yesterday to remind you not to go overboard if he treated you well. You asked me to tell you to hold off for a week or longer, to make sure it was a real change."

Israfel nodded.

"It's permanent if you go back," Ophaniel said. "Isn't permanent worth waiting a week?"

"I— Why do you have to make sense?"

"I'm a Cherub. God made me to make sense." There was no trace of sarcasm on Ophaniel's face. "But God made you too, and I acknowledge that sometimes we don't need to make sense. If your heart tells you to rush back, maybe you should."

"I can't," Israfel said. "You won't let me near."

"In an hour or two, you'll be near again."

Israfel let off a long breath. Ophaniel rested his hand on her knee.

"Is my absence from Heaven a problem?"

"Not as such." Ophaniel shook his head. "To be honest, they may not attack again if Camael tells them he saw Gabriel."

Israfel said, "Didn't Uriel do a memory-edit?"

"Yes, but Uriel didn't realize Camael was still conscious when Gabriel arrived. Consequently, no edit on that. Uriel hasn't left the throne of Glory since realizing—apologizing. I think God wanted it that way, to be honest, since God permitted the rest of the edit. But we shouldn't count on Satan's previous failure for protection." Ophaniel's eyes lowered. "We still need to tokenize you."

"We have a verb for it now?"

The Cherub's brow furrowed. "It's better than Sidrielizing you."

She smirked at him. "Only marginally."' Israfel rested her elbows on her knees and gazed over Sixth Avenue. "Are you ready for me now? Or can I have a few minutes?"

"A few minutes is fine."

She waited, then looked at him.

"Oh, you meant alone?" He bit his lip. "I really dislike leaving you here."

"Gabriel was within thirty feet of Raphael when they grabbed him."

"Then I intend to be within twenty." Ophaniel's wings raised. "Or you can just come back with me into Heaven. Park Slope is the only place to get a pizza, but it's hardly the only place to pray."

Israfel smiled. "You forgot zeppoli."

"I never forget anything," Ophaniel said. "A zeppolo is like deep-frying a golf ball and then dusting it with powdered sugar."

"You do remember!" Israfel exclaimed, and they both laughed.

Ophaniel looked into her eyes. "Come back with me."

Israfel nodded, but then when he left, she remained.

God? she prayed.

In the next moment chains wrapped around her, and even as she lashed out, a Guard enclosed all of her, entangling her wings.

Screaming, Israfel shed all her Godly light against her attacker, brilliant and fierce.

"Quick!" Belior was shouting. "I can't contain her!"

Even as Asmodeus moved closer, a thousand angels appeared around them; dozens had run for help even as others disregarded Michael's directions and tried to intervene. Immediately a legion of Asmodeus' armed forces surrounded Israfel while Asmodeus pressed right up next to her, wrestled her to the ground, and covered them both with his wings. In the next moments she stopped struggling and lay limp.

Ophaniel reappeared on the rooftop, Raguel and Michael and Saraquael in the next instants, their swords shining like stars, but Asmodeus and Belior only glanced at them before flashing back to Hell, their faces afire with triumph.

Gabriel awoke to a frenzied touch in his heart. He opened his eyes to find Raphael before him.

"They have Israfel," he whispered.

Gabriel bolted out of the bed, instantly armored. Raphael wrapped him in his wings and flashed them from the room.

Gabriel doubled over, nauseated and disoriented, but Raphael kept a hold on him. He looked up to figure out where he was: the staging area just inside Heaven's gates.

Michael was calling for the chiefs of the orders, and more angels were arriving every second. Gabriel backed into Raphael, who stood with his hands on Gabriel's shoulders.

"It's no good," Raphael called to Michael. "He's not able to transport without losing equilibrium."

Michael looked at Gabriel. "Can you take charge of keeping Israfel alive?"

Gabriel nodded.

"He can't travel!" Raphael yanked Gabriel backward. "What is he supposed to do?"

"Something." Gabriel turned to Raphael. "I can do something." Then to Michael, "Let me enlist some of the other Cherubim."

"Take whomever you need," Michael said, "but do it quickly because we're leaving."

Gabriel's first impulse was to flash himself to those he wanted, but considering the vertigo, he instead spread his wings and flew through the intervening space. As he departed, Raphael wished him God's grace, then diverted his attention to the order of Seraphim. He was going to stand in for Israfel.

God, Gabriel prayed, *let us find her. Let us save her.*

The angels had arranged by orders. Even the humans had arranged and ordered themselves, led by Peter, James and John. There were no Thrones at the staging area: they would provide prayer support.

Gabriel cupped his wings to land before Ophaniel. "Find a replacement for yourself. I need you and Zophiel, plus six of Israfel's secondaries."

Ophaniel put Sidriel in charge and then called the names of seven Cherubim.

When all of them had assembled, Gabriel said, "We're the Israfel team. Our job is to keep her alive long enough to be rescued."

The Cherubim awaited instructions.

Gabriel realized he didn't have any at the ready.

"One of the biggest helps for me," he said, spinning up a plan even as he said it, "was the strength of the Seraphim. We need to empower her the same way through our bonds."

"They have her Guarded," Ophaniel said. "I wasn't able to follow."

"Was she conscious when they grabbed her?"

Ophaniel's eyes lowered. "No."

"They need her conscious in order to work. Was it the same location?"

"It felt that way."

Gabriel shivered.

"You had Remiel on the inside," Ophaniel said. "Without someone on the inside to pry open the Guard, our energy won't penetrate, not even to prolong the struggle, let alone avert the outcome."

Gabriel grabbed Ophaniel's arm. "I'm going to try to be on the inside."

With a frown, Ophaniel said, "Is Satan going to invite you in?"

"He thinks I'm dead," Gabriel said, "and we believe he's covered with my residue. I'll be able to force my way in."

Ophaniel paused. "Get a picture of his face for me when he sees you. But keep in mind, he might know you survived."

Gabriel said, "I can only hope I'm sufficiently startling that Michael can break into the room."

Behind them, Michael was already dispatching legions of angels into Hell.

Ophaniel said, "You and Israfel combined should be enough to hold off Satan for at least a little while."

Gabriel's shoulders dropped. "It had better not come down to a fight. I'm not at full strength, and she and I aren't bonded."

"She wants to rebond." Ophaniel opened his hands. "Do it, save her life, and worry about the rest later."

Gabriel paused. "That's good to know. And we have the token as backup if all else fails."

Ophaniel looked uncomfortable. "She never made one."

Gabriel's wings flared. "Why not? Did you do anyone?"

"We did, but—"

"I asked you to do her and Raphael first!"

"I couldn't get near her," Ophaniel said. "She was livid. You know Seraphim. We were going to do her next now that she'd gotten calm, but we ran out of time."

"Always time to do something else first." Gabriel's eyes glimmered. "Isn't that going to be the ultimate irony, if we lose her because once again, we put off helping Israfel because there would be time to do it later?"

Ophaniel closed his eyes. "That was my bad decision."

Gabriel shook his head. "There's nothing to be done about it now. You guys start trying to feed her power. I've got one place to go before I head out."

Gabriel focused on the Vision and flashed to the Throne of the Lord, fighting the panic that engulfed him when he moved.

He raised his eyes to behold God, so struck by glory that he forgot the fear, forgot to bow, forgot how to do anything more than absorb the light of God. Simultaneously beautiful and terrifying, the sight completed him—every hunger, filled; every need, met; every question, answered. Gabriel basked momentarily in love stronger than any Seraph could give, and he opened his heart to return a love equally fierce.

Lucifer had never understood this, that love was a choice every moment, that God would never compel what they offered freely.

Gabriel leaned into the heart-fire so much that he nearly tumbled in head-first. For a moment he was only a son of the Lord. God held him at arm's length and kept him individual.

Gabriel shook himself, bowed at last, and presented himself properly. *I need your help.*

Speak, Gebher'li.

"I need help to save Israfel," Gabriel said. "I need your strength."

Abruptly Jesus was before him, guiding him to a stand.

"I'm still not at full strength." Gabriel lowered his eyes. "Can you please complete the healing process in me?"

Gabriel felt himself abruptly topped up to full power, like a hose with the faucet turned on.

"You're not healed yet," Jesus said, "but your normal power is yours for the time being. It won't replenish once it's used."

Gabriel projected his gratitude.

"You're welcome. Now," Jesus said, "you need another weapon."

He opened his hands and created a large grey square about four inches thick.

Gabriel squinted.

Shaking out the fabric, Jesus said, "This belongs over your armor."

It turned out to be a grey cloak with a loose hood and a silver clasp that pinned at the neck ("It's your seal," Jesus said, because Jesus was even more detail-oriented than Gabriel.) At the wrists were silver bangles. An amazing volume of cloth spread around Gabriel as Jesus fastened it, and the black silk lining slipped easily against his armor.

Gabriel shifted uneasily. "I'm going to look ridiculous."

Two slits in the back allowed his wings free movement. Jesus finished fastening the buckles. "We're operating at the level of a carnival trick, but the humbler the power expended, the greater the shame when Satan falls for it. You look great, but I'm not done yet."

Jesus turned Gabriel's silver chest-plate to a scuffed black. The metal on Gabriel's sword, belt and boots transformed likewise, and the rest of his clothing went uniformly grey.

Jesus touched Gabriel's eyes, then opened his hands so a silver light appeared between.

Gabriel looked into the mirror and took a quick step backward. "Okay—I'd attack myself now."

His face had turned chalky, and his smoke-quartz eyes swirled with the chaos of the Void. He couldn't stop looking into them in the mirror.

Jesus winked out the reflection. "The light in Hell will provide the rest of the illusion. Make sure to use the cloak to its best extent too, for the supernatural effect."

"Super-preternatural," Gabriel said reflexively. "I'm already super-natural."

"One thing more." Jesus handed Gabriel a helmet that framed his eyes. Then he kissed Gabriel on the cheeks. "You have my blessing, Gabri'li. Rescue Israfel."

Gabriel bowed and flashed away.

Beelzebub and Mephistopheles arrived in Lucifer's office to hear him berating a smug-feeling Asmodeus and a self-assured Belior. "I don't care about the opportunity! We weren't ready!"

Beelzebub said, "What—"

"We captured Israfel," Asmodeus said. "Go kill her."

"We aren't ready!" Mephistopheles said.

"The army is," Belior said.

"And you should be ready too," Asmodeus said. "Belior was expected to do the impossible in twenty-four hours, and you were only asked to improve on something you'd already done."

Mephistopheles said, "Have you *got* a defense yet against Gabriel?"

"We don't need to do this now," Beelzebub said. "Tie Israfel together with Asmodeus and hand the two of them over to Michael when he comes with his forces."

"Enough," Lucifer said. "I want all four of you coordinating the defense against the enemy. They're going to invade, and they know which room we're using."

Mephistopheles said, "We could move her in here."

"We set up that room specifically for that purpose. We'll keep using it. For the moment she's not conscious, but as soon as she is, we'll start." He turned to Asmodeus. "I know perfectly well which of you was responsible for this sabotage. When this is done, I'll deal with you and your Cherub."

A call came from the main gates. The invasion had begun.

Hell's sentries met thousands of angels. Asmodeus had positioned a sizable chunk of his forces at the bottleneck of the entrance.

The invaders encountered some difficulty, but the first wave consisted entirely of Angels and Virtues instructed to engage one sentry each and keep him inhibited, allowing the following groups unimpeded passage to any spot in Hell. The inhibitors locked sword-to-sword with the sentries and bound them with their wills, then removed them to other locations.

Next came the Archangels, flashing to the open spaces where their superior fighting skills could be brought to bear. They met a room full of armed defenders in the common area, but new Archangels appeared everywhere a space opened to admit them. The chaos burgeoned. Cries of surprise, curses, calls to God, exclamations to friends, and orders all added to the din.

The defenders began fleeing to the remoter corners of Hell: the peripheries and the deeper levels where they could ambush an attacker and rip out his throat. These places began filling with Dominions and Powers. Principalities flashed to the ice fields; that choir functioned as one unit under Raguel's direction.

In the midst of the chaos, even before all the angels had arrived, Satan showed himself to rally the damned.

With Asmodeus at his left and Belior at his right, Satan sent a nonverbal order to all Hell: the angels felt it roll past with the force of a body blow. The demons revived in the presence of their leader and the commanders of the armed forces, regaining their organization. They spread out like oil, no longer fleeing as much as repositioning. Half in the great hall disappeared. Satan vanished with these.

The Cherubim and Seraphim arrived with the human saints. Michael dispatched the whole order of humans to the lab areas where the higher-order damned had set Guards as road-blocks and were organizing pockets of resistance.

A dozen demons extinguished every light in the great hall. In order to see, the angels now had to shed light on their own, making magnificent targets for demons curled into nooks of stone, lying prone under benches with drawn swords, or lining the walls armed with bows and arrows. Well-used to their own territory, the demons functioned fine blind.

The remainder of the order of Angels arrived, carrying shields and making use of the narrow headroom to deflect whatever arrows they could and to expose the demons waiting in ambush.

At one end of the hall, Belior stood shouting orders, coordinating complicated defenses in several different areas. At the other end, Beelzebub stood on a table where fighting was thickest, hacking at angels with his sword in flames.

Michael flashed to the clearing closest to Beelzebub, as near as he could get without taking to the air. At his back, Saraquael provided cover, and Zadkiel followed on his left. The three worked their way toward the rallying point of Hell's defense.

The Seraph focused on them with a sheen of double-intellect in his eyes.

Zadkiel gasped, "Mephistopheles."

A Seraph-Cherub pair in combat are almost impossible to defeat in this kind of situation: the Cherub ensconced, unseen, empowering the Seraph while providing surveillance to guide his raw force.

Saraquael sent an order to the angels in his immediate command: find Mephistopheles. Then he separated from Michael and Zadkiel, working his way in the opposite direction so they could surround Beelzebub.

Stopping to confront a new demon, Saraquael hesitated when he realized how much pain surrounded him.

Everyone had been wounded at least once. Angels and demons' spiritual bodies recovered from wounds that would kill a human being, but in some cases that meant only replenishing them for the next strike. Their forms did this naturally. The pain came as it would in a man, but recovery overtook the wound before it crippled. What the demons fought for (when defending) was not to take lives but to resist control. Their frenzy sprouted from a fear of chains. Humans proved useless in angelic struggles until they compensated for this cardinal difference: angels fought to restrain, not to kill. Demons on the offensive fought to hurt.

Even to humans, the dangers were psychic more than corporeal, and Saraquael had just encountered one of them: the carnage sickened him. He swung his sword, but the room tilted at him.

A golden glow split the darkness at his side: Remiel, laughing like a lunatic. She whirled like a dervish, a sword in each hand.

The demons thought her mad. They fled wherever she danced with her sunshine blades. Beside her, Saraquael recovered his footing.

Her back to his, Remiel said, "A poet's soul shouldn't be here."

"I'm the standard-bearer." Saraquael looked into her eyes and tried to regain his balance. "We need to stop Beelzebub."

Remiel charged Beelzebub, even as Michael jumped him from the other side and Zadkiel sliced at his legs.

Saraquael gasped as Beelzebub avoided all three attacks simultaneously while striking back at them as accurately as if confronted by only one.

Saraquael sent the order again: *You have to find Mephistopheles!*

One of the Dominions replied, flagged the Cherub in Saraquael's thoughts. High in a nook on the wall, Mephistopheles was discorporated as he directed Beelzebub's every movement to keep him unhurt. He paid no attention to himself. The demons near him had formed a living fence.

Zadkiel! Saraquael sent.

The other standard-bearer followed his thoughts to Mephistopheles. With the fury of a comet she charged, plowing through the guards at his front, her sword dragging through his dissociated form and forcing him solid with a scream.

Ten Virtue archers fired on Mephistopheles the moment Zadkiel made him solid.

As Mephistopheles took the hit, Beelzebub dropped in pain, and both vanished.

Saraquael and Remiel followed Beelzebub, while Zadkiel pursued Mephistopheles. Michael remained in the hall.

Raguel sent that Asmodeus had been isolated in the ice fields. He wasn't captured, but he couldn't get out either.

Sidriel sent that they had Belior fully engaged at the Lake of Fire.

At the far end of the hall, answering the need for a commander, Satan appeared.

Michael surged with relief—he was here, not destroying Israfel—and then terror—had he already done it?—and then rage. Either way, it was combat.

Focused on Satan, Michael didn't realize until too late when a demon slashed at him. Even as Michael turned to avoid the blow, a brilliance arced from the ceiling to divert the demon's sword. Raphael touched Michael with one hand, healing him while striking with his sword in the other hand.

For the moment, Gabriel's power resided in Raphael, but Michael couldn't tell where the Cherub had established himself.

Michael called Remiel. *I need all the Virtues scanning Hell for Israfel. Flush out any individual demons in hiding.*

Forming teams of three, she replied from a distance.

Michael looked again toward Satan, and he tingled all over.

"Go to him." Raphael's voice had a repressed laughter out of place in the middle of a battle. His double-shined eyes glistened in anticipation. "Please."

Michael hadn't heard the last word, nor anything after "go". He found an open space, and instantly flashed to it to lock himself in hand to hand combat with the first enemy creation had ever known.

Satan met Michael's blade, a sword searing with blue light. Michael's whole soul glistened, warm, charged with the might of God.

Swords clashed far too fast for human eyes to see as they pressed for an advantage, each seeking a moment, an opening, and a solid hit. Satan brought all his power to bear, a power second only to God's own, and it would have shattered Michael where he stood except that God inhabited all Michael's soul. In response, Satan marshaled everything he had, hating the person of Michael, hating even more the one to whom Michael had ceded control.

For the moment, it was God versus Satan, no pretense, and both would win: God would win the battle, and Satan would win the only way he could, by refusing to do the thing God had asked of him. Satan's fury consumed him—the frustration, the unfairness, and the iron determination to persevere regardless because in his heart, he knew he was right to refuse to submit.

Michael felt God's warning. He dropped as Satan swung at his head.

Something shot out of the floor right through Michael, extending itself like an underworld manta ray, its billowing form rippling out to three wingspans and suffusing the chamber with a red light.

Satan looked up in horror.

Gabriel, thin, black, and infuriated, thundered, "Lucifer!"

Satan recoiled from the form curling over him, fear exploding off him like radiation from an atom bomb. His Seraphic fire whipped through the room, enveloping everything around him.

Every last demon cleared the area.

Gabriel raised his arms, that cape whipping all around him, and fixed Satan with a glare that could blister granite.

Satan fled. Gabriel pursued.

Reality thickened around Gabriel as he tried to pass through a Guard not designed to admit him, but inch by inch he pressed through, forcing it to recognize himself as a part of Satan's form, forcing himself toward Israfel, toward her killer.

As Gabriel arrived, he erupted with fear, no idea where he was, unable even to hear God in the darkness of Hell. Then he forced himself to get calm: he could sense Israfel; he could sense Satan as terrified as himself and probably feeling the fear as his own. Oddly enough, the darkness helped by giving Gabriel less data to assimilate. He knew where he was now. He was in the room where Satan had tried to destroy him.

I'm in! he sent to Raphael, and the Guard admitted his thoughts to the outside because it recognized him. He pulled, then pushed at the Guard until he managed to open a keyhole for Raphael's spirit latch onto his.

God, give me strength, Gabriel prayed, and he felt Raphael relaying his prayer to God.

"You're awake," Satan said. "Perfect."

Satan faced Israfel chained as Gabriel had been, and he pinned her with his will. There was no power focus, no team forming a Guard on the room, no one Guarding her immobile. Perhaps all that had been an affectation; perhaps Gabriel's unlacing had proven so easy that Satan dispensed with the formula. This meant it would be either easier or harder to defend Israfel; insufficient data—Gabriel couldn't predict.

Israfel shrieked, and Gabriel's heart jolted.

"It's over for you," Satan whispered between heavy breaths. "They're trying to free you, but not in time."

Israfel tried to strike back, and Gabriel felt panic wash through her when she couldn't. Her head whipped around, but she couldn't move any other part of herself.

Hands inside— The feeling of slipping apart—

Gabriel rose behind Israfel, unleashing red light to shatter the darkness like a flawed opal. Even as Satan stared in shock, Gabriel shouted, "Never again!"

Satan returned his attention to Israfel, who cried out once more and tried to blast back at him, frustration swirling from her as he kept her will frozen.

Gabriel slipped behind Israfel, reached into her soul, and re-laced her.

Satan tugged her apart again. "I'm glad you're dead. Alive you were my inferior, and death changes nothing."

Gabriel secured Israfel a second time, then tried to reach through the Guard for her other bonded Cherubim. Raphael fed Ophaniel's strength through the opening to Gabriel, and once they had a line in, Ophaniel's and Zophiel's energies found a home in Israfel's heart. Momentarily her secondaries joined the stream.

Satan worked faster. Gabriel counterattacked, retying Israfel as quickly as he could to undo any damage before she got hurt, but Israfel was still the pawn, still in the center. Gabriel called for more help, desperate as he watched her partially destroyed and partially fixed again and again.

Satan's eyes gleamed, and then Gabriel felt his grip change to grasp a different part of the beadwork. As he struck the new spot, Israfel's whole soul shivered.

Israfel cried aloud, "Gabriel!"

Diving back into her, Gabriel could feel the damage: a whole area of Israfel's soul was unsupported, vibrating—and he didn't know how to fix that.

He grasped for Israfel's heart, and she clung to him.

All over Hell, demons were surrendering. They had learned instantly: Gabriel had returned from annihilation, and such a terrible Gabriel that not even Satan dared face it. The Archangels were collecting the wounded and chaining them together, fastened to the walls and ceilings. Virtues rousted out the stragglers in the deeper levels. Principalities carried in prisoners from the ice fields, and Angels stood guard over the restrained or unconscious demons. Constantly the victory became more total as more Guarded pockets were opened and the inhabitants flushed out, captured, and secured.

Inside one of the final strongholds, Gabriel tried to shore up Israfel's buckling spirit. His fading strength left his form misty. The silence remained unbroken now even by Israfel as Satan and Gabriel each attempted to gain an advantage.

Gabriel realized, *I'm constantly defending.* And then, *I'm not as strong as I was.*

Raphael pumped energy through the keyhole for Gabriel to absorb however much he could.

Satan struck again, a second pressure point, and more of Israfel's spirit collapsed.

Gabriel slid himself inside Israfel's soul: inhabiting it, loving it, doing his best to contain her within his heart, maybe slow Satan's progress. Ophaniel and Zophiel were filling her, but the strength leaked away through the broken parts. Whereas before Israfel had held tight to herself, now she was flagging.

Hang in there, Gabriel urged. *Stay with me.*

Israfel reached for him, and in the next moment she offered Gabriel her fire.

It came over him like cold water to a traveler in the desert. Like a hungry serpent, his soul uncoiled, absorbing it all and swamping her at the same time in rings of steel, his Cherub strength.

Satan radiated disgust, trying to block the flood or break the bond off at the socket, but there was so much. Gabriel swirled into Israfel and she into him with joy because even fighting for her life, even on the brink of one or both their deaths, a bond was goodness. Was purity. Was love.

Strong again, Gabriel reinforced her soul with his own material. He could feel both Raphael and Ophaniel urging him to open the Guard wide, but he couldn't make more than that keyhole. He might have escaped himself, but he'd never leave Israfel.

Satan's eyes sparkled. Then, with one spiritual "hand" in Israfel's soul, he reached the other into Gabriel's.

Gabriel moved. Satan couldn't hold him, but that shifted him away from Israfel, so Satan hit that major juncture again. Israfel was losing cohesion.

Knock her unconscious, sent Ophaniel. *He can't touch her then.*

Not while she's partially disassembled!

You were unconscious.

Raphael was keeping me together. If I do that without him here, we're going to lose the unfastened parts of her.

A moment later, Raphael's urgent voice: *God says "Remember your strength."*

Gabriel shored up Israfel, slipped out of Satan's hold again, and then had to brace Israfel once more.

Quit being cryptic, he prayed. *I've got a lot going on here.*

Satan hit the second pressure point. To Gabriel's horror, more of Israfel's soul collapsed.

In a panic, he reached into Satan's soul for that burning cord holding his soul together, and abruptly in his hands he felt the beads nearest the end: hard, raw, strong. He unlaced them.

Satan blasted at Gabriel, then turned his anger full-on at the Cherub, locking his will on Gabriel's own soul.

Raphael was screaming in his heart, but Gabriel couldn't spare a thought from the fight, because Satan was doing it all over again, wrapping his hands and his power around Gabriel's personality and trying to slide the beads off the string, and he was so much stronger—so much more—

Raphael again: *Remember your strength.*

I have no more strength!

The clatter was deafening as Michael attacked the outside of the Guard, but Gabriel knew he wouldn't break through in time to save either of them.

Gabriel forced enough of himself free of Satan's binding to attack again. Too much information: disorientation as Satan struck down at him while he had his hands in the Seraph's heart, his own substance within Satan welcoming him back, and a moment's sensation of how pliable their souls were toward one another because of their respective choirs. And oh, how much more vast Satan's was than his own, how his cord hypercoiled around itself so it left the beads looser but simultaneously harder to disconnect.

They had completely engaged with one another now, Israfel hanging half-unfastened behind Gabriel but otherwise forgotten.

Satan pushed. Gabriel felt himself give. Again Satan pushed, and more of Gabriel yielded. There just wasn't enough of him.

Remember your strength!

What strength?

Gabriel bubbled with frustration, with horror as Satan unfastened still more of him. Raphael within was trying to keep him tight, but it was a matter of time—

Michael landed a blow that vibrated the whole Guard, but it didn't shatter.

Satan had forced Gabriel back against the chamber wall now, side by side with Israfel. Gabriel wondered if he'd lost the war for both of them because here he was wavering on the brink of delirium with Israfel no closer to freedom, and Satan still had more energy than both of them combined.

Michael slammed the Guard again. It buckled, then re-formed partially around Gabriel.

As it did, he felt the chain anchor for Israfel's left arm at the back of his neck.

His eyes flew open.

Remember your strength.

The chain anchor. His attempt to survive the first time.

Gabriel extended his soul behind him into the wall, grasping the anchor. His heart racing, he vacuumed out all his own power.

With a gasp, Satan watched Gabriel double in strength, in a second becoming his equal in power, and in next surging ahead of the one angel so strong he had though he might be God's peer.

Gabriel himself marveled, intoxicated, flushed, astonished by his own glory and by the might he possessed, the things he knew he could do, the sudden insights into the universe and God's heart and God's intentions. There was nothing he couldn't know now, no mystery he couldn't unravel—and for a moment he beheld himself and marveled at the glory of the God who had created him.

In the next heartbeat, Gabriel came back to himself, was smart enough to see the trap into which he was plummeting, and returned his focus to Israfel. As the infusion of strength settled in his heart, Gabriel pushed Satan to the opposite wall with his will, repairing himself even as he grabbed Satan's heartstrings. Then, his eyes fire, Gabriel wrenched with a stranglehold on that one pressure point Satan kept hitting on Israfel.

Satan cried aloud as he tried to secure himself, but now for the first time in eternity it was a fair fight.

Israfel stared, bedazzled. Raphael cheered him on, crazed. With his hands in Satan's heart, his will pinning the Seraph in place, Gabriel blazed a light entirely Godly. That light shattered the lab area darkness, vibrated the Guards from within, and forced wider the keyhole Ophaniel and Zophiel used to access Israfel.

In the corridor, Michael was flinging himself at the Guards, which buckled without breaking.

"Peter!" Michael shouted. "Peter!"

Armored and sweating, Peter arrived instantly.

"Peter," Michael gasped, "You're the Rock, and on that rock he built his church—"

Peter's eyes gleamed. "And the gates of Hell won't withstand it!"

He landed one powerful kick at the Guard, and the whole framework ruptured.

Michael rocketed inside, tackling Satan.

Gabriel dropped around Israfel, covering her in his mantle, shattering her chains.

Satan hit the granite, Michael's sword against his throat. The Archangel's eyes swirled white and blue, and for a moment the presence of God flowed around him.

"Thus says the Lord," he shouted. "You will never, never attempt another annihilation. Creation is reserved unto me, and annihilation is mine."

Satan spat in Michael's face.

Still God's mouthpiece, Michael didn't notice. "If you make a third attempt, I will disembody your will and pin you in place, strip your power, and leave you alone and impotent for the rest of time until you're only a forgotten fable, all but annihilated yourself."

Raphael forced his way into the room and came beside Gabriel trying in desperation to rebuild Israfel for the final time. Israfel had her arms around Gabriel's neck, and she shivered like an ice-covered branch in the wind.

Raphael focused his amber light on them. "Let me help you."

Gabriel faced him in confusion: Satan had hit the same eyelets so many times—she was raw, she wasn't holding where he fixed her—

"We'll do it," Raphael murmured, stroking her soul to send his power through her.

"Ophaniel!" Gabriel shouted. "Zophiel!"

Michael didn't turn his head from the demon before him, his eyes locked with Satan's. God was bringing him back to himself. "Do you concede?"

Satan said, "No."

Michael flashed him to another part of Hell.

Ophaniel dashed to Israfel's side. "Hold on. Israfel, please, just hold on." Grabbing Israfel's hand, he looked to Gabriel. "Help her! You have all this power, do something!"

Gabriel gathered her closer, bowed his head so his blond hair mingled with her black. *Respond,* he urged. *I'm holding you together. Raphael is pouring in power. This is the last time. You just need to knit together now. Just once more. You're safe. Just once more.*

Zophiel rushed into the room, casting aside her sword with a clang against the stone. "I'm with you, Israfel. Stay focused."

Gabriel tried again to restring her, but everything crumbled: metal fatigue of the soul. He directed Raphael's healing power onto those spots like a searchlight, and he prayed.

"Do something," Ophaniel begged.

"We're trying," Raphael whispered. "He's doing everything he can."

"It's not enough."

"It'll have to be," Raphael said. "Gabriel, what else can we give you?"

"I need ideas." He looked from Ophaniel to Zophiel. "Bounce something off me. We need another means of patching her up."

With her shredded heartstrings and eyelets in his hands, Gabriel sent his enhanced mind into the problem and engaged with it on every level possible, attacking it from twenty directions at once, discounting each idea as useless or dangerous. Ophaniel and Zophiel offered suggestions, but batting them back as other suggestions gave him no breakthrough. He abandoned that and went further inside, reviewing everything that had gone into saving himself and wondering what use it would all have been if he in turn was not able to save Israfel.

He raised his eyes to Raphael's, and he sensed the key lay with him. The Spirit pushed him to remember...something. Raphael had saved him by letting go, but that had worked only because of what Raphael had been holding. Gabriel had none of that; letting go in this state meant Israfel's dissolution.

Pray for us, he sent, and Raphael nodded: he hadn't stopped praying.

Israfel felt soft in his arms, like jelly. Gabriel looked to Ophaniel, who went immaterial and slipped inside Gabriel's body, then solidified as Gabriel went desolid so that Israfel had been transferred to him. Ophaniel stroked her cheek, but even that pressure left a shining distortion over her.

Zophiel said, "If we're going to have an epiphany, we need it now."

Gabriel went after the problem again, engaging and returning as rebuffed as if he hadn't tried at all.

He looked at Raphael. "This is so frustrating. I might as well not even be here!"

And with those words he remembered Raphael saying the same to him: that with his mind engaged in a problem he might as well not even be there. And then he nearly wasn't, never again.

How many times hadn't he been there for Israfel, all the little abandonments and the unshared moments? And now Gabriel wasn't even "here" when she was dying, rendering her last moments like so many others, with Gabriel physically near but mentally far.

Gabriel bowed his head and whispered, "I'm sorry."

He disengaged. He focused on Israfel, on the poppy he'd braided into her hair, and he leaned forward so he had his arms around her as she lay on Ophaniel's lap. He sent his mind back into her soul and pressed his will around the crumbled parts to support what he couldn't repair, and thought only about Israfel, only about this moment. Because if all he had left to give Israfel was these few minutes, then this was what he would give.

Zophiel whispered, "Could Uriel help?"

"Uriel gave back the knowledge," Raphael replied in a similar hush. "I already asked."

Israfel's hair felt brittle even as the rest of her felt soft. As the minutes passed, Gabriel dissolved a little too get his form closer to her, determined just to be near, waiting. Just being present.

Raphael murmured, "Try her again."

Gabriel gave Israfel access to his power, and there came a response: weak, but she'd taken it. Raphael's glow still enveloped her, and Gabriel tried again to direct it to the weak spots.

What if there was another technique, some way—

Whatever you're doing, quit it, Raphael sent.

Chilled, Gabriel forced himself to stop looking for alternatives, just to be there.

Raphael sent reassurance.

For so long, Gabriel felt as if he were only waiting, watching, and so useless. But he was holding Israfel together, and he was guiding Raphael's efforts to best effect, and he could sense the prayers all around them, Uriel's and Mary's, Michael's, Saraquael's, Zadkiel's— so many. At some point he looked up from Israfel to realize many others had come into the room as well, that Zadkiel stood behind Raphael with her hands on his shoulders, that Michael had checked in on them, only he'd been so absorbed in Israfel that he hadn't noticed.

And next he saw Raphael smiling, realized Ophaniel had relaxed, that Zophiel breathed easier, and in the next moment he gazed down at Israfel as her eyes fluttered open.

"You're still here," Gabriel whispered.

She groped for his fingertips.

Gabriel probed into her soul. The parts that had crumpled were firmer again, not yet ready to be laced but rapidly reconstituting.

"Thank you," she whispered. "You gave me everything you had."

"No," Gabriel said. "Just the only thing I could."

Ophaniel carried Israfel to Heaven where Mary and the Thrones awaited, Gabriel and Zophiel accompanying.

Wings flared, Uriel stared at Gabriel. "What happened to you?"

Gabriel puzzled until he remembered Jesus had turned him pale and dark-eyed. He didn't answer but just stayed by Israfel's side.

After laying her on the bed, Ophaniel whispered to Israfel, trying to get her hands loosened from his wings, but eventually he just went desolid to stand free.

Uriel inspected her. "Everything seems to be here."

Gabriel sighed.

Uriel peered at Gabriel. "And there's more of you than before." The Throne touched him. "Satan tried to unlace you too?"

"I returned the favor." Gabriel shivered. "I had to repair myself. Does it feel like I did it right?"

"You're raw, but it's all there."

He felt Raphael ask for him, so he flashed back to Hell. The infusion of power seemed to have had at least one permanent effect: there wasn't the terror any longer when he traveled.

She's stable.

Raphael nodded. "You still look terrible."

"Thanks. I scared Satan half to death."

Pivoting, Raphael took a step toward him. "You scared me half to death too." Raphael's eyes flamed. "I couldn't get to you."

Gabriel brushed his wings by Raphael's.

Raphael stopped to heal an injured angel, then returned attention to Gabriel. "Remiel was having trouble with Mephistopheles. You should join her and pull your up-from-the-grave stunt once more."

Gabriel sighed. "This isn't a practical joke."

"They deserve to have the daylights scared out of them." Raphael paused with a glimmer in his eyes. "Satan sent out a wave of terror that could have cracked open a planet when you surprised him, and pretty much every demon tried to hide after that."

"Asmodeus and Belior too?"

Raphael shook his head. "Raguel had to cinder Asmodeus." He looked downcast for a moment. "We tried to hand him over to Belior until he reconstitutes, but he doesn't want anything to do with him."

Gabriel's shoulders dropped. *What a waste.* Then he looked up. "So it's only the three stars of the show remaining."

In the lab area again, Remiel, Saraquael and Raguel worked on a Guard Gabriel found too familiar.

"They're both in there," Remiel was saying to Raguel, "and we can't crack it open." She tapped the Guard. "Have you ever felt anything this strong?"

"I believe I have," Gabriel intoned.

Gabriel caught the glances the other three exchanged when they saw his eyes and clothes.

"It's just me," he said with a laugh. "Gabriel 2.0, the scary version."

"Don't mind me." Saraquael shifted to stand behind Remiel. "I'll just make sure I keep the lights on at night for the next century."

Gabriel grinned. "I'm testing out my Halloween costume."

"Dibs on the cloak," Remiel said.

Gabriel touched the Guard, sampling the power of the Seraph-Cherub bond that fueled it, and at the same time realizing with an intoxication that he still was far more powerful than ever before. He could crush that Guard and laugh while doing so, maybe squeeze the pair tight and pull them out through their own web.

Instead he made his presence known to the Guard, and the Guard, recognizing him, trembled with surprise.

As it did, Raguel smashed it open.

While holy light flooded the chamber, the two inside scattered like roaches, flashing to any other part of Hell. Prepared for this, Remiel and Saraquael flashed after them, and within seconds, each returned with one prisoner caught and chained. They dropped them in front of Gabriel.

Mephistopheles fell to his knees. Beelzebub glared first at one Cherub and then the other, although one disturbed him visibly.

Gabriel folded his arms.

"Go ahead," Beelzebub said. "Annihilate us."

Mephistopheles rolled his eyes. "No, you idiot."

"We changed you," Beelzebub said.

Gabriel studied him.

"Quit over-thinking everything." Head tilted, Beelzebub smirked. "Are you going to destroy us, or did death only make you more annoying and less effective?"

Gabriel's brow furrowed. "You haven't made a compelling enough argument for me to return the favor."

Beelzebub squared his shoulders. "Simple revenge. We killed you, so you should kill us."

"I would never," and Gabriel smiled slowly, "take you out of Hell."

Mephistopheles got to his feet and stepped closer to Gabriel, touching his cloak. "How are you here? Is this a new transitory state, or were you re-created?"

"I'm still the same angel." Gabriel lowered his light a little. "You failed. I'm alive."

Mephistopheles cocked his eyebrows. "Do you attribute your survival to a faulty technique? Did the pieces regenerate as we suggested they might?"

Gabriel said, "Actually—"

"Actually," Saraquael interrupted, "two Cherubim in a debate here and now would be a terrible thing, so let's just leave it as a mystery to further torment you during eternity in Hell."

Gabriel glared at Saraquael, who shrugged.

"They need to calm the lower order demons," Remiel said. "We're having a hard time keeping them chained thinking there's something returned from the other side of annihilation powerful enough to make Satan scream like a school-girl."

Beelzebub's eyes flashed. "There's no way you'll get as much mileage out of that as I will."

"I intend to try."

As Saraquael chained Mephistopheles and Remiel led Beelzebub away, Gabriel said, "Wait." He looked Mephistopheles in the eyes. "Do you want to be chained together or separately?"

Mephistopheles looked over his shoulder at the Seraph, who looked at him and met his eyes.

"Together," said Beelzebub.

"Then cooperate." Gabriel flashed Mephistopheles and himself across the room.

Mephistopheles muttered, "Two Cherubim debating would not be a terrible thing," looking at his cuffed hands. Then his head picked up. "You do look different. Was that an undocumented effect?"

"It will be gone soon," Gabriel said. "There won't be any lasting changes."

Mephistopheles let off a cloud of frustration.

"Did you really think God would permit it?"

Staring at his feet, Mephistopheles said, "We had to at least try."

Cherub-to-Cherub they regarded one another momentarily.

"The idea was," said Mephistopheles, "that I could solve the problem—the logistics of the thing—and I never considered facing the consequences. Like with the hydrogen bomb—like J. Robert Oppenheimer, for crying out loud—I said, this is the way you do it, but I didn't think we would."

Gabriel folded his arms. "You never believed they wouldn't."

Mephistopheles couldn't look him in the face. "I got so engaged in solving the problem that I never considered the practice which would come after the theory."

Gabriel kept his voice low. "These things have to go to completion."

Mephistopheles' wings dropped. "I wouldn't do it again."

Gabriel opened his hand.

Mephistopheles tried to take a step back, but Gabriel's will held him.

"No!" He shivered, his blond curls getting in his eyes. "But I just promised not to use it."

"Satan will beat it out of you," Gabriel said. "He'll engage you and give you everything you ever wanted. Consider me as saving you the trouble of being beaten or seduced."

Swallowing, Mephistopheles concentrated until his eyes glowed. He arched his neck and sparkled all over, and then fine tendrils of light extended from his eyes, from his skull. His arms flexed from his sides, and his fingers spread.

Gabriel opened both hands and called all the light filaments together. "All of it," he murmured, then gathered them together into an orb.

Mephistopheles opened his eyes, shaking. He was crying.

Gabriel ignited the orb on his palms, and it crackled as it flared. When the flame exhausted itself, nothing remained.

Chalky pale, Mephistopheles wrapped his arms around his stomach.

Gabriel resisted the urge to put his arms around the other Cherub, but with a soft voice, instead he said, "I have a question for you, something our own Cherubim never managed to answer."

Mephistopheles dragged up his gaze, a spark in his eyes.

Gabriel took a step closer and whispered, "Can't? Or won't?"

Mephistopheles drew a short breath, first looked at the ground, then up and over Gabriel's shoulder. Gabriel could follow the trajectory of his gaze without turning his head: he'd just looked toward Beelzebub. Gabriel didn't pivot to see if Mephistopheles' bonded Seraph was looking at him with anger or with concern or perhaps even with fear, or if he wasn't looking at him at all.

Mephistopheles said, "Won't."

Gabriel's hands unclenched. He hadn't realized he'd tightened them.

Michael appeared alongside Gabriel. "If you're done with him, I'll take over."

Gabriel relinquished control over to Michael. "Chain him together with Beelzebub."

Michael huffed.

"I gave him my word."

Michael waved to Saraquael to bring over Beelzebub, and they chained the pair to one another.

"There will be no further annihilations," Michael said. "You will not re-perform the research."

Beelzebub held his head up in defiance even as Mephistopheles slumped.

"What will you do to us if we don't comply?" Beelzebub said while Mephistopheles murmured, "Will you just shut up?"

"Well, what is he going to do?" Beelzebub shrugged. "More pain? We've been in Hell for so long that pain is redundant. We'll cope."

Michael explained in exceedingly simple terms what it might feel like to exist as an awareness and a will stripped of one's faculties, self-aware but unable to affect the world around oneself in any way.

Mephistopheles said, "Your unsubtle implication being that compliance prevents this scenario."

Michael shrugged.

The demon pair stood without speaking for a moment, but Mephistopheles had his wings against Beelzebub's. Finally the Seraph said, "If that's all—"

Michael grabbed Mephistopheles by the wrist. "It's not."

Beelzebub tried to lunge between them, but Saraquael tightened him up so he couldn't move.

"This one's personal. Open your hand," Michael said.

Mephistopheles did, revealing the sigil ring.

Michael touched it so it returned to himself.

Then he looked at Saraquael. "Take them through the ranks of the prisoners and have them calm everyone. Let the prisoners know it will only be for a while longer, until we have everyone accounted for."

Saraquael flashed them away.

Michael looked around to find only Remiel. "Where's Gabriel?"

Gabriel stood less than a wingspan from Satan in the deep dark. If Satan could detect his presence, he hadn't reacted.

When Gabriel adjusted his cloak, Satan turned toward the sound.

"It's just us." Gabriel filled the cavern with a red light. Satan was chained to a rock wall, but not so tight he couldn't stand freely.

Satan's eyes bored into Gabriel, measuring and re-measuring the power confronting him. "You want some sort of concession?"

"I'm not expecting a sincere one." Gabriel let Satan's study proceed. "You make promises only to break them and then call us fools to agree. You could swear anything and I wouldn't believe you."

"Then why return?"

"You didn't kill me." With folded arms, Gabriel stared icily. "You missed the mark again. Are you prepared to finish the job?"

Satan smirked. "What makes you think I'll try again? One of the Almighty's mouthpieces already issued a string of impressive-sounding threats."

"Because you're stubborn, and you'll agree to the system in the short term if it meets your wants over the long term. Michael promised vengeance if you try again. I don't want you even to try."

Satan met Gabriel's gaze, his eyes glistening, his smile calculated. "How do you propose to do that? I have my own free will."

Gabriel reached out in a nonverbal expression of what could not be said. As only a Cherub can, he educated Satan about the brilliance of a single soul: the uniqueness of an individual's memories and perceptions, the unique fit of a soul into the matrix of creation, the love only that specific soul could give and the unique way in which only that soul could reflect the light of God, an individual sculpted and endowed with life by the Father.

"Why should that change my mind?" Satan shuddered. "I knew all this. The worth of a soul is the reason I tried to destroy one."

Gabriel's black eyes burnished the rest of his face. "God can re-create anyone."

"He won't. He'll remain non-involved that far. Eventually I'll succeed, and you'll have lost one of your brilliant and unique lights."

Gabriel looked down. "You're set on trying again."

Satan's eyes glinted garnet in Gabriel's distorted light. "When I have nothing left whose loss would affect me, why not? I've burned too long to be afraid of more pain. Someday the returns will diminish enough for me to try again to annihilate you. Or Michael. Or Raphael."

Gabriel breathed deeply, and his eyes softened. Relaxing first his wings and then his shoulders, he hummed out a long breath with his eyes half-closed.

The presence in the room changed as Gabriel diminished and Another took over.

Satan looked right at him and said, "I hate You."

Possessed by God, Gabriel embraced Satan, who pressed back against the wall and the chains. Gabriel's fingers came up to touch Satan's head, and then with closed eyes he departed.

The Guard came down, the lab became solidly dark, and the knowledge of annihilation went from Satan.

Twenty-Five

Gabriel crouched by Israfel's bedside as she awoke.

Ophaniel threw himself over her, tangling his wings in hers, hugging her with an unCherubic desperation as she sighed. Gabriel could feel her drawing strength from Ophaniel, so he offered his own even as Zophiel offered hers.

She raised her head, taking in the wide windows, the bead-curtains, the bird-filled trees and the crystalline sky, and finally the bare wooden walls and floors. "I'm home?"

Ophaniel only held her tighter.

They were in Uriel's bungalow again, a place Gabriel would gladly avoid for the rest of eternity if it meant everyone remained intact. While Israfel sat with Ophaniel, Gabriel probed into her heart, avoiding direct contact with her frayed heartstrings. "Stay still a moment." Without fanfare, he hooked the healed pressure points back together so quickly that Israfel didn't get a chance to do more than rattle the windows.

"Thank you." She looked at all three Cherubim, then took Gabriel's hand. "I was so scared he was going to take down both of us."

Gabriel squeezed her fingers. "It was a near thing, but we're both safe."

She shook her head. "You look awful."

"Thanks." He grinned. "It's not real. Remiel has dibs on the cape, though."

Israfel frowned. "Surely she can't wear it all the time."

Ophaniel made room for Gabriel to shift closer to the bedside.

"There's one more thing." Gabriel felt his cheeks go hot. "If you can try to hold still, I'm not sure if this is going to hurt, but it should be quick."

She recoiled. "What are you doing?"

"We re-bonded." His gaze dropped. "I needed your energy to defeat Satan, but I can break it for you now."

Israfel's spirit armored against him.

Gabriel felt Ophaniel brush his wingtips against his legs where Israfel couldn't see.

Gabriel forced himself to look into her eyes, into a blueness he wouldn't be able to plumb a few minutes from now. "God's going to require the knowledge back soon. I won't get another chance. You'll be stuck with me again."

She squeezed his hand so tight it hurt. "Then we'll just have to try harder to be present to one another, won't we?"

Gabriel trembled. "Breaking it now wouldn't preclude re-bonding at a later time, when you're more sure."

"I'm sure."

A flash of silver crossed his eyes. "Do you think you'll be up for trick-or-treating in a couple of weeks?"

She snickered. "Only if I get to wear that cape."

Releasing her hand, Gabriel unfastened the neck only to realize there were too many clasps to do this gracefully. Instead he flashed himself out of it, catching the cloth before it rippled to the floor. "Deal. Remiel can wait."

Raphael flashed into the room, beaming broadly. "It's checkup time. Everyone out but Israfel."

The three Cherubim flashed away to their choir loft, the third ring back from the throne after the Seven and the Seraphim.

Ophaniel said, "You're aware that if you hurt her again, I'll happily beat you half to death?"

"Please do." Gabriel bit his lip. "She deserves better."

Zophiel said, "Are you really going to surrender the knowledge?"

"I'm not sure I have a choice."

Ophaniel said, "Only Satan will have it? Is that really in our best interests?"

"The details blur after a certain point," Gabriel said, "but I think God stepped in and took it from him."

"This stinks," Ophaniel said. "I don't like a mystery."

"Mephistopheles figured it out." Gabriel's eyes glowed black. "Surely he's not *that* much smarter than you."

Ophaniel and Zophiel snickered. "Plus, we can cooperate."

"Maybe after the fifteenth time God removes the knowledge from us, he'll get tired of doing it," Zophiel said, and they all laughed.

An Angel appeared before them, then turned to Gabriel.

"It's my turn?"

The other two Cherubim projected reassurance and condolences. Gabriel went with the Angel.

Together they flashed to the throne, and the Angel departed with a bow.

Gabriel knelt. "My Lord. My God."

"My strength," said God.

Gabriel prostrated himself and presented himself properly, and God gave his approval.

He stood again, regarding God face to Face. "May I ask a few questions?"

"Certainly."

"Will Israfel recover fully?"

"She will."

He let out a long breath. "Thank you for all your help. I couldn't have done it alone." His fists tightened. "Will Satan ever attempt it again?"

"I removed the knowledge from him," God said. "None of them have it now. The one who learned it the first time is too unwilling to study the matter again, and the others don't have the same ability to reverse-engineer the soul."

Gabriel waited.

"There will never be another annihilation." God sounded amused. "You wanted me to spell it out."

Gabriel's eyes flashed, but he looked aside. "Did you take the knowledge from Satan after you assumed control in the lab area?" When God assented, he rubbed his chin. "That feels odd. I'm supposed to impart knowledge, not obliterate it."

"Education had no effect."

"I trust you," Gabriel said. "Removing knowledge is a first for me. I functioned as an antiCherub."

God chuckled.

Black-eyed and hopeful, Gabriel looked up. "Father, are you pleased with me?"

God made it known in Gabriel's heart how very pleased he was. Ducking his head, Gabriel grinned.

Jesus appeared before Gabriel and took his hands. "You did everything I wanted. Thank you."

Even as Gabriel shivered, Jesus turned his armor from black to grey, and then the armor vanished entirely to be replaced by jeans and a sweater. His touch on Gabriel's eyes returned them to grey, then changed his skin and hair to their normal color as well.

Gabriel trembled.

Jesus held him at arm's length. "Are you ready?"

"No." Gabriel's hands knotted. "Please let me keep it. I'm not going to abuse the knowledge. I won't even admit to still retaining it."

Jesus shook his head.

"We had that whole conversation," Gabriel whispered. "I don't want to forget that too. Please don't leave me an antiCherub."

"You're fully a Cherub." He gestured that Gabriel should kneel. "But there are some things even Cherubim need to forget."

He rested his hands on Gabriel's head and then pushed his fingers up beneath his hair.

What if you only took part of it? Gabriel sent.

"Then you'd piece it all back together and you'd have to go through this again," Jesus said. "Remember your words to Mephistopheles? *Consider me as saving you the trouble of being either beaten or seduced.* Satan's not going to leave you alone if he thinks you still have it, so you can't."

"Afterward?" Gabriel said, fists clenched. "Maybe then?"

"No promises, Gabri'li." Jesus ran a finger along some strands of Gabriel's hair, tracing down his forehead and over his eyebrows. "Relax."

Gabriel tilted up his face to look Jesus in the eyes, and Jesus brushed the tears from his cheeks. "It's done."

With Gabriel shaking all over, Jesus crouched and kissed him on the forehead.

When Gabriel was ready, Jesus had him stand, then called for Raphael and Israfel. Raphael held Gabriel while Jesus took the memory from Israfel of how Satan had manipulated her soul. She didn't object.

"Now," he said, facing the three of them, "what's this about a fun bet?"

Gabriel and Raphael grinned simultaneously.

"You're both crazy," he said with a laugh. "Gabri'li, go blow up something, will you? For the only time in Eternity, you've got more power than Lucifer at his peak. Don't wear it down. Spend it all at once."

Israfel and Raphael both ignited.

"I know just the thing!" Israfel stood on her toes, her wings spread. "There's a star nursery four billion light years from Earth that hasn't turned out a decent star in millennia."

Raphael gasped. "That's perfect!"

Gabriel folded his arms and glared at Jesus sidelong. "Thanks."

"And Rapha'li," Jesus said, but Raphael interrupted, "I know—get him the stupid root beer float."

"*Get* it?" Gabriel said. "You have to *make* it! There's a microbrew root beer they sell in New England called Virgil's, and a place called 'Promised Land' in Texas that makes the best vanilla ice cream on Earth."

Raphael glared at him while Israfel choked on laughter.

"The glass has to be ice-cold," Gabriel said, ticking off the points on his fingers, "with a little chocolate syrup around the inside rim. You pack three scoops into the bottom—"

Raphael said, "You have got to be kidding me!"

"Of course I'm kidding!" Gabriel gave him a shove. "Take-out from Friendly's is fine."

Jesus said, "Oh, and Zadkiel wants to borrow the cloak after Israfel and Remiel are done with it."

"Zophiel wants it too," said Israfel.

Gabriel sighed. "I'm never getting it back, am I?"

"Eternity is a long time," Jesus said. "You'll get it back. But I suggest you start a sign-up sheet."

Israfel escorted Gabriel to the star nursery where they located a spot with two brown dwarfs in close proximity. Raphael excused himself while Israfel selected an ideal vantage point to view the show.

Michael appeared, his signature suppressed. "Gabriel doesn't want an audience, does he?" When Israfel nodded, he said, "So don't mention I'm here." As she snickered, Michael added, "And if Gabriel asks, Remiel is *not* also watching from other there. With a video camera."

"Gabriel just signaled," Israfel said. "Where's Raphael?"

"Right here." He reappeared, holding a tall mug. "I hope this is cold enough for him."

"Absolute zero should suffice under most definitions of cold." Israfel smiled. "No take-out?"

"He nearly died, and then he saved your life." Raphael tossed the mug from one hand to the other. "The least I can do is procure some chocolate syrup."

"Second signal," both Seraphim said (with Israfel bouncing in place, hands clasped together).

The nebula flared with a white light, followed by an afterglow that shimmered on all the stardust and gaseous matter as it swirled around the gravity wells. Raphael whooped, followed by a deep awe that rolled from the depths of his heart. Next a visible chain reaction as a brown dwarf tripled in size, trembled, and collapsed on itself; it ejected matter that reflected light in every frequency of the spectrum.

"Oh," Israfel murmured. "My God."

As the glow waned, the show repeated with a second brown dwarf in the same cluster.

How many is he going to do? Remiel sent.

I told him to do at least three deep discharges. Raphael's thoughts sounded faint, so much of him was absorbed in the light show. *The rapid recovery afterward will rebuild substance in him.*

Does it work? asked Remiel.

It's efficient, Raphael sent, *but I don't mind the side effects, either.*

With that, a third star ignited, and everyone applauded.

Gabriel flashed to them, shaking, breath heavy, but with pink cheeks and bright eyes.

Coming up close, Raphael inspected him. "How do you feel?"

"Pretty good," he managed between gasps. "You're right. I don't get to do that very often." He looked up to spot Michael, then Remiel. "You didn't videotape that, did you?"

"It's content for my website," she said, the camera still rolling. "I was just thinking it's too bad I don't have a rusted pickup with a gun rack and a six pack."

"You're a lunatic," he said. "Quote me on that." Then he looked at Israfel. "Was that worth the price of admission?"

She smiled. "I think so."

"Come on." Raphael tossed him the mug. "I owe you a root beer float."

"Not yet." Gabriel gazed on the lighted nebula. "I want to watch it burn for a while. It's beautiful in its own way, how it's going to reform eventually and not just be snuffed out."

Epilogue

An eight-year-old boy in an angel costume ran ahead of a black-haired woman in an ankle-length grey cloak. "Hurry up!" He tugged at the door to the nursing home.

"Don't you think you've trick-or-treated enough?" the woman said as she hauled open the door for him.

The boy turned his bright grey eyes on her. "Just this one more, please? And then we're done. Come on!"

A number of the residents relaxed in the main lobby. The little boy ran right up to the closest cluster of elderly ladies, adjusting his gold-wire halo. "Trick or treat!"

A chorus of "Ooh!"s from the women. "Who are you?" one woman said.

The boy stood straight and tall. "I'm the archangel Gabriel!"

The women gave him another chorus of "ooh"s, and one said, "What a little angel!"

He clasped his hands behind him. "Thank you, Ma'am!"

"And so polite, too." They gave him candy to put in his pillow case. He ran to the next group, and one of the residents turned to the grey-cloaked woman. "That's an incredible costume. Did you make that for him?"

Eyes sparkling, she said, "His Father did."

"You must be very proud of him," said another.

"He certainly is energetic," the woman said, then called, "Gabriel! Don't go far!"

A moment later the cloaked woman saw the grand piano beneath the tall windows. "Is that in tune?" When the residents assured her it was, she settled at the keyboard while Gabriel did his rounds through the whole room. By the time he returned to her an hour later, his pillowcase was full of candy and his head full of anecdotes from the residents. Taking requests, Israfel was astounding everyone with a faultless rendition of every song.

"Your mom is really talented," one gentleman told Gabriel, rubbing his hair.

"I know, sir." He straightened his halo. "She's been good to me."

Seeing Gabriel, Israfel stood from the piano bench, and the residents all asked her to return sometime with her charming son. Israfel tousled Gabriel's hair and told him to say goodbye.

Not yet, he sent. *There's one more upstairs.*

He grabbed her hand, leading her along corridors that smelled of antiseptic and waste at the same time. The sterile light from fluorescent fixtures glared against the polished floor as they walked, occasionally stopping at a resident's room, announcing "Trick or treat!" and then producing for the resident a treat from the pillowcase. Each time Gabriel did this, the resident would exclaim that it was his favorite, and how had he known?

At the end of the corridor, Gabriel said, "Last stop. I promise."

Israfel sighed. "Did we just cover the whole Earth?"

"That's why Raphael doesn't want to do it anymore." Gabriel squeezed her hand. "It makes for a long day. But it's a chance to talk to people when they don't expect an angel."

"I have to admit," Israfel said, "name-that-tune was fun."

Gabriel turned into the corner room, a double with one resident out; the other lay in the bed beneath the window, muttering in a monotone.

Gabriel climbed onto the bed and got her attention with a soft, "Trick or treat."

The woman's guardian sat on the edge. "She won't understand."

Gabriel withdrew a handful of hard candies from the bag, then handed one to the woman.

She took it with translucent-skinned fingers, unwrapping it with a light crinkling. First she slipped it into her mouth, then whispered, "Horehound drops."

Gabriel looked into her eyes, his gaze riveting her as only an angel's can, bringing her a pinpoint of clarity.

"Grandma brings these," she murmured, half submerged by the dream that was her life. "My father goes to work. Then Grandma comes."

Gabriel stroked her hand while the woman sucked on the candy, and its long-ago flavor evoked a dozen locked memories.

The woman's guardian touched her hair wistfully.

Gabriel said, "Does Grandma come every day?"

"She does." She gazed into the angel's eyes as if there was no one else. "I think she does. So hard to remember," and she returned to chanting beneath her breath.

Gabriel said, "Talk to me."

She stopped, looked only at him. "My father leaves. Grandma comes. When will my father come home?" Her eyes filled with tears. "Where am I? When will I go home?"

Gabriel lined up five of the brown candies on the woman's bedside tray, counting out loud. The woman focused.

"Every day," Gabriel said, "Grandma will bring one to you. Every day, you can have one." She still watched. "Five candies. When you have the last one, your Father will come get you. And you'll go home."

"After the last candy," she said.

"One a day," Gabriel said. "When Grandma comes."

The guardian looked startled and relieved at the same time. "She may not remember. She's lost so much."

It's hard to have parts of you slip away. Gabriel stroked the woman's bony hand. *But she'll get it back. Just a little longer and she'll be whole again.*

Outside once more, Gabriel walked with the pillowcase in one hand and Israfel's in the other. The Seraph was quiet.

Gabriel moved closer to Israfel. "Thank you for coming with me."

She looked down at him in his wire halo. "Do I get first pick of the take?"

"I get all the Smarties."

"Naturally."

"Everything else I would put out in the jar in the library." He slowed his steps, and so did Israfel. "So you can either take a pile now, or maybe," and his voice lowered to almost inaudible, "you could come get your share a piece at a time."

She met his eyes as they turned the corner. In the next moment a breeze blew through, and then there was nobody there.

Acknowledgments

Special thanks to my beta-readers: Ivy Reisner, Wendy Dinsmore, Amy Deardon, and Normandie Fischer, without whom this story would be one convoluted sentence that had too many adverbs (Jane gushed thankfully.)

I would like to thank the hard work of everyone at *The Sword Review* and *Dragons, Knights and Angels* and *Mindflights* magazines, who encouraged my efforts by "releasing my angels into the wild" and who published this book's first edition. Many, many thanks to Madeline and Evan, who know why without my enumerating the reasons.

A special shout-out to Stephen, Caroline, Thomas and David, four awesome children who are brilliant, sensitive, energetic, and also just happen to be my own. And finally, much love to James Lebak, who married a work-in-progress but doesn't seem to mind the editing process.

Thank you so much for reading *Annihilation*! Please consider leaving a review at Amazon or Goodreads (or both.)

You can check out the start of the story at *Seven Archangels: An Arrow In Flight* and *Seven Archangels: Sacred Cups*, both coming soon. (One sooner than the other, of course. I may write about angels, but I myself am quite human.)

Also:
Tabris is a guardian angel who killed the boy he vowed to protect. Only instead of condemning him, God gives him a second chance – another assignment. But in protecting this other child, Tabris can't be sure he's not fighting the wrong enemy.

If you'd like to hear from me when new books appear, feel free to email me at JaneLebak@gmail.com. I've also got a Facebook page at http://www.facebook.com/JaneLebakAuthor.

Thanks again for reading my story, and I hope to hear from you.